## MARCELA SERRANO

# Antigua and My Life Before

Marcela Serrano was born in Santiago, Chile, in 1951. In 1994, her first novel won the Literary Prize in Santiago, and her second book won the Sor Juana Inés de la Cruz prize, awarded to the best Hispano-American novel written by a woman. She now teaches at the University of Vicente Pérez Rosales in Mexico City.

## About the Translator

Margaret Sayers Peden is an award-winning translator and has worked closely with numerous illustrious Latin American writers, including Carlos Fuentes, Isabel Allende, and Octavio Paz.

# Antigua and My Life Before

Translated by

MARGARET SAYERS PEDEN

Anchor Books
A Division of Random House, Inc.
New York

# Antigua and My
# Life Before

A Novel

MARCELA SERRANO

FIRST ANCHOR BOOKS EDITION, AUGUST 2001

*Copyright © 2000 by Marcela Serrano*

The Library of Congress has cataloged the Doubleday edition as follows:
Serrano, Marcela, 1951–
[Antigua vida mía. English]
Antigua and my life before: a novel / Marcela Serrano; translated by Margaret Sayers Peden.—1st ed.
p. cm.
ISBN 0-385-49801-2
I. Peden, Margaret Sayers.  II. Title.
PQ8098.29.E725 A5813 2000
863—dc21
99-056680

Anchor ISBN: 0-385-49802-0

*Author photograph © Valeria Zalaquet*
*Book design by Dana Leigh Treglia*

www.anchorbooks.com

Printed in the United States of America
10  9  8  7  6  5  4  3  2  1

To Violeta Parra

To my sisters:
Nena, Paula, Margarita, and Sol Serrano,
the women who complete my "we"

# Preface

Until 1973, Chile provided an unusual example of democratic continuity and republican tradition in Latin America. Strong political parties, with free elections and an ever-expanding social program, were part of its history. All that changed on September 11 of that year when, after a stormy period of political confrontation, the military seized power by overthrowing President Salvador Allende, a Socialist who had won the presidential election in 1970 and subsequently imposed a strong agenda of social changes that included agrarian reform and expropriation of many large enterprises.

The dictatorship that resulted from that coup, which was headed by General Augusto Pinochet, quickly acquired international notoriety for the harsh repressiveness of its policies. Hundreds of thousands of Chileans were forced into exile, several thousand were executed or disappeared, all critical thought was proscribed, and a systematic attempt was made to erase all the old symbols and values of popular culture.

Pinochet's dictatorship, which lasted nearly seventeen years, was unexpectedly disrupted in October 1988, when he lost a plebiscite in which he sought to extend his hold on power for another eight years. International solidarity, and the Chileans' strong preference for a democratic form of government, succeeded in defeating one of the worst dictatorships of the continent. Pinochet did not, however, lose all his power. He directed the orderly retreat of the military to their barracks and from that base he exercised a firm control over democratically elected governments obligated to govern under a constitution dictated by Pinochet himself. The Chilean transition, as a result, has been very problematical, and Chile's citizens are still experiencing the malaise of living their lives under the shadow of military power.

This novel is set in the early years of that transition to democracy, and evidences the nostalgia Chileans still hold for the true democracy that until a few decades before had been a way of life.

# Acknowledgments

To the Fondo de Desarrollo de la Cultura y las Artes, for underwriting the first section, "End of the Fiesta."

To Paula Serrano, for everything.

To Elisa Castro, for her generous readings and suggestions.

To my friend—whom I promised not to name—for the scope of his contributions.

To Alberto Fuguet, for his complicity.

To Sol Serrano, Gonzalo Contreras, and Héctor Soto; each of you knows why.

To Karin Riedemann and Mónica Herrera, for their help, and for loving and supporting me.

To Marcelo Maturana.

And, of course, to the city of Antigua, Guatemala, for giving me the gift of this novel.

*Poetry is the one*
*concrete proof*
*that man exists.*

—Luis Cardoza y Aragón
illustrious Antigueño poet
(CASA DE LA CULTURA DE ANTIGUA)

# Part One

## END OF THE FIESTA

(Inspired by an engraving by José Clemente Orozco
Hospicio Cabañas, Guadalajara)

# 1

The day the Berlin Wall fell.

Everything began that November 9, 1989, with the fall of the Wall. Who could have imagined how much more would come down with it?

Which was what I told Violeta Dasinski that day.

I ought to have been a witness; if only I'd paid more attention.

In the photograph there is a forlornness in her expression I hadn't noticed until now. As if her consciousness were dissolving in her eyes.

The date of the beginning of Violeta Dasinski's public life was the day her name appeared on the front page of the Santiago newspapers: November 15, 1991.

I was awakened. Suddenly came the end of dreams and beginning of recall. Abruptly I went back, picking up the memory that preceded the long stroll through my unconscious. Andrés was bringing my breakfast, and there on the tray was the morning paper. Then I saw her.

I studied that face in the photograph. But it is a different Violeta who pursues me: fuchsia glitter on her harlequin mask—clown or Pierrot?—and the hands of the makeup artist transforming her into a sad Venetian with gold and red confetti on her neck.

There was something I had to do.

I got the car keys and left.

"Every reporter in town will be there, Josefa. Don't go!" Andrés could not hide his concern.

"I have no choice."

"Then I'm coming."

"No, this is something between Violeta and me."

As I came closer to the Ñuñoa neighborhood a shiver ran down my spine. When I turned into Calle Gerona to park in front of Violeta's house, I saw two policemen guarding the front door. In fact, all the press *was* there, lying in ambush. Recognizing me seemed to give them new vigor, and they rolled toward me like an avalanche. The policemen came to my defense. One took my arm.

"It *is* you! What are you doing here?"

"I need to go in, I have to talk to her daughter."

"No one's in the house. They took the girl away."

"Please, let me go in. I'm a friend of the family. I have to get something." The cop looked puzzled. "There are things of mine I left here a couple of days ago, things I don't want to fall into just anyone's hands." As I lowered my voice the confusion in his eyes deepened. "Please . . ."

I had no doubt that he wanted to let me go in, but it wouldn't go well with him if he did. He looked at his partner. He was holding back the journalists, who hadn't given up and were trying—at the top of their lungs—to ask me questions.

"You come with me," I proposed. "That way you can see that I'm not up to anything."

"It isn't that, señora. Well, since it's you . . . I'll come with you."

I went inside, hearing the cop's footsteps behind me and sensing his curiosity: I could almost have touched him. Once in that long, dark—all the shutters were closed—typically Ñuñoa corridor, I went straight to the back, to the sunroom. Unhampered, the morning light was pouring in through thousands of tiny panes. Beyond them, the deserted, nostalgic patio. I felt a shock, as if Violeta were waiting for me, sitting in the flowered linen armchair. On the air was a hint of her incense, her perfumed candles. Violeta and that sunroom were one and the same, one passed its feelings to the other, absorbing, fusing. But of course she wasn't there.

To the right, sitting against the thick green wall, was the trunk. A rectangle of yellowish-brown varnished wicker facing the thousand little panes of glass, waiting for me. "My grandmother Carlota saved it from the Chillán earthquake," Violeta had told me many times, as if I didn't know. I hurried to open it—the key never worked—and dug into the disorderly order: books, notebooks, stationery, clippings, drawings. My mind raced: where are they? I can't hunt through everything, they're supposed to be mine, I should know . . . I saw them. Several notebooks of assorted sizes tied together with a simple cord. And on top of them, a large notebook bound in dark brown leather. If I hadn't given it to her myself, I would have had a hard time recognizing it. I took it out confidently and the policeman seemed relieved.

"Is that everything?"

I hesitated. And the others, the ones tied together? The single notebook in my hands seemed innocent enough, credible, something I might have forgotten. But the others? I didn't have the heart to leave them there. You owe it to Violeta, my conscience dictated, stiffening my spine. I took them.

"This is everything." I looked at him, radiating assurance, as I tried to stuff the whole bundle in my purse.

"S-S-Señora," the poor man stammered, his dark eyes moving from the handbag to my eyes, from my eyes to the handbag. Then I did something out of character: I offered him an autograph. That wavering gaze lighted up.

I went to Violeta's desk. She always had paper on hand. Beside the clean stack was a book opened to page ninety. I asked the policeman's first name and wrote a long and affectionate inscription.

My exit was triumphal. (Poor Andrés, how could I explain to him that he couldn't have pulled it off?) I'd been so focused on my task that I had forgotten the press. I was furious when as soon as I stepped out the door I felt the heat of their spotlights in my face: the TV crew had arrived. Without missing a beat, I asked the policeman—who had his autograph in his pocket—to escort me to the car: I had nothing to say.

Three blocks away my façade of assurance collapsed. When I had gone to Violeta's desk I had seen page ninety of the open book. I couldn't help it. I suppose it was the last thing Violeta read. Those two verses, falteringly underlined in brown ink, swept over me.

The page was Adrienne Rich's "Poem of Women." Oh, Violeta, I wasn't eager for us to go our separate ways. No, believe me, I didn't mean to be a heedless witness to what you were going through.

I can reproduce the underlined words, I know them by heart:

*And all the limbs of a woman plead for the ache of birth.*
*And women come down to lie like sick sheep*
*by the wells—to heal their bodies,*
*their faces blackened with year-long thirst for a child's cry . . .*
*and pregnant women approach the white tables of the hospital*
*with quiet steps*

*and smile at the unborn child*
*and perhaps at death.*

Violeta, tell me that your smile was for the unborn child, but don't tell me if it was for death.

A forgotten image had come back to me during the night. That image, in the difficult moment of waking, established a relationship between the present and the previous evening. Andrés brought in the newspaper. I began to be aware of this new reality only after I felt the stab of pain in my temple, not before.

An image from childhood.

Violeta coming to my house with a cardboard box in her hands. It was fairly large and her slight trembling betrayed the effort it had cost her to carry it so carefully on the bus from her house to mine.

"Can you keep this for me?"—her little girl's eyes, at once questioning and distrustful.

With the same disinclination you feel handing over booty in your care, she held out her hands to deposit the box in mine.

"Where is the most secret place in your house, the place no one comes but you?"

Her words sounded so serious that I tried to answer at the same pitch of intensity.

"My bed."

"All right. Let's go."

Silently we went up to my room. She took the box from me and pushed it under the bed herself.

"That's it."

She was turning to leave when I asked her to explain.

"Tomorrow is the famous move, and I know no one will look after my things. The grown-ups think my stuff is junk. That's why I want you to keep all my treasures until the danger is over and they have things set up in the new house. That way, no one will throw them out."

As she left she looked hard into my eyes.

"You will look after them, won't you, Josefa?"

The next day she came to me during the first recess.

"Did you sleep over my papers? No one touched them?"

"Papers?" I asked, amazed. She hadn't forbidden me to open the box, but she might as well have, because even though I was curious I hadn't dared. "Didn't you say they were treasures?"

She looked at me, half arrogant, half surprised.

"Yes, they *are* treasures."

At the end of a week, I reminded her of the box.

"No, I don't want it back now. I'll tell you when."

After a period of time she thought reasonable, she came to get the box. I walked with her to the bus stop. She was deep in thought. As we said good-bye, she said, "You really trusted me. You will be my friend as long as we live."

*Connection through secrecy + privacy*

Violeta always wrote. Diaries? She never called them that. Notes. "To keep my head straight," she said. It was easy to please her. I brought her some pretty notebooks from every trip. *Notebooks, but not golden.* I remember one with a photograph of Virginia Woolf on the cover. Another with Paul Klee's *Senecio* on the glossy binding. And the ones bound in bright cloth, those were her favorites. These smooth, virgin pages, Violeta would say as she ran her hands over them, are as inciting as a young girl's body to an aging man.

Pistachios and notebooks; Violeta was easy to get gifts for. I never had to think about it.

They piled up. She had a large, pretty, undisciplined, generous hand. She filled the books quickly, especially if she got them at some moment of crisis. I would venture that during her marriage to Eduardo she filled more notebooks than in all the rest of her life.

I had been able to rescue them. I couldn't bear the idea of seeing her private thoughts in the hands of the press or the police—whichever might be the least charitable.

She was so casual that day a couple of months ago. We were in the sunroom—you were never anywhere else with Violeta in her house—and she interrupted the conversation to look toward the wicker trunk, as if remembering something she was afraid she would immediately forget.

"You know, I can't remember anything anymore. I don't know what's happening to my poor head; the day it explodes you'll find thousands of tiny squares of paper with notes on everything I don't want to forget, a thousand stupid things a day. That's all a head is good for, it seems, or at least mine . . . And behind the little squares the black dust that is the measure of the effort I've made to remember each of those things. Believe me, there will be more dust than notes."

"And what is it you don't want to forget about that trunk?"

"Oh, yes. That. If anything happens to me, Josefa, say I die unexpectedly, a heart attack in the middle of the street, whatever, my diaries are in the trunk. Please, do something with them. Keep them safe."

I laughed.

"Then why do you write them?"

"Because I can't help myself, it's my one bit of order. You promise?"

"Yes, I promise."

"Good, that's that. One less thing to worry about. I can't tell you how many times I've said, I have to ask Josefa . . . Then I see you and I forget. What were we talking about? Oh . . . Pamela. Go on."


I didn't have to see the newspapers the next morning: the telephone calls from squads of journalists let me know. It was *my* photograph this time, going into Violeta's house, and the press speculating about our relationship.

What was I doing there? That was the big question.

No comment. I wouldn't accept a single call. If I can't bear them in normal times, imagine how much less I wanted to talk that day. I closed myself in the studio. I didn't even open the door to the children.

I asked Andrés to come home early and take over. The whole house is vibrating, in upheaval. We are all equally restless. I try to hide it. I have to get a room ready for Jacinta. It surprises me how she keeps repeating the story of how my mother brought Violeta to our house when we were little girls. Well, the circumstances were different, although I don't suppose that the abandonment Jacinta is struggling with now is any greater than Violeta's was then.

Sooner or later I will have to say something.

What will I talk about? Our childhood? School? The blue pixie eyeglasses with tortoiseshell frames? No, that won't be enough. I'll have to tell about the costume party, about how Violeta was late the night my makeup man turned her into the darling clown with a fuchsia face. And about the gin. And also about her fear. "Josefa, you tell him, I'm running so late. Eduardo is going to be angry."

But that won't be enough, either. It would be impossible not to talk about the Last Forest, the place of refuge, Violeta's dream. And about the mill house. Yes, that's all I should say.

Tell one woman's story.

A woman is the story of her acts and thoughts, her cells and neurons, her wounds and enthusiasms, her loves and hates. A woman is  inevitably the story of her womb, the seeds that were fertilized in it, or not, or stopped being, and of that moment, the one time she is a goddess. A woman is the story of little things, the trivial, the everyday, the sum of the unspoken. A woman is always the story of many men. A woman is the story of her people and her race. And she is the story of her roots and her background, of every woman who was nourished by the one before her so she could be born: a woman is the story of her blood.

But she is also the story of a consciousness and of her internal battles. And a woman is also the story of her Utopia.

Violeta.

This wanted to be the story of Violeta, if only mine weren't so interwoven with hers. But our biographies don't allow me the necessary distance. Or the things that marked us both, such as a sense of loss, of exclusion, and of a certain scorn for the opaque.

Probably she would define her life as a story of passion. Even so, if I look far enough, I think not; not just passion. The story of Violeta is a story of longing.

# 2

Despite our differences, Violeta and I had things in common. For example, honesty, and our love for silk blouses. And dazzle. Dazzle has always been important to us. Not the usual or the obvious. We needed a certain light focused on us. Light that could save us from the immediate, that could distance us from vulgarity. We detested the ordinary. And for that reason we shared a desire for solitude. Physical solitude. As the years went by we valued it even more, as if the lack of it stood in the way of our flowering. Without it, Violeta and I shriveled. We recognized each other as women of our time, and we were not so foolish we didn't understand that our time conspired against that innocent desire. It was in looking for solitude that Violeta found the place: the mill house.

An unnamed, secret place. A place of unrelenting wind, abandonment, disconnected from anything around it. Cut off, self-sufficient, where the sum of all the features of the landscape were independent of any others: a small universe reserved for us. And it was Violeta who made the analogy between the mill house and Paradise.

"Where but in the south of Chile can you find a place like this?"

It was ten years ago when Violeta came back to this country. After her long absence she immediately headed south. That time she set up a tent near Puerto Octay, on the shores of Lake Llanquihue, and then drove on toward Ensenada. When she left the town of Cascadas behind, following a primitive road, elevated and scenic, that snaked along the lake shore, Violeta suddenly caught the full scope of the view, along with the full impact of its majesty. It was a clear day and before her stood the Osorno volcano: the emperor of volcanoes, as she baptized it. On either side she could see the clear profiles of Puntiaguda and El Tronador. Their snow-covered peaks harmonized with the intense blue of the waters of the lake and varied greens of the vegetation. (On the other hand, she later would learn that on rainy days the water and sky encompassed every shade of gray and even the plants and trees became hazy, with that indefinable color you associate with the rare combination of strength and serenity.) She drove on along the winding road, more and more enthralled with the panorama of the lake. At one point as she came to a fork in the road she watched all the drivers unhesitatingly swing onto the main branch. What matters is that Violeta saw the side road and decided to take it. The friend traveling with her protested, that wasn't the way. Violeta insisted, and turned down a steep lane that curved so sharply you could not see what lay below, and with enough bumps and potholes to discourage the most enthusiastic adventurer. But it is nearly impossible to discourage Violeta. The road straightened out again and before her was a bay, no more than a kilometer long, surrounded by a path bordered on the left by open fields and on the right by the lake. Violeta's eyes were drawn to that field flanked by hills and green knolls on which she recognized the native trees and bushes of the area. Small, roaming groups of domesticated animals and fowl—some ducks and geese, goats and sheep and cows, mostly—animated the scene. Then she turned to the other side of the track: thick rows of pines curtaining the long beach.

She got out of the car. She ran to the sand and knelt down in it. This landlocked and peaceful bay was sheltered by its geography, the two points curving out into the lake, creating a large haven of calm water. *This is its own place,* thought Violeta, bewitched, *and it's the bay that gives it the sensation of a private space.* She contemplated the silence. She told herself finally that this was a small world separate from the rest of the large world. The hills surrounding it, with their ancient, towering trees, heightened the sensation of a miniature kingdom.

Through the pines she glimpsed the ruins of a mill. And beside that, a house. The typical house of the south, two stories, with a larch shake roof and gray wood siding that once had been dark reddish brown. It seemed abandoned to its fate. On the railing was a narrow, planed, pine board with the words: *Casa del Molino.* She walked on toward the broad entry, with its classic steps and landing of planks secured by four beams, and found the door. But there were two doors, not one. She knocked on both at the same time, intuiting the silence that was in fact her answer.

She walked back down the steps, turned into a narrow pathway between large chestnuts, and almost immediately found a second house, a cabin. As she started to knock on that door, as if it were the house of the woodcutter from her childhood stories, she saw another small wood sign: *Casa del Castaño,* House of the Chestnut Tree. Why were they named? Who had named them?

Finding Señor Richter a half hour later was easy. Violeta's enthusiasm led her to him.

"When they closed the mill, they put the houses up for rent. My grandfather divided his for many years, so he and the miller's family could both live there. He also built a hut under the chestnut trees for storing wheat, I converted that into a cabin. My married daughter summers there, we don't have enough room here with the grandchildren. And if you walk a little farther, a few steps beyond the *Castaño* house you will see the pitched roof of the house where some campesinos live. Aguayito and La María. They have a garden and supply the renters' vegetables; they bake bread, milk the cows, smoke the salmon. And they have a son, a handy guy who does everything: he cuts the wood, repairs the outlets, takes the bottled gas tanks into town . . . everything and anything the people in the big house need."

This was in November of that year, and Violeta left the place only after renting both houses for the first of February.

"Don't ever tell anyone you were here," she told her companion, the only witness.


"You act more like someone who likes to rough it than a summer renter" was Eduardo's comment when he came to our sanctuary for the first time. "Only Violeta could choose a summer place that looks like the wildest Irish coast," he added, looking at me.

"*Ryan's Daughter,*" I agreed.

"No one is going to fight you two for this place, you don't have to keep it a secret." He wrapped us both in his arms. "No one in his right mind would want to live in all this wind."

Violeta, surprised, thought a few seconds and then laughed.

"How strange! I'd never really thought about how the wind never stops. For me it's just part of the place and it never occurred to me that there are spots where the wind *doesn't* blow."

"You can relax. That's why the Beautiful People never come here; this wind kills any possibility of water sports. You don't have to be so secretive about it, Violeta," Eduardo insisted.

That first night, at dinnertime, still amazed at the mill house,

Eduardo said with a certain irony: "With Violeta, even the style of her summer vacation becomes an act of commitment."

"Well, if you lived in South Africa, the mere act of breathing would be an 'act of commitment,' " she fired back.

Andrés, who praised nearly everything Violeta did, came to her defense: "I think it's more exact to call Violeta's committed views a sense of responsibility."

"Mmmm." I looked at him with my usual skepticism. "I wonder if Violeta doesn't get weary of always being responsible."

"How do you mean?" Eduardo asked.

"I don't know, this thing of constant responsibility . . ."

"It's a question of having some kind of discipline in your approach to the world," threw in Violeta, maintaining her good humor. "I think that's what Andrés is referring to."

"No, I think he's referring to your famous causes," I said, keeping it light. "So many causes. How exhausting!"

"Right, a real bore. Can we change the subject? It doesn't take much for Eduardo to laugh at me; don't give him any more excuses. After all, you're supposed to be my friends, aren't you?"

That night Andrés put down his book a minute and turned to me, very serious.

"Violeta is not a simple woman, is she, Jose?"

"No, of course not. Why do you ask?"

"I don't know. I have the feeling that she's struggling, looking for a satisfactory answer to something quite simple: living."

It was true. Violeta's nightmare, her terrifying dream, was that empty silence would be the answer to her questions—those she formulated without formulating them—about the fairest way to walk this earth.

Every year as February drew near, our ritual would begin. This year, as before, the closer we came to the first of the month, the more the telephones rang. And that night, the eve of our departure, as we loaded the cars we talked at least ten times from house to house.

We had agreed earlier about books. Andrés and I, for obvious reasons, docilely submitted to Violeta's judgment, although I have to admit that it was the one concession we made to her. I was in charge of the videos, which my son Borja had taped during the winter. The first few years we took old films, a lot of classics, a lot of black and white. When videos got to be almost contemporaneous with the movies, we watched in the summer the films we had missed during the winter. I never went to movie theaters anymore. I hated to be recognized and dreaded the inevitable person in the next seat opening her candy with all that cellophane crackling in the silence of the theater, ruining any possible enjoyment. And then when she began chewing or started with the gum, I would have to get up and move. (I will never forget the first time I went to a movie in New York and saw those gringos with their enormous cardboard buckets of popcorn. I took the sensible course: I dropped out of line and never went into a theater again. I'd never dreamed that a custom like that would make its way to my country.)

"Are you taking the waffle iron this year? Right. And the grill? I can't find a place for the gridiron, I can't get another thing in."

"You want to leave the Swiss coffee maker? I'm bringing my Bialetti."

"And your guitar?"

"Shit, Violeta, don't bug me. I'm going for the rest."

"Then Jacinta will bring hers. Don't think you can get away with a whole summer of not singing."

As the years went by we got more sophisticated.

"Cell phone? Don't be an ass, Josefa! Why will we need it? The idea is to block out the rest of the world."

Violeta was right: that was the purpose. If it weren't for the poles for the electric lines, we wouldn't have known what century we were in. Even the lack of a store helped us construct our refuge against the distinctive markers of our civilization. Not long ago I read a poll; two percent of the population doesn't know who the President of the Republic is. I thought about the campesinos in Llanquihue: I had no doubt that Aguayito was part of that percentage.

*Time* was the key to the mill house.

It removed contingencies. We turned into some kind of vagabonds without an anchor, or wardrobes, or obligations. It gave us the opportunity, once a year, to examine our lives objectively, and this led us to believe our roots were lasting. A rare quality of the times. The one place on earth where I never worried about time, to the point that I couldn't be sure whether two weeks or five days had gone by, whether it was Tuesday or Sunday, whether I'd just come or it was time to leave.

That atemporality rejuvenated me and softened my edges. (I had known that sensation when the business of Roberto happened. Except that then time was suspended, absorbed in the horror. Now, in contrast, we were in charge of time; it neither dominated nor subjected us.)

In the mill house we cooked for ourselves, something we rarely did during the year. We sang, something I denied myself in my everyday life. We talked . . . in circumstances in which I nearly never shared with anyone, except some nights with Andrés.

All our everyday acts lost their routineness and became surprises.

We would settle into my large kitchen and while we talked about our work—my concerts, her architecture, our husbands and our children, or about the book the other one had just read—plum compotes, strawberry marmalade, or waffles on cold evenings would fly from our hands. Violeta had brought her hammock and hung it between two chestnuts in the field in back. The wind never daunted her.

We needed a place that was both bucolic and on the water. Bucolic wasn't enough. The water, as always, gave us an outlet. For our feet; for our thoughts.

Violeta took the miller's house and I took grandfather Richter's. It was a division based on the size of our families. We went up the same stairs to our two doors, which were never closed. The children ran in and out of both. One house, Violeta's, looked toward the volcano. Mine, the lake. Violeta, who had a true passion for houses, would stop to gaze lovingly at the gray boards. Even with all the traveling she had done in her lifetime, and knowing that she was only passing through, she always wanted to have a house in the country she was visiting, or in each city or town that stole her heart. She never lost her fantasy of putting down roots wherever she was, of designing her own house at each stop along the way. "Some day, if we can convince Richter to sell us this place," she told me, "we will build two houses. I have them all designed in my head. Not just mine, but yours, too. You'll see. Divine. Built entirely of larch. They will both have views of the volcano and the lake. And we'll not spare any expense, Josefa. Be ready!" It was true that as she inhabited places, she appropriated them and flooded them with her person. A rare quality, hers. One I've seldom encountered.

We heard each other's every sound, which was why the place could not be shared by people who didn't know each other. The division was amusing: I got the large kitchen, Violeta the large bathroom. Her house had two bedrooms. Hers was nearly monastic; it was small, with a double bed and a chair. Nothing more. The second bedroom was enormous, with very high ceilings and lots of cots. Jacinta took that over, keeping it filled with her girlfriends. In that regard Violeta was much more permissive than I was. It wore me out to have people in the house every minute, and I limited the number of friends my children could invite. Not Violeta. "Look, Josefa," she would say. "Nothing is more important to me than the memories Jacinta will have of her vacations: they will give her stability when she grows up, I know. I don't want her to go through what I did."

My house had four bedrooms, two small bathrooms, modern, with showers. Violeta's bathroom and her enormous tub were the envy of all my family.

Violeta always got up at midnight, or dawn, and gravitated toward the warmest place in the mill house: the bathroom was her favorite spot. The great water heater, with all its plumbing exposed—as if its antiquity or precariousness were the forerunner of the boldest vanguard—and the heat those pipes released seemed to call to her. Violeta didn't really know where that heat came from or where it was going. Her body moved toward it almost independent of her will; she slipped about like a ghost, incorporeal, a wisp, the hint of warmth from those radiating conduits.

Violeta and I would sing. Those were Andrés's favorite moments, when we laid a fire at night and through its orange tongues I saw his love quietly surfacing. "I fell in love with your voice before I fell in love with you," he used to say. "Doesn't matter." I would forgive him. "My voice and I are one and the same."

There were long periods when Violeta used to sing with me. Drawn to any form of art, "to breathe in life," music was not something she could do without. In various settings—school, university, country, parties—always the same scene: Violeta harmonizing with me. Her voice was high, fragile, and sweet, a soprano had she been a professional. I sang the melody in my strong, resonant contralto:

*La pericona se ha muerto, no pudo ver a la meica . . .*

She would come in at the exact moment:

*La pericona se ha muerto, no pudo ver a la meica . . .*

And then in unison:

*. . . le faltaron cuatro reales, por eso se cayó muerta . . .*

At that point we would look at each other; our mood would change, and we would continue with joyful intensity.

*Asómate a la rinconá . . .*

We always argued about the songs of Violeta Parra, our favorite singer. We agreed that her two best were *"Gracias a la vida"*—Thanks to Life—and *"Maldigo"*—Curses. Violeta insisted that the latter was best of all, by far, while I wouldn't yield *"Gracias a la vida."*

"It's gut-wrenching, Josefa. *'Maldigo'* is the essence of being torn apart!"

The mill house was the only place that Violeta sang with me again. I with her, she with me. We sang to pain, to love, to hope, to the future. We sang with love. I kept on singing; Violeta kept the pain and the hope . . . Hope, in Violeta, more than anything. For me, a glimpse of such hope inevitably meant ending up with pain.

Yes, Violeta sang life. She sang it until it cursed her. Always with the hope that opening her eyes in the morning, every morning, would be worth the pain, her dream intact that man's lot would change, trusting that those who sorrow would not have to wait for the end of the world.

3

*I am damned by the catastrophes of my country.*

Corral. The Berlin Wall and Corral earthquake were to blame, Violeta writes in her diary, which finally I had found the courage to open.

*That day in May, 1960.*
*I was young then, but not Eduardo. He was twenty years old. And he often told me the story: the sea drew back, back, back, many kilometers. People were surprised, amazed, they ran to see the expanse of sand they had never seen before. They sank in their heels and gathered shellfish, astonished, contemplating the secret treasures that lay in the open. Suddenly they hear a loud noise approaching from the horizon. It was deafening, as if the sea were bellowing. A strange sound no one*

had ever heard before and that probably no one ever will again. *Eduardo looked up and thought: something very bad is going to happen. The sky had changed color; everything grew black. In the distance, far away, an enormous wave was moving toward the coast, thirty meters high, black, and the sky began changing color: with the roaring came red, then blue, even green was seen in the heavens. Eduardo starting running up the hill like a madman. The luminous sky blinded him, those changing colors. He pulled off his scarf, tied it around his eyes, and peered through a little slit at the hill he was running up, frantically, up, up . . . As soon as he reached the top, leaving the stony land behind him, he turned just in time to see the gigantic wave crashing down on the coast of Corral. The water covered everything. Everything. Voraciously, it swallowed absolutely everything that lay in its path.*

*Eduardo stared. With his own eyes he saw how the sea consumed all he ever had. He was <u>completely alone</u>. His house and his parents' houses had disappeared. His family, his wife, son, father and mother, every member of his family swept up by the sea, engulfed by the sea, drowned in the sea.*

*Until then, Eduardo had believed that orphans existed only in storybooks.*

The story of Corral is in the big notebook, the one with the brown cover. I don't open it to just any page. I examine the dates meticulously: nothing at random. Since I didn't listen to her then, I mustn't fail now.

*9 November 1989*

*I have the feeling that today is an important day.*
*Two things happened.*
*The Berlin Wall came down.*
*I wandered around the house, uneasy. I didn't know exactly what*

*I wanted to do. Until I went to the bookstore; I needed to see Papa, hear his opinion. I have always enjoyed looking through the shelves at the last hour of the day to see what new book has come. But today I wasn't interested in the books. I felt a strange restlessness.*

*My father was talking with a man behind the counter, a middle-aged man, about medium height, with dark hair and beard and dressed very casually (no necktie, sport coat, khaki trousers). Papa called me over to introduce me, and once I looked at the man I recognized him.*

*"I didn't know you were back in Chile," I said.*

*"Neither did I," he answered.*

*I laughed, and hoped he would stay. At that moment Carmencita called Papa; she was arguing with a difficult customer.*

*"Excuse me, I'll be back," Papa, always well mannered, left us alone.*

*I looked at him. "The Berlin Wall fell." I didn't know what else to say.*

*He told me he had heard the news.*

*"What are your feelings?" I asked.*

*He: Nothing in particular. Good for freedom. And you?*

*I: Yes, good for freedom. But . . . I don't know, I'm a little disoriented, as if things have gone off course.*

*He: What does that matter, if there are no superior causes. You are very young . . . but when you are my age you know nothing exists beyond the dementia of fanatics or the emptiness that makes them so.*

*Oh, God, if you're going to propound some thesis, I can't take it, I thought. Which was why I didn't answer him. This wasn't the moment to tell a stranger something that wasn't clear even to me. We stood there, not speaking, and automatically began to look at books we didn't really see.*

*Eduardo: Are you a good reader?*

*I: Rather good. Do you have a suggestion?*

*Eduardo: You sound very formal.*

*I: It's just respect, I guess.*

*Eduardo: Or else my age. If you loosen up a little, I'll recommend a wonderful book.*

*I: All right, I will. What?*

*Eduardo: Have you heard of Agota Kristoff?*

*I: No, not even the name.*

*Eduardo: Look, your father has her novel,* The Large Notebook. *She's Hungarian, although she writes in French. She isn't very well known. Take it with you now, you won't be able to find it anywhere else. Of course, once you've read it, I expect a report.*

*I didn't hesitate; nothing gives me as much pleasure as knowing I have a good book in my hands. Even more since he recommended it, he's a serious writer, not someone fashionable.*

"Come on," I said. "I'll buy you a cup of coffee as a sign of my thanks."

*We walked along Providencia—no longer the center of town as it was when I was a girl—and had to go a long way to find a good place.*

*I reiterate that the business in Berlin had me upset; it wasn't a normal day. My intention was to talk and, I hoped, to make friends a little with this man whom I felt I knew through his books. Maybe we could talk about the seaquake in Corral, his losing his wife, his unusual life story. In fact, for a magical time, we did. I told him my favorite authors and listened to his comments, almost with devotion. One point in his favor: he immediately noticed my ring.*

"That's a piedra cruz," he said.

"I know."

"It's from the south, the Laraquete river, near my part of the country."

"I know that, too."

"I was surprised to see it on you. I've never seen another person wearing one."

But then he went for the easy move: he asked me to go to a hotel with him, within a half hour of having met him. Pretty subtle!

Just in case, I told him no.

I'm annoyed with Susana. She's nothing to me, nothing but a would-be writer who hangs around the bookstore. But I'm angry anyway, as if she'd beat me at some game. Actually, she did, and Carmencita, of course, couldn't wait to tell me the minute she saw me. Although it's not all that clear that Susana won: after all, I rejected him. I told him no, and that's why he asked Susana. I feel superior to Susana; I am a less easy prey, and that always gives one a certain class. Even though it's nasty to say so, and I hate undercutting the bond of sisterhood, Susana takes my leftovers. I'm annoyed with Eduardo, too. He told my father how sensitive and intelligent his daughter was, how well we'd got along, things like that. But just the same he must have thought of me as interchangeable if one minute he could proposition me and the next go after another woman. I'm terrified at the thought of turning into a Susana overnight. After all, he treated me just the way he did her; the only difference is that I said no and she accepted. I'm not sure whether I won or lost. I am a single woman, with a slightly dreary love life, and I handed another woman an opportunity on a silver platter. Of course, I hate like hell to end up in bed the first time—as if I never have?—or say yes out of fear, the pure fear of being rejected the next day, probably by someone worse than Eduardo. Don't they say that time narrows every single woman's selectivity? That frivolous—writer he may be, but frivolous just the same—man must be thinking: you lost your chance. Or maybe: you're not the only fish in the sea. He couldn't care less that I turned him down. I'm upset, but the truth is that, Susana aside, I realize it's not actually Eduardo I'm annoyed with. It is so difficult to say no! In that arena, I never really know what I want. It's me I'm upset with. My head is swimming with powerful and uncomfortable emotions, but none of them has anything to do with Eduardo directly, just myself.

Beginning of December

I'm moved by his story. Any violent geographical event fascinates me. Why not? Josefa says that vulnerability hooks me sexually, that I'm the perfect refuge for helpless narcissists. That's her opinion. It is true that that was the case with Jacinta's father, but a lot of years have passed and I hope not in vain.

My superego did well not to accept the external demarcation between one woman—another—and me. I am *Susana* and she is *Violeta*. We must recognize ourselves in each other. I went to bed with him. The second time, not the first.

We ran into each other again in the bookstore. According to him, he was looking for me. He said I owed him my thoughts on The Large Notebook. I had so many, and such passionate ones, that after the coffee shop we went to have a drink (which he didn't drink) and then on to dinner. Between the cold Venetian eel and papayas in their own juices, I heard his story. I knew, from the signs, that the hotel was close by, and that I almost had one foot inside.

At the age of twenty, following the seaquake, Eduardo was absolutely alone. He went north. He stopped in Chillán. Not even he knows how he got through the next two months, day and night in a bar. His drinking companions, out of pure sympathy, kept the luckless fellow drunk, and in the process created the thirst that haunts him to this day.

Then, the usual . . . He started driving a truck, going to nearby rivers to load riprap. A woman asked him to move in with her—food for body and soul—and then came the classic moment of intellectual emptiness: he decided to enter the university. Law was his choice. He didn't last long. He worked for a notary until he earned enough money to move to the heart of Santiago and become part of the bohemian scene that was flourishing in those years and write a book.

That first novel, At the Bottom of the Sea, *set in the south and using the seaquake as the central element, was a huge success. It was read, it sold, it was reviewed and reprinted, royalties rolled in, it was included on reading lists, and new editions came out one after another. He started a number of second novels, which he didn't finish—every author's drama, he told me—until at the beginning of the seventies he published* Terra Australis, This New World. *Now the subject was contingent, nothing to do with the way of life in the south. But almost nothing happened. Eduardo left the country, imagining that in another country verve, imagination, and strength would breathe new life. He settled in Canada, where in the eighties he published his third novel. I remember very well when it came to Chile; it was a good edition and looked handsome on the shelves of Papa's book shop. I read it and liked it. It was pure nostalgia for his country, and in those days we were all engulfed in nostalgia: both those who were still here and those who had left their land behind identified with it. But the critics didn't credit that identification, which they attributed to "extra-literary" (and therefore not valid) reasons. That was seven years ago. The success of that first book has never been repeated. The next novel—he says—is writing itself.*

*"It is still to be seen whether I am truly a good writer or whether it was nothing more than the power of the seaquake," he told me as we were enjoying dessert.*

*And I left with him.*


*Note: going into the hotel, I threw a question at him. "What about Susana?" His confusion wasn't a pose, or his answer. "Susana? Who's she?"*

# 4

Jacinta takes a silvery ball from her pants pocket and nervously plays with it. She rubs it, passes it from hand to hand without looking at it.

"Is that the one from her necklace?" I can't help asking.

"Yes."

"What about the chain?"

"It broke."

"When?"

"The night of the party."

I swallow hard and instinctively reach out to take it. Jacinta handed it to me.

During a trip to Mexico Violeta had bought a silver ball she wore on a chain. She explained that it was for good luck (wasn't the *piedra cruz* enough?) and that to prove it was silver—good silver—the artisans had put little pills of silver inside that jingled every time she budged. This made Violeta a kind of walking sleigh bell. The *tinkle-tinkle* of the sphere sounded with every movement, preceding her; with my characteristic vigilant ear I could hear her coming, as if I had a presentiment. Violeta's fingers, those long, agile fingers, nervously played and toyed with her necklace. She could center her energy in a single act as insignificant as that, and truly concentrate. She had an incredible capacity for spending long periods doing absolutely nothing—something I detested. For me, time was voracious, its only objective to be well used. I had a thousand ways to spend time, living with guilt when I squandered it and genuinely suffering for all the things I didn't get done, left for tomorrow, or simply forgot. Not Violeta. She would stare at the ceiling or the leaves of the acacias where she hung her hammock at the house in Ñuñoa, eating pistachios or playing with her new necklace, as she had the last time I'd seen her, and time would pass tranquilly before her eyes, without a worry. Where was Violeta at such moments? Her remoteness was swept away in the tide of my own symptoms: the pace of success, the traffic, the busy life I have chosen. Now I find out through Jacinta, her daughter, that the chain of her necklace broke that night, November 14, 1991. Violeta could not count on her silver ball for good luck. And she must have asked herself why the ring wasn't enough, with the history and strength that earth-brown and black stone carried with it.


Jacinta has inherited the skin that was so much her mother's. At times I thought it was ivory, but when I held a piece of amber I realized that was Violeta's coloring. In a year or two, when she turns eighteen, Jacinta will be taller than her mother. According to Violeta, all children of that generation will be taller than their parents. "It's what they eat," she told me. "What do you think happened? When did everything change? When did we begin to eat and have children like North American women?" So, soon—two or three years will fly by—Jacinta will be rather tall. Her build, too, neither thin nor heavyset, is hereditary. She is one of those females who doesn't have to worry about weight, one—how I envy them!—who can happily commit the sin of gluttony without consequences. I despise bodies like that because I would give anything to have been born with one; only my envy made Violeta realize that it wasn't natural to *be* like that, and after that she was grateful for her good fortune. The only other characteristic Jacinta got from her mother is her thick, wavy hair. When we were girls, Violeta dreamed of having my straight hair; not all the hair presses from the early sixties could tame those curls. Jacinta inherited them. And that's all. Her eyes and good vision come from her father.

Violeta's glasses defined the stages of her life. "What year was that, Josefa?" she would ask me. "What glasses was I wearing?" Four Eyes, they called her, because of those horrible blue tortoiseshell-frame pixie glasses. We were in the third grade when she first attended our school. Violeta showed up in those glasses, and some of our schoolmates said, during recess, Did you see the new girl? Did you get a load of those glasses? They all stared at Violeta and laughed. She didn't know what they were saying, but she smiled, blushing. She was standing alone in the courtyard; no girl would go near her as long as the popular girls didn't give a sign. Four Eyes. They laughed. The truth is that Violeta never has seen much, or, more accurately, she has seen a lot of things, but hazily.

Toward the end of adolescence, along with pretensions, came the contact lenses. As scatterbrained as she was, she lost them a thousand times. I remember—and I still get a little ticked—how many places that happened, and always at the least convenient moment: the movies, on the bus, in a store. Violeta would grope around on the ground for her lens, on all fours, making me feel guilty if I pretended not to notice. Inevitably, both of us would end up crawling around looking. The amazing thing is that we always found them. I rejoiced when she entered her intellectual phase and from the vanities of the world passed to the next-to-last phase: the contact lenses were replaced with eyeglasses like the ones in old photographs, the kind you wear perched on the end of your nose, with round lenses and narrow wire frames. "Do I look like Mia Farrow?" she would ask, wide-eyed.

# 5

*We, the others,* we saw Jacinta born.

The child was born in Europe and was named after a trapeze artist. She was conceived in Greece, in the Peloponnesus. Violeta and Gonzalo had married in 1973 and left the country shortly afterward. They waited just long enough for her to get her architecture degree. For Gonzalo, on the other hand, architecture had been a way station on the road to painting, and he didn't care about the degree. He was going to devote himself to art without a concession of any kind. Rome was the city they chose. From that ancestral city they did a lot of traveling. Violeta spent long hours, eternal hours, bent over the drawing board in the drafting room of a Roman construction company, earning their living while Gonzalo, brush clutched in a hand streaked with oils, was learning, painting, dreaming. His were dreams of greatness, success, recognition. Violeta, for her part, would come home to the tiny apartment in the heart of the *Centro Storico* so exhausted that she had no dreams of her own: she dreamed and labored for him. When there was enough money they closed up the apartment, or sublet it to some friend, and jumped on a train or ship or bus.

Greece was their destination one of those winters. From Athens they went to the Peloponnesus. As they crossed the isthmus, Violeta fell in love with Corinth, with its enormous fortress. To her those gigantic stones melded nature and architecture, seeming to reach the heavens, while the small houses of ancient tiles might have housed dwarves. But it was before the temple of Apollo, standing all by itself in the middle of old Corinth—how long had that small, neat, abandoned temple been there?—that she decided to stay. "It's so barren, Violeta, let's move around a little, the wind is too strong, I'm freezing to death." Gonzalo finally tore her away from that strange place and they went on to another even less hospitable: Mycenae. Violeta crossed the threshold of the Gate of the Lions over and over, as Gonzalo whispered in her ear: "Walk there again, it will be the first and last time your feet touch something millenary." Before the tomb of Cassandra and the piles of stone that once had been the guardian lions of the entrance, Violeta brooded about the long-ago, forced exile of that other woman, alone, carrying the weight of her family jewels, prisoner of Agammenon. So, perhaps, she had been welcomed by these stone lions and this strange city, hostile as the wind, indifferent as the unchanging sky that had looked down on Cassandra, her mind filled with premonitory images of blood and forsakenness. Cassandra, alone with her shattered history and her death. Violeta did not want to leave. The wind blew incessantly; it was the coldest she had ever known, worse than the wind in Corinth. Even so, they stayed. There in that place of ocher earth, they met the performers in a circus that traveled from city to city through the Peloponnesus. Violeta would sit on the ground with a sack of pistachios and as she tossed them in her mouth—breaking her fingernails as she shelled that hard, green fruit—watch the indefatigable trapeze artists practice. (That was when she discovered pistachios. She never stopped eating them, and when she went home to Chile and could not find them anywhere, she always counted on Josefa to bring them back from some trip. When at last you could buy them in Chile, it was too late for Violeta.) She never missed a single practice during that time. Her eyes would grow wide at the spectacular acrobatics, staring, hypnotized, while Gonzalo filled his artist's pad with sketches. Jacinta, the woman trapeze artist, wore a silver ring on her fourth finger. The stone was a small black oval encircled in heavy silver. The world in her hands, thought Violeta. The world on one finger, Gonzalo told her. Mexican obsidian, said Jacinta, and Violeta would search for that ring until she found it, years later, in Mexico. Jacinta had not lied.

Jacinta came from Canada. (When, after what seemed centuries to Violeta, she learned that Eduardo had lived in that country, she asked him if he knew her. Eduardo laughed.) Jacinta's partner was Maxx, with two *x*'s. Maxx the trapeze artist, the acrobat with the fabulous muscles that gave Jacinta absolute security in the air. Captivated, Violeta and Gonzalo accepted when Maxx and Jacinta invited them to share their tent for a few days. One of those nights—chosen?—the second Jacinta was conceived.

Back in Rome, Violeta learned she was pregnant and thought of herself as a queen and of her daughter as a chosen of the goddesses. *After all, her seed was fertilized in the land of the gods*, she would write later in her diary.

*And when she grows up I will teach her about goddesses. I will tell her about Hera, the matriarch, and about earthly power and the way to solidify a marriage. About Artemis, the Amazon, with her love for nature. And Athena, with her great civic sense and the intellectual logic that originated in her father's world. Aphrodite, too, the goddess of the sacred body, sacred in passion and the arts. And last I will tell her about Demeter, the fecund, nourishing earth mother, and Persephone, mistress of the underground and the occult, with her dreams of death and transformation. Knowing their stories will help her become a woman. Yes, I will ask her not to identify with one only, because that one might be the source of unthinkable sorrow. Let her know them all, and recognize something of herself in each of them. Let it not be a vulnerable goddess like her mother, who has lived only as a link in a chain.*

Thence the name of the girl whom a pregnant Violeta never once dreamed of being a boy. Many times she was specific: Jacinta is my daughter. But the original Jacinta was a trapeze artist.

# 6

Mauricio calls me on the telephone. He is shocked.

"It's her, isn't it?"

"Yes, it is."

"But Josefa, what the devil happened?"

"I don't know, Mauricio, I don't know. You can imagine, I'm shattered."

I refuse to interpret, or give explanations.

"I can't stop thinking about her clown costume," Mauricio insists. "She was so pretty that day when I finished. That's when it all happened, isn't it?"

"Yes. Like you, I haven't stopped asking myself what might have happened if you hadn't painted her face. She wouldn't have been late, and maybe things would have turned out differently."

"I could tell she was nervous when she saw it was getting late."

"Was she? I didn't notice, I was concentrating on other things . . ."

"Oh, Josefa . . ."

No, I'm not up to listening to Mauricio's boo-hooing. I have enough with Andrés, and Jacinta, and my own children. My own are enough.

That prophetic night, the eve of Violeta's leap to the front page of the newspapers, that night, the night of the party, of the harlequin, she came by my house.

She was in a rush.

"The shoes, Josefa. Do you remember you were going to lend me those clodhoppers for my costume?"

She says she's going to the party as a clown. I can barely see her in the mirror because Mauricio is doing my makeup. I can't live without Mauricio; I can't take a step without him. I can't imagine going out if I haven't first checked my face and hair with him. He asks Violeta about her costume. She describes it.

"But that's so plain!" Mauricio comments.

He keeps doing my makeup, but he is studying Violeta out of the corner of his eye, and he hasn't given up. He finishes with me, and sits her down before the mirror.

"Come here a minute, my precious, I'm going to work on you just a little."

He warms to his task, and decides to transform her from the clown in a second-rate circus to a fabulous Venetian harlequin.

"Pierrot? The patchwork or chessboard one?"

"No, forget Picasso's harlequins," Violeta answers candidly. "Just red and yellow patches."

Mauricio is delighted with his work on her face. He can't let her go.

"Your friend is delicious," he tells me, "but so neglected by the hand of God."

Violeta laughs and surrenders to him. Minutes go by and still Mauricio can't stop. He opens his makeup case.

"Total magic!" says Violeta, dazzled by the colors and glitter.

"The hair! I have to do something inspired to your hair. Jose, my darling, give me all the ribbons you have."

"Can you find us some ribbons?" I yell to my daughter, Celeste, and feel a twinge of jealousy.

Then comes the glitter, the thousands of gold and fuchsia specks. Violeta is being transformed before the mirror. The other Violeta appears, the one who is not she, the one she likes so much.

"Hurry, Mauricio," I urge suddenly. "We'll be late."

"It doesn't matter if you get there late, look how gorgeous your friend is going to be."

"Eduardo is going to be nervous, I know him," says Violeta.

He is still working on the harlequin. By now I'm enthusiastic. (The jealousy has faded.)

"A work of art, Mauricio," I exclaim. "She's fantastic!"

Violeta looks at her watch. She touches the red and gold confetti on her neck.

"You call him, Josefa, I don't dare, he'll scold me."

"But who, please, is this monster?" shrieks Mauricio in his affected voice.

"My husband, that's who. He isn't a monster. He's just . . . a little upset these days."

"Don't pay any attention, don't call him. Just show up, and the minute he sees you he will fall at your feet."

That fuchsia glitter on her harlequin mask.

In fact, Violeta does get to the party late. Eduardo was waiting with a gin and tonic in his hand and his lips screwed into a grimace of reserve. As she told me later, at that very minute they had the first discord of the night. Of that night.

On my retinas, on Mauricio's, on those of anyone who attended that party, was imprinted the image of Venetian tristesse.

It was getting hot toward the end of 1989, the year the Wall came down in Berlin. At the time I was recording in a studio just a block from Violeta's house. I had already begun to sink, slowly, into my iso-lation, and was in touch with very few people. I saw her strictly because the studio and her house were so close. When we took a break for the sound engineers to have a beer, I would walk to Gerona and we would have a cup of coffee.

That afternoon Jacinta opened the door, and I went straight to Violeta's bedroom, pausing only a moment to study the design in the largest living room rug. Violeta's house was like a mosque; it was filled with rugs. What differentiates a *house* from a *home*, she always said, are the rugs. She talked about knots per square centimeter, the blend of cotton with wool and silk. She bought a Herecker in Istanbul that was signed and had a name: *Flowers of the Seven Mountains*. When I came in, I always stopped before its garden bordered in deep blues.

I found Violeta stretched out on the bed, clasping her tense, focused face with both hands. Beside her, a plate of beautiful cheri-moya fruit. Music was playing at an earsplitting volume. That was the only way Violeta knew to listen.

She looked at me absent-mindedly.

"Dear God, Debussy is so difficult!"

Amused, I returned her look.

"And is that a problem, Violeta, that Debussy is difficult?"

"It's just that I would like to understand him. Not just Debussy; I would like to understand any artistic production, whatever it may be . . ."

"Especially literature, these days."

She laughed. "Is that why you came!"

"I have ten minutes, tell me quick," and without asking, I began eating the sweet cherimoyas.

Those were the days Violeta was talking with her dead. Conversing with them before their photographs in that kind of traveling carnival of a bedroom. At the base of the umbrella stand, the central piece in the room, amid the clutter of hanging things—hats, kerchiefs, mufflers—and next to the copper slot intended to hold umbrellas streaming rain, she had put up a photograph of Cayetana and one of her grandmother Carlota and the aged Antonio. She also had put a photo of Gonzalo next to the dressing table, lost among earrings, beads, bracelets, and necklaces. "But Papa isn't dead," Jacinta complained. "That doesn't matter, darling, the concept of death has more than one interpretation." The red candles were dancing. Violeta was always surrounded by lighted candles that sat side by side with her inevitable incense burners. Now they multiplied before her dead. She felt protected by them, and asked them to ignore the horrible black insect that had frightened her, and join her to Eduardo for a lifetime.

Because a couple of weeks after the first hotel, Violeta and Eduardo go to Cajón del Maipo for the weekend. They eat mushrooms in a modest inn and facing a large window overlooking the foothills of the cordillera swear undying love.

She confides to him her obsession to be a mother again, speaks of her diminishing possibilities and of her fear that Jacinta will repeat her own life as an only child. Eduardo doesn't seem to be scared off, unlike others who had pretended to be receptive to this speech. He has his own ambitions; he needs a wife. After the loss in the seaquake in Corral suffered when he was so young, he had for many years resisted any love commitment. "I've lived a dog's life," he tells her. "A stray dog, a free, libertine dog, but a dog nonetheless." He believes the only thing that will allow him to write his great novel will be a home and a wife. A domestic structure that will support him as he creates. "Wives lend a sense of something sacred to man's writing," Eduardo comments, and Violeta laughs because she knows that is true. "I need a wife myself," says Violeta. "That's a good deal for anyone." "Since you can't have one, be mine," Eduardo suggests. Violeta is astonished that a man in his fifties would have so little fear for those words. "If you want a home, I have one. You want a wife, I can be one. You want structure, I can give it to you. All I ask in return is a child." All this said amid laughter and cuddling, but uttered nonetheless.

Violeta tells me that after that agreeable conversation in his arms, she gets up to go to the bathroom, leaving Eduardo in bed. When she opens the door, she nearly steps on a black cockroach. "The biggest one I ever saw in my life, and the ugliest." Violeta stands transfixed.

December went by with its cherries, sweeter than ever that year. In February we left for the mill house.

It was there that Violeta talked to me the first time about "the Last Forest": her *nowhere*, a place in her consciousness, that unifying space that her mind began to construct out of a desire not to lose her dreams.

"It isn't a place to get to, Josefa. It's just strength to escape the immediate. If the *grand ethic* no longer exists, I would like for the Last Forest to be my small personal ethic."

She was expecting Eduardo.

The evening before his arrival, a windowpane broke in her bedroom. She runs to Aguayito; everything must be perfect for the next day. Aguayito sends his son with a new pane. I come in behind him. Violeta is on her bed with a book, still in her swimming suit. I see her bra and panties tossed on the only practical chair. Aguayito's son, nervous, cannot take his eyes off those silky undergarments. Violeta doesn't seem to notice.

"What treat can I offer him, Josefa?"

"How about smoked salmon?"

"It's already in the refrigerator. I was thinking of something more intimate, like something special to wear. But I don't have anything here. I know! You do my makeup for me!"

"Do you have cosmetics?"

"Me? What do you think, I barely have any in Santiago."

"I have kohl."

So typical, not to have anything to do her face. The next day she comes to my house. She's taken off her blue jeans, replacing them with a long Indian skirt.

We both sit on my bed as I do her face: I shape a depth in her eyes that they don't have. My daughter, Celeste, watches. She lowers the photo album she's looking through. She interrupts: "Violeta, look at these photos! They're from five years ago and you have on exactly the same clothes."

Celeste can't believe it. Violeta laughs.

"That doesn't surprise me, I've had this skirt ten years. But it's pretty, don't you think? Do you like it?"

"Ye-es . . ."

"Such enthusiasm, Celeste!" Violeta jests.

"As you can see, it flaunts its years," I put in.

When Violeta leaves in a halo of sandalwood, her eyes very black and the orange of her skirt shooting sparks, Celeste turns to me. "Violeta sure is behind the times, Mama. About everything!"

"It's one of her great virtues, Celeste. Don't undervalue it."

Even today, looking back, my eyes can wonder at the spectacle of the furious lake lashing the shore. And the volcano, enormous, majestic, the only witness: the hills sown with green are silent.

Violeta comes out wrapped in a blanket, and slowly walks toward the beach, pensive. She finds me there. She sinks down beside me without a word and stares at the waves.

"Eduardo's in the same mood as the water," she comments after a while.

"Angry?"

"Seems to be."

"What did you do?"

"Absolutely nothing. That's what's surprising."

My solitude that afternoon was total: the children were in Ensenada—they'd gone to have tea at the Bellavista—and Andrés was in Santiago for a few days. I hadn't seen Violeta and Eduardo all day; I assumed they were taking advantage of a time all to themselves, something rare between adult couples.

"The way his character is changing makes my head swim. It's got me down."

I wait for her to say something more.

She's afraid of being dramatic, I know her. She's the first to despise gravity. Serious, yes; grave, no, let's make a distinction. It's one of her maxims.

"What happened, Violeta?"

"He raped me."

I couldn't help laughing.

"But that's the one thing you want—or am I wrong?"

"I'm serious, Jose. We made love, everything perfect. Then we took a siesta. When he woke up he wanted to make love again. I didn't want to and told him, very affectionately, that I wanted to read a little while. He got out of bed and went into the living room. I picked up my book, thinking that everything was peaceful. I heard him opening the refrigerator and thought he'd woken up hungry. After a while he came to the room, looking very different. I don't want to go into details, but he was very odd. He smelled of alcohol, and he had a kind of perverse twist to his lips I'd never seen. He threw himself on me, literally. You know he doesn't drink, that's why I was so surprised. I asked him what the matter was and he just spouted obscenities. And now here's the worst about me: the obscenities got me all hot. And what started as rape ended up as wild passion. He's sleeping now. And I feel ashamed; it's left a bitter taste in my mouth."

"It had to be the alcohol." I, too, am amazed.

"It must be that . . ."

She gets up and hugs herself in the blanket. Still on the sand, I tug at one corner when I see she's about to leave.

"How do you feel?"

"I don't know," she tells me.

It was my opinion that Violeta indulged herself a little and that from time to time she allowed herself a certain indiscretion. I remembered her love for walking on the blade of the knife, of flirting with the edge, the outer limit. Which was why Violeta was more vulnerable than I.

"The black cockroach, you remember? Now it's the broken window pane. You think *el Espíritu Malo* is circling round?" ~ *omen*

"I don't know, I don't need evil spirits to justify anything."

"You're so logical, Jose!"

"It's always been clear to me that the human creature is perverse, dear Viola."

"And you keep so calm?"

"It's just there's nothing to do about it. Don't you realize that civilization and standards are all that keep us from eating each other alive? I don't know how you can still have hope for the future and the evolution of the species."

She seemed to be the old Violeta again, with laughter in her eyes. Again she clutched the blanket to her body, as if in fact it were warding off danger. She started back to the house, slowly. My eyes were fixed on her bamboo-like fingers, and I barely heard her when she said: "It's a familiar feeling, Josefa. I must dig into this. My gut instinct is giving me signals. The way you always have."

## 7

$\mathcal{W}$e, *the others*, know what Violeta was referring to. We were at her side that first day in school. Also the second and the third and all the days thereafter.

We watched her that Friday during recess as she took her thermos and sandwich from her schoolbag. The teacher, standing in the doorway, checked the filling in the bread of every girl in the line. She took Violeta's, examined it, and made a scornful face.

"Paté! Listen, girls, the new student has brought a paté sandwich. And remember this well so you learn what not to do."

Many faces—too many, in the eyes of the small Violeta—turned to stare at her.

"Today is Friday: the Catholic Church prohibits the eating of meat or any of its by-products on this day."

"I'm sorry . . . I didn't know."

"And your mother? *She* didn't know?" The teacher's disdainful tone was incomprehensible to Violeta.

"I don't know."

"Confiscated!" cried the teacher, throwing the sandwich into the trash bin.

Violeta went out to the courtyard alone. At least she had the thermos to dull her hunger.

She sat down on a bench and screwed off the top. Some of her classmates watched from a prudent distance. As she poured the reddish-brown liquid into the cup, one of them exclaimed: "Coca-Cola!"

They rushed toward her, ready to speak to her for the first time. Violeta was happy, maybe they would forgive her sky-blue eyeglasses and the paté. She offered to share the cup, smiling.

"Yuuugh! It isn't Coca-Cola," the first girl who tasted it said with horror.

"No." Violeta explained. "It's tea."

The other girls fell back: for the second time that morning there was disdain on their faces.

"She brought tea." The tone did not admit appeal.

"You drink plain tea? At your age?" another asked.

"That's what poor people drink," a third added.

"Let's go!"

Once again, Violeta was alone in the courtyard, with her scorned tea in one hand and the thermos in the other. She hated her mother at that moment. Didn't she understand that you can't bring *tea* to a school like this? She would tell her that night. But she had already told her about the glasses and she hadn't paid any attention.

"Your father bought them for you in the United States. You know, immigrants have never been known for good taste."

"Get me different ones, Mama, they all laugh at me."

"Please, Violeta, learn to be your own person. You will see when you're grown how important it is to be different."

Maybe, was her thought, but all she knew was that she was a little girl, and the only thing that interested her was being as much like the others as possible.

She didn't succeed.

Don't let it rain, don't let it rain, she used to pray in the winter. Rainy days were the only time her mother came to pick her up at school. With the rain came nearly all the mothers, and hers *was not* like the others.

Cayetana had straight hair and wore it long, really long. Before she came to the new school, Violeta loved her mother's hair, that shiny chestnut cascade that swung like magic following Cayetana's lively rhythm and energy, wet when she came out of the shower, air dried even in winter, the drops of water trembling on her shoulders as she walked around the house half naked: she would cover herself with a short towel she held in her left hand as her right beat time to the music she listened to at full volume. Her husband always scolded her, not too convincingly: "What a getup, Cayetana, God in heaven!" And Violeta would study her, fascinated by the freedom of those movements duplicated by her mother's hair. But now that same mane embarrassed her. Hers was the only mother in all the school with long hair. During the fifties, teased hair or a perm were the only acceptable hairdos. Urbane women wore their hair short and in a bouffant. And you never saw them in trousers. Cayetana was still under thirty, but her daughter saw her as an older woman; so she should look like one!

Cayetana's house in Ñuñoa was Violeta's cradle. The back patio, large and nostalgic, taught her love for trees and grape arbors. Violeta walked to the store on the corner, while her schoolmates were not allowed to go out alone, not even to the street door. Later she would invent her own "strict rules" for her mother (who never had any) because she felt out of step with the permissions Cayetana always gave her and that she never acknowledged in front of the other girls. "You want to stay over at Isabel's? Sounds like fun, Violeta, of course you can!" Cayetana would tell her; in contrast, the other mothers in the class thought it bad taste. "No, she wouldn't let me," Violeta would tell her friend Isabel, who would say with resignation, "Just like a mother; mine never lets me, either."

The storekeeper always greeted Violeta by her given name and, before she even asked, invariably said: "An umbrella for our Violet girl." He would turn to the colorful shelf that to her looked like a carousel and choose a cellophane-wrapped sweet, a red-and-green "umbrella" or "pine tree." She would take it and hand him her coin. Violeta was intensely bonded with her neighborhood, she felt she was a participant in its every ritual. She *was part of* the intelligent-looking gentlemen who were always in deep discussion at the Las Lanzas bar and sandwich shop and waved as she went by, or the old men sitting reading in the small plaza. If she went to the big plaza, someone had to go with her, but the small one, the one on the corner of Calle Richards, she could go to by herself. Once she was older, she learned to smoke in that plaza, buying single cigarettes at the kiosk on the corner. Her friends in the neighborhood had mothers like hers. One boy was the son of artists, another of a city representative; the girl who wore the ruffled dresses was the daughter of a writer. And the father of Alicia, her very closest friend, was a philosopher. The fact that her father owned a bookstore was normal among those friends. As it was for Violeta to go with her mother when she marched in street demonstrations before elections. Nothing like that seemed to happen in her school, however. Violeta loved her neighborhood and never suspected that it would be what finished her off among her new schoolmates.

She decided to celebrate her birthday. Cayetana was excited about it and prepared a big party. One by one, she drew each invitation by hand. Violeta would never forget the red gelatin in the scooped-out oranges; Cayetana had made them herself, she who almost never cooked. They were beautiful.

At four o'clock in the afternoon of that August Saturday, Violeta, in white from tip to toe, was waiting to greet the friends who would help her celebrate her ninth birthday.

It was a long wait. The doorbell obstinately refused to ring. At a quarter to five, finally, the first little girl came. Cayetana went to open the door. She smiled at her daughter's schoolmate: dark, shy eyes, short, straight hair, and wearing a heavily starched dress under her lightweight blue coat.

"What is your name?" Cayetana asked.

"Josefina."

"Josefina what?"

"Ferrer."

"Come in, Josefina. Welcome."

They went to the room in the back where the children of Carmencita, the clerk in the bookstore, were playing; she never missed a family event.

By five-thirty the silence was deafening. Violeta was afraid it would shatter if she spit out the knot swelling in her throat. Carmencita's children on the floor with some toy, Josefina in a chair, Violeta in another, paralyzed, as only hope can paralyze.

At six they went to the table. Fifteen minutes earlier some friends from the neighborhood had showed up, although they weren't the ones who'd been invited. Violeta was thrilled to see them, fearing, in that loneliness, that all the delicious treats on the dining room table would be wasted: the meringues, the gelatins, the open-face sandwiches spread with egg salad and chicken salad, the enormous birthday cake. The very worst would be to have all that food left. She never learned that at Cayetana's orders Marcelina, Violeta's nurse, had gone to the houses of the neighborhood children and brought them back to the party. That meant they could cut the cake with some dignity. No one else came. After they had sung and eaten, Cayetana went over to the one girl from Violeta's school.

"Josefina, why do you think your schoolmates didn't come?"

"Because Violeta lives in Ñuñoa."

"What?"

When she saw how dumbfounded Cayetana was, the child didn't know whether to go on or not. But Cayetana urged her, and that opened the floodgates of her feelings.

"There's a group in our class that are the bosses; all the girls do what they say. They don't like Violeta: they say she's Polish, and that the glasses she wears turn their stomach. They look down on her because she drinks tea and eats paté sandwiches. When they received their invitations and saw that Violeta lives in Ñuñoa, they got together and agreed they wouldn't come. That's what they told everyone, and the joke was not to tell Violeta."

"And why did you come?"

"Because I turn their stomachs, too."

"And why do you turn their stomachs?"

"Because my father is a baker."

"And that's all?"

"I don't know."

Cayetana ended her questioning there, not knowing whether to cry or, given her character, simply burst out laughing.

Violeta remembers clearly overhearing the discussion that night in her parents' room.

"Does Violeta really have to pay such a high price to be fluent in English?" Cayetana asked her husband.

"It is precisely this school that will ensure that she's not left out when she grows up. You don't have any sense of that, Cayetana; the middle-class intellectuals you go around with don't know much about such things. I do."

"There are two alternatives here, Tadeo: either we are raising a malcontent who will turn into a social climber, or we're shaping a revolutionary."

Those words sank into Violeta's being; they lodged in her memory even though she did not consciously understand them. That child always did listen more with her instinct than her reason. And that

*patronizing*

54

never changed; she approached persons, events, feelings by observing rather than fully comprehending, as if merely by making room for things internally she made them hers.

That night, in bed, the curls falling over her cheeks were wet with tears. When she scrubbed her cheeks dry she decided she would not give up in that minor war. She dreamed of herself, alone—or perhaps after that afternoon with a partner—facing the cruel, implacable hostility one knows only in childhood. She would stay in that school and she would get the best of all of them.

# 8

I often got weary of Violeta.

I got weary of nurturing our friendship, as I did of nurturing anything that wasn't my voice. If I did it, it wasn't out of generosity, as she believed. Or out of loyalty, as others thought. It was simply my fear of being alone.

I was made aware of this fear in San Miguel de Allende, in Mexico. Amalia, a famous and elderly Mexican singer, someone I had admired and listened to forever, had come to my concert. She invited me to have a drink one afternoon; I was honored, and accepted. I knew that in her retirement she had chosen to live in that town, but was surprised to find that her address was a hotel.

On the enormous patio surrounded by red colonial arches and exuberant greenery, rocking on the gallery with tequilas in our hands, she warned me about it.

Amalia gave her last concert at the age of sixty. And that night, completely tranquil, she shut the door. She did not intend to expose herself to the humiliation of diminishing contracts, of clubs instead of auditoriums or theaters, of audiences that compared her live performance to records from earlier days. In answer to my eagerness to understand why she was living alone in a hotel, she described the progression: the closer she came to the peak of her fame, the more the world began to be intrusive. The first thing she got rid of was her husband, who couldn't accept being relegated to second place. Then it was her children: before long they decided to live with their father, who seemed to have more time for them. Then it was the house: without a family, it didn't make sense to look after *that* enterprise, when the enterprise of her success was so much more seductive. She rented a large storage space, moved all her furniture and belongings there, and began living in hotels. Finally she felt independent. She confessed to me how much people bothered her, how she felt pursued. How she was crushed with guilt for not answering even her lifelong friends, the ones who became a weight on her shoulders rather than a pleasure. She saw only the people she had to, no one else. She composed her best songs during that period. Finally she was taken seriously and considered a professional. When she passed through San Miguel de Allende on a tour, she told herself that she would retire there. "Nothing original," she added. "Many people have done the same; artists from everywhere live here, especially our neighbors to the north." She kept her promise and here she was, right before my eyes: two rooms on a bit of a gallery that was nearly hers. Nothing more. Her children visited reasonably often, and an occasional friend came by to say hello when in town.

San Miguel de Allende, cautiously in my memory.

I chose Violeta from among all my women friends because our histories went back so far that no explanations were necessary. She was part of my childhood, almost another member of our family. That's why I was so comfortable with her: anything we did together was like doing it alone. And my fear of emptiness did not allow absolute privacy. Then as very gradually people became superfluous—and that phenomenon heightened despite my will—I feared that if I broke the last link I would pitch face first into total solitude. No, I said to myself one night: someday Andrés won't be here for you; who knows that better than you do? Your children will be living their own lives, and then you, you who have had fewer and fewer friends the higher you climb the ladder to the stars, will have no intimates. And no one will want you to be theirs. Do you know, Josefa, what it is to live without a true friend?

San Miguel de Allende comes back to me because of my first—and only—fight with Violeta. Remorse is having its way with me, Viola, Violeta, Violetera.

First came the business of the dining room, and then the story of the sauna.

But the sauna was preceded by the tale of the "love nest."

For years I would eat lunch with my younger son Diego in the bright, inviting kitchen of my home. Until the period Violeta calls "the process of making yourself inaccessible." The first symptom was that on my return from a tour I surprised everyone by asking María, the cook, to set the table in the dining room. We would have lunch there. I was irritated by the proximity of the maids; just the idea that they had access to me put me in a bad mood. I couldn't bear being exposed for forty-five minutes every day. If I had moved to the dining room, it was so they couldn't talk to me. So no one could get to me.

"Careful, my love," Andrés said affectionately one day. "One of these days we won't be able to find you."

That's when Violeta started calling me "Miss-I-Don't-Have-Time-My-Life-Is-Too-Important." I would laugh, a little uncomfortable. I felt permanently obligated. My career seemed meteoric, and each step took more effort than the last. The contradictions in my professional and my private lives cut through me like a poisoned lance.

I don't need to elaborate on this point. For today's women it's already a commonplace. I prefer to address myself instead to feelings: the calls I haven't answered always pressing on me, the people I've left waiting, the basic affection I haven't returned. I come home to lock myself in. I have to work: words are pounding in my head with their respective notes; I have snippets of a song I can't get down because the conditions aren't right to do it. I come home and it isn't my retreat anymore.

It's strange, the darkness in this house; so often it seemed the only possible source of light. I go in, I open doors, I see sour faces in front of the TV, the light in the garden being wasted, bodies flopped on beds as if disjointed. Everyone waiting for the vital notes to come out of my poor throat. Andrés comes home for dinner, happy and self-satisfied. Unlike me, he has had twenty-four hours—he has them every day—to think how to do things well. He kisses the children with the weariness born of satisfaction. And I resent it: my relation with the children is always neither here nor there, I'm always shooing them away to be able to work, and always want them home because I can't get along without them. I have opted for their eternal presence because I'm afraid of being forsaken. How can it be that what I love most becomes what most disturbs my everyday existence?

Then I begin to pay for every minute of solitude. I give everyone tickets: run along to the movies or take a taxi to the museum, with ice cream as you leave, and when the door shuts I savor the silence they've left behind.

"Zulema, I'm going to be working. I don't want to be interrupted."

In Zulema's mind, however, I am at home. The interruptions begin. At some moment I run out of the house, furious, run, with no idea where I am. I'm walking and find myself standing in front of a building under construction. Studio apartments for sale. I brighten. I wait for Andrés with enthusiasm.

"What are you talking about? You're thinking of a love nest?"

"A love nest? No, Andrés, nothing like that . . . it would be an office, somewhere I could work."

"And would you have conferences with the musicians?"

"Maybe."

"And maybe you could also use it for photography sessions? Have you thought about putting in a bed?"

"At least a sofa-bed for a nap," I reply in all innocence; I'm so absorbed I don't notice his irony. "And I wouldn't give anyone a copy of the key! Imagine, darling, the control I'd have over my own time."

The discussion continued until Andrés changed his approach and adopted that man-to-man tone he likes to use with me at times. He didn't utter the words *love nest* again, but he didn't think much of the idea.

"No, Josefa. No. It's a bad investment. It's very expensive. That building is not well constructed, and the finishing trim is terrible. No one will want to rent or buy it from you later! And we're not even talking expenses. And who would take care of it when you're on a trip? Who would clean it for you? I don't see you doing it, you'd end up keeping Zulema at the apartment. Besides, Josefa, this is no time to have extra square footage with all the poor people there are, with the problem of so many who have nowhere at all to live except with relatives. Don't you agree it's frivolous to buy an apartment just to have a few hours a day alone?"

That's a typical Violeta phrase . . . as if they were in cahoots.

It took me several days to realize what he had done, and to feel fenced in. Everything *in our house.* He wants me home, at any price. The house and me: joined together until death do us part.

"He's partly right," Violeta tells me a few days later. "It's already hard enough to put up with a famous wife when he isn't famous himself. He thinks he's forced to take care of the children when you're on tour, even the ones that aren't his. And he sees you constantly surrounded by musicians and rock stars and sound engineers and newspapermen, sees you getting yourself up in sequins for your star appearances, when a million eyes are studying every centimeter of your body. You can't ask that of him, Josefa. He is a husband, after all . . ."

I closed off a second-floor room we never used because it was too dark and had a sauna built. Everyone thought it was for health purposes, or vanity, but I had discovered that a sauna is like a bathroom: a place of absolute privacy. It was going to be the one place where no one would be able to talk to me. *La señora* is in the sauna, Zulema would say on the telephone; she wouldn't even have to lie.

I installed my sauna. I became an addict.

Next came the telephone. I asked them to change the number one more time. I brought in a line for the children's living room, with the promise that no one would use it but them. The second line would be for "the house." We agreed with Andrés not to give the number to anyone, only the family, in case of emergency. We both could be contacted at our offices. With that system, I relaxed for the first time. The damned phone didn't ring anymore and finally I could enjoy my house without interruptions, without the constant fear that I would be trapped against my will. I told my friends, without batting an eyelash, "I don't have a telephone; leave a message with my secretary."

But I made the mistake of giving Violeta that same story. I hadn't learned to make the necessary distinctions.

I was working with Alejandro one morning in my office, going over contracts, when the secretary interrupted: "Violeta Dasinski wants to see you."

I was surprised. Violeta was very discreet and never came to my office without warning.

She was sitting in front of my desk. She was playing with a yellow pencil, and she was not smiling.

"I brought you an idea for your next song."

"Yes?"

" 'The soul selects her own society. Then, shuts the door,' " she recited with her perfect pronunciation. "That's Emily Dickinson."

"Nice," I commented, disconcerted.

I asked for coffee for both of us; I had a vague presentiment. Then she got up—long, Violeta's skirts, heavy her boots—and, looking out the window, said accusingly: "Are you aware, Josefa, of the level of your voraciousness?"

Strange coming from her. Caring and warm, she did not usually speak that way.

"What are you talking about?" I heard the defensiveness in my voice.

"Details. Symptoms. Have you noticed that you smoke your cigarette down to the filter, as if it were the last one you would ever have?"

"Don't say that, you know I'm not supposed to smoke." Trying to appease her, divert her a little.

"And when you drink wine? How many times do you fill the glass? In a social situation, I mean."

"You're not saying I'm an alcoholic?"

"No, that's why I said in a social situation. And when you go home, you yourself have told me, you go into the kitchen and eat half a baguette—particularly if you're dieting."

"Where is all this going, Violeta?"

"I've spent the last three nights analyzing you. I learned from your children that it's a lie that you don't have a telephone. You didn't remember that they tell everything to Jacinta."

"Oh, so that's it."

My mouth was dry from pure anxiety. I can't stand the idea of a quarrel with Violeta, I can't stand it.

"Violeta, I'm sorry. Don't judge me, please. I'm exhausted."

"You're always exhausted."

"It's just that it's not easy! It's not easy, this being . . ." I couldn't find the right word.

"Famous?"

"That word makes me sick."

"But it's short . . . and precise."

She wasn't going to ease up, I felt it in the air.

"You should understand. You better than anyone! All the years I was my mother's daughter, who sang! Then the music student, who sang, and later Borja's and Celeste's mother, who sang, and the music teacher, who sang, until finally I've become, flat out, a singer. You think it's been easy?"

"No, I know it hasn't. And no one has enjoyed your success more than I have. The problem is what fame has done to you."

"Forgive me, but you exaggerate. No one is complaining."

She laughed ironically.

"It's just that no one says anything to you."

"Maybe. The worst is that I doubt I'd care."

"Of course you wouldn't. You always were a skeptic, that didn't come from fame. But I didn't think you would also make that classic leap from skepticism to cynicism." She cut herself short with a reflective look, an expression very typical of Violeta when she is wound up about something. "I believe that fame favors intricate paths of disconnectedness, and that you've plunged into one of them."

"You truly believe I've become a cynic?"

Spurred by her own certainty, she answered, and there was no quiver in her voice.

"I understand, Josefa, that cynicism works like a drug to create distance, an analgesic against the danger of existing, until it becomes toxic. At first, no doubt, it was a relief; you could mock your fears. But in the end it has poisoned you." She hesitates a moment, looks at me. "A cumulative effect, like morphine, higher and higher doses, until your addiction becomes irreversible."

She got up. She picked her up purse and coat, walked to the door, and hurled her judgment.

"Be careful, Josefa: cynicism is a highly dangerous disease."

I sat frozen. I made no move to stop her. Let her go. I lit one of my five daily cigarettes . . . which usually I saved for other times. I smoked voraciously, as Violeta had described.

I felt like a house with nooks, memories, and intimacies that no one else could appreciate in its true dimensions. The blue wood box Robert sent me once, filled with colorful candies, large sweets with caramel and shredded coconut: that box is seen as a *objet* but I see it as a token of love. My legitimate reserve gives me the right to open the door of my house and let people come in as far as I choose: some into the entrance hall, others as far as the living room. No farther. The bedrooms, the study, the back patios, are mine. What did Violeta say about intricate paths of disconnectedness? No, those paths aren't intricate, it's just that reserve operates there, and that allows no vulnerability. Of course, it is also a mark of internal poverty—no doubt of that!—but that way I am safe. I have a right to keep my house closed. Yes, Emily Dickinson is right: *then, shuts the door.*

It is true that to survive I attributed to people a certain measure of inherent malevolence, probably more than they had. Thus fortified, I eased through the turbulence of human relationships. Not Violeta. She was naturally confident, and so went through life evenly, openly, with less baggage than I, with the illusion she would find what was best in others. Today I'm looking back, and although in hindsight things become evident once one knows the plot, I insist—without any of the seer's presumption—that Violeta was mistaken.

It was easier to wound Violeta than to wound me.


I got nothing out of trying to intellectualize. By the second cigarette I realized that although human relationships have always been complex for me, I was now experiencing clear evidence of that complexity. I was thinking about Violeta's words and measuring the caliber of her resentment. When had it begun? I'd never even noticed. I'd been more careful with her than with anyone; I'd told the story of San Miguel de Allende, and Violeta was the one I chose. I'd been talking about reserve, and suddenly it comes to me how much we keep back even from those we love most. It's like everything else: reciprocal. Every relationship has its own, its instinctive, division: what is revealed, what is held back. God, I really do love Violeta. But . . . And the list of *buts* is enormous. My always relative reaction to her enthusiasm; the quantity of opinions I don't listen to because I attach them to her defects: no, I won't pay attention to that because Violeta is *excessive;* no credence to that, Violeta is *rigid;* I won't argue it with her, she's a *fanatic.* Nevertheless, aside from Andrés and the children, she is the person I'm closest to in the world. Close? If this is closeness, what is distance? What others feel toward me? I never analyze what I stir in others. I ask myself very few questions, because, unlike Violeta, I have never wanted for basic affection. Most of all, my parents'. Or what Andrés feels for me. Yes, Andrés; he gives me such security that I look at other people without anxiety, entirely calm: so that person likes me; that one hates me; I leave that one cold. But now I'm afraid because I haven't learned shadings, taking "that person likes me" as absolute, without further consideration. Violeta's eyes were accusing, *no one says anything to you.* No. My distance probably has inhibited them. No one dares tell me anything. And Violeta has.

yourself ←  Something is suffocating me. I ought to go into a convent. Have no relationship but one with an unseen being. The subtleties of affection and the lack of it are oppressive. What a temptation, to get into it with Violeta, to jam the accelerator to the floorboard and not choke back what I've kept silent! I reach for the telephone: call her right now and throw her aggression back in her face. But I stop myself: a spark of lucidity. No, Josefa, stop; it would be so difficult at your age to make new ties, don't blow those you've kept for a lifetime. Cherish them. And in my very pores I feel the fear of losing Violeta. There are some luxuries I don't dare give myself, like complete sincerity. That time has passed.

I get up from the desk. I ask my secretary for some aspirin. Alejandro and I go back to work. I turn the page.


Why didn't I go to look for her with a huge sack of pistachios and just give her a hug? It would have been enough. Violeta had a special capacity for turning my defects into virtues. She took them, infused a little ideology, and returned them as positives. No one else in the world did that for me. She would have forgiven me instantly, she didn't know the word *rancor*. Why did I let her go off to Bahías de Huatulco alone like that?

"Do you want me to take you to the airport?"

"Don't worry, Eduardo is taking me."

"Do you have enough money?"

"Yes, Jose, yes." She would never have called me Jose if she were angry, I consoled myself. She, Andrés, and Mauricio were the only ones who called me that.

I should have said right then, before she left, Violeta, I miss you, let's forget that conversation. Her feelings were hurt and I knew it. But I did nothing.

"Write me, all right?"

"But I'm only going for three weeks."

"You always send me a postcard, even if you're going a week."

Violeta was fond of rituals, and she had a lot of them. She was painstaking in their execution, especially if they involved others. She always bought a postcard for me, looking for something beautiful or amusing, another for Jacinta, and a third for her father.

"Yes, I'll send you a card."

And as if I were incapable of any other subject, I began talking about Mexico, one of our shared loves.

("Mexico is an outrageous country" was Violeta's characterization. And in that exuberance we let ourselves be seduced, each in her own time. For me, it was when I cut my first record; for Violeta, when she made her pilgrimage in search of Cayetana. And the excess of that country invaded different chinks in our beings. Stayed with us. "Forever," said Violeta.)

"Let me know if you're going to build a house in Huatulco," I said (yet another house for her list of fantasies).

When the first card arrived, why did I decide to ignore the symptoms of her sadness?

*To the degree that the world I knew is coming apart, my grasp on things growing weaker, hostility is making me weaker and I cannot find—it's fading—the human hearth I knew growing up. I am speaking of the collective hearth . . . the great one.*

*The truth, Josefa, is that I don't feel at home in this world.*

There was a second.

*I met a North American, his name is Bob. He is a combination newspaperman and social scientist. In my words, he's a "romancer." He's made the same pilgrimages through Central America I have, and that's made us closer.*

*Do you know that Bob knows you? He attended your triumphal performance in Radio City Music Hall, in New York. I told him that you felt like a "star" the first time you saw one of your CDs in a window on Fifth Avenue. It must be destiny—no?—that he went to hear you because you're Chilean (like every well-bred gringo, he was interested in the subject of our country) and that today I run into him here in these bays on the Pacific.*

*It's very rare to find someone on the planet who feels about things the way you do, isn't it?*

*Bob, too, sometimes thinks that we could create something like heaven here on earth, that history cannot go on being the story of human suffering forever.*

Again I look at the photograph of Violeta in the newspaper. Her curls are in disarray. Her body sparks an aura of ice, that body that knew nothing but warmth.

Calm did not help Violeta, because there was no calm. This time she wasn't accompanied by her sainted hope.

Did the Last Forest fade away without my realizing it? Did it fail to protect her from the storm? Maybe there were many forests; Violeta lost her way in their labyrinths and the last one stood empty: she could not get there in a straight line.

# 9

"I'm a slave to my body, Josefa, and I hate myself for it."
"Do you think marriage might be the solution?"
Apparently it was.


From Violeta's diary:


*My wedding night was the first night of love-making without an orgasm; just the opposite of so many women who begin to come once they know they are going to marry.*

*When I met Eduardo, I was, you might say, ready to tuck some tenderness in my kit bag. Tenderness is something I never wanted to be without.*

Eduardo has taken over my house, even though that wasn't my intention. Tonight, Sunday, he stretched out on the bed with a legal pad in his hands and sat me down in front of him. He asked me, rather severely, to get my glasses. Then he dictated a list of chores I was to accomplish during the week. All domestic, such as call the handyman who needs to clean out the gutters or make the annual inspection of the stove in the hallway. When I asked him if he was joking, he told me he would be checking my efficiency the next Sunday. I have taken it as a game.

"In this house the intellectual is me," he warned. I suppose there can be only one if the couple is to function.

Eduardo was writing on his yellow legal pad at the iron table in the garden, after lunch, while I was watching the sky from my hammock. I interrupted: "What would your Paradise be like? Tell me, quick, without rationalizing."

"You mean, how would I like the world to be?"

"The ideal world . . ."

"Let's see . . ." He thinks for a minute and turns the question back to me. "What would you change in this world?"

"Me? Two things. The body and the poor: they escape my Paradise."

"How is that?"

"The body is decay, the perishable, the painful. And the poor: the global stigma."

Eduardo looked at me with light irony, and then brushed me off: "All I know about my personal Paradise is that it's in my writing. I've never thought about the other one, and it doesn't worry me."

We've made love; husband-and-wife lovers, perfectly legal.

I am the consummated Eros of an excited and eager Eduardo. I get excited and eager myself. Everything goes as it should, and I lose control, as always with him, and that makes him crazy as a blinded horse; our cries are almost embarrassing. *Everything was great until just after orgasm, his orgasm. It's not for nothing it's been called* the little death! *Come. Climax. Get it off. The result: pleasure, relief, peace. And with him, from there straight to sleep. Straight, I said. Without a breath. Not even opening his eyes to tell me he loves me or, there at the last, to watch me loving myself. Nothing. He pulls away as if he had never been near me, moves into a well-being that is solely his. After love, Eduardo shares nothing. He comes and he falls asleep, that's the cycle. Not a trace of tenderness, of closeness, of caring. I lie in bed, eyes wide open, still suffused with the intimacy I have just experienced, and my only impulse is to caress him. With tenderness, not passion. When I hear him snoring, I realize that my caresses are out of place. He was gone the moment he finished.* I am left absolutely alone, *his semen inside me, his smells clinging to my body, my love wandering around the room. Without a friendly hand to reaffirm me after our mingling.*

*Once again I have been Eduardo's depository, once again he has taken me and left me.* I am nothing to him at this moment.

*I think, I should charge him the next time.*


*At least if I have demons I'm aware of them.*


*Today, as we were eating, I told Eduardo the amusing conversation I had with Josefa when she came over from the recording studio to have coffee.*

*Josefa: I can't understand, Violeta, I simply can't understand that success isn't your overall goal.*

*I: What do you find strange about that?*

*Josefa: Well, I don't know . . . You could go a long way.*

*I: I'm not interested in "going a long way." Not in that sense, Jose. Not as me, the architect. I would like for the world to go a long way, can you understand that?*

*Josefa: No, I don't understand.*

*I explained that the only thing that interests me is doing my job well.*

*Josefa seemed incredulous. Then the concept of triumph doesn't matter to you at all?*

*I looked at her, almost with commiseration in my eyes, and said no.*

*Eduardo kept twirling his fork. That was when he said, "The big difference between you two is that Josefa is a winner and you're a loser."*

*I looked at him, partly in anger, partly in shock.*

*"The word* loser *makes me sick! It can only come from the lips of someone with a terrible complex or someone clawing his way to the top—which is nearly the same thing—and you're not that, Eduardo. Besides, that's a concept invented in the Chile of this decade; we Chileans didn't use to divide ourselves into categories like those."*

*I've been boiling ever since.*

*So typical of our day to make nouns out of adjectives and . . . how ghastly! adjectives out of nouns.*

*If I were capable of planning objectively and not getting personally involved, I would have devoted myself to politics. But I always go around digging my own grave. How I would love to know prudence and moderation! (Or lack of transparency?)*

*Her voice is unique; she is supergifted, no doubt about it! How many singers have been given that timbre, how many know how to use it?*

*Today was Josefa's long-awaited recital. It's the first one Eduardo's been to. We had the best seats in the theater.*

*The ovation that welcomed her did not in any way affect her bearing: elegantly static and remote is always her way on stage. No one would suspect she is suffering. It is her panic that makes her seem distant; it is part of her persona, something the public loves without perceiving that her remoteness is merely fear, her eternal fear. But we, we who know, are calm, because once she starts singing her pleasure begins, her vertigo, and nothing or no one can stop her.*

*She was wearing a dark lamé dress, floor length and severely cut (except for a fairly low neckline and a slit to the knees). The rest: pure lamé and Josefa's body. "Stu-pen-dous," I say to Eduardo, and he adds, "And sexy!" That night she didn't wear her hair loose the way Andrés likes it; it was pulled back tight to her head; her only accessory was a small crownlike clasp that held her hair in a perfect coil (but I know she's added an extension; her hair isn't that long).*

*Nothing on the stage but a chair. (How inexpensive it must be to mount one of Josefa's productions when she decides to sing alone with her guitar. Lighting, nothing more. I explain to Eduardo that for television she uses an orchestra, and sometimes she takes a couple of guitarists on her tours. But not when she's recording or it's live performance. He shushes me.)*

*The order of songs is in the program: ninety percent are hers. All she added were the famous tango* Malena *and Chavela Varga's "Amanecí en tus brazos"—I Awoke in Your Arms. I was surprised she didn't include her beloved* Macorina; *after all, among the songs written by someone else, it's her biggest hit.*

*With the first chords of the guitar came a nearly sacred silence. And from that silence emerged her song. Once again I am struck by the effect her voice produces on those who hear it. Are they transformed, do they fly, are they transported to heaven? What is it exactly that happens to them?*

*Eduardo scarcely drew a breath until the intermission. Only then did he ask: "Is this really the same woman we saw this summer? The one with the old espadrilles and three faded sweaters?" He didn't know I sang every song with Josefa—under my breath. It's my way of encouraging her from afar.*

*Everything was perfect, as always. No miscue, no false-step. That's why she has the program distributed in advance, to have everything set, everything under her control. Josefa says almost nothing between songs. At most she gives the title and says what album it's from. On rare occasions she tells when or why she composed it. This economy is part of her legend.*

*When the concert was over, the applause summoned her back to the stage. She made a move to exit, but the public wouldn't hear of it. "Macorina! Sing Macorina for us!" She hesitated, then something changed in her expression. She took up the guitar and began: "Put your hand here, Macorina, put your hand here . . ." Josefa's pleasure in singing that song is contagious, you feel it along with her and— say what you will—what this vocation means becomes palpable: savage pleasure. ". . . your lips were a blessing of ripe guanábana and your tiny waist the benediction of that danzón . . ." Yes, Eduardo was bewitched. ". . . the heat of that danzón." The ovation that followed managed to bring the man down to earth.*

*Well, I can't go on all night writing about the recital, I sound like a stupid fan. Which I am. And today I've become more important in Eduardo's eyes, just for being Josefa's friend.*

*Eduardo came home late tonight. I was waiting with dinner ready. He finished his lasagna with gusto and slowly savored his wine, a Tarapacá I've become fond of and which, to my surprise, he drank to the last drop.*

*"Very good," he told me. "Everything was very good."*

*"You see," I said. "I'm not such a bad housekeeper after all."*

*Eduardo: What I said has nothing to do with you or whether or not you're a good housekeeper.*

*I: (surprised): Why not?*

*He: It's all automatic.*

*I: The lasagna made itself automatically?*

*He: Rosa made it.*

*I: And who told Rosa how to make it? Or do you think a maid functions automatically, with no directions from me?*

*He: Well, the wine came automatically in the monthly order. They even bring it to the house.*

*I: But Eduardo, I place that monthly order; if I didn't the wine wouldn't come.*

*He: It's on your list, it's automatic.*

*I feel completely removed from the picture.*

*And to add insult to injury, late in the night I am awakened by sharp stabs in my ovaries. It's my period: perfect, cyclical, punctual.*

*Last night I reached orgasm before he did and stayed mounted on him, moving frenetically, so immersed in that frenzy I didn't notice his ejaculation. I opened my eyes only when I heard him laugh. "I came," he said, still laughing. Was that mockery I saw in his eyes?*

*I moved off him, slightly humiliated.*

*I get my domestic self mixed up with my sexual self, and don't know which I am, as if they were so incompatible that I don't recognize myself in both simultaneously. Something must be going badly.*

*Speaking with Josefa about sexual pleasure: that wave of heat that fills us, erases us, that we easily recognize as desire, is what humanizes her. And what destroys me.*

*Antibodies form only in response to known emotions. Confronted with unknown ones—contempt in bed, for example—no antibodies form, they don't recognize the sentiment; you don't put up your shield and your heart isn't resentful.*

*I never learned to isolate myself from desire, which may be why I've been generous: a well from which I still haven't learned to filter out things that have fallen in.*

*This state of my being is not innate.*

*Bored with waiting for Eduardo, I turned on the television. A young political figure was being interviewed. They asked him about nostalgia. He replied: What is that? I don't know it.*

*I turned off the TV and knew I would never vote for him.*

*I remembered being in a restaurant and running into an old student leader who had been a close friend. I was at a table waiting for Josefa so we could go to Channel 7 where she was going to participate in a program about the 60s. When I saw him, I thought: who better to give me an idea I can pass on to Josefa.*

*He: The 60s? Only one thing to do with them, Violeta.*

*I: (eager for an intelligent answer): What? Tell me!*

*He: Forget them!*

*Today we had dinner with Josefa and Andrés. It was Celeste's birthday and since Jacinta couldn't miss that, all three of us went.*

*Marginal note: Jacinta took me into Celeste's bedroom to see the new decoration: new bed, dressing table, bed table with little painted flowers. All the paraphernalia needed to make a girl her age happy. "It's precious, Celeste!" I said enthusiastically. "Your mother is an angel to do this for you." "It didn't cost her anything," she answered, annoyed, "since money is all she has." "You're not being fair. What about the time, the effort? Doesn't that count?" But I stopped, and I see a pout forming on Celeste's lips, a quintessentially childish expression. "She doesn't love us," she tells me. "All she wants to do is get rid of us." I sat her down on the bed and gave her a lecture. I must remember to tell Josefa about it. Damned teenagers!*

*Eduardo was enchanting, clever and amusing. I realize that I'm using this notebook only to complain and I feel I'm being very unfair— almost as unfair as Celeste. I wonder why I never need to write when I'm happy? When we were in the kitchen lighting the candles for the cake, Josefa asked me how things were going in my new marriage. "There are adjustments," I answered. "The famous adjustments. How long do you think it takes a couple to iron them out?" "A lifetime, Violeta," she replies.*

*I called Josefa to talk with her about Celeste. How everything ended was that Celeste went to her mother today, perfectly happy, and* said: "*Violeta's funny, Mama. She uses affection when she's dealing with men and with women she uses her mind.*" *Josefa replied:* "*That must be one of Violeta's little nuggets of wisdom, to treat each individual with what they need most.*"

*Good for her, good for me.*

*Eduardo is, like every man who prides himself on it, a complete egocentric.*

*Have I turned into one of those neurotics of addictive love?*

*What drives me crazy is that he doesn't listen to me. Every night I could write a brief three-act play here, illustrating three situations a day when he doesn't hear me. What's the matter with him? Does it bore him to answer? Doesn't he have any personal time for me? Is it just that his ego fills all his needs?*

*It's going to give me cancer. I am going to grow a cancer out of pure desperation at not being heard.*

*Why do I think about penetrating and not about enveloping? The penis penetrates, the vagina envelops.*

*I recall Agustina, a woman from a squatter's camp I took in because her husband beat her. She was working in the village's communal kitchens. That first night, telling me about her life, she said: "He occupied me last night, compañera, and then after everything else he dared hit me."*

*Eduardo is snoring, I have got out of bed and tiptoed to the sunroom, swamped with anguish. The thing that happened in the mill house has happened again. What can I call it? From one moment to the next he was transformed into a brute. I fought it and fought it, until it was useless, until I gave in with revulsion. It is his obscene side that confuses me, hurts me. Nevertheless, that is the side that ends up winning.*

*Agustina and I are alike: woman/depository. All liquids are deposited in us: semen and sweat. Could sorrows be liquid? They should be, like amniotic fluid, like blood, like tears.*

*Tonight I was occupied by my husband.*


*I decided to confront the subject of his thirst. I prefer to call it that, I want to embroider the despicable.*

*It was still early and the bar was nearly empty. Listening to New Age music, I ask him who the customers usually are. "Certainly not the people who live in developments on the outskirts of the city, or office workers from downtown," he replies sullenly. "Goddamn bourgeoisie," he adds. "The bar calls itself a* pub *and substitutes Vangelis for boleros. They set out peanuts by the whiskey, talk English at that corner table. There aren't any bars anymore like the ones where we used to come and get drunk when I first came to live in Santiago. They don't even have wine in a pitcher anymore, only sophisticated drinks. This doesn't seem like my country." I look at him, completely in tune, and join him in remembering a country we both loved but that has been transformed without our say.*

*He is telling me about* Los Tres Mosqueteros *bar. It was enormous, and dark; the tables disappeared in the shadow. A long brass foot rail gleaming below the counter. Under the arches of the main room, the suitcases of vendors who sold books door to door. The sound of dice rattling in leather dice cups. There were men, only men. On an old radio, the voice of Lucho Barrios. "And beer and wine were both welcome in that world," he says with a faraway look, and adds: "Those men never had anything to say, but I could feel the invisible bonds among them. It was then, Violeta, I recognized the unspoken solidarity of those who, despite themselves, had elected the depths of alcohol."*

*He asks for a second gin and ginger ale. "Loneliness is devastating," he says. "And tonight threatens to be eternal. My private hells are so many—you know them—don't judge me for a drink or two too many." "What loneliness do you mean, Eduardo? I'm here." He looks* at me, uncomprehending, and I realize that he goes places I cannot go with him, and I am overcome with remorse and love; painful love, spreads through my body. I order a gin for myself. And before long, another. I am with him, inside his skin. He takes me in as one of his. And tells me: "You will need gin, Violeta, only when your comprehension approaches the metaphysical, only when you no longer are tuned to this piece of life in this piece of a too real world, when your intelligence can no longer ignore pessimism. Then you will belong with us."

I thought, the gin was in his blood even before he began drinking it.

"I despise you for your strength," was the last thing he said to me, "and I love you for it. It's strange that the gods haven't managed to cloud your eyes."

I think that after that night in the pub I began to live a demented existence. I have no other way to live with him. Maybe the price I'm paying to become a mother again is too high. How to know?

# 10

$\mathcal{W}$e, *the others*, we know what Violeta was talking about when she named the refuges. We were there when the first disintegrated.

No refuge would have been possible without an organizing element: Violeta's love for art. Gonzalo's painting, Josefa's music, Eduardo's writing. The muse/mother. She could paint, but she wasted her eyes on the planes she drew in that Italian office to nurture Gonzalo's painting. She was born with music in her ears, but she always sang the second part to Josefa. Words bubbled from her even in the cradle. Bubbled, but she did not choose them.

She chose architecture. As Josefa always said, Violeta deduced people's houses. And she maintained that spaces condense everything that happens to people. She just acted as the go-between. Later, she wanted to go farther, ponder collective spaces, so she studied urban development. Eventually she conceived beautiful housing projects that could be developed through nongovernmental organizations. But she would have to wait to see them built.

Because she loved Gonzalo.

Because she was busy all those years in Europe, playing the role of provider, working on behalf of her husband's painting, being his most rigorous critic and acting as his manager in the sale and exhibition of his paintings.

They traveled constantly, they saw things through each other's eyes, they shared a thousand desires. Violeta did not have time then to answer life's questions because she had to have the quick answer for Gonzalo, whose own questions made him falter. Any weak structure in Violeta was shored up to protect Gonzalo from his own weakness, to keep them seeing one another in the bottomless reflection each offered the other.

Violeta, Gonzalo, and reflection.

Gonzalo acted as a sounding board of love and abandonment, of protection and discouragement. His sentiments were so strong that she was obliged to feel them, too. And she got used to *feeling* in Gonzalo's image. (Josefa later tells her: "Just as well you left him; in the long run those levels of mutual dependence are asphyxiating.")

*I looked in his eyes,* Violeta writes, *I found his forlornness, his found mine, and we both traveled in it; we rode on his croup; there we galloped, there we rode through the world and returned exhausted, the two of us dead of forlornness.*

Jacinta was born.

Something changed.

Once a week, at night, Violeta would braid Gonzalo's hair, her long, patient fingers weaving the light strands, one over the other. Now the baby cried and she had to go to her, and the braiding was interrupted.

Violeta did not welcome the changes between them, she who had always loved change. She did not embrace them, because she suspected that if the rules of the game were changed, the mirrors in which she and Gonzalo looked at one another—at themselves, at the other—would shatter.

"We could go back," Violeta said one day, "where we belong . . . to Latin America."

*Our America, queen of nations.*

She convinced Gonzalo; she spoke of roots and of the color of other skin and light. She harbored more than one intent for that voyage. They sent Jacinta to her grandparents and crossed the Atlantic. They started down through Mexico, and in every city Violeta left her heart. Bolivia was the last stop, the anteroom to Chile.

Violeta's first piercing memory is of nothingness become flesh. A pair of unwary strangers, totally Europeanized, reaching Santa Cruz de la Sierra on the day of Carnival.

Once in their hotel they had a hint of the force of the aloneness that would later engulf them. After breakfast, the employees began to disappear. They told the *patrona* good-bye with a triumphal air: you could read the license of the fair on their faces.

Violeta and Gonzalo's plane from La Paz had landed that morning at seven. Walking toward the hotel, two blocks from the main plaza, their skin told them they had reached the tropics. Violeta's hair was wet with sweat beneath her straw hat, her cotton clothing clung to her body, her hands were perspiring. And the town was deserted. "Doesn't surprise me," said Gonzalo. "After all, it's Sunday." At eight, sitting in the Hotel Italia drinking coffee, the dark-skinned girl waiting on them announced, with great charm, the day that lay before them: Carnival.

When the time came to explore the city they went out to enjoy the centenary trees around the main plaza, green with that prodigal green only the jungle—or its environs—bestows. Until they realized, after a brief walk, that they were the only people out strolling that day. Until even breathing began to choke them.

No one in the streets. Empty sidewalks. Shops and restaurants tightly closed. And groups of carnival participants—the crews—

sounding their trumpets and drums, walking with a strange rhythm somewhere between dancing and dragging. All around them painted, bedaubed youths with bags of water, paint, garbage. Their role seemed to be to attack anyone on foot. From beneath a colonnade on the plaza—colonnades of arches, the old and beautiful colonial tropics—Violeta tried to cross the street; she felt something sharp hit her right side. She had no idea what it was. She shuddered with sudden cold, and felt pain like a knife in her ribs. She screamed for Gonzalo. He had made it across the street and was hiding behind a column. When he saw it was safe, he ran toward Violeta. His eyes held impotent rage as he bent down to his wife's feet and picked up a dirty plastic bag containing sharp-pointed sticks.

It was twelve o'clock noon on a Sunday in a strange and strangers' country. Alone, wet, in pain, they would find no ally in the streets.

Gonzalo purposefully seized his wife's arm and they headed for the hotel, moving fast, heads turning, seeking a clear path. Violeta was hungry—they had got up at dawn to catch the plane—and could think of nothing but food. He, however, brooked no discussion; he had to get out of sight. They reached the hotel running, hiding every time music announced an approaching crewe. The sun was blazing. Once they left the plaza behind there'd been no more canopies or shade. Pure sun, with no shelter.

The hotel was empty, too. The dining room closed. At the desk they found a slightly microcephalic boy whose one ability seemed to consist of handling out room keys. Along with the vague information, perhaps invented in the face of their urgency, that the Pamplona, a restaurant opposite the hotel, might open sometime later that day. Violeta and Gonzalo could see the door from their window.

Nothing to eat.

Violeta picked up the Jack Kerouac book she was reading. From time to time she looked out the window, hoping to see that door open. By mid-afternoon she was staring compulsively, as if suddenly a magic key might open it. Her hunger increased as the hours went by and the impossibility of satisfying it became more and more vivid. Violeta's eyes were strained from staring at the Pamplona de Santa Cruz restaurant. In the distance, drums and trumpets poisoning the air, that weary, exhausted sound, terrifying in its monotony.

"Violeta," Gonzalo, lying on the bed, blurted out in the pristine silence of the room. "I want to talk to you about a couple of things I've been thinking over."

"What things?" she asked, surprised that he was talking to her when her mind was on something else.

"About my painting. About Latin America and Europe, and the two of us . . ."

Violeta looked at him, not disguising her uneasiness. She choked back the brusqueness that came spontaneously.

"No, Gonzalo. I'm too hungry to talk. Please, let's leave it till later."

The crewes kept passing beneath the window. Less and less impressive now, the costumes increasingly slapped together, dirty, mismatched, worn. And the air in the room, more and more humid. The fan was ineffective, and no book seemed capable of distracting Violeta from her edgy exhaustion.

At five, Violeta decided to go out. She had to find something to eat. Gonzalo, furious, preferred hunger to that dark, ambiguous fear, that fear made up as a fiesta. They went out. The sun blazed down, the tropical sun of eastern Bolivia turning opaque a city already weary of its revelry. Violeta thought of Graham Greene, of Malcolm Lowry. Latin American palm trees, in her hallucination, blending into those of Jakarta, of Vietnam. The dust with that of Mexican towns on the Day of the Dead. The same uneasiness of not knowing what or where the limits are.

Then suddenly, rain.

The downpour of Carnival.

And Violeta's rain-soaked body unable to distinguish among sweat, crewes' projectiles, and the heavens.

At last, down the block, she saw a small store with its door open. She ran to it. A gang followed. They smeared her with mud, soaked her yet again, something struck her back. Nothing mattered: there was food on a counter. Goat cheese. And some potato flour crackers, hard, old, brownish. And beer. Violeta felt a bond with the woman who was tending shop, like that of a little girl for her mother when she has waked her from a nightmare. Gonzalo, his face black with paint and smarting from some blow, watched from a distance, as if he were not involved, alien as a madman looking at his own asylum. Violeta made up a skimpy packet and undertook the adventure of getting back to the hotel with her treasure. She met their enemies again, and they began to be invisible. Hundreds of glassy eyes, brains cleft by alcohol, coke, and the sick music, advanced toward her. The accursed dancing, continuing as if it couldn't stop. It was near dusk, and the water bags being thrown now contained rocks: disheveled, the members of the crewes; disheveled, Violeta and Gonzalo; and those drums in their ears like a bad augury.

Violeta expanded her desperation and hateful feelings to include the entire city, all the people in it. A continent of incurable ills, she thought, every ounce of our misery become flesh in these streets and in these brutes stupefied in their dementia.

With the percussions in their minds now, not just their ears, they reached the hotel as the sun set. Soaking wet, with mud and filth plastering their bodies, their hair, their faces, their immeasurable fatigue, they went to their room along deserted hallways and there, tearing open the package with grimy hands, Violeta gulped down cheese, swallowed, gulped down more. She cracked the cap off the beer, feeling the liquid spread through her body. Gonzalo's eyes never left her. Gonzalo, not eating at all.

She threw herself on the bed, fully clothed in her disgust and despair. It was then he spoke her name, as if from the dark.

"Violeta."

*male gaze*

She did not look at him, waiting. There was a seriousness in his tone that alarmed her.

"Yes?"

"I have something to tell you."

"Now?" she asked, incredulous.

"Yes. Now. Once and for all."

Silence.

"I'm going back to Europe."

"You're what?"

"I'm leaving you."

# 11

Nostalgia of lands wounded, divined. That was what Violeta breathed in her return to Chile.

"Blessed homeland," she murmured.

"Now I begin my own life. I always knew that a woman's story exists to the degree that she seeps into the story of men. If she doesn't, she's relegated to oblivion. But I don't intend to resign myself to that."

That was what she told me.

And she set about it. She began with what was most basic: a house in Santiago for Jacinta and herself. She asked her father for her inheritance from her mother.

"The bookstores are yours, Papa, and you have several children who have no claim to Cayetana's money. I want it, I'm her heir."

"I'd have to liquidate part of my capital . . . capital that will also be yours at some future date."

"I'm not interested in the future. Times are hard in Chile, Papa, and I'm going to have to keep on my toes if I'm to keep the system from swallowing me up. I want to do well. I'm sorry for your sake, but you're going to have to liquidate some of your assets and give me what's mine."

With money in hand—and to the surprise of her father, who after all those years found himself facing an assertive daughter—Violeta attacked the task of looking for a house.

During that period she went with me to see a dressmaker who lived on the outskirts of town. From a distance we could see a scene that looked familiar, a scene of an upper-class neighborhood. Perfect house, but in miniature: front garden, but tiny; balcony with flowers; dog by the children's side. They are well dressed and look as spotless as the house. Everything in place, a woman, colorful children's clothing, everything to suggest the standard model.

"I didn't remember La Florida like this," Violeta says, surprised by the new aspect of this part of Santiago.

The vision changes as we drive closer. The house is not quite so white, the paint is peeling. The woman's hair, which seemed to be so well cut, is straggly and her breasts are drooping. The children's polyester clothes—not the cotton they first seemed—cling with static electricity. The dog is just a mutt.

"This is a parody of better neighborhoods," I say. "But considering the poverty, it's a good imitation."

Violeta looks at me, distraught.

"And identity, Josefa? Who are we, after all?"

Disturbed by a city whose physical appearance she scarcely recognizes, she goes back to Ñuñoa, her childhood neighborhood.

From Plaza Ñuñoa, she walked and looked and questioned. Until one day she found the house on Calle Gerona, three blocks from Cayetana's old house. A grape arbor, a palm tree, two acacia trees where she could hang her hammock, crown molding, Oregon pine paneling, leaded glass windows, and the sunroom with the thousand squares of sun.

"Think it's big enough?" I couldn't help asking when I saw the huge dimensions.

"There's never a square foot that isn't good for something. Ask me, after my eight years in the Via del Pavone. Those poor Europeans die of suffocation in their cramped spaces."

"Won't you be afraid in such a big house, just you, alone, with a child?"

"I brought my father's revolver."

"Violeta! These aren't the best times to have a gun in the house. Isn't that madness?"

"Maybe. But it's registered in his name; all legal and proper, don't worry."

"And you know how to shoot it?"

"Perfectly," she laughed. "Have you forgotten I'm the grand-daughter of a marshal?"

She filled her house with music, with paintings, with books, and with rugs. They were her only capital, all she needed.

"There's so much you don't have," I told her one day.

"That's my freedom," she replied. "Doing without. It's connected with a certain way of looking at the world."

Violeta did things that surprised me because they were so different from me. She cut her own hair, trimming curls close to her neck, without looking in the mirror, without ever going to a beauty shop. Her loathing for modular furniture, for voguish restaurants, for women's magazines, for shopping centers, for reproductions, made me seem mundane though really I wasn't.

The first time she came to my house after her return to Chile, she told me straight out: "It's beautiful, Josefa, but you have to get rid of all these reproductions. They're pretentious and vulgar." "Why?" I asked. "If they were posters, just framed, without glass, respecting their nature as an advertisement, they'd be fine. But to treat a simple reproduction as if it were a painting . . . No." "You're exaggerating," I told her. "No, I'm not exaggerating. The only thing that deserves to be hung on a wall is an original." "But Violeta," I protested. "I don't have enough money yet to buy originals." "Then leave the wall empty, that's always more respectable. And if you can't do that, you have several alternatives: a pretty photograph, an amusing piece of fabric, your children's drawings. There's no such thing as a bad child's drawing."

I envied her lack of interest in clothes—but why not, since she looked good in any old thing. She was always in long skirts and boots; never a dress made to order, never a two-piece suit, never a high heel, never a mini in winter. Violeta and I had always dressed modestly. Our families didn't have money for luxuries, and that was how we were brought up. We followed that standard as adults. Until my work demanded I change. The day I bought my first garment for five hundred dollars, I told Violeta. It was a white jacket, quilted, made of different fabrics: white, cream, pearl, ivory, a patchwork of silks, brocades, and satins. She touched the jacket, surprised, and tried it on before the mirror. So much money for something you just put on your body! When I bought my first dress for a thousand dollars, I told her that, too. But the day she saw the beaded dress for my concert in San Francisco, she didn't ask the price. Our slow divergence had already been driven home.

Violeta's concerns when she returned were perfectly defined: the Chile of those years, which broke her heart, and art as everyday life. Her sense of being a protagonist was intense, something she had never felt in Europe. As defense against the dangers outside, she decorated her interior spaces. She found nothing more effective than those things that moved her, betting on that as the only possible manifestation of art.

"Why 'what moves you' as a form of art?" I asked, I the pragmatist.

"Why psychoanalysis as a manifestation of love? It's the same idea," she replied.

I thought she had been reading too much Julia Kristeva and didn't argue.

Everything connected with Violeta seemed either romantic or patriotic.

I observed her uneasily: art, artists' colonies, friends, delirium, energies divided and squandered in a kind of dilettantism. "In the end, there is no art but the quotidian," she said, and invested all her passion on behalf of the ordinary. The house on Calle Gerona flourished, evenings there were a refuge for her circle. Violeta as queen, sharing everything, listening, giving everyone else the same attention she would have wished for herself. Answering every call. Her ears tuned to all voices, pouring out her lifeblood to answer a multitude of expectations. No one asked her about herself. Violeta, with no time of her own, generously giving it away. Until the day she runs dry? I asked myself. You heard the best music in her house, listening to New Age when no one was doing it yet, talking about books not yet available in our country, going to cine-art functions, drinking coffee brewed in a real coffee maker. ("Three things have impressed me very negatively in coming back," she said. "Nescafé, the absence of central heating, and machismo, and in that order.")

So much life in her. Why did she go around lending it?

Going to the movies with Violeta was the best way to know her. The way she gave herself to the screen was nearly shameful, like a child, believing everything, frightened, suffering, as if everything were real from beginning to end. Her body ached, physically, after a difficult or anguishing film. Oh, well, Violeta was like that about everything.

That was the period of her greatest external beauty: her body and her house as props. Disguise, colorful clothing, sensuality, all enlivened her and everything around her.

(One Sunday morning I go by to look for her, expecting to see her in her perennial Sunday blue jeans. No, she explains. She needs to be innovative and pull herself out of the rut of daily life. That sunny Sunday morning she puts aside her blue jeans and opens her closet, taking out and combining different clothes, black and a blue like petroleum; she ties a beautiful scarf in her curls, circles her neck with an African necklace she keeps for grand occasions. And what is the occasion today? she asked herself suddenly, surprised by her own rules. None, was her answer. Just a sun-filled winter day that could slip away any minute; and inevitably there will be less time when Sunday is gone. Adorning time so it won't get away so quickly, Violeta tells herself as she tries new fragrances among her Oriental oils. She studies herself in the mirror, stroking the African silver and horn, and is reminded of grand occasions. "If not now," she says to me, "when?"

To be Violeta's friend then was a gift. Her affection seemed amplified, honored, blessed, poetic. I myself felt privileged, always important in her eyes. If you told her some simple personal story, one of those silly, important stories, in her hands it escaped triviality.

But Violeta spread herself thin, and her energy flowed out in those gestures. Nothing coalesced. It was a beautiful life, but crazy. Violeta, seduction and personal style: no, she wasn't a flirt. Even so, she was terribly seductive. She was surrounded with lovers, and she seemed to love them all, she had room for them all, and when she tired of them she sent them away with a feather-light touch. She lived on the edge, with risk as a permanent option.

That scene in the hammock: it was one summer at the mill house. Violeta was playing with matchsticks, swinging between the two chestnut trees. She was arranging them on the cover of a sketch pad in her lap, forming a long line.

"What are you doing?"

"I'm right in the middle of an accounting session," she answered, smiling.

"You're counting matchsticks?"

"No. Men. Each match is a man I've made love with. I'm concentrating, I don't want to leave anyone out."

"<u>Don't you think that's a lot?</u>"

She looked at me. "No. Why? Actually, I'm proud of it."

Some constraint kept me from counting, and I looked away. But up to that moment, there must have been at least twenty-five.

Later, during my daily walk toward the hills, aside from acknowledging that her view of *sin* and mine were very different, I thought about Violeta's love affairs: however many there may have been, they never seemed casual, but full, tender, dedicated, and wanted. Violeta and vulnerability. In her eyes, probably, I was living a vulgar moderation. And to mine, she has lived with a systematic lack of deliberation. Well, that's not so strange, I told myself, Violeta doesn't know the *word* deliberation.

"I am drowning in platitudes in this country: swallowing them, breathing them. What can we do, Josefa?"

"Make a choice. Heroic or prudent, darling. The two don't go together."

"The thing is not to lose confidence in the world about us. We mustn't, for any reason, lose that."

"I already have," I tell her.

"You aren't an example, Jose, you have already given up."

"I haven't given up, Viola. I've just forgotten."

Violeta refuses to recognize the opacity of forgetting.

We park the car on Providencia; we go to the bookstore with the list she has drawn up of books I must read. It includes authors as different as Mishima, Carlos Fuentes, and Christa Wolf. I know I will find them; if there is something I admire about Uncle Tadeo, it is his ability to keep up with what's new.

Before we cross the wide avenue, we see a group of people standing around, enough to make a small crowd.

"What's going on?" I ask her.

"I don't know, let's go see."

We walk closer. In the center of the tumult is a girl, pretty and well dressed, protected by several ladies—the kind who have time to stroll down Providencia any day in the morning—exquisitely turned out and carefully made up. A man, probably the husband of one of the women, is manhandling a young boy, nearly ripping out his skinny brown arms. The suspect can't be more than fourteen, and he's poorly dressed—if the rags he is wearing can even be called clothes. Someone tells us that he tried to steal the pocketbook of the girl, the pretty little thing, and that they've called the police to hand the culprit over to them. But the kid is yelling that he hasn't done anything, that he didn't try anything, that he's not a thief. Violeta looks deep into his eyes and I don't know what she sees, but she is enraged, and confronts the man holding him prisoner.

"Are you sure he was going to steal something?"

The man is flummoxed. Was it possible that someone who looks like Violeta could take up the cause of this miserable little runt?

"Well, I didn't see it, but if she says so . . ."

"Did anyone see him?" Violeta shouts, while I'm hiding and taking breaths down to the pit of my stomach; I wish I could disappear behind the crowd, skip all this hassle. I don't care about the ragtag kid, or the robbery, or the girl. My one concern is to get away without attracting attention. I hear the ladies shrieking, and Violeta giving it back as good as she gets. I see her pull the boy, not violently but firmly, from the hands of the man who no longer seems quite so confident, and watch her open a path and walk gracefully through the bystanders, guiding the boy carefully, almost tenderly, by the shoulders. Violeta's defiant gaze as she walks away with the boy, that dignified and assured gaze, is not new; I know it well.

"The poor are unhinged by their very poverty" was the only explanation she offered me.

I have seen that look more than once. The first time was when she took Marcelina's hand in the aisle of the church at school, pressing it, walking forward haughtily, shouting with her eyes: Let's just see anyone try to humiliate her!

It was our confirmation ceremony. Each of us had to select a godmother. I never understood what that sacrament was supposed to mean, except for the part that attracted me at the time: the godmother bit. Not the one from your birth, whom you had no voice in selecting, but one you chose yourself.

Marcelina Cabezas was a Mapuche Indian from the south who had taken care of Violeta from birth. When it was time to choose a godmother, it seemed clear: Cayetana was already her mother; grandmother Carlota was her birth godmother; who but Marcelina deserved such an honor?

All our classmates came to school that Sunday in white, holding the hand of their pearly godmothers: aunts, older sisters, grandmothers. Everyone's head turned when Violeta appeared with Marcelina. Dressed in her best outfit, all sky-blue organdy, with her jet-black hair proudly straight, Marcelina Cabezas entered the church holding the hand of her baby, but her stoic march slowed before the looks she was receiving, marking her, piercing her, setting her apart, depriving her of the right that had so honored her. Violeta turned red: with fury, she would tell me later. She pressed Marcelina's hand, did not move a centimeter from her side throughout the ceremony, and stayed for the hot chocolate and cookies, alone with her godmother, without a friend— except for me—to come anywhere near her in all the enormous refectory. When both of them had drained their cups, Violeta again took

Marcelina's hand and together they went down the long, long hallway, through a thicket of eyes and whispers.

"You know, Josefa," was Violeta's only comment afterward, "if there's anything we should learn from being born into our world, it's that we should try not to humiliate those who weren't—and there's a lot more of them. As long as I live, no Marcelina is going to feel alone. I swear by my life."

That was all she said.

(Many years later, the psychiatrist she was seeing concluded that credit for getting Violeta through the many losses she had suffered rested solely on Marcelina's shoulders. Violeta knew how lucky she had been to have the protection of Marcelina's affection, and it seemed not at all strange to her that sanctuary was given by the same person who taught her the basics: language, her first words, her first stories, her first look at the world. In Marcelina's stories, in her account of her land and her ancestors, in her oral tradition, Violeta learned from the tutelary spirits. And that was a weapon that would help her endure the things that were to happen in her next lifetimes.)

She tells me later, in the mill house: "The revolution was glorious. It was so *there* . . . And anyone who wanted could join in. Its great capital was that anyone at all could become a hero! And thanks to the revolution, anyone could be a person, even the poorest. Today, to be *someone*, a hero has to begin with money; that's the only capital that counts. The *sine qua non* requisite."

Later she wrote with those always ink-stained fingers:

*The revolution/the great female: it filled everything, furnished all the answers. It was total.*

*Without a Utopian dimension the ephemeral envelops me, traps me, and tells me that life is barely this: what I see and what I touch. Nothing more.*

*Is Utopia still possible?*

The avaricious eighties, they called them.

Someone brought me apple tea as a gift from Turkey. I invited Violeta to share it. She goes with me to the kitchen and as I boil water I take cups from the cupboard. I have the sugar bowl on the tray when my eyes focus on the heavy white cups crazed with tiny cracks. The reddish yellow of the tea emphasizes the vulgarity of the pottery.

"Come with me, Violeta."

"Where? I thought we were going to try this tea."

"No. Not in these cups. Come on, let's go."

We climb into the car. In ten minutes we are in a large department store and Violeta is watching me, mouth agape, as I ask to be shown a porcelain tea set.

"Don't you think that's a bit much?" she asks.

"No, there isn't any *too much* when seeking beauty. You're the first to champion that idea."

"But not like this, I never meant this."

"No matter. Everything must be *perfect*."

We wore the decades branded on our skin, like cattle. She repeated: those avaricious eighties. The explosion of greed, I called them later, when the nineties gave me perspective.

She was swinging in the hammock between the two acacia trees—in the winter she would pick the little yellow balls from her hair—while I climbed rung after rung in the ladder to success, swathed myself in organza for my performances, accumulated savings accounts—so much money earned in the eighties—as I sang and bargained my soul to be able to do it, receiving applause in tour after tour, signing contracts for television, cutting new records. But in theaters I sang like Joan Baez. Not to sell myself out completely, I told myself, as I did just that, nursing the fantasy that I hadn't completely joined the philistines.

Crazy, successful, and complex, the eighties for me.

We also lived silly everyday scenes.

Andrés and I were in our bedroom getting ready to go to a wedding, and Violeta, lying on my bed, was leafing through a magazine.

"Tell me, Violeta, what do you wear when you're going to a wedding?" Andrés asks as he splashes on cologne.

"I don't have *ad hoc* clothes because I don't go to weddings," she replies absentmindedly.

"You're not invited or you don't go?"

"No, no one invites me."

"But that's strange, Violeta. Why?"

"Because it's something that never happens around me. No one gets married. Not my friends, not their children."

"What do they do, then?"

"I don't know. I hadn't given it any thought."

Andrés laughed. I remembered Violeta telling me a few days before, "My social needs are diminishing as yours are increasing. Believe me, Josefa, mine are more and more minimal."

And while Violeta was struggling on behalf of humanity in the housing projects and getting her feet muddy while learning the tangled processes of a housing subsidy, my passion for singing was escalating. It was nearly my only passion, and my physician kept me in pills so I wouldn't faint from stage fright, and I was finding protection in Andrés's strong arms. How far apart had we drifted? What Violeta suffered most in modernization was feeling the loss of roots.

No, the famous modernity did not do well by Violeta or by me.

Not by her, because it marginalized her. Not by me, because it devoured me.

Sometimes I thought that Violeta belonged to an extinct species.

And as always when Violeta talked about the past she did so as if inspired, and I crept into that inspiration. And I knew that one thing saved us from being lost: the mill house. It was the one bond that was sufficiently strong. Violeta and that unnamed place were nearly one and the same. Their spirits coverged; to describe one was to describe the other. And by offering me refuge, it saved us.


But this summer there will be two empty windows. Violeta will not be in the third. How to imagine the lake without her presence? What will I tell Señor Richter? What shall we do with that house?

How will I explain that Violeta won't be coming?

# 12

$\mathcal{I}$'m looking for the center.

This is what Violeta writes when she travels to Mexico. Inexorably, I am approaching the blank pages in her diary, the end of this story. It has been only three months since Violeta's last trip. How could I not have realized she was running away?

To understand her flight, I have to talk about Violeta and light.

She sought it incessantly, even within herself. Because of that, her homes always bordered on the transparent. Demanding of herself, she set limits on her thirst for experience. She would not allow her life— always a little off center—to be turned into a game without rules. And the dignity of her feminine self was an important part of the game and the luminosity. Every day lived beside Eduardo was in a way exposing that dignity to harm. She knew it. Light was fading. She did not forgive herself those steps into the shadows.

It was no surprise, then, that she chose Mexico—where the air is clear—to cleanse herself of darkness.

The boundless sea of Bahías de Huatulco brought the sea into Violeta's eyes. And peace settled into them. But didn't last.

*First dialogue with the North American who silently accompanies me late afternoons on Playa de la Aguja:*

*He: Aside from the things we know already, what do you dedicate yourself to?*

*I: It depends on what those things are . . .*

*"The usual," he tells me with a smile.*

*"Those are things I don't dedicate myself to," I answer, smiling myself.*

*The laughter on his lips spreads to his eyes.*

*He: Then, where are you from?*

*I: From Chile.*

*"Chile?" He seems immediately enthusiastic.*

*"Yes, Chile" (that deep fissure, as poetry named it).*

*He gave me refuge.*

*He's from Boston but he speaks Spanish almost like a native. Good thing for me, I can't be intelligent in another language. His name is Bob and he's handsome. Finally he spoke to me; today is the third afternoon we've been here at the same time on this small beach where no one comes but people who bring their books.*

*Fidelity: indispensable or necessary?*

*The second is more attractive; it implies an option, and lacks the ugliness of the norm.*

*Between the indispensable and the necessary runs a stream of crystal clear water that not merely refreshes, but rushes over rigidity, softens it, shapes it, and bathes it in a surface that as it hardens turns into confiture, not stone.*

Today I described to Bob a table set on a summer afternoon. Diced green pepper in olive oil, shredded onion with red ripe tomatoes, corn on the cob—which they call elote here—a large cheese on a cutting board next to a sharp knife, raspberry juice. And in a wicker basket, a loaf of bread, the crust golden and crisp, the center soft and smooth. All on a blue-and-white checked cloth, under the chestnut tree.

It was an opening to tell him about the mill house.

In Chile the days rained misery, the days rained sorrow, the days rained loneliness. And although the rains stopped, I fear the memory-less country.

Here I am safe, amid these red ants and the toads that hop from the stairs at night, as they do in the country.

I think of the difficulty of defining desire with precision, because desire has no language.

I go back to fidelity. What happens when there are secret zones in a couple, spaces of blocked and crystallized communication where you can never again enter? What happens when intimacy begins to be constricted and impoverished? Where does it go?

I came to Huatulco. I chose this place on the map carefully. I came here in order not to be the complaining and grieving woman I'm turning into. Accustomed to my own obstinacy, I must become another.

I've watched the iguanas crawling along beneath the sun, up the stairsteps, kings of all they survey. They blend into the stone; iguanas are stone, some black and white, the next one gray. They move like spry old ladies, quick and broody as hens, with their feet splayed wide. The iguanas' mimicry suggests a couple of ideas I cast aside because I don't like them.

I have sent Josefa a postcard, telling her about Bob. Today I explained some things to him, and he understood. My vague ideas—vagueness floods all my perceptions—are received by him with exactitude. They don't bother him. I couldn't help talking to him about uncertainty. I fear it, I explained; I see myself surrounded by it. That's how the nineties began for me. I don't want that, I'm looking for a way to get away from that. This is not the end of the century I deserve.

Bob was born in the United States and is "politically correct." Although we're on the same wave length intellectually, can he know what I'm talking about? Can he know about pain? What I have found out is that he knows about compassion.

I spent a glorious day in Oaxaca. Late in the afternoon, as I was sitting on the steps in the plaza eating a red, red watermelon, I set things in order; I summoned my goddesses, the ones who are always with me. Persephone told me, very wisely, to look around in my present surroundings.

I bought a ceramic piece for Jacinta: indigo blue, with a sun and moon playing around the outside.

Could Eduardo not have read what Pavese once wrote? That one has to pay for every luxury, and that EVERYTHING is a luxury, beginning with BEING in the world.

I remember how amused Josefa was that I instituted a "bitch session" in the mill house. A half hour on the clock. We women would get together—any age was accepted—and let it all out, all the things we carry inside us. Many things came out, some unexpected, some fantastic. I would look at the clock and, very serious, cut short the sighs or huffs of rage.

"All right, enough! Time's up."

And each of us would go her way or take up her chore, renewed. (Oh, that our burdens were lighter!)

I am very surprised, and must tell Josefa, that I haven't needed my bitch session here in Huatulco. I always have believed that women's capacity for revitalization is unique. The regeneration of their cells is better, even, than that of snakes, and definitely better than men's.

Huatulco as medicine. Here there's nothing to fear, no Sunday afternoon lists on yellow paper, no glass of gin that explodes into abuse, no ambiguous body—mine—that rejects and accepts without rhyme or reason.

For now, and, it is to be hoped, forever, only Bahía Tangolunga, and the water that is green when you touch it but blue when you look at it. Only those fish forming an enormous triangular school, all sizes but identical in design: black-and-white dots on the body, brilliant yellow on the tails: a modern Japanese drawing, these millenary fish as they flash by the coral, in unison, obedient, harmonious. If I could translate that to tangible expression, I would make a tapestry. (I promise some day to learn that art.)

My body is remembering what my mind has forgotten these last two years.


Always on Playa de la Aguja, we have talked until sunset. I told him a story.

It was about that woman abandoned in adolescence. I started rather timidly, but as I went along the words came on their own, no one could have stopped them, forgotten details, various embellishments, all roaring in my head. Exhausted, I end my story: "It isn't that this little girl, an adult today, longs for those women of her childhood. No, it isn't that she longs for them. They're always in some corner of her being. Forgetfulness is merely doing its duty, like a cloak that warms or a refreshing breeze. And memories . . . they can filter through, like a ray of light. But aged by light or the past, they still *pulse. She lives in the spirit of her ancestors, and they are always there, their whispers."*

*I fall silent. Bob asks: "Were you with this woman a long time? At her side?"*

*"All her life," I answer.*

*Then, after a long silence, he looks at me.*

*"We need to take a small trip, you and I. A necessary trip."*

*And we set off.*

# 13

"I picked up some Beethoven at the Duty Free in Buenos Aires, all nine symphonies for twenty-eight dollars," Violeta said when I went to see her on her return from her trip.

Eduardo opened the door and led me to the bedroom: the *Fifth Symphony* at full volume. Violeta in a trance, wrapped in a towel, sitting on the floor with her legs crossed. One hand held the towel at her breast, the other was following the music, directing the orchestra. Eduardo pointed to her, with that casual and detached air typical of one of the two who make up a couple, the one who doesn't suffer.

"Look at her. She's a madwoman."

I smiled, wondering to myself why my friends' husbands almost always seemed to be idiots.

Violeta greeted me, happy. A good look, her back-from-Mexico face. Although it's been only two months or so, memories mill around me: the dogs, the transition, the big news, all of it mixed in with the songs I had to record, the ones Violeta didn't like.

"Wait for me, I'll be dressed in a flash."

She threw on beautiful cottons, long rosy-pink cottons, fastened three different necklaces around her neck, and we went to the sunroom. She asked Rosa to make us coffee, and then she handed me a small, black cloth bag. I opened it, looked inside, and got up to kiss her, very moved. Was she forgiving me with this gift? Were the walls of reserve between us coming down? Since Violeta spoke a different language, probably a necklace for me was a way of bringing me close to her. Because Violeta adored necklaces; she looked for them, pursued them, collected them. Touching the delicate silver filigree, I ask if it is Mexican.

"No," she answers and lowers her voice. "It's from Guatemala."

"You went to Guatemala?"

Again the lowered voice.

"Secretly." Spied on in her own house; that's the impression she gave me.

"But Violeta, that's a big deal! Were you there? In Antigua?"

She says yes with her eyes, with almost a hunted look.

Jacinta bursts into the sunroom, interrupting us.

"Mama, come help me, I can't handle the serum."

"What serum?" I ask, startled.

"Amiga had pups," Violeta answers. "The world is backward in this house. She has nine and I have none. Come along with me."

We go to the kitchen patio. The nine puppies are huddled around Amiga, small, soft, black lumps cuddled together in the middle of a certain amount of filth.

"No one wants to clean up their vomit or their shit," she says, resigned. "The veterinarian brought the serum and it makes Jacinta nervous to give it to them. I'm mama to everyone."

"Violeta, this is pure chaos," I protest, terrified of slipping on a patch of excrement.

"But look how sweet they are . . ."

She takes one in her arms; her gesture reminds me of when my children were just born. Violeta seems happy, as if taking care of them demanded nothing of her. I sat in the kitchen, trying to be a part of it, but the dogs devoured all her attention. I'd gone to a lot of trouble to find a minute to run by her house. If it hadn't been for my bad conscience about the argument before she left, I would simply have postponed it. I took advantage of Eduardo's coming into the kitchen to leave. Violeta accompanied me down the long hallway to the door.

"Just give me a quick rundown. How did it go?"

Surprisingly, her eyes filled with remembrance and she answered, dreamily.

"Well."

A thousand times in recent days I've remembered that *well* I didn't at first decode: sensual, loaded, mysterious, that word when Violeta spoke it.

"Will you tell me about Guatemala later?"

"Yes, later."

At the door, she asked when we could get together under calmer circumstances.

"I don't know, I just don't have any time . . . I'm writing some songs, I've been wrapped up in that since you left. I'm focused on that."

"Can I see them?"

"You want to?"

"A lot. If you'd like, I'll come by your house after work tomorrow and give them a quick once-over. Is that all right with you?"

"Sure. I'll expect you," and I added, "You look really good."

She looked at me, very serious.

"I feel wonderful. Mexico is like a balm. Distance, another balm. But I have a strange presentiment."

Ever since we were little girls, I have always thought Violeta had something of the witch about her. She says she inherited it from her grandmother Carlota.

"I go around feeling possessed with this fantasy."

"What fantasy?"

"About leaving the country."

It sounded like a sentence. It took me back to that day in December 1989, the day when we were hurrying to vote in the first elections since those years that had seemed eternal to her.

"The democracy you've yearned for is coming, Violeta, it's coming."

And she had answered in a forlorn voice: "Something strange is happening to me, Josefa. Everything about those years is painful to me. I've thought about it carefully, and I realize it's a pain I'm *never* going to lose. But something tells me I'm not going to be here to enjoy the new phase."

Some days I waked filled with words. Those were marvelous days, recognizable to those closest to me: absent-minded, a little frown, my eyes slightly unfocused, as if I were near-sighted, as if I had Violeta's eyes, I couldn't handle two stimuli at once. I wafted through my house, touching the walls of the hallway as if I were on a ship in rough seas. My wanderings ended in the back room, where finally I had set up a kind of studio: at the back, near the patios, as was fitting. Always stopping first in the large square kitchen—which fascinated Violeta; hers was rectangular and she swore that in her next reincarnation she would have one that was square—I lingered at the shiny white contrivance that cooked our food, resting my fingers on the burners, lifting the lid of a pot—something always was steaming there. Something happened those days when there were fewer interruptions. I'm talking about the interruptions endemic to our kind: the ones that produce divisions and subdivisions in our attention. As Andrés vowed, those days I went into a trance.

114

And that was the peculiar state I was in when Violeta came back from Mexico.

I was waiting for her the next day in my studio with coffee and cigarettes, eager to know her opinion of my songs. I'd gone through this same rite a thousand times, always respectful of her evaluation.

"You have to grab me while you can," she laughed when I handed her the sheets of music, already in clean copy. "When I got back, Eduardo had a big project for me: the nearly complete manuscript of his novel. It seems he really was working while I was away."

"But he's been writing it for years. At least as long as he's been with you."

"I know. And now he wants me to correct it, act as his editor. I don't know why he's putting so much trust in me."

"He'd be stupid not to . . ."

"I'm a carousel of synonyms. God help me if I don't immediately pick up each page as it comes out of his typewriter! All right, let's see yours."

I left her alone for a while. She didn't even look up when I went back. Her concentration has always fascinated me; I used to tell her it was her masculine feature.

"Can I be honest?" she said after a period of silence, music in hand.

"Of course."

"It's as if your sensations are so limited that you have to squeeze every last drop from them. There's something lifeless here, Josefa."

"In fact, I do squeeze every sensation dry when I sing. Afterward, I'm empty. That, basically," I added with a smile, "is my famous indifference."

"I'm not talking about that." Violeta was serious, committed to my songs, feeling a responsibility for them. "There's something empty, deserted, about these words. They're beautiful, but they give me the feeling that you're not being touched by either life or reality."

What she didn't add was that that effect is achieved only with extreme coldness. Her mood when she was talking to me was an alternating current of contained impotence and sad disillusion.

"It's strange. As if normality, democracy, muzzles you, muzzles all of us, and just the reverse, that dictatorship, urgency, living on the edge, vomited words over us."

She gets up, goes to the end table and pours more coffee for each of us. That must have been the last coherent conversation I had with Violeta. I have a clear impression of her slightly confused expression as she told me: "There's no outpouring here, Josefa."

"Should there be?"

"Yes," an emphatic *yes*. "I don't know whether it's self-control or self-censorship, but I know that fear of letting things flow out is paralyzing you."

I looked at her thoughtfully. She continued.

"It's the internal breakdown of this era. What happened to us, Josefa?"

I don't clearly understand the plural Violeta is using, but I intuit a sense in which it is possible that she and I are both on our way down.

"In this society tied to efficiency of production, voracity of consumption, in this Chilean transition, our outlook gets poisoned with pure distaste." Her tone lightens. "It's distasteful, this business of moving from a poor society to a rich one. The truth is, Josefa, that these are not good times for creativity." She slowly lights a cigarette. Inhaling, she continues. "I feel a great nostalgia for the times when we were growing up. The nineties are barren of ideas. Ideas! My God! Where did they go?"

She stops. I don't want to interrupt her, I'm afraid of a deeper discussion, I don't want to argue with her. Not right now.

She picks up the sheets of music, looks at them distractedly.

"I'm out of synch with these minds today; fear of dissension, lack of irreverence, pragmatism . . . And don't tell me that such things pay off. You know what I feel? That there's no such thing as an innocent relationship any more. Even friendships have changed from being something that's simply there, to something that has to be negotiated. Nothing seems to come free anymore." → comes @ cost

"It isn't strange, then, that I'm reflecting all that. It's the mood of the times."

"Well, as an epoch, it's not one hospitable to me. I wrote you that from Mexico; I feel as if I'm in a no-man's-land. I don't even recognize what our desires are. The world is old and tired, Jose." *Borderlands*

"No one was as eager for democracy as you, Violeta, and I'm seeing that no one has paid as much to live in it as you." My tone was measured; I fought my urge to shout in her face: Get over it, Violeta, do me a favor and get over it! It's a new day!

"It's true. And I criticize myself for that, if you want to know. I feel guilty."

I smile at her with irony. She elaborates, innocent.

"I wish we could recover a sense of the sacred! That *something* would be sacred again! Look for the enchantment, find it, restore it, redeem it. Can't your songs go there?"

I was thinking about what she said when I saw her turn pale. Her tone changed and she said: "You know? I don't feel so good. Let's finish up another day."

"What's the matter?"

"I don't know, I feel bad . . ."

"What hurts?"

"Everything."

"Should I call a doctor? Or take you to the clinic?"

"Don't be silly. It's just a twinge of something."

"Let's go to my room, at least lie down a while."

As she curled up on my bed, reminding me of the black puppies, I went to brew some herbal tea. Waiting for the teakettle to boil, I thought about our aborted conversation. We were now almost at the end of 1991. It was so frowned on to long for the past that Violeta was ashamed to recognize it. And she was arming herself with an array of abstract ideas to disguise what so clearly was happening to her. She was heartsick.

The call the next week came from Jacinta: Violeta was pregnant.

Now things do speed up.

As she waters the geraniums neatly arranged in their red pots, all identical, ten flowerpots on the balcony on Calle Gerona, she looks at me queasily. I see an ugly bruise on her cheek.

"I got overtired. I fell and struck the basin in the bathroom."

"What did the doctor say?"

"That I should live in low key until I'm past the first trimester."

"But Violeta, were you still expecting to get pregnant?"

"No, I thought about it a lot, but I'd given up hope. It's been quite a while since I counted days and did things according to the calendar. Maybe that's why it finally happened."

"What does Eduardo say?"

"I think the novel is more important to him than this. He goes around in a trance. He isn't going to be at all pleased to learn the conditions I'm supposed to follow these next months. I haven't told him yet."

"What conditions?"

"It seems it's no joke to have a baby at forty, Jose. Things were touch and go when I had Jacinta, too, if you remember. I have to take care of myself; it's my keeping the fetus that most worries the doctor. I have to prevent spasms or contractions of any kind."

"Are you trying to tell me that you can't have an orgasm?" I tried to make a joke of it, but she answered very seriously.

"Exactly. That's what the doctor told me."

"Why don't you ask for time off, or a leave without pay, and devote yourself full time to looking after yourself?"

"Because I took my vacation time to go to Huatulco." And she adds, "And because I don't want to be home all day. Not with Eduardo working here."

"You sound like he's possessed . . ."

"He is."

Several days went by without my hearing from her. Just one quick telephone call to ask about her health. I was immersed in my songs, revising them after the conversation I'd had with Violeta. I was concentrating so hard I even forgot something as crucial for her as her pregnancy. Sometimes my children came in; they'd been with Jacinta and gave me reports. Those weren't easy days, Violeta was not feeling very well.

I had to go north, to give concerts in Arica and La Serena. The night before my trip I again got a phone call from Jacinta.

"Josefa, Mama is spotting."

"Shit! Did the doctor see her?"

"Yes, but now she's locked in her room; she's been crying all day and she won't let me in."

"And Eduardo?"

"He didn't come home last night. I don't know where he is. Come see her. Please."

I was packing my suitcase and planning to be with Andrés once I'd finished. It was always hard to leave him. Every time I did I needed him to spoil me and give me confidence. Besides, I was meticulous when it came to my suitcases. I couldn't leave anything out: from antidepressants to fruit salts for my stubborn acidity, from earplugs to tampons (several times my period had come early because of the stress of going on stage). My wardrobe and makeup I left to Mauricio, who went with me on every tour, a condition of my contract. But even so, the suitcases required all my concentration.

"I'm leaving tomorrow at dawn, Jacinta. You know these damned schedules for national flights . . ."

"Make time, Josefa. I bet she'll open the door for you."

I hadn't noticed the presence of my son Borja in the room. He was avidly following the telephone conversation. And his look—the judgment in that gaze—was enough.

"I'll be right over."


I should have canceled my concert. The picture that greeted my eyes when I went into Violeta's room frightened me. Why didn't I take her home? Why didn't I rescue her?

In fact, she did open the door of her bedroom. I was repelled by the dense, fuggy, fetid air. Again I thought of Amiga's pups when I saw her holed up there, seeking refuge and warmth. But there was no nurturing mother to gather *her* in. The room and the bed were a mess. Her hair, uncombed. No amber or ivory: her face, streaked from crying—like a child's—showed new bruises.

"Violeta! You've fallen again!"

She didn't answer, as if the evidence was enough.

"I'm not going to lose this baby, no matter what!" she said finally. Her determination seemed positive to me.

"Are you bleeding?"

"Yes. I know I will never get pregnant again; I know it. That's why I want to keep this one even if it's the last thing I do in this life."

"Why are you spotting? Haven't you taken care of yourself?"

She didn't answer, and hid her face in the sheet.

"What is it, Violeta! Tell me!"

"Eduardo. It's Eduardo's fault. It's so hard to say this, Jose, I feel disloyal."

"Why the hell are you covering for him? How long must you play the doormat? It's doesn't suit you!"

"Don't scold me." A thread of a voice. I hated my own harshness. "What happened?"

"It was last night . . . He'd given me a few pages of his novel to correct. I was very tired and I told him I'd do it today, that I wanted to get some sleep. He stayed at his desk, angry, and I came to bed. Half-asleep, I heard him go out. He came back late. He woke me up, he'd been drinking. You could smell the gin from the doorway. He wanted to make love; I told him we shouldn't. He got obscene, you know . . . Then, really violent . . ." Violeta's voice was trembling; she was ashamed and having difficulty finding words. "He told me this pregnancy was stupid . . . I told him that was why I had married him. He was furious."

"He's a sonofabitch bastard." Rage boiled up in my body. "He raped you, didn't he?"

"Yes."

"And you, what did you do?"

"I did what any woman would do faced with brute strength: I fought back. And suddenly I thought, This will do even more harm to the baby, and gave in. It was as if I weren't there. When it was all over, I told him that if it happened again I'd kill him."

"And he took you seriously?"

"He hit me."

"You have to report him to the police."

"He's my husband, Josefa, I wouldn't get very far."

I stroked her head, finger-combed her hair, as you would a neglected child's.

"What are you going to do, Violeta?"

"Keep this baby. As for the rest, I'll think about that later. For now, I know he'll come back repentant and ashamed. And that will give me a period of truce."

"I'm going to talk to Andrés. He can help."

"No! Not a word. I mean it. I haven't told anybody. Eduardo isn't just my husband, he will also be the father of my child. I don't want anyone to know anything. Don't tell Andrés, please."

"All right, all right. If that's what you want."

And I left for the north.

# 14

The last pages of Violeta's diary are undated. The color of the ink has changed, and I think about those fingers forever stained with traces of pencils and pens. The ink on the last pages is brown.

Short sentences, brief paragraphs . . . Everything she writes is an abstraction. Was that intentional? Did her delicacy keep her from a more flesh-and-blood report? Who knows what she left out of her diary? Maybe that very omission was what suggested—should have suggested—to me the action that was not detailed.

*Except my womb.*
*Let my body be profaned, my very existence be profaned.*
*Except my womb.*

*I seek singing light, the dawn light. If only it would cleanse me . . . it has never failed me.*

*Hours go by, he with him, I without him.*

*In sex, one is very alone.*

*In my hours of leisure I caress my stomach, holding it, apprehending it, nesting it. There was an instant of blessed eternity: the instant of conception. That is what my heart holds to the fore.*

*There is not a single demon left in hell. They have all lodged in my head.*

*Finally all blood reaches the place of its quietude, says the Maya* Chilam-Balam. *I must believe that.*

*One by one he tore off the petals: the deflowerer.*

*To be introduced deep inside a space. To introduce one body into another through its pores. With excess, with daring, with boldness. What it has done is more than penetrate. It has dissolved into pieces.*

*I suppose there must be some conquest—whatever it be—that is forever. Or is it that all conquests require daily effort if they're to be preserved?*

*I'm afraid of the nightmare. It comes again and again. I dream that I'm giving birth to snakes, tiny, slippery serpents slithering from my vagina. No, not children. Snakes.*

*I am vigilant. I am alert. I am on the eve of . . .*
*I think obsessively about death and its allies.*
*I do not fear heroic danger. I fear unheroic danger.*

*I sense the bad spirit, the Invader. I seek my refuge. The Last Forest; the protected place, where shadows suggest the Utopia of the sun that will sift through the treetops and some day warm us at noon, where we will mock the rains with the certainty that they have not come to stay, where there will be a roof over everyone's head, where everyone will be secure, where geography will be more solid than terrifying. The place of compassion. A place no nostalgia lurks.*

*More than anything, I fear ethical orphanhood.*


*Women are goddesses when they give birth. The power to give life is absolute power. I am all-powerful.*

*I invoke the goddess Demeter, who will help me.*

*I am ready. The last rosy flower of the azalea has withered, I can finish now.*


*The body is a trap, is a trap, is a trap.*


*ABUSE KILLS SOMETHING VERY VALUABLE: MERCY.*


And on the last page before the blank pages, in enormous, hysterical letters, I read her last anguish, the last she wrote:

*Her daughter has lost her reason. Tell Cayetana to come take me.*

# 15

Although there is not a lot of talking in my dreams, last night I dreamed of Violeta, and Violeta spoke to me. Not the way she usually talks; this time her words and the atmosphere in which she spoke them was somber.

She told me:

*I have been all moments this summer. In dark moments, I did what I did. And in sunny moments I became a queen, and Eduardo was king. And that instant was luminous, the one on the way from your house to mine that night, Josefa.*

*The glitter on my face, the way my hair looked, seeming like another person, made me feel like an angel. In my pocket I guarded the best look I knew of all Eduardo's looks, and clutching it tight to my body, I set out to meet him. To open myself, to make things better, to rebuild.*

*I am an angel, I tell myself.*

*I run my fingers lightly over my beribboned head. Fluttering colored ribbons. I ask myself how they are fastened; they seem so firmly attached to my new harlequin being. This will be a crazy night, I smile to myself. I want to forgive. I want to be radiant, as I was once, as I have often been. My outward appearance, in the nearly sacred hands of the makeup artist, has plotted a lucky, celebratory night for me.*

*Eduardo will be recaptured by my spells.*


Violeta faded away, enveloped in airy pink; she faded and I could not hold her back. Something like a cloud carried her away; I couldn't speak to her, I didn't have a chance to ask her anything.

I lay awake, sleepless, like so many nights since that night. Violeta took even my sleep with her. I went into the living room; a fire was still burning in the Bosca stove. I had smoked my daily quota of five cigarettes, but decided what the hell . . . With a glass of Amaretto and my sixth cigarette, I focused my full attention on Eduardo. A puzzle become a nightmare. The great writer. That's what the press is calling him now, after what happened.

Why did he draw away from Violeta so totally? She reminded him of his body, something he preferred to think of as external. How superfluous the body is to men—excepting the specific moment they want to unburden themselves of it. They can experience passion only in limited, restricted doses. Even from that finite moment they return fearful and drained, which is why they fall asleep. Fusing is too much for them. Our bodies are nothing but a rest stop along the road, a pause between something important before and a still more important afterward. Between art and power, we exercise the vulgar ability to draw them toward the earth. That's the great problem: they see us as a familiar and often occupied rest stop. Accustomed, ordinary. A rest that demands fusing. I must get on, the man thinks; I must hurry on to important things (which never are *feelings*): the great novel, politics,

*gender roles*

money, diverse and precise undertakings. *Toward what* isn't important, but they must hurry.

Woman's body as interlude. How strongly Violeta understood this! A draining interlude that reminds them they are alive. Alive in themselves, not for the purpose of great causes: alive, period. They abandon those bodies, terrified of how much the dissolution of their person interrupts them. They always have to be off. Sleep as the most familiar of departures; sleep to recover from that so abjectly alive instant in which they felt and did not think. Or analyze.

Passion, always, as a short-term project; merely an interim in the flow of important things . . . which never are in us, only in something beyond. Our bodies and their demands are left behind, superfluous.

Maybe, Viola, they truly desire us. But to endure that truth, they must think of it as a banal desire. They cannot bear the fact that we are a desire in ourselves.

One of Violeta's strange characteristics was that she forgot the origin of her scars. "Don't be silly," I would say. "How can you not remember what happened to your arm, what made that mark?" "But I don't remember," she would answer, guilelessly. Which is how she forgot what Hell is.

Violeta and her Hell: Fragility.

(Fragility of principles, of affection, and, the most awesome, of life.)

And inexorably we come to the present.

Mid-November.

We go back to the fuchsia glitter on her neck, to Mauricio, thrilled about his handiwork, the gold on her cheeks, to the night of the party.

To the thing Violeta did, which abolished the helplessness of every living woman.

"I talk to myself," she told me that night during the party. "For two years I've been talking to myself."

She offered Eduardo a phyllo-wrapped shrimp, but he kept talking with Andrés, ignoring her.

"Everything went to hell. I arrived in such a good mood, and went to look for him, but my being late set off something about . . . He was surly, aggressive. We got off to a bad start. It's a shame, I was so happy."

I had scarcely seen Violeta since my tour in the north. We had exchanged quick telephone calls; everything was going well, the spotting had stopped. Eduardo hadn't been drinking, and every day that went by played in Violeta's favor. She was winning time in this battle, she told me in the midst of my rushing, and I was reassured.

Out of the corner of my eye I saw Eduardo ask Andrés to hand him the bottle of gin. I looked at Violeta; she was shivering.

"Oh, God, no!" I heard her murmur.

"Tell him not to . . ."

"I'm afraid to . . . he's capable of throwing a fit right here, in front of everyone."

"You want me to do something?" A strange courage came over me at that instant.

"No, no. That could be deadly."

Violeta crumpled. Only someone who had known her all her life would have seen it beneath the mask of her disguise.

"Violeta, you're trembling."

No response.

"What are you afraid of? Losing the baby?"

"Yes. But there's something else, too!"

"What?" I had to ask, she hesitated so long.

She looked at me with those kohl-blackened eyes.

"Jacinta."

I didn't comprehend what she was saying. I would have asked if Andrés hadn't interrupted us to ask her to dance. They went off together. She seemed better, and I satisfied myself with watching them. They looked handsome on the dance floor. Andrés disguised as a musketeer, with balloons bumping the brim of his hat and streamers embracing them both. The music was gay, the laughter noisy, there was copious food and drink. A fantastic party, I said to myself, and congratulated myself for having invited Violeta. Parties like this weren't part of their milieu, and I had thought it would be entertaining for her to come, to see faces she had seen on the screen or in magazines. Violeta enjoyed such things and later told funny stories about them.

I went over to Eduardo. Gin in hand, he was following the dancers' steps. Andrés and Violeta were very close; he was saying something into her ear, and both were laughing.

"They get along well, those two."

"Very well," I replied.

"Did you know she's thinking of you as godmother?"

"She hasn't said anything to me." I was moved; I, the least maternal person, godmother; it seemed to me a lovely honor. "I'd be delighted if she asks me."

I was surprised by the greediness with which he emptied his glass and immediately poured another.

"Hey, careful," I said, trying to make a joke of it.

He didn't hear me, or he didn't care. He poured a big drink and, to my stupefaction, drained the glass again. That was when he told me what has been pounding in my head ever since that night. Boring in, boring in.

"You're such a good friend of Violeta's, did you know the baby isn't mine?"

"What are you saying?"

"When I lost my wife and child in the Corral seaquake, I decided to have myself sterilized."

"Are you serious? You did that?"

"Yes. It was my way to prevent that ever happening to me again."

"And does Violeta know?"

I heard a sinister, unfamiliar laugh.

"I never told her. She wanted to get married to have children, why would I tell her that?"

"You were dishonest!" I couldn't help letting my discomposure and scorn show through.

"Dishonest enough to hope someone would look after me," he said with contained fury, "to hope not to be flung into the gutter, to hope to write in peace, to hope to be supported financially . . . and to put up with that bitch coming back pregnant from a trip and trying to pass me off as the father. But I won't tell her . . . the bond of paternity is sacred to her; that protects me."

"And why are you telling me?"

"So you will know the kind of friend you have; so you won't be so protective of her. You could take my side sometimes."

"I could tell her all this."

"No, you won't do that. I know you. You never get involved in other people's problems, you don't have time."

Again that laugh, brief and strange. And as if nothing had happened, he added, "Come on, let's dance. Let's see if we do as well as those two."

He grabbed me by the waist. I didn't want to dance with him. Against my will, I suffered the roughness of his embrace.

Something had come loose in Eduardo. All the fraternal feeling of our relationship seemed to evaporate, and I felt his hands and legs pressing against me. In the commotion of the dancing, he overtly tried to rub his sex against mine. At that instant, my instinct understood what my mind hadn't: Jacinta. At my age, intuition is merely the result of experience. Rage shook my body. Rage, oh, my God, the rage. The sickness of the end-of-the-century woman. We should not direct it, I told myself. No one person is guilty. But my rational thoughts did not last. I caught Andrés's eye and sent him my most desperate look. I saw that he was bewildered, but his reaction was immediate. Letting go of Violeta, in a friendly way he suggested to Eduardo that we change partners. I think that Eduardo scarcely noticed. I melted into Andrés's arms. Never leave those arms; never let other arms touch me. "What happened, Jose?" he whispered. I was incapable of answering. "Later, darling, later." And danced clinging to the only possible place for me.

My eyes met Violeta's only once. It reminded me of the butterfly Violeta, the childhood friend. Her grief like the final aria of *Madame Butterfly*. But there was no threat—none—of death in the categorical ivory of her eyes.

I did not see her leave. I repeat, in light of everything that happened, I did not see her leave. The freshness of the scent of Andrés's neck swept away Eduardo's filth; I forgot Violeta.

Was it my responsibility to distinguish between a love story and the story of a mistake? The consequences were not foreseeable. That night, this woman, with her pregnant, deserving body, underlined, highlighted, showed her other side. And I had no way to know it. We never saw, none of us ever saw, the true striations of that heart. Could I have suspected, then, that it would be only instants until the beat of compassion in Violeta was stilled?


We learned the rest early the next morning.

Rosa called the police at three in the morning.

At three in the morning, Rosa was awakened because Jacinta had forgotten her keys and called her from her party—a different party—to ask her to open the door. "Mama will get home later than I, so she won't know," the girl said, and Rosa, to cover for her, waited up.

At three in the morning, my Celeste—in bed, with only the light on the night table—was writing a love letter. Taking advantage of her parents' absence, she was listening to Bob Dylan at full blast, checking to see if the present Violeta had given her was worth her time. She went through seven drafts. At three in the morning, she was writing the final version.

At three in the morning, Borja was dancing the last rock number with Jacinta as she looked at the time and said: "They'll kill me." "No," my son answered. "I know what that party's like, they won't be home until dawn. Cool it, Jacinta, cool it."

At three in the morning, Jacinta was dancing the last dance with her friend Borja. At three in the morning, she asked him why he hadn't said anything about her new sweater. "It's pretty," he answered. "Where did you get it?" "My mother brought it to me from her last trip." "But it doesn't look Mexican" was Borja's comment. "No," said Jacinta, "it's Guatemalan." She toyed flirtatiously with the many tiny bead necklaces she was wearing, and kept dancing. At five after three, she said, "Come on, Borja, let's go, please. I don't want to make Mama mad, she's already feeling bad enough."

A little before three in the morning, I was telling Andrés, "I can't last any longer, let's go." "Don't be a party-pooper, we never dance," he answered. "But I don't like the last agony of a party, I don't like to see everything on the floor, the burst balloons, the wrinkled streamers, the spilled glasses. I don't like seeing people drunk after having seen them arrive looking so composed." "All right, this last dance," Andrés said. It was a Beatles song; Violeta always quoted it: "Life is very short, and there is no time for fussing and fighting, my friend." Andrés sang it in my ear. The last notes sounded, and I told him: "Let's go do our thing; *life is very short*, let's not waste time, my love." Andrés was excited at the prospect. He looked at the hour and said, "It's three o'clock, let's go."


Five to three: Rosa heard the shot. Rosa had tiptoed into the hallway when she heard the señora come in. She was worried, knowing that Jacinta wasn't home yet. The girl's bedroom had two doors. One onto the hallway: it was the one everyone used to go in or out of the room.

The other opened into Jacinta's bathroom, and the bathroom, in turn, had its own door to the hallway. Rosa, still tiptoeing, went into the bedroom and slipped the bolt on the official door, then came out the bathroom door. If the señora stopped by to tell Jacinta good night, she told herself, she will think her daughter is sleeping and not go in. That was when she heard screaming in the master bedroom. She couldn't make out the words, but she recognized Eduardo's and Violeta's voices. And blows. That sound, she told me later, is not something a woman from her world can ever mistake. Frightened, she ran to hide in her room. A half hour later, she heard the shot. She crept out of her lair and her eyes could not believe what they saw: Eduardo's body lying in the hall in front of Jacinta's door, blood, and Violeta a few feet from him, kneeling on the floor, head bowed, clutching a revolver in both hands.

The police came immediately. After them, Borja and Jacinta. They were alarmed when they found the door to the house open and the police cars in front. They ran in and the scene was exactly the same as Rosa described. As if it had been frozen in a photographic instant.

"Mama, Mama!" cried Jacinta. "Mama, what have you done?"

That was the first and only time Violeta reacted; she had not acknowledged the presence of the police, or Rosa's screams, or anything happening around her. She looked up, wearily, dully, at her daughter, and in a low voice spoke the only five words she would utter:

"The spirits weren't on duty."

The noise and the shot: Violeta's revolver filled the air with the smell of gunpowder, and in it lingered silent, millenary laments.

Violeta fired for all of us.

Intermission

$\mathcal{W}$e, *the others,* were with Violeta that night many years ago, when alone in her father's house she searched through the books in the coigue-wood bookshelves. We saw her, clear as day, walk to the poetry section, raise her hand, and pull out a hardcover edition bound in gray: *The Fact of a Doorframe.*

"Adrienne Rich," she murmured to herself, and twice repeated the author's name. It's thanks to a doorframe that I exist, was her obvious reflection, and she left with the book. She never put it back.

She made a note in her diary; we don't remember anymore which of her many notebooks. But she wrote down the part about the doorframe.

Farther on, visiting the poems one by one, she found "Poem of Women." Again she took her notebook and wrote two lines of the poem in capital letters:

## MY LIFE IS A PAGE RIPPED OUT OF A HOLY BOOK
## AND PART OF THE FIRST LINE IS MISSING.

And she ended in her characteristic hand: "This was written for me, I know it. I must find that missing first line."

We have always heard Violeta say, emphatically: "My mother's loneliness was sealed on a Tuesday, at eleven o'clock at night, January 24, 1939, the day of the Chillán earthquake."

*The fact of a doorframe*
*means there is something to hold*
*onto with both hands*

When she copied those three lines of Adrienne Rich's first poem, "The Fact of a Doorframe," in her diary, she thought perhaps other poems might define her better than that one, but she left it for later, when poetry would acquire its true dimension, greater than the trembling of the earth.

Because the earth trembled. (Yet despite this indisputable fact, Violeta was, long afterward, to choose to live in a zone of volcanoes. Challenging them? The sea trembled for Eduardo, and the water swept everything away.)

But it was real, we saw it. It was night that summer in 1939 when Oscar Miranda decided to go to the club. A game of dominos and a couple of drinks, that's all, he promised his wife, Carlota. She, combining patience with indifference, said good night at the door, and with no further thought went to the bedroom to put her daughter, Cayetana, to bed.

Oscar Miranda did not return home, or ever see his wife and ten-year-old daughter again. The body of Oscar Miranda was trapped beneath a wall of the lounge he called "the Club." The earth opened, walls fell, and the city came down.

When things began to shake in Carlota's house, she had not yet fallen asleep. The small pink-crystal teardrops on her lamp began to dance as she lay staring at the ceiling, wondering why God had put her on this earth. Not immediately alarmed—she never lost control—she waited to see if the pink drops would stop jiggling. They did not stop. Then she went to her daughter's bedroom. Without waking her, she picked her up and, holding her against her sturdy body, went to the front entrance, to the frame of the one large door in the house. The child opened her eyes; confused to find herself beneath the eaves, she hugged her mother as the world reeled like the snow in her globe when she shook it. No, it wasn't that gentle. This movement was stronger and sharper. Until the wall of the hallway to the bedrooms began to crack, until the foundations sagged and the house split in two.

Both of them would remember all their lives the screaming in the street, the lost and faraway howls, like background music for what was coming immediately: the fall. First, all the objects they lived among, and then the walls of the house they lived in.

Carlota and Cayetana, beneath the frame of that doorway, did not move, did not breathe, did not speak, did not weep. The house fell, but they were saved.


Carlota looked around her, bombed by a war absent a human hand, and ran, carrying her daughter, to the one other house in the city that meant anything to them. It was flat on the ground. Only the next day did they succeed in digging through the ruins to the residents; that night, between the two of them, they hadn't been able to do it. No survivor. Carlota looked at them: her mother and father, dead. And there was nothing else. She had already gone by the lounge; Oscar Miranda was dead, too.

Carlota looked at her city for the last time, and abandoned it. The belongings she was able to save were so few she wondered if it was worth the trouble to take them. Then, on second thought, she stacked them in a wicker trunk, varnished a brownish yellow, and, hoping to make her load light as possible, sent them south on the train. She took a suitcase in one hand and her daughter in the other and, after burying her family, she left.

She set a course toward the sea. They got off when the train stopped in Concepción.

Once installed in a boarding house they could afford—where, proudly, she paid in advance—she bought her daughter a lead pencil and a notebook with graph paper, handed them to her and said: "Draw. Or write. But don't sit here doing nothing. I fixed you a cold lunch, eat it at one. Not before, so you don't get hungry in the late afternoon. I'm going to look for a job."

The first day was disheartening. She applied in shops and groceries. She went nowhere near offices. Why? With the limited skills she could demonstrate?

On the fourth day she came back at ten in the morning. Cayetana was writing a poem about volcanoes.

"All right. I have a job. With the salary I'll earn, we won't be able to stay in this boardinghouse. No matter, we'll rent a room for the two of us in a less expensive neighborhood."

"Where did they give you work?"

"In a variety store. I'll sell everything from buttons to pencils."

They moved to Chiguayante. After much pleading and insisting on their situation as victims, they obtained a place in the neighborhood school for Cayetana.

Neither Cayetana nor Carlota thought of herself as unhappy. They had a roof and food. They had each other.

The room they rented was furnished, and Carlota kept it spotlessly clean. The only thing that belonged to them was the wicker trunk, which followed them to every house they lived in. They had only one table, a bed they shared, two chairs, and a little charcoal brazier at one side of the room. The bath was communal. The chamber-pot under the bed helped at night. Cayetana missed the tub in her home in Chillán, but she didn't say anything; the tub buried beneath the rubble of the earthquake was less important than the body of her father, similarly buried.

Everything went along well until the day the cashier at the shop said the register was short, and accused Carlota. She, insulted, immediately resigned.

A dark time followed. Brief, but dark. That is how we remember it, and they do, too. Employers asked for references. Carlota had none. Some time had passed since the tragedy in Chillán, and now it didn't work—as it had at the school and the variety store—to present herself as a victim. And since her former employers had accused her of stealing, there would be no recommendation from them.

The woman they rented from was understanding. A little time on credit, but just a little. They had no friends, only a few acquaintances. It was becoming difficult to eat.

(Many years later we heard Cayetana tell her daughter, who was born when this story we are telling was long forgotten: "I knew hunger; you have no idea what that anxiety can be. I think humankind must be divided into two groups: those who have been hungry and those who haven't. That's what separates the haves from the have-nots. I have excuses for a trauma or two that you will never have.")

The family that rented the room next to theirs had a daughter of seven. Sometimes Cayetana played with her, even though she considered her a little girl. If she helped her with her homework, the mother invited Cayetana to stay for tea. She prepared a long French roll for each of them. When that happened, Cayetana could skip dinner and have some for Carlota besides.

But it didn't last. Carlota found a job at a lounge. She had to learn to serve and prepare different kinds of sandwiches. Her schedule changed. She went to work late; that gave her time to clean in the morning and prepare dinner. But she never got home before nine at night, and the thick of winter made the darkness worse at that hour. Many times she came home to find Cayetana in bed, often half asleep. Those times, she curled up on the bed before taking off the high-heeled shoes that hurt her feet, and hugged her daughter. She held her to her bosom for long, timeless, moments, unique and irreplaceable, playing with that rebellious chestnut hair.

Once the child asked:

"Is life going to be like this forever?"

"No, oh, no!" her mother answered roundly. "If that were so, God would not have put us on this earth. Since he did, it was for some reason. Wait, we will soon know his reasons."

God was a vague figure to the girl; probably for the mother as well. Like a friend who accompanies us from afar, thought Cayetana, but who is not overly concerned about us, or we about him.

Both of them were lonely with this new schedule. But they could pay the rent and have enough to eat. Sometimes Carlota brought ham and cheese from the lounge that the employees were allowed to take home when the food was getting stale.

"I don't like for you to work so hard," Cayetana told her mother.

"It's just my feet that hurt. I have to wear these high heels to please the clients; I'm going to end up with cramped toes."

There were Sundays—Carlota's one day off—when she did not have the strength to get out of bed.

"I ought to take you to the park, like the other mothers do," she said guiltily.

"I'll trade the park for stories. Long stories, Mama. That way you won't get out of bed, and I won't either."

Those were the same stories that would enliven and spur Violeta's imagination years later. Cayetana told them all her life, and then Violeta told them to Jacinta. "A family of storytellers," Carlota used to say.

One day Cayetana, tired of being shut in, decided to go to the lounge after school. It wasn't more than twenty blocks from home, and she walked them happily. She never took the bus, she didn't have money for that. And when she went in, she smelled something on the air. She saw no one but men. It wasn't tea they were drinking at that hour, but beer. They were shouting at her mother as if they were her masters. It hurt Cayetana to see her mother there.

I will study and study, she promised herself; I will get an education so I will have a decent job when I grow up. And my mother will not have to work.

One night Carlota came home very angry. She seldom was angry, so this surprised her daughter, who by then had quite a pile of graph-paper notebooks—small ones of cheap paper—filled with poems and drawings. She tore her attention from the words she had finally got to rhyme.

"What happened?"

"A customer went too far. I complained about it to the boss, and he didn't back me up."

She did not give further details, but Cayetana's little heart shrank. She counted the days. It wasn't more than ten until her mother was out of work again.

"Your job is hanging by a thread, that's where you are!" her boss had told her.

"And I have my honor," Carlota answered, as she pried the hands of her boss himself, not just a client this time, from her buttocks. "Pay me what you owe me, I'm not coming back."

And she didn't. She had no doubts. She left, with the same con-viction she had felt when she abandoned her native city the day after the earthquake.

"We come from a breed of survivors, Cayetana. You and I. As your daughter and her daughter's daughter will. I can feel it."

The next day Carlota went to pick up Cayetana at school. She took her time, breathing the air, looking at people in the streets, paus-ing before the shop windows. Walking like this is a luxury; time is the greatest luxury, she told herself. It was in the window of a bakery that she saw the sign: NEEDED: DOMESTIC HOUSEHOLD EMPLOYEE. GOOD SALARY. INQUIRE WITHIN.

Carlota could not take her eyes from the sign. Then she went on to school and picked up her daughter.

The next day she followed the same route. The sign was still there. The next day, she went in.

That same night, Cayetana told her mother: "Don't die, Mama. What would happen to me? I'd be all alone in the world." And Carlota replied with conviction, "I'm not about to die; I am a strong woman. The day I die I will be an old woman, and I will be very tired but I will die with my boots on, as befits tough people. You'll see that what I tell you is true."

Carlota and Cayetana moved into a nice house near the Parque Ecuador, close to the Universidad de Concepción. Don Jorge Gallardo—Carlota's employer—taught philosophy in the law school. He was single, a widower, father of one girl. What Carlota most feared when she started her new job was having to reveal the existence of her Cayetana. But that caused no problem at all. To the contrary: given the master of the house's situation, the girl was welcome.

Two long years went by without surprises, mother and daughter very close. The only thing that still bothered Cayetana was saying, "My mother is a domestic servant." And it hurt because she knew that something in Carlota was destroyed. Might it be hope? Cayetana asked herself when she saw this woman courageously serving meals, washing dishes dirtied by others, cleaning the bathrooms. Hope you can always get back.

She did not wash or iron clothes. For that, Don Jorge employed a young girl orphaned by her Mapuche Indian mother and mestizo father, whom he had given work to augment her income. The girl was very drawn to Carlota; she treated her with great respect, like the mother she had lost, suspecting that this woman was not living the life she deserved to live. For two years, every Tuesday and Friday, they had lunch and dinner together.

"You are a very wise woman, Señora Carlota."

"In life, girl, sorrow makes us wise."

Cayetana was the one who benefited most from this girl's presence. Finally she had someone who could take her out for a walk, go with her to the movies, and help her in small tasks. And there were the stories. Cayetana, sitting beside the hearth, listened to the Mapuche girl's stories of her race and learned from them. She told Cayetana about the tutelary spirits, about her ancestors whom the *machi* summons with a twig of cinnamon, sprinkling it with *mudái*— blessed wheat liquor—about the husband chosen for the *machi*, the one who must provide her with everything so she can do her work. "That is what I would like to be, a *machi*," said Cayetana. "You can't," she replied, "you're not Mapuche." "But I'm mestizo," the girl answered proudly. "Or do you believe the Spaniards had only Spanish children?" She told Cayetana about the *pillán*, explaining that it isn't the devil, as Whites believe, but the spirit that looks after them. She called heaven "the land above," and that Cayetana never forgot. Or respect for the oral tradition, the voices of the elders, parents, grandparents, great-grandparents. Cayetana listened to the dreams the girl could summon: "We choose the flight of the condor overhead or of the caterpillar that has not moved a leaf but will become the butterfly that will move imagination." (Much later, Cayetana would tell her daughter: "The best aspect of that culture, Violeta, is that emotions and ideas are combined in the same words. That is the greatest difference between us." We cannot know whether or not the girl understood.) And Cayetana, once she had absorbed the meaning of the word *lamién*, thought a lot about brotherhood. She asked Carlota: "Mama, why is it that all Mapuches are brothers and Whites aren't?"

The girl who told so many stories to Cayetana was named Marcelina Cabezas.

As we were saying, that tranquility lasted two years, until the pirate came, the one who supplied Don Jorge with seafood and flour. He was a man of the sea. During some uprising, he deserted from the navy, took the radio he received instructions on and, because he considered them confusing and contradictory, tossed it into the ocean. He disappeared, boat and all. He returned after four years, with money. Aware of his crime, he turned himself in and paid his time in jail. When he emerged a free man, he bought a mill: that was the one place you could get bread during the period of the depression.

Don Jorge professed a mixture of admiration and affection for him.

One day, while Carlota was serving tea in the living room, the guest asked her straight out: "You, señora, why are you working here?"

"Because it is honorable work and I must give my daughter an education."

"Have you never thought about injustice?"

"Why? What happened to me happened, and I have to face it without asking questions."

"Well, it wouldn't hurt you to ask a few. You know as well as I do that this job isn't right for you."

"Since there isn't any other . . ."

"What is your day off?"

"Thursday evenings, and half days Sunday."

"Well, next Thursday I will come get you and take you where some of my friends are having a meeting. So you get to know the world a little, and ask those questions you never ask."

Carlota looked at him. Tall and robust, how wide were those

shoulders? Yes, it was vigor he communicated, like a scent. His black, very lively eyes moved restlessly. His hands, large as he took the teacup, large and rough, looked very strong. The first day she saw him, she had noticed a ring he wore on his little finger. It was a black-and-brown stone he called a *piedra cruz*; it contained a cross formed in the stone itself, not engraved or carved. Carlota was moved by its beauty and uniqueness. And those hands must have done many things. And that was why she agreed, not for the meetings or the questions.

Carlota was afraid she would forget what a man's hands were.


That was when she learned about comrades, manifestations, and socialism, all very foreign to her. And of course—and why not—her bosom swelled with libertarian airs. She wanted to study, to read about those things in the books this pirate made available to her, and many Thursdays, instead of going to the Parque Ecuador or strolling along Calle Barros Arana, she stayed with her daughter, studying. They did it together, one as interested as the other. At times Carlota read paragraphs to her daughter—some idea that seemed beautiful or inspired—and she understood better than her mother.

But all that smoke did not go to her head. The comrades provoked her, urging her to seek better horizons, but every day she decided to stay with Don Jorge: there she was not cold (the south is inclement in winter), or hungry (Cayetana ate the same balanced diet as the professor's daughter), no one mistreated them, and her Cayetana—her only child, the light of her eyes—could study in peace.

Until the day Antonio Sepúlveda—for that was the pirate's name—asked Carlota what her dream was.

"To see the capital" was Carlota's firm reply.

"Nothing original about that, coming from a provincial woman."

"But that is my dream."

"You will see the capital, woman, if you marry me."

One week later, the *piedra cruz* was ceremoniously slipped onto Carlota's ring finger. And Antonio Sepúlveda told her its story, so she would know *what* he was giving her.

The Sepúlvedas were eleven brothers. They lived in Talcahuano. One day, gold fever struck one of them, Guillermo, and under its spell he left home. The years went by and Guillermo did not return. Each brother, all of them bound to the sea, took it as his task to look for him. Nets of every nature were cast to haul in news of the missing man. Nothing . . . Guillermo had disappeared.

After five years had gone by, the youngest of the brothers, Antonio, was sent by his father to New York, following a reliable trail, with the mission of finding his brother. As the Sepúlveda patriarch bid his son farewell, though playing down the solemnity of the occasion, he had presented him with a medallion. The pendant hung from a silver chain, and set in the mounting was a *piedra cruz*. It was one of the stones of that region, from a nearby river, the Laraquete, that have the natural cross in earth colors, somewhere between black and brown, and are found in only two rivers in the world. "It's a good luck cross," Sepúlveda told his youngest son, "and may luck be with you."

The eleventh of the brothers set out. After much wandering and no few hardships, he heard of a small place in Harlem, sunk in the midst of poverty, called Chile Chico. It was a fringe of the fringe area where Chileans gravitated. He was taken to the patriarch of the barrio. "He is the one who calls the signals, the only one who can help you and give you information."

Antonio was received by a tall, heavyset man with a colorful tattoo on his left arm. Next to a glass of wine, a weary Antonio spit out the story of his brother. He was heard with attention and amiability. But no. Guillermo Sepúlveda had not passed that way. No one with that name. No. We know all the Chileans who have come through this part of the world in the last five years. No one of that description. No one.

As Antonio got up to leave, disappointed and unconvinced, the large man said, "Wait." He left and in an instant returned with a small cardboard box. It was sealed. "A gift for whoever sent you here," he said.

The youngest brother returned to Talcahuano and delivered the box to his father. He opened it. Inside, mounted in a ring, was a *piedra cruz*.

A year later, when Cayetana was fourteen, grandfather Antonio—as Violeta always called him—bought a house in the capital, in Ñuñoa, the neighborhood where his friends and comrades lived. They were very near the main plaza of the municipality.

It was a proper house. Very large, two stories, with many rooms, patios, and a grape arbor.

The mills and fishing boats of Antonio Sepúlveda were bearing fruit. He left one of his brothers in charge of his properties and set out for Santiago to indulge in his grand passion: politics.

After the first month, Marcelina Cabezas took the fast train to Santiago and came to live with them.

Cayetana never wanted ever to leave that house. Until she left everything, every possible house.

Violeta was born there. The first time she heard the word "move," she was twelve, when she had gathered all her papers together in a cardboard box and hidden them beneath the bed of her friend Josefa until the new house was ready. But that was much later. We, *the others,* must respect the order of this account.

Life in the house in Ñuñoa was the closest thing to a happy life we have ever known. Grandfather Antonio filled every space of life and of the house. Cayetana he treated like his own daughter. Carlota like his one true wife. He came and went among Santiago, Concepción, and Talcahuano, always with his hands full. There was never any shortage of good supplies for Marcelina to transform into splendid meals: fish, seafood, assorted sausages.

There was music.

There were books.

Grandfather Antonio bought Cayetana all the books she wanted: novels, poetry, history.

There were always people.

Grandfather Antonio closed his doors to no one.

And he did not close them to the young foreigner Tadeo Dasinski.

Tadeo was the son of a Polish marshal who fought against the dictatorship of Pilsudski between 1926 and 1935. Daszynski, as he originally spelled his family name, was a socialist. At a moment of political crisis, he decided to send his youngest son out of the country. Temporarily. He chose Buenos Aires, where a brother of his lived. Tadeo arrived there in 1931, when he was only sixteen. (In that country he called himself Dasinski; to simplify, he explained to his uncle.) He struggled to complete his basic course work in Buenos Aires. As the general had insisted on the provisional nature of that exile, his son did not study or do anything significant, awaiting a summons from his father that never came. And although he forgot nearly everyone from his country, the image of the dictator Pilsudski, with his thick black mustache, was forever engraved in his memory.

Because of discord over money, Dasinski fought with his Argentine uncle and came to Chile.

"He's not completely adapted," was Antonio Sepúlveda's comment when he met him.

"That's what I like about him," Cayetana replied.

And they swept him into their circle, integrating him into social evenings, political discussions, fritters on rainy days and toasted flour on sunny ones.

Tadeo Dasinski was the color of amber and seemed to be master of his body. He had the Europeans' languidness and looks, along with their fear and uprootedness. Cayetana fell in love with him.

They were married under a condition set by her: they would live in the Ñuñoa house. It was so large there was room for everyone. They could arrange the second floor as a private apartment. But Cayetana would never live apart from Antonio, Carlota, and Marcelina. And considering Tadeo's limited economic resources, this turned out to be less a burden for him than a relief.

Antonio did not want his daughter to suffer any economic hardships because of marrying a poor man without a profession.

"I didn't have one myself, and things haven't gone so bad for me; it's all a question of hard work and effort. But he's not going to get anywhere in that office where he's working. He'll be a low-level employee all his life. And the man isn't stupid. I'll set the two of you up in your own business."

Two things came as wedding gifts: the *piedra cruz* ring that the mother removed from her own finger to place on her daughter's, and the capital—so eagerly desired by Cayetana—to set up a bookstore.

"I will be able to read all the books I want!"

"But on one condition," Antonio warned. "That you don't interrupt your studies. Tadeo will manage it until you finish your courses."

Influenced by Don Jorge Gallardo, Carlota's former employer, who from the beginning had noted Cayetana's interest in learning, and who had taught her many things, she entered the Universidad de Chile to study philosophy.

"You'll starve with that degree," Carlota told her, not terribly worried.

"And what am I for?" replied the bigger-than-life Antonio Sepúlveda. "Let her study whatever she wants. Maybe with those courses she will go into politics later."

So Tadeo took charge of the bookstore and Cayetana continued at the university.

*We, the others,* accompanied Cayetana, shortly after her wedding, through her pregnancy. The only one she would have. She lived it jovially and with illusions, and the entire Ñuñoa household took pains to indulge the future mother. Arguments about the name were a game everyone enjoyed.

"A Polish name? Never!" Cayetana exclaimed when Tadeo tried to put in his oar. "It's enough with that family name. At least in the given name you should see roots in the south. The south of Chile, Tadeo."

Every suggestion was rejected by Cayetana.

Until one night, returning home, she ran to her mother.

"I have the name for my daughter!"

"So headstrong, child. What if it's a boy?"

"It's going to be a girl, I'm sure of it. Let me tell you, Mama. We went with some friends from the Education school to a large inn out on Gran Avenida."

"Why so far, baby?"

"Because there aren't any places like that in Ñuñoa, Mama. To have fun you have to branch out a little. We drove as far as the 22 bus stop, all crammed together in the same car, because one of my classmates had been there and he wanted us to hear a duo, two sisters who sing boleros and folk songs. The inn is called Las Brisas. And one of the women caught my attention."

"Why?"

"Because, Mama, guess what? I knew her. This woman with the long, unruly hair and a voice stolen from the angels reminded me of someone I knew. I thought and thought as I was listening. Where do I know her from? I've heard that voice before . . . something from my childhood. Until it came to me. You remember when we were living in Chillán and that wonderful old woman, La Pancha, worked for us? You remember she was singing all the time?"

"How could I ever forget La Pancha, baby!"

"And you remember how sometimes a young woman who went

around with a guitar over her shoulder came to see her, and La Pancha showed her the songs she made up?"

"I remember how proud La Pancha was, not that a folklorist was interested in her songs . . ."

"It's her, Mama. She's one of the sisters who sing. As we left, I went up to her and asked her if she was the person I remembered. And she told me she was. You should hear her sing! Pure talent, pure popular tradition. Believe me, Mama, she inspired me."

Carlota was surprised by her daughter's enthusiasm.

"And what is this woman's name?"

"Violeta Parra."

There was a brief silence, as if the chords of the guitar were flashing through the future mother's brain.

"My daughter will be called Violeta."


"Hire someone to manage for you and handle the cash register," the father-in-law advised Tadeo. "And you learn about books in earnest. It can become your profession."

And that was how Carmencita came to the family. An intelligent young girl, hard-working, discreet, she soon started to share their Sunday lunches, and took Violeta into her arms almost the moment she was born. A year after Violeta's birth, Carmencita had a baby of her own. She was unmarried. Antonio Sepúlveda, as a good freethinker, forbade anyone to ask her questions, and took in this son of an unknown father with all the naturalness in the world. He was Violeta's playmate from earliest childhood. Two years later, Carmencita's second pregnancy again surprised them.

At Cayetana's insistence, who protected her and sympathized with her, Carmencita was given a raise. A single woman with two children to raise is no joke, she argued. Since this baby was a girl, all the clothes, toys, and later, uniforms, everything that was Violeta's, Cayetana passed on to Carmencita.

So the family seemed to grow and grow, and everyone found a place in it.

About this time, Cayetana decided to visit a seer. A kind of witch who could read the future. The first thing she did was ask her to tell Violeta's fortune.

"Your daughter will have two lives," the woman prophesied.

"What does that mean?"

"She will have two lives, that's all I see."

Cayetana came home with this prediction, and among them they came up with a thousand conjectures and interpretations.

"As long as you love me a lot in each life, I don't care how many you have," Cayetana told Violeta.

"And what did they say about you, Mama?"

"Not much, not much at all."

No one could get anything more out of her.

The only fight anyone remembers from those years had to do with Violeta's starting school.

Cayetana believed in public education and planned to send her to a neighborhood school supervised by the Universidad de Chile and only a block from their house. Several of her friends had chosen this coeducational lay school for their children; it had an excellent academic reputation. Cayetana thought it was the natural place for Violeta.

But for the first time, Tadeo did not agree and spoke up rather stubbornly.

"I want a private school for my daughter where she will learn foreign languages and make contacts for the future. I don't want Violeta to go through any of the things that happened to me, the way I've always been an outsider, or you, who had to suffer being the daughter of a domestic servant. I hold the highest yardstick for my daughter."

"He may be right," Carlota intervened, captive to who knows what recollections.

"That is social climbing," was Grandfather Antonio's opinion. "They will make her a misfit. Besides, on principle I'm opposed to bourgeois schools. Catholic most of all!"

"We are all baptized, there's not a single pagan in this house," his wife replied.

The argument went on for some time.

"She absolutely must speak English," Tadeo insisted. "The world of the future is English, Cayetana. Look at what a handicap it's been to us not to know it."

That argument softened her resistance. She thought of her passion for reading, and of the possibility of not having to read translations but having access to the originals. In the end, she decided that it didn't matter: one's true formation was in the home, and school was secondary.

"How are we going to pay for it?"

"We will send her to the public school on the corner for the first three years, until I get the money together," said Tadeo. "The business is going well, trust me."

And that's what they did.

While Carmencita's children stayed on at the school on the corner, and the children of Cayetana's friends as well, three years later Violeta was sent to a school run by nuns in an exclusive neighborhood, so she would learn English.

It seemed strange to Cayetana, but once it tickled her sense of humor, which she had in large doses, she ended by finding the whole thing funny.

Carlota was happy.

Antonio always said it was stupid.

Tadeo, every time he went to the school, swelled with pride.

"My daughter will not have any problems in life," he boldly conjectured. "She will be cultivated, refined, a worthy granddaughter of a marshal, and will be able to adapt to anything that comes along."

To tears, too, said Marcelina—to herself, since no one asked her opinion.

A diversion in Cayetana's eyes.

Despite her studies, which went on forever, and a busy life filled with activities, Cayetana developed an uncontainable tenderness for her little Violeta, trusting she could share the traditional role of mother with Carlota and Marcelina. She called Violeta "my little apple," and nibbled her. The child would look in the mirror at night and ask herself if she looked like an apple. Her mother made her laugh, and it was that laugh, reflected in Cayetana's eyes, that she loved most: Violeta always looked for her eyes.

One of the worst memories of her childhood was the episode of the Polish vase. It was an enormous flowered jardiniere, very fine, one of the few possessions from her father's past life. Sometimes Violeta played "getting dizzy" in the front room: she would spin in circles a hundred times, with her eyes closed and her arms held out straight, until she lost her balance. Her father told her again and again not to do it, that she could fall on the vase or knock it over with her extended arms. Until it happened. She broke the vase. Tadeo was on the verge of losing control. Violeta, terrified, sought her mother's eyes: in them she found a blend of confidence and lightness. Without a single word from Cayetana, those eyes placed the importance of what Violeta had done in perspective. So breaking the Polish vase stayed in the girl's mind as a mistake, a bad bit of mischief, not something awful. Thanks to Cayetana's eyes.

Violeta came home crying one day because in her new school her classmate Carmen Brieba had accused her of being a Pole, telling her that all Poles were Communists and that they were going to ex-communicate her and her father because of it. Cayetana burst out laughing.

"And how does Carmen Brieba know that?"

"They told her that at home. The problem, Mama, is that she always knows everything."

"And why is that, Violeta?"

"Because her cousin is Queen Elizabeth."

Cayetana could not hold back a belly laugh.

"A cousin of Queen Elizabeth?"

"I swear it Mama, that's what she always says in class."

"And you believe her?"

"Yes, Josefa and I believe her."

Cayetana hugged Violeta, and her laughter filled the child's heart, who never again worried about being Polish, or whether or not they were all Communists.


We, *the others*, would like to respect Violeta's memories, which at a certain point began to be fragmented. It isn't our memory that's fragmented, it's hers.

There is something in the air of the Ñuñoa house. Violeta perceives it but doesn't know what it is. She is close to adolescence, and we know that her eyes have registered the image of Cayetana crying in her room because Grandfather Antonio has been hard on Tadeo. They have asked him to lend them money to enlarge the bookstore, and he has refused. Violeta knows that her grandfather never denies anything without a good reason. Something shrinks inside her.

Her next memory is of Carmencita's third pregnancy. Cayetana decides to take charge of the new baby.

"I will be the godmother," she announced, and Carmencita wept at her offer.

It was during Carmencita's pregnancy, almost the end, that they had that dinner for the Latin American visitors in the house in Ñuñoa. It produced a strange mixture: Socialist leaders, intellectuals, international officials, and even a few *guerrilleros,* it was said. Grandfather Antonio knew them all; he had his networks and contacts. Some nights he sat Violeta on his knees and told her about the most famous of these famous people, one they called "Che." And telling her about Che, he would praise the value of solidarity and generosity. This doctor, who had given up a comfortable and stable life to gamble his life on the poor, and not only the poor of his country but those of the entire continent, was like a star to Violeta . . . Grandfather Antonio used these opportunities to talk about how all of Latin America ought to be one entity, sharing the same destiny, and that good men ought to take chances for that. He quoted José Martí: "It is a crime not to be a useful man." Violeta listened, oh, so serious, absorbing her grandfather's words. Then the memorable dinner took place, and Violeta recalls herself curled in a ball beside the fireplace, trying to pass unnoticed, as she saw her mother's eyes frequently glancing toward the green, half-fierce, half-protective eyes of a Guatemalan guest. Violeta perceived something she did not know how to record in her consciousness, but she could not escape the almost magnetic waves issuing from the man. He was young and very handsome. She kept staring at him, fearful that maybe she should remember that face, fearful of the vibrations from her mother's body.

The attack came a few days later: Grandfather Antonio's heart stopped without warning. One morning, quite simply, he did not open his eyes. Mourning cloaked them all from head to foot. Life without Antonio was not life at all. An opaque rain fell upon the house, something Violeta swore to combat during those inconsolable nights in her bedroom when she wept for her grandfather. Dazzle cannot come from outside; another person cannot give it to you, it has to be from you, she concluded.

Carlota decided to give up. Or just began gradually to do it. Violeta was very angry. "Why don't you fight, Grandmother? You're the strongest of us all." "Because I don't care anymore, baby, I'm through. I'm old now, I want to go and be with him."

In the meantime, Carmencita's baby was born. Since Cayetana was to be the godmother, the house had to come alive. Marcelina cooked for several days; Carlota found strength to join in, and Cayetana to build enthusiasm. The baptism took place with all the proper trappings, and even today Violeta would recognize the pink dress they bought her for the occasion.

The night of the baptism was the darkest time after the death of her grandfather. Violeta remembers Carlota and Cayetana locked her mother's room: Cayetana was screaming and, though weak, Carlota was consoling her.

"Thank God Antonio's gone," Carlota sighed. "He never liked him at all, he suspected something."

Violeta listened, her ear glued to the door.

"That's why he didn't lend you the money to enlarge the book-store."

Violeta went to Marcelina to ask her what was going on. She got no answer.

The next day, Tadeo moved out. He told his daughter good-bye, and promised to see her very soon.

"When you grow up you will understand and be able to forgive me."

Cayetana immediately left on a trip, but not without giving a full explanation to her daughter about what had happened. She was honest, as she was in everything. She did not try to cloak obvious facts in shadows.

"The day the baby was born, I was sitting in the main waiting room. Since the delivery was taking so long, I went to the maternity ward to see if there had been some problem. And to my amazement, I heard Carmencita screaming Tadeo's name. You know what came to me, Violeta? I remembered a Russian spy novel in which the heroine, who had passed herself off as a German, and whom everyone believed was German, cried out in Russian as she was giving birth. That made me nervous. Suspicious, in fact. But we had the baptism to go through, and I'd given my word to be godmother to this baby. So on the day of the ceremony, observing the interaction between Tadeo and Carmencita—with my eyes opened now—and seeing little things I previously had ignored, I understood it all. I spoke with him that evening as soon as the guests had left. I told him a true lie, a horrible game you allow yourself only in circumstances that are equally horrible. I told him that in the delivery room, Carmencita, afraid that she was going to die (women do strange things at that moment), had confessed the truth to protect her children. Which was how I knew that he was the father. Tadeo's pallor made any confession unnecessary. Yes, my little apple, that is the truth. Your father has been with Carmencita ever since you were born. It has been a savage betrayal. But in spite of everything, he is your father, he loves you, and you will find a way to forgive him some day. I will not."

Violeta listened to this story as if it had happened to someone else. With her emotions paralyzed, she wasn't paying attention as her mother concluded.

✻ "The perfect chess piece: the man protected by women, using the shelter of their shelter to destroy them."

Violeta thought she was going to lose her mind. If Grandfather Antonio hadn't died, none of this would have been possible. Her father was a good person. How could she believe he had stayed with her mother just because it was to his advantage? How could he *not* love her mother, that adorable woman her daughter saw as irresistible?  "A man can love two women at the same time," Tadeo would answer much later.

And Cayetana went away, too, leaving Violeta with Carlota and Marcelina. "Latin America," she answered when they asked her where she was going. That vague. The child received a few postcards that she kept for a long time. She remembers one from Colombia in which her mother mentioned the Tequendama, an orchid garden and a coffee plantation. Nothing more. The one from Lima is the one she remembers best: her mother called it "a thrice-crowned city, beacon of the great Pacific ocean." She remembers an altar in the San Francisco de Jesús de Lima church, the one of the Patrón de los Imposibles, and her mother telling her she was attracted by that name and that she prayed for her before the Patron Saint of Impossibilities. Violeta kept forever the card written in Guadalajara, Mexico. The splendid building that appeared in the photograph was of the orphanage they called the Hospicio Cabañas. Cayetana describes the twenty-three patios, the orange trees and the whitewash, the generosity of light and space, the Orozco frescos, and of having found a sacred place there. *Some day your eyes will see this light, my little apple*, she writes her daughter, *and you will be enslaved, as I was*. There was also a postcard from Guatemala, and the girl rejected what it said, without knowing why. She knows only that she doesn't remember anything about that part of her mother's trip. That was all, until Cayetana's hasty return when Carlota believes her time has come. Cayetana manages to get there and give her mother her love. The next day, throughout the night, Carlota lay dying. And at the appointed hour, she got up in bed to die with her boots on, as she had promised her daughter. She imitated Grandfather Antonio's instrument: the heart. But Violeta knows that Carlota has died of love.

Then chaos crashes over the child's head. After a few days she finds herself in the house of her friend Josefa, because Cayetana has decided to close the Ñuñoa house, sell it, and go away. She leaves Violeta the wicker trunk. When she is ready, she asks Marcelina to stay and take care of her daughter in Tadeo's house, promising that she will send for her soon. Very soon. Wait just a little while.

Marcelina does not want to move into Tadeo's apartment. It is small and crowded. But the real reason is that she dreads being around

Carmencita. "How can I put up with her?" "For Violeta's sake," Cayetana tells her. "For Carlota's and mine."

Tadeo, happy to have his daughter back, and making future plans for everyone, rents a large house and moves Violeta into her own bedroom. "But this is just temporary, Papa," she tells him. "It doesn't matter, I want you to be comfortable. We don't know how long it will be before your mother comes back to get you." That was when Violeta moved for the first time in her life; and in the midst of all that uproar took her papers to Josefa.

The day Cayetana left, as she hugged her daughter, she did something that betrayed her because it seemed definitive (Did she sense her fate? Violeta would ask herself a thousand times afterward). She took off the *piedra cruz* ring and put it on her daughter's finger.

"It's a little big for you, but no matter. This is the ring for the hands of all our women, all the women of our family Through it we pass down the best of ourselves to the one next in line. Don't lose it. I leave it to you as my pledge, because it is the thing I love most. You can give it back to me the next time we're together."

Violeta waited and waited. She acquired the habit of pausing at the street door of her father's new house and looking down the sidewalk, hoping to see that graceful figure, that long chestnut hair the other mothers didn't have. She received cheering letters. *We'll be together again, my love, wait just a little longer.* When Violeta was thirteen, she received a letter she did not understand very well and that didn't interest her. Seven years later, when she was twenty, on the same day, her birthday, the letter turned up in a book. She was struck by the coincidence; it seemed very like Cayetana. Then she read it and kept it, so she could later pass it on to Jacinta.

*On this the day of your birth, my beautiful girl, I want to remind you of something: you are very privileged. Today you turn thirteen, and these words will sound strange to you, but I need you to remember them when you are older.*

*Your equals probably will not need you, they know how to take care of themselves. It is the others who will need you. And this, Violeta, does not refer only to your courses and to the profession you will have some day, but to the world.*

*Normal people, Violeta, are simple people. They are not particularly intelligent or interesting, not especially well educated, or successful, or destined for triumph. That is, my dearest, they are not anything special. These common people have made their way into history as statistics; as individuals, only in records of births, marriages, and deaths. A society worth living in is the one devoted to these people, not the rich, the brilliant, the exceptional—although a society that does not give them space would be suffocating.*

*The world is not made for our personal benefit, nor are we here to benefit ourselves. A world that proclaims such an objective is not a good one, and should not endure.*

*I would not want you to forget this as you grow up.*

*Happy Birthday, my love.*

Until the day the news came that would end all Violeta's hopes. After that she did not go out to the sidewalk to wait for her mother. Not then, not forever after, would she seek Cayetana's eyes. Never.

"The guerrilla war," Tadeo told her. "She set her own rules and now she's died by them."

The green eyes of the Guatemalan came back to Violeta. Was she with him all this time?

"I don't know," was her father's unadorned answer.

Tadeo went to Guatemala to claim Cayetana's corpse. He did not allow his daughter to go with him because he took this as a matter to be dispatched as quickly as possible. He came back without it. The list of betrayals was going to kill Violeta; that was how she felt. Not even a body. Her father's explanations were unsatisfactory. That they had taken the cadavers to a small town in Guatemala, that they buried them there, that the cause of death was unclear. The authorities insisted that it was an outbreak of fever; others said they'd been machine-gunned. The coffin was sealed. That was it.

Not to see your face again, Mama.

Never to see your face again.

(Violeta spent years looking for things in her father's house that Cayetana might have touched. Violeta needed to touch the things she had touched.)

Violeta knows, and we as well, that her salvation in those days was Marcelina. She alone held Violeta's shattered world together. The fragments were mended only in her dark body, fruit of a mestizo father and Mapuche mother. What equilibrium Violeta conserved flowed from this woman's roots, like the herbal remedies she had so often used to heal her during her childhood. It is Marcelina to whom Violeta declares an eternal debt.

When Marcelina felt Violeta was capable of fighting her own wars, she considered her mission complete. But before she left, she had to settle two matters with her little girl.

First: "We're going to a place that would have been important for your mother. She would have taken you there herself if she were alive."

So one night she took Violeta to the barrio of La Reina to hear a folklorist who sang in a tent.

"She has become very famous," Marcelina explained, "even outside the country. Everyone comes to hear her. A voice stolen from the angels, that's what your mother said."

Violeta listened, enchanted.

"You are named Violeta after her."

(When Violeta was a grown woman, she often visited the long house on Calle Carmen, right in the heart of Santiago, the official site of La Peña de los Parra. As she drank the warm wine, she always thought of the rudimentary tent in La Reina, and how much Marcelina and Cayetana would have liked this new place.)

Second: "His name was Rubén Palma, in case no one tells you. The *guerrillero*, the one with the green eyes. They died together. They lived out their love and in it they died. Always remember that, butterfly."

And she left.

Violeta demanded, kicked, cried, but Marcelina, very quiet, told her, "My homeland is the only thing that will save me from all this pain. I must go there. A person must always go back to her origins. It's time for me."

Marcelina Cabezas died in her sleep, peacefully, in her own land. It was ten years later, when Violeta was living in Rome. Again she wept, and kicked, and accepted it only by remembering the last words she heard from Marcelina.

The name of Cayetana was erased from the house where Violeta lived with her new family. No one spoke of her; it seemed healthy to everyone not to remember all the turbulence that had surrounded them in the past. The appearance of happiness and normality was possible only without her memory. Tadeo begged his daughter to allow them all to preserve the tranquility that was so precious to them.

One day when Tadeo was angry with her, requesting that she not ask any more questions about her mother, Violeta promised him this would be the last.

"At least tell me one thing: where, exactly, is she buried?"

"In the town of Antigua, in Guatemala."

Then, certain now that poetry was going to have more space in her life than the trembling of the earth, Violeta went back to the book by Adrienne Rich, to her "Poem of Women." She made a new note beneath the names "Carlota, Cayetana, and the others."

*The faces of women long dead, of our family,*
*Come back in the night, come in dreams to me saying:*
*We have kept our blood pure through long generations*
*We brought it to you like a sacred wine.*

Then she reread what she had underlined so many years ago.

MY LIFE IS A PAGE RIPPED OUT OF A HOLY BOOK
AND PART OF THE FIRST LINE IS MISSING.

And realizing that her adolescence had come to an end, she set out
to seek that missing first line.

# Part Two

## The Last Forest

It is we, *the others,* who observe Violeta before her mother's empty chair. We hear her repeating to her absent figure, "I can't forgive you. I can't."

It is we, *the others,* who watch Josefa in her tight-fitting beaded dress, her body static, unmoving, as she sings, microphone in hand, deathly the silence in the auditorium, and we know that Violeta will not come to this performance, or the next, or any to come, and Josefa needs Violeta to tell her that it's going well, that everything's fine, that everything will be fine.

# 1

$\mathcal{I}$ am the one who should be named Violeta, I was the depository of her song. But that isn't how it was.

My father baptized me Josefina Jesús de la Amargura.

I lost long afternoons of my life dreaming about having a special name: sonorous, majestic, like the names of so many musicians of the old world. Rimsky-Korsakov. Or Sergei Rachmaninoff, for example. Rach-ma-ni-noff. How beautiful Russian names can be. How evocative! And my name is Ferrer.

When I was three I learned to recite "The Capture" and "The Death of Antoñito el Camborio." ("Some day we will return, we will all meet at the Guadalquivir," my father predicted when he read us "Lament for Ignacio Sánchez Mejía" in bed, my brother and I under the covers, listening.) At three, already reciting García Lorca by heart and dreaming of dying in profile and with the soapy leaps of the dolphin, mysterious words I came to understand long after I could recite them. I was tagged as *an intelligent little girl.* Years later, my therapist opined that that was not a good sign, nor did it reveal intelligence: it was merely an indication of sadness and death in such an early stage of life.

Despite that, my childhood was stable.

Stability that doesn't help me today.

Jesús Ferrer was born in the south of Spain, in a small town near Seville, in the region of Andalusia. He lived through the Civil War, fighting for the Republicans, and crossed the Atlantic on board the legendary *Winnipeg,* the shipload of Spanish refugees organized by the poet Pablo Neruda. There were three brothers. My uncle Marcos stayed behind in Franco's jails, later to go into exile in France, and my uncle Senén accompanied my father to this remote country.

They say that Jesús kept his ardor alive during the first years of his life in Chile. Violeta seized on this to insist that I had revolution in my genes. Those are not my primary memories of my father.

I have the impression that he was slowly giving up. (Isn't it likely *those* are the genes he transmitted to me?) After a while, the *Winnipeg* and the Spanish Civil War faded, as if a powerful instinct of survival removed him from some accursed marginality, situating him in the comfort of the center. We never again heard his heavy voice telling us (or telling us the story of?) *"No pasarán."* They shall not pass. Marginality had already wounded him, irreversibly. Why didn't he fight? He adapted to this country, and changes in the Chilean political situation left him indifferent; he stayed outside those swings of mood. I prefer to think that this attitude was born spontaneously, not calculated.

For a wife he chose Marta Aliaga, the most classic of uncommitted Chilean women, middle class, unaware of the ocean, the Republic, or the Fifth Regiment. It was not a casual selection. My mother was everything he needed to pass unnoticed, to be *just another* normal citizen. So that no *idea,* as idea, would be relevant. The mixture of insipidity and veiled ambition in my mother was seductive to him. My father was filled with contradictions. Or perhaps simply a weak man. This is, clearly, a family characteristic. It leaps to view in his two brothers.

Senén was active for a while in Chilean politics, working vigorously on behalf of the radicals. One of his best friends came to be the President of the Republic. When this happened, the man called Uncle Senén and literally offered him anything he wanted. "All you have to do is ask," he told him. And Uncle Senén answered: "I've been thinking it over carefully, I knew this moment would come. I want to be the Secretary of the Public Wardrobe." His friend looked at him with amazement. "Secretary of the Public Wardrobe? But, Senén, I can make you an ambassador . . . I can give you important posts. What you're asking is too easy, no one asks for that because there's *nothing* to do, it's mind-boggling boring." "That's exactly why I want it," Senén replied.

Then, after many years of exile in Paris, on Franco's death, Uncle Marcos returned to Spain for the first time. It's a different country, it's no longer the one you knew, his friends told him, but the dictatorship is over. He traveled to his birthplace and after greeting the few members of his family who survived he walked to the plaza. He sniffed the air, recognized what he had been missing, filled his chest. Suddenly he noticed an unfamiliar shadow to his left, from the back of the plaza. He saw an equestrian statue that had not been there before. Intrigued, he walked to it. Francisco Franco on horseback. A statue of Franco in his town!

He immediately returned to Paris.

That is my father's family. This is who I come from.

I should add that Jesús, until his seventieth year, when he died, loved me very much.

I never have liked the term *famous* applied to me. I prefer to say that things have gone well for me. But my mother is fascinated by that word.

"My daughter doesn't need to learn about domestic chores" was the phrase that determined my upbringing. "I am raising her to be a queen. Since when do queens have to learn stupid little chores?"

She was gambling that I would not be invisible. One day she told me a short, insignificant story.

She was the next-to-last of several sisters. The two elder ones shared a bedroom and, since they were well into their teens, the world of that room held a great attraction for her. Everything was lively, fun, filled with secrets; and in that room the wardrobes smelled good. One of the sisters, Aunt Juana, is getting dressed for a visit from her boyfriend. Aunt Adriana is helping her. Juana has tried on at least five dresses, with accompanying cries of admiration from Adriana.

"Shall I wear the blue jumper?"

"Yes," Adriana answers. "Victor hasn't seen it."

"With what blouse? Has he seen me in the lilac blouse? What blouse did I wear last week?"

"You wore the white one, so I would put on the lilac one today."

"Good."

From a corner, watching this girlish fiesta, which to her childish eyes signified importance and freedom, Marta asks: "What about me? Did I wear this skirt last week?"

Both sisters turn, as if only now noticing her presence.

"You? Who cares what you wore last week? No one looks at you."

From that moment, Marta swore to be an attention-collector. Not for herself, because she considered that impossible; but when I was born, she knew for whom. The quality or intensity of the attention didn't matter, only the amount.

The boyfriend Victor married Aunt Juana and, to the family's shame, returned her shortly thereafter. No one ever knew exactly why. Once this happened, my grandmother was seized by a strange affected piety. Piety, I insist, though it was merely external, not the faith or compassion one carries within. And my mother inherited it, with the same superficiality.

"Look, daughter," she told me a thousand times during my youth. "In life it is better to be respected and admired than to be loved. Get that in your head."

Of course, Grandmother Adriana always said it, and my mother repeated it. The problem was that all my aunts were spinsters. The youngest, Aunt Chela, lived with us for several years, and when there wasn't room in the house any longer she went to a convent. Victor had *loved* Aunt Juana, and look what happened. And if it hadn't been for that half-crazy Spaniard half-disoriented in a strange country, Marta's fate might have been the same as her sisters'. At least, that was what she believed. She managed to marry, despite her grandmother's sing-song voice in her ears: "Between saint and saint, a high wall ensures restraint," and, "Because man is fire, as everyone knows, the woman lays kindling and the devil blows."

One afternoon I was studying at my grandmother's house, religion notebook in my lap, surrounded by all my aunts—each busy with some chore. One by one, I was writing down the cardinal sins: alarmed at so much evil, I asked them what the *cardinal virtues* were. None of them knew. And that is the true picture of these women, I concluded: they know all the sins and none of the virtues.

On the wall above my bed was a crucifix. One day an old black-and-white engraving appeared beneath my Christ. Large letters spelled out L'ORGUEIL beneath the illustration. "Well, aren't you studying the cardinal sins?" my brother Patricio asked pugnaciously. "I hung it right beside your bed so you don't forget that pride is the sin Mama invented for you."

I have to say in my mother's defense that she never felt about me as I did about my daughter, Celeste. As Celeste was growing up, I didn't know how to situate myself, how to see myself. As my daughter grew older, I was forced to abandon the last traces of my childhood, pushed to grow up once and for all and play the role of mother that the world and my daughter expected. I felt I was still too young, and that that role was too big for me. It was very difficult for me to adjust to being me—the enterprising, vivacious woman—and Celeste's mother, all at the same time. Borja never posed questions of lost identities, but because she was a girl, Celeste did. In contrast, my growing up never gave my mother any problem. She was intrinsically a *mother*, as if she had been born for that task alone, and felt entirely at home with it. She never had fancies about youthfulness, as I did facing the microphones, or Andrés's delicious body. The model I received, therefore, was perfectly clear, passed down to me cleanly and precisely. Worse in so many other senses, those models were certainly more clear-cut than the ones I gave Celeste.

My father, with a Spanish partner, opened a bakery. It began as a modest business in the Club Hípico barrio where we lived, and the earnings were rather scant. I lived my early childhood in that barrio, and remember with happiness the nearby Parque Cousiño—today Parque O'Higgins—which my children scarcely know. This was also the time when my father taught me to sleep with both hands on the bed, a habit I have kept till this day. Every night Papa came into my bedroom and as I slept lifted the hand I had thrown over the edge of the mattress. So the mice wouldn't eat me. "In the war, the mice were hungry, too, and they ate little children's hands." To each his trauma. Violeta had to sleep with a clear path to the door, always ready to run out at the first sign of an earthquake.

By the twentieth of every month, Papa's money ran out. The quality of our food immediately declined:, potatoes and cornmeal, corn chowder, stew. Papa would borrow money from Uncle Senén. On the first, punctually, he repaid him. And on the twentieth we were again penniless, and the cycle started all over again.

The bakery grew and we began to have more money and more

needs. An expensive school for Josefina, my mother said. That was her priority. Her premise: "We must raise her to be someone in life," and, "Josefina will not be a woman whose fate could have been greatness only to have life cheat her out of it."

We moved to an exclusive neighborhood, because I could not go to an expensive school while we were living near the Club Hípico. We went to Las Condes, to a smaller house in Villa El Dorado. Fewer and smaller bedrooms; we didn't have room anymore for Aunt Chela. This person who had been fundamental in my life disappeared overnight; the one who waited for me every afternoon when I came home from school to tell me all the latest atrocities: assaults and accidents were her favorite themes. But quite aside from that, she wore gorgeous vintage slips. I asked her to give them to me when she went to the convent; years later, Andrés thought they were very sexy, with that retro look . . . She would have been scandalized had she known. Aunt Chela's petticoats, indestructible, still exist. Time didn't pass for her, always exact, growing more and more herself with the years. She was the only person in the house who had any common sense, and that had given us a certain equilibrium.

Aunt Chela and the Old Fortune-Teller hag. She was a gray-haired tramp who had lost both legs and went around on cut-off crutches, dragging the rag-wrapped stumps. A terrifying image, nothing but torso and hair piled on top of her head, crafty eyes, and a hand always out, trying to stop passersby to tell their fortune. I was irrationally frightened of her: if I saw her from a distance, I would walk blocks and blocks to avoid going past her. Her mere presence evoked evil spells. One day she came to the door of my house, begging food. I screamed when I saw her and she responded with fearful curses. Aunt Chela consoled me, and, surprised by the intensity of my fear, asked me the most lucid question of my entire childhood. "Might it be, child, that your problem with her is just the fear of becoming like her some day?" The Old Fortune-Teller was an obsession, like so many I've had. But I believe that this one is tied to a profound intuition about myself: the fear of spilling over, of the fall. The Old Fortune-Teller lived in me as a kind of fear of going beyond limits.

Aunt Chela was the essence of a minimal life. In some strange way she was happy about the move: finally she had something she was at risk of losing. But I never forgave my parents, who had sacrificed her in order to live in a better neighborhood.

Once we were asked, in my new school, to fill out a form about our antecedents and family: the number of brothers and sisters, the father's activities, the mother's, and so on. In the box that said father's profession, I wrote *baker*. My schoolmates laughed at me. They had all proudly written *lawyer, engineer, doctor*. Josefina's father is a baker! They whispered and shot sidelong glances at me. When I told my mother she turned pale; her upper lip trembled as it did only when she was irate.

"Whatever made you put that! *Entrepreneur*, you should have written. *Entrepreneur!*"

She did not speak to me all afternoon. My mother was poisoned with impotent bile she could not direct toward any individual, only toward life in general, when things are not as one would like.

The difference in the way my mother and I felt about being poor is that I didn't feel dishonored by it; I saw poverty as a passing phase, an illness that does not leave any scars.

When I began to show a gift for music, I asked to take classes at the Conservatory of Music. My father thought it was a whim, and laughingly said, "And how will you do that, Josefina? Where's the money coming from?" My mother, in contrast, took it very seriously. What grieves me today is that though she made the effort, it wasn't for love of music or to make me happy. No, her determination was directed toward a possible way for me to become "somebody." For three years my mother sold eggs and cheese, house to house, to pay for the famous Conservatory.

Marta Aliaga went to such lengths so that I could glide smoothly toward the world of the wealthy. But her perseverance and her eagerness caused me to stumble, not glide; it set me on guard; it made me feel it was a privilege to be where I was. Not natural.

When I won that first prize in the Festival of Song in Viña del Mar, when no one had expected it—I least of all, and made the leap to "celebrity" overnight, I was grateful almost exclusively for my mother; it was my gift to her voraciousness. Also for her were my thoughts when I held the cover of my first record in my hands. A prize for her, I said to myself. I could have said, in more straightforward terms, a prize for her social ambitions. But . . . it isn't easy for a daughter to recognize her mother's defects, especially such a revolting one.

In my opinion, I have paid her back, with interest. I do not feel indebted to her. First it was the singing. And then, the thing that crowned all her ambitions: Andrés. Deep down, I thought, fame wasn't enough. It was fame added to prestige that would finally provide serenity. And that I gave her when I married a lawyer, Andrés Valdés.

At last I have made her happy.


And at last I don't fantasize: we are our parents and the circumstances it has been our fate to live, nothing more. (Jesús Ferrer and Marta Aliaga, the Festival of Song in Viña del Mar.) The sum of what our parents contributed and what has molded us through circumstance. Nothing more.

When I proposed this idea to Violeta, years ago, she asked me: "Then, husbands and children, who are supposed to play such a part in who we are. What about them?"

"Circumstance," I replied. "Nothing but circumstance."

# 2

Violeta.

> *Accursed heart*
> *With no thought for me, no, no thought for me.*
> *Blind, deaf, mute,*
> *from birth, yes, from birth.*
> *How you torment me.*

Violeta, almost the other half of my being, committed a murder. Violeta was taken to jail. Violeta was later absolved. Violeta went away.

Our stories blend together. Today I came to the surprising conclusion that I am the one who leans on her, not the reverse, as I had often thought. Violeta killed, and saved herself. Precisely then, at that moment, my decline began.

Summer came, the summer of '91, but I was still in winter, in the internal winter from which I have never emerged.

When Violeta went away, I felt that the same materials of the present were being used to build my future, and that this condemned any prospect for growth. Violeta's eternal drive to push forward went with her. Now there would be no voice to say, "Josefa, Josefa, let's think about what's to come!" Now no one would urge me to let my thoughts drift. And when some day, some day of days, she asked, "What have you been leaving behind you, Josefa?" I would have no answer.

She gave me the answer: anything you can't find room for in your heart will be weak. If what Violeta left me as a token was that, my heart is empty. Unable to assume reality, as the philosopher would say, because of existing on the outer fringes of Utopias. Or should I understand that Violeta's token was her mourning, which in the end cut a channel for my own?

I should have let go of everything that drained my energy, but I couldn't. What happened is that the restless devil, the one that possessed her, took hold of me.


For her, anything except uneventful triviality.

That was her judgment.

You were right, Violeta, to quote Hernández: *except your womb, everything was dark.*

I would never have approved such an extreme: murder. That she has done. I remember asking Andrés, in all seriousness: "In strictly conventional terms, isn't Violeta immoral?"

"Maybe," he answered. "But that isn't what matters most to me."

Nevertheless, time and events have led me to conclude, after much analysis, that *every* woman—on the edge, experiencing that spilling over we fear so much—is capable of killing her man.

And to my amazement, I was not the only one to reach that conclusion.

Chilean society was quite disturbed by this murder. If it had happened in a marginal community, Violeta commented later, it would have been just another case. But a well-known writer murdered by a professional woman "from an expensive school," as Mama told it? No one was indifferent. How many photographs of Violeta in the newspapers! How many speculations! How many attacks and how many defenses from various social movements! Some virulent, others going so far as to ask for the death penalty: that woman as example. The scandal went on and on, seemed not to end.

> *Daughter of rebellion*
> *followed by twenty plus twenty.*
> *Because she gives her life*
> *they want to give death in return.*
> *Run fast, run fast, run, run, run.*

Andrés took on her defense. Violeta confessed her guilt from the very first moment, and that made things much easier. She was taken to jail. No visitors were allowed at first, they were very strict with her. We all went to give statements, and I took her diaries; I handed over parts of them to the judge, under seal of secrecy. I know that the diary helped her. And that her pregnancy also played in her favor. ("Words and lyrics will pour from the blood. And if you are godmother, Jose, the music, too. My child will be an artist.")

Besides Andrés—her lawyer—Jacinta was the first to see her. She tells me she has spoken with her mother in jail. Violeta has asked her not to lose faith in her, despite what she has done. Faith? Jacinta looks at her unforgivingly. But after a pause, under the force of those imploring eyes, she replies: "I have no choice. I'll have faith in you only because in life you have to have faith in *someone*."

Jacinta did not want to go back to the house on Calle Gerona.

"I can't ever look at the door to my bedroom again," she said. Although she was living at her grandfather's, my house was where she spent her time, her real home, as my parents' house had been for Violeta when Cayetana disappeared. Borja turned out to be the white knight for this helpless princess, who, in addition to her own and her mother's sadness, had to put up with being hounded by the public, along with accompanying insults and humiliations.

A shrewd publisher produced Eduardo's novel like lightning. That contributed to the publicity about the case, and there was scarcely a single writer who supported Violeta's cause. All of them, as a guild, denounced her, except for one or two women. I do not need to go into the success of the murdered author's novel. Finally Eduardo stopped being thought of as narrator of the Corral seaquake and was again being read by everyone. Had he known, he might have asked Violeta to kill him sooner.

I remember the night Andrés locked himself in the study to go over Violeta's defense. At two in the morning he came into the bedroom wearing a look of triumph.

"Josefa," he told me, "I have reviewed codes and laws up to here. And it's a poet who has given me the answer. None other than Shelley. He says that the great secret of moral conduct is love."

That set the tone.

Violeta's case came to be a paradigm for every sector of society.

Everyone spoke up.

Many supported Violeta rationally, but no one wanted to stand beside her. It was a unique occasion, one in which everyone had some banner to fly. From the feminists, who had found the perfect vehicle for denouncing masculine oppression of women, to those opposed to divorce, who thought the best defense against abuse, mistreatment, and crime was a solid family structure.

If this tragedy had happened to a woman of the people, the criticism would have been milder. Among the most conservative groups, the main theme was loose behavior among the intellectual strata. They clashed among themselves, because the anti-abortionists—although repelled by Violeta's image—did not dare condemn her; she had, after all, acted to save the child of her womb.

The Catholic Church itself asked for moderation in the sentence: however bad the deed, she had protected a life.

Organisms of the State spoke of intrafamilial violence.

Everyone, absolutely everyone, had something to say, and often those "somethings" were contradictory.

The press did their usual thing. The sensationalism knew no bounds. Thank God, they had no direct access to Violeta. So they tried to reach me. It was ugly.

The first symptom of women's reaction was the appearance on TV of an important intellectual on a program with high ratings, saying: "Violeta Dasinski spoke from the straitjacket that is the language of our gender."

"Violeta kills for life!" was the chant of many fervent women in front of the courthouse, where they had brought signs demanding, FREE VIOLETA.

Some female sociologists elaborated the following thesis: what happened to Violeta Dasinski was that *she lowered her guard,* as women always do at a time when they are infused with the fullness of their female being.

One important women's magazine came out with the following header: "Violeta Dasinski not only has invaded male bastions; in the process she is transforming them."

A very prestigious female historian went back to the beginnings to make her denunciation: "Did not Vicuña Mackenna himself tell us that the point of departure for the Chilean woman's moral and intellectual education during the colonial period was suspect?"

A singer, neither a feminist nor an intellectual but very popular with her public, dedicated her latest record to her.

Some called her "a woman bewitched."

I would wander around before dawn, imagining her prison. What were early mornings like for Violeta in jail? She was always obsessive about the dawn. She wouldn't be warmed now by the water pipes in the bathroom of the mill house. An *ulmo* in bloom. If only her eyes could see an *ulmo* in bloom on the way to Puerto Octay!

Finally they let me see her.

I drove to stop 10 on Vicuña Mackenna, to the Buen Pastor jail.

It was a small room, damp and bare, furnished with nothing but two chairs turned toward each other. Violeta was sitting with her back to the door, facing the empty chair. She stood up when she saw me. We looked at one another an instant, devastated. I opened my arms: come, Violeta, come, I was screaming inside. I enfolded her, hugged her, held her.

"He was going to rape Jacinta . . . he was going to rape Jacinta . . . and Jacinta's room was empty . . . but I didn't know . . . he was going to rape Jacinta . . ."

"I know, Violeta, I know that. You don't have to explain anything to me."

I took her face in my hands, I needed to look at her.

Her hair was pulled back. She was pale, with dark circles under her eyes, and although she had never worn much makeup, now her face looked scrubbed, completely bare of artifice. She was wearing her usual long skirts, but no earrings or bracelets or necklaces. Only the *piedra cruz* ring, which she played with the whole ten minutes of my visit. She seemed to be somewhere else. And I knew that it wasn't she who had gone away but her nostalgia.

I didn't blame her. Your eyes, Violeta, mistook their heaven.

She talked about her accursed race.

When the time was up and I was starting to leave, she said in a flat voice: "I would do it again, Josefa. Today the only difference between Eduardo and me is that he will not open his eyes again."

Violeta feels she is dead. It is obvious that the new times were not right for defending the best part of herself.

On my second visit to the jail, which also lasted ten minutes, I asked about the baby. I wasn't sure how to approach this subject, it was so delicate. I was obsessed with my conversation with Eduardo that last night.

"What will you name him?"

"If it's a boy, Gabriel. Like the archangel."

For exactly one minute, neither of us said anything. I remembered the pistachios I had brought her, and took them from my purse.

"It isn't Eduardo's child," she blurted, forestalling my question. And added, "Thank God!"

"I knew that. He told me himself that night."

"That's why he started the fight. The last one."

"Then?"

"It's Bob's. Do you remember him?"

"Yes, of course I remember."

"Even so, I'm planning to test the baby's DNA, in case Eduardo lied. But in my heart, which is the only place you truly know things, I know the father is Bob. I've thought of nothing else since I've been here."

"But Violeta, why didn't you take precautions?"

"Because I thought I couldn't get pregnant any longer. I'd hoped for so long, but nothing . . . In any case, Josefa, it was just one crazy night, as you might call it, just one when I didn't use any protection. It was the first time we made love. After I was back in Chile and learned I was pregnant, I thought it was Eduardo's. No one gets pregnant from one night! Especially at my age."

"Was it in Bahías de Huatulco?"

"No. In Huatulco I held myself back, repressed my feelings, as hard as it was. When Bob learned my story, he wanted to take me to Guatemala. I felt there was no reason to deny myself loving a man capable of doing that for me."

The guard arrived. My time was up.

"It was in Antigua," Violeta tells me, from behind the broad uniformed figure.

"In Antigua." I smiled at her, and we hugged.

At the door, she turned to look at me.

"I was wrong about the prediction. I thought my two lives were before and after Cayetana. Now I understand that if I can conquer my horror, Josefa, this will be my second life."

She knows, without the least doubt, that this is the end of the time she breathed up to the moment she pulled the trigger. That all the rest, come what may, will be different. That her life will be forever divided into two parts: the part that came before the shot—that precise instant—and what she will call her second life.

"Your daughter will have two lives," the fortune-teller had told Cayetana. The first was over.

"Thanks for the pistachios."

On my third visit, I could finally see she was showing. Impending motherhood was evident. They had eased the restrictions, and she was living the life of an ordinary prisoner. Visits were regulated, and outdoors; we could walk and talk with relative tranquility, but always with lots of people around. As soon as the doors opened at the prescribed time, several visitors would arrive to see her. I was never again able to be alone with her. That was the last time.

She told me about the women in the jail.

"The difference between men's and women's crimes is that men kill in robberies, in street fights, because they're drunk, and their victims are nearly always people they have never seen or known anything about before. Women, on the other hand, never kill anyone they don't have feelings for. I've talked with them here, and have never heard of one who murdered a stranger. They kill lovers, children, husbands . . . only what they have loved. I'm no exception."

I could see she was depressed.

As we said good-bye, she cloaked her feelings with a smile, and said, "Jose, if things should go badly, you know what my last wish would be? For you to come the night before with your guitar and not stop singing until everything was over."

One day when Andrés came back from the jail he brought me some notes from Violeta: lyrics for my songs. Her long hours of idleness had been put to good use. I read them. My first reaction was to lock myself in for an entire day with Erik Satie and Philip Glass, listening to them, absorbing them. They always wielded a magical effect: creativity invaded me, followed me, pursued me. Putting music to Violeta's words was born of my very gut, with a spontaneity and freshness I hadn't felt for a long time. I rediscovered an enjoyment nearly absent from my last record, the one Violeta criticized so harshly. In less than a month the songs were ready. I had never worked with a collaborator. I composed the music with meticulous care, but with a strange internal haste. Producing this record broke every rule: poor musicians, poor sound engineers, I didn't give them a minute until the job was done. My haste had to do with Violeta. For me, it was vital to present the record to the public before they judged her case. I knew my own power.

I had problems with my agent. His first reaction was that the songs were sad, that they wouldn't sell. That they went against the grain. I forced him to tell me the truth: the obvious effect on sales and marketing: Alejandro believed that my being connected with a crime could spell the end to my career. Soil my image, so clean and carefully crafted. He was willing to accept the songs only if we kept the author of the lyrics anonymous. I was furious, I called him two-faced, a coward. I repeated words Violeta sometimes hurled at me. I threatened him: if he didn't go along with me in this venture I would consider it grounds for breaking our contract. "You've changed," he replied, bewildered. "You're someone else; you've never acted this way, not for anything or anyone." "Well." I smiled at him. "Who said it's too late to begin?"

I am the most important thing in Alejandro's life. And that isn't fair; he is just one more person in mine. No symmetry.

As the jacket was being printed, he asked: "Josefa, with all this uproar, we haven't talked about the title."

"Don't worry, I already have a title, and the production crew knows what it is."

"Oh, and what is that?" He was not at all happy to be left out.

*"Violeta Dasinski, or a Story of Longing."*


I launched the new record on television, to the whole country, with an enormous splash. I myself made sure there would be enormous publicity. Suddenly, standing in the middle of the set, I realized it was the first time in my life I was on television without a tranquilizer in my body. My mouth dried up. With so much excitement, I had simply forgotten. But the show must go on. I took the microphone.

"When Peter Gabriel was asked what the subject of his latest album was, he answered, 'A good part of this record is about ties.' I would like to make his words mine."

That was all I said. I just sang.

No record of mine had ever been listened to, sold, publicized so much. THE SINGER AND THE MURDERESS, blared the sensationalist press. For the first time, the word *committed* was applied to my singing. To me, who had carefully avoided that label. For the back of the jacket I had chosen lines by Violeta Parra, which expressed everything the album was about:

> *I do not take up my guitar*
> *to get your applause,*
> *I come to sing the difference*
> *between what's true and what's false;*
> *otherwise, I do not sing . . .*

What I didn't show Andrés, or anyone else, were the two pages Violeta had mistakenly mixed in with the songs she sent me. They were hers, in her familiar handwriting, copies of some Quechua poems. The title was in two languages:

*SANK'AY/ETERNAL PRISON*

*For this, Father,*
*You engendered me?*
*For this, Mother, you gave me birth?*
*Corrupt prison*
*Devouring—O sin!—*
*My lonely heart . . .*

*My heart?*
*Here is my song of atonement,*
*House of the captives!*
*House of the chains,*
*Set me free!*

On the second page, beneath the title *Harawi*, Violeta writes an explanation. "According to Waman Puma de Ayala, the offender—who was hanged by his hair at the edge of a cliff called *yawar-qaqa* (cliff of blood)—endured the cruel punishment, crying out with pain, until he died, and in those last moments of his life he sadly sang an elegiac *harawi*, invoking the birds of prey to do him the enormous favor of notifying his father and his mother."

*Father condor, carry me!*
*Brother falcon, lead me!*
*Inform my mother*
*That I have been five days*

*Without food*
*Without drink!*

*Father messenger, take note*
*Carry my message*
*My wandering voice*
*My heart.*
*Take me to my father!*
*Take me to my mother*

After the birth of Gabriel, of that true miracle, Violeta was absolved and set free. With her child in her arms, she left immediately; she boarded a plane for Mexico and promised to notify us of her final destination. She asked Jacinta to wait for her, she would send for her very soon.

And so the sepulchral maiden took off, deserting the scene.

# 3

It isn't as if I were an easy person. No.

I am a phobic woman.

Antidepressants in very small doses all my life. At least they have no side effects.

My phobias are not conquered. Only reduced.

Closing my doors to the world as I have done, isn't that another phobia?

I remember something Violeta said once when she was defending me to Pamela, a friend we have in common. All because Pamela had asked me the following question: "Deep down, Josefa, do you hate the world?" I answered cuttingly: "Deep down and on top, darling. Unabashed."

"We can't even hate her to her face," Pamela complained to Violeta, "because she has enough pain to carry that we have to forgive her. I hate successful people with sad pasts, it gets in the way of hating them!"

"But don't you find her frankness disarming?" Violeta had asked her.

"Yes, I do, but how smug she is about her neuroticism! You tell me; hasn't everything gone swimmingly for her? It wasn't enough for her to be the best singer, she had to nab the best husband besides. And on top of that, she has beautiful children. How can everything go so well for someone and she still give herself the luxury of being neurotic?"

"Josefa is very bold," Violeta told her. "She has a great virtue not all public women can claim. She wasn't invented by others, as so many famous women are. She invented herself."

Violeta. Always defending me.

I'm sure all my women friends thought more or less the same as Pamela. She was a fabulous woman, lots of fun, and sometimes I wanted her around. But I was cursed: inevitably I projected distance. (Even so, I got Pamela a job with Andrés, in his office. She was desperate following her separation, and needed a better-paying job.)


After I won the Festival of Song, offers for appearances and concerts began to pour in. I didn't know how to handle so many things at once, and went to Phillipe, my psychiatrist. That was the beginning of the pills. Today I am amused when I remember those telephone conversations that he, despite being the busiest physician in Santiago, always had time to answer.

"Phillipe, I have a program on Channel seven in two weeks, and one on thirteen next week. What do I do?"

"You're already taking the Aurorix and they should be taking effect in another ten days. You're safe for the program on Channel seven. Can't you put off the program on thirteen a couple of weeks?"

"But Phillipe, how can I ask the station to change the dates to adjust to my panic? These are scheduled programs."

"Then we'll have to change the dose."


I realized I was a "star" the first time I saw a photograph of myself without recognizing it: that is, without knowing when it had been taken, by whom, why, or how. I mentioned that strange sensation to an experienced singer who was very cordial to me when I was beginning. We were sitting in the living room of her house, she in a filmy white dressing gown, her hair dyed and lifts on various parts of her body. I see her as a prototype, and I project myself forward in time. No, I will never be like that. She consoles me; she tells me about the habits you acquire with practice, with training: it's like any other profession. "The one problem, dear girl," she tells me, "is that with the years you get slower in changing one habit for another; but you can do it, believe me." We are in the middle of this conversation and she reaches out and presses a bell with one finger. The maid appears.

"Irene, my amphetamines, please."

Irene returns promptly with a small silver tray. On it is a glass of water and a saucer with four or five white pills.

"Here you are, señora."

And she disappears as my friend, her eyes closed, gulps down the pills that are her form of facing this "profession."

I go back to Phillipe.

A great deal has been said about my style, about the hieratical airs I give myself on the stage, my static, stony, almost stoic, posture. It wasn't an option: from the first, terror paralyzed me, I couldn't budge—neither my legs nor my torso would respond. Even so, they sometimes described my grace as "Andalusian." Well, of course, I *am* Andalusian. But, grace? I know nothing about that. Maybe from Andalusia I inherited what critics praised as my "versatility," the way

I assume different "voices," as if they were truly mine. I recorded an album of boleros, and they said I seemed born of the very depths of Latin America, as if I had sung boleros my whole life. And when I recorded some *rancheras*, they said the same thing about Mexico. Yes, my grace may come from Andalusia. My bearing? Definitely not.

It was during that summer, the summer of the Viña del Mar Festival of Song that my perspiration began to smell different.

Panic came to be part of my passage through the world. Not just on stage, but getting things done. Panic that I would be late to a recording session, panic that Mauricio wouldn't bring my dress to the set in time, and I wouldn't be ready, panic that I would miss my planes and not get to a performance. Adrenaline wasted on a thousand little commitments, filling my life twenty-four hours a day.

I began to need audiences, as if my only objective were to rain sensations over my head . . . but I was always so busy I scarcely had time to perform. Violeta never forgave me when I stopped calling her and asked my secretary to do it for me. I didn't have time. That was when she put a name to a certain attitude of mine: "When-Josefa-Pulls-Out-Her-Mona-Lisa-Smile." When I turned inward and used this smile as an enigma: no one knew what was happening behind it. I didn't know, either. Only one thing was clear to me: the joy of singing, the passion of lifting my voice, the thrill of composing a song. That pleasure, oh, lord . . . I wouldn't have traded that for anything! And when Celeste came to me to complain about the way her math teacher was acting, how could I explain I was living in another world, one where math teachers didn't exist and where adolescent daughters—and only with great effort on my part—barely fit in.

"Josefa has shiny satin dreams," Violeta said one day.

"You're mistaken," I replied coldly. "I don't dream."

Part of my phobias have to do with food. Celeste is where she is with good reason. I loathed any human being who ate in my presence. If it were someone close to me, the hatred was more intense. I watched that person eat—whoever it might be—and the process of detesting began, of thinking he or she was a brute, worthless, obscene. The only times I have understood the act of murder have been in those circumstances. It didn't happen in open places or in restaurants; it had something to do with intimacy. One friend who chewed gum became so repugnant to me that I got rid of her as humanely as possible. I am speaking in the past tense; since taking antidepressants, I am a little better, but not totally. I never have been able to have a romantic breakfast in bed with a man. The first piece of toast does me in. Both Roberto and Andrés looked on this as an illness and did not provoke me. I have always had background music wherever I was eating. Instinctively, I was constructing an infrastructure that would allow me to live with my phobia. Blood-curdling—for their viciousness—have been the thoughts I have had about ordinary people in the moment of the innocent act of eating. If I see a scene of people eating on television, I immediately punch Mute, especially if it's one of those gringo films where everyone talks with a mouthful of food. I know every last detail of the way people around me eat, the precise sound of their jaws, the way they swallow and use their tongues. I have come to believe that eating should be as private as urinating and defecating; if only dining rooms could be converted into bathrooms so I would never again have to be forced to witness such a disgusting activity.

My last lunch with Pamela was frightful—and awful for plenty of other reasons besides. She was eating greedily, shooting me nervous and apologetic glances, lewdly chewing, chomping as only an obsessive woman can do. I detested her forever.

Another of my phobias was night terrors. If I was left by myself in a house, however well protected it might be, my fantasies darkened with blood and knives. When I lived alone with the children, and didn't have enough money for a maid, my poor brother had to come stay in my house. If he couldn't, my mother came. Violeta was living in Rome then, and God only knows how much I missed her.

At least I have no phobia about money. I balance my bank account only when I have to wait at a doctor's office or for an appointment with someone important. Then I work on my checks, only to pass the time. Otherwise, I don't worry about it at all. Which is also a way of saying that I don't have to do the addition and subtraction because I have enough money.

My personal slogan became: *No, I'm not here, I won't be, I don't want to be.*

I can safely say that I never heard the imperious and charitable call to save the masses, or anyone in particular. People were all the same to me. I have never felt charitable even toward this woman I carry in my bones. My eyes have always been focused on the next event. I couldn't waste time on trivialities. I have very little sensitivity for understanding the simple functioning of just any person who happens to come along. The percentage of people who do nothing but eat, work, and sleep is far too high. Aren't we destined, after all, to do something more than that?

According to the lyrics of my songs, I was singing to people and to love. As I became more skeptical, I began to feel like a liar: I was deceiving my own public. I told Violeta that the last summer at the mill house. She proposed that I make a list of people I was fond of, writing down the names of those I don't want to stop loving, and then check the list the following summer. "If it begins to grow shorter," she told me, "you will have cause to worry; if not, you can attribute general loss of affection to the selectivity that comes with age. And that, after all, Josefa, is a sign of maturity."

I didn't make the list, just in case. At any rate, it would have been very short.


I realized, soon after I began, how difficult it was going to be for people to take my singing seriously. As a woman, dear God, what a job it is to be taken seriously in any field!

I was listening to Marlene Dietrich one evening. Velvet and throatiness in her voice, and not even in her own tongue: that little accent in the English of her songs in the thirties transformed into pure sensuality. Celeste interrupts. "I didn't know that Dietrich ever sang."

"Please, sit down here with me and listen," I ask her.

"Oh, Mama, I have much more important things to do."


One day we were filming a documentary video in my home, with a large production crew. I was being interviewed on the subject of discrimination against women in the arts. As I have mentioned, cameras make me miserable; that was why I asked them to do the interview at home, not on the set, so I could be more relaxed. Right in the middle of the filming, a terrible racket: the vacuum cleaner. There, only yards from us, Zulema was merrily working away. The director, very patiently, says, "All right, from the top." I look at Zulema with murderous eyes, wondering whether she would dare run the vacuum during one of Andrés's meetings. She disappears.

"Tell us, Josefa," says the journalist. "In what way do you feel you are discriminated against compared to a male colleague?"

I am beginning my comment, explaining why women are not taken seriously. And I hear the cameramen laughing. At that moment Andrés comes out of his study and as he opens the door, trips over one of the tripods.

"Sorry, I'd forgotten that the TV was . . ."

I look at the crew.

"Report this scene instead of interviewing me," I tell them, giving up. "It is much less theoretical than my words."

There was nothing to be gained from confronting Andrés. His intentions were never anything but good.

The image of these new women we are is enough to bring on a stroke. Besides running a house, giving birth to and bringing up the children, working (financing ourselves!), and—it is to be hoped—

nourishing our spirits, we must be intelligent and sexually competitive. Not just that, we must offer our partner the chance to feel he is someone more than a mere provider. (Of course, it should be said in passing, however he feels on the subject, in objective terms he really *isn't* the provider anymore.) That is, leave room for him to develop his *affective self.* We pave the way for men's new *ego* and waste our energy in making them believe in it, when in our heart of hearts we know that it is upon us, and solely upon us, that the responsibility for all affective life rests. Affection, in the family and anywhere else, continues to rest one hundred percent on our overburdened shoulders.

Mine had carried more weight than normally falls upon a woman.

We were coming back from the country, Roberto and I. He was driving; I had put a Satie tape in the player. It was a sunny afternoon. We had left the children with my parents, and had planned this getaway like a pair of teenagers. We didn't even have to verbalize it: we were young and happy. Roberto's arm was bare, he was wearing a short-sleeved shirt. I had an irrepressible impulse. That arm, those thousands of tiny hairs, light against the afternoon sun, and, as always when at the wheel, the hand attentive to shifting the car, inattentive to me. The erotic impulse; I touched his arm. This is the last thing I remember before the truck racing toward us.

Nothing happened to me. Roberto died.

I would never smell his scent again.

After that day, fragility came to be my most lacerating obsession. I have disguised it in a thousand ways in order not to live with awareness of it in my mind. But it envelops me, strangles me, as if its pressure on my bones were a winding sheet asphyxiating me, killing me.

Taking care of my two children was arduous: thousands of hours of classes in three different schools, being both father and mother . . . Music, forgotten. All pleasures suspended, because the mandate was house and children first. Those times were dark, very dark. And the way I looked did not contradict that. I didn't groom myself, I didn't buy clothes—I didn't have a cent, anyway—I didn't take care of my body, I ran from one side of town to the other to pick up the children and still get to my classes on time. In the middle of all that, I found slices of time to dash by the supermarket, cook unappetizing meals (leaving no one satisfied), wash dishes, keep uniforms and knapsacks ready, and at the end of the day I fell into bed exhausted. I didn't smile much during that time.

I clung to Celeste as my only accomplice. We women are born— or were we brought up to be?—attentive to the needs of others, and very little to our own. In the language of the unspoken, always pointing toward, preparing ourselves for "the other goal": maternity. The boy child sees nothing, he simply plays ball; the girl, in contrast, worries because Mama's face is so sad; she knows from birth the signs of sadness.

My grandmother Adriana knew, my mother Marta knew, I knew, and my daughter Celeste knew.

That time is colorless in my memory. Permanently cloudy and gray. It was so long. I thought nothing pleasurable awaited me in life. That everything would be like that forever. Why does one never have enough sense to realize that crises—and bad times—pass?

(Sunday, mid-afternoon at my parents' house. Boredom is discoloring everything. I am bored, the children are watching television, they're bored too. My parents are escaping the same boredom with a siesta. I pick up a magazine. Suddenly, looking at the life of the stars, I think: I will be there some day. How? Why? "Let's claw our way out of opaqueness, Jose, let's claw our way out," Violeta had told me a thousand times. My life can't be this lousy, with nothing more. Duty fulfilled among four walls: the walls of my house, our three schools, my city. I cannot bear the darkness of my fate, and I am afraid it will always be like this if, through sheer will, I don't turn it around. My students, my inadequate salary, the same routine year after year, the triteness of it all. NO! Again I study the privileged people in the magazine. At least they have done something that deserves a paragraph, a photograph. I get up from my chair, restless. Something has happened to me. A light: an indication that there might eventually be a different world, and that it all depends on me.)

Then, for a few instants, the drabness was broken because of a green dress. Only a few instants. I didn't know the feel of silk, real silk. A friend lent me the dress to go to a wedding. I tried it on before the mirror in the solitude of my bedroom, another mid-afternoon. Something powerful passed in front of that reflection. There are people who wait a lifetime for a vision and never have one. You don't improvise one, it isn't, well, let's have a vision. But in front of that mirror I had one. I saw that the world was broad, waiting, and I felt voluptuous in it. Wings. The world revealed its breadth in my reflection and I sensed there were heady, sensual fantasies possible to bring to life. It was absurd to feel that way considering the life I was living. Nevertheless, touching the silk of that green dress, seeing how I looked in it, I knew with certainty that something extraordinary was waiting in the future.

Only at night did I allow myself to remember Roberto.

I pinched my arms until I hurt myself. Sometimes my legs: I left purple bruises on them. Not out of masochism: I did it to be sure that I was alive.

That it was true Roberto was not.

My sexual life began with him; everything that went before was nothing but childish games. We felt a great physical interdependence. I had been possessed by him, with all the fullness and infinitude those terms can represent. Never by anyone else. His touch was irreplaceable. I came to think at certain moments that touch was *everything*. I wept those nights, thinking that I would never again be flesh with other flesh, that only one body in the world could give me what his had given.

Until Andrés came along. How fragile sex is! The first time Andrés kissed me, I realized that my skin was burning. I would never feel that again: that was what my body had told me, and yet I had. Traitorous body. No touch is unique and definitive; that was my lesson. It is the weakest link, the whole chain is broken there. And the woman who does not believe that, who locks up her sexuality believing in the indestructible circle of a single body, is—thank God!— mistaken.


Violeta was living in Rome when I won the Viña Festival. The country was in the hands of the military. Probably she thought it was bad of me to compete when so many other singers were in exile, dead, or disappeared. Star of the dictatorship. It was a musician friend who convinced me to perform, and he himself accompanied me on the guitar (and has done so a thousand times since). And this spiral began. It was in the midst of this coming and going that I was introduced to a prestigious lawyer named Andrés Valdés. He came up to me at a dinner to tell me how much he liked my songs. I thanked him, as I always did, but I also noticed the bones of his face, very squared, and the two creases that formed in his cheeks each time he smiled at me.

"Brahms and you," he told me, "are the only cassettes I have in my car."

Even though I was with someone, he offered to drive me home. I said no.

Shortly thereafter, I happened to sing at the casino in Viña del Mar. In the dressing room I found roses, all red, with his card.

I mentioned that to Pamela, who was his colleague.

"Careful, Josefa. Andrés is a seducer," she told me. "Great attorney, criminal lawyer. He has an office and a life like a movie. But he's been married for at least fifteen years."

"And what is wife like?"

"Well, the other day I saw them having tea at the Riquet, in Valparaíso. He was reading the newspaper and I didn't see them exchange a single word. She was ordering for the children . . . they're pretty big by now. But he didn't give her the time of day."

"And looks? What does she look like?"

"She has that upper class look, very refined, with expensive clothes and stylish hair. I wouldn't say she's gorgeous, no. She's *elegant,* which isn't the same thing."

When I sang at the Teatro Municipal with a well-known pianist, roses again awaited me in the dressing room. All red. And outside the door, Andrés. This time I didn't have the willpower to say no, and I went with him.

I think something happened to Andrés that happens to many sensitive men with certain women. As if in another reincarnation he had given me certain qualities, and as he left them with me, he rid himself of them, allowing him be male—lock, stock, and barrel. When besides being a man, he wanted to be a *human being,* he went looking for them. And found them in me.

Andrés needed his union with me to restore in himself parts that would make him feel he was a complete human being.

# 4

$\mathcal{V}$ioleta's unfolding has begun.

When her first letter arrived, I wasn't surprised that it was post-marked Guatemala. It was addressed to Andrés and to me.

*Dears, dears:*

*I am living in "la Antigua," as they say here, the sleeping beauty of Latin America.*

*I am working in a furniture shop called* Reminiscencias Españolas, *Reminiscences of Spain.*

*Bob is with me these days.*

*Gabriel thinks he's king of the walk.*

*I arrived with all my pores sealed. Only in Antigua have they opened. This place wears all the skins of America on its skin.*

*We are living in a pension while I look for a house. I have a school for Jacinta.*

*That's all for now.*

*Because if I tried to thank you two properly, there would be no way to do it. No way.*

*Violeta*

She never doubted where she would end up. I think she knew it from the first day she was in jail, although she didn't say anything to anyone. Of course, the plane took her to Mexico. There she would think things over. I'm sure she didn't see anyone: she went immediately to Guatemala, as she had planned with Bob, whose letters had come through Andrés as intermediary.

Would she stay with Bob? Could he, would he want to, gamble everything for a woman with her history? And if he does, could he live and work in such a remote place outside the stream of history? Well, if his trade is reporting, or writing political essays, he can do that anywhere in the world.

The house on Calle Gerona sold at a good price. Violeta's father has packed up everything in a huge container and is waiting for her notice to send it to a permanent address. *Everything* is a manner of speaking. While in jail, Violeta made a list of things she cared about; there weren't many. Uncle Tadeo showed it to me, and it was amusing, so like Violeta. "All my books, all my music, including equipment, my rugs, my paintings, the hammock, the umbrella stand, the wicker trunk." She asked him to give all the rest away, and have Carmencita take her winter clothing, because she would never be wearing it again. "Have Josefa choose some piece of furniture she likes." I chose a wooden cupboard painted bright green, with drawings on the doors. "The design looks Mexican," she had told me, "but it's from Poland. Strange, isn't it, how cultures can coincide?"

Since the house sold well and Violeta has the money, why is she working in a furniture shop? It's not very clear in her letter. Is she designing or using a screwdriver? Could it be a form of atonement, or did she want to learn some technique?

All this was discussed at length during dinnertime. For one reason or other, my family feels it owns Violeta. Borja is the one who seems best informed and interested. Could he be writing Jacinta without telling us?

I think of Cayetana and about how much Violeta is like her. No, I can't accuse Violeta of putting convenience first. She gave up everything she knew, all that was comfortable; the easy way was never an option for her. Just like Cayetana.

The next note said:

*I'm in the middle of intensive therapy. "Without the checks of belief, the balance between life and death can be perilously delicate." Do you agree?*

There were several notes after that, always very brief, a mixture of the cryptic and the informative. In one of them she wrote:

*There is a wonderful custom in this region. They have some small, brilliant yellow coins that are worth a hundredth of a quetzal (that is, nothing). When a couple gets married, the tradition is to put seven of those coins in a piggy bank. They assure fortune and good luck.*

*They are few and far between.*

*Bob and I managed to find seven of them, and are using a red wooden tiger for a piggy bank.*

This was Violeta's way of telling me that she and Bob have formalized their union.

They have bought a house and are restoring it. They will have a permanent address: the Calle de los Peregrinos: Pilgrims' Street is not inappropriate.

I send her the following fax: "What can I say, Violeta? Your luck is unique. I believe that Jesus Christ himself loves you."

She has traded architectural plans for brightly colored embroidery wools. Violeta has now dedicated herself to making tapestries. She tells me she is learning every kind of technique. She would seem to be genuinely committed to it, it doesn't sound like a passing fancy.

*Did you ever read the medieval legend of Philomela? Keats wrote about her. A feudal knight, lord and master, married to an older woman, falls in love with his wife's younger sister. He closes the circle about her, and finally he rapes her. To keep her from telling, he cuts out her tongue. The girl locks herself in her chamber and weaves a tapestry in which she tells the story of what happened to her. When the feudal lord discovers her work, he decides to kill her. And does. As she dies she is transformed into a nightingale. That is why the bird sings at night while other birds are still, so it can be heard.*

*I know the legend of another bird; it comes from the Huichol culture on the coast of San Blas, in Mexico. It has enormous, almost concave wings, as if it could gather in all things. It is charged with closing the gates of heaven to prevent evil from visiting the earth.*

*I have come to Antigua with the inescapable baggage of my European culture and here, exchanging the nightingale for the bird with huge wings, I am transforming my past, making it American. (Like the cupboard you chose.) I have many stories to weave.*

Later on, when she was mastering her art, she had a couple of shows in Antigua. Because of them, people in the United States began to buy her tapestries. Today she sells through a prestigious gallery in New York. *The owner is a friend of Bob's,* she tells me, as if apologizing for doing so well. *They pay me astronomical sums. I can live quite a while from a single piece.*

I am thrilled—and surprised—that she is successful.

I thought that when she committed her crime Violeta was beginning a cycle with no exit. How wrong I was! Today I can testify that, after an act of courage, she has been visited with grace.

Her latest letter came last week.

*Jose, do you remember when Carlos Fuentes talked about a "constant temperature"? I am living in it.*

*Antigua is feminine.*

*Antigua ends with the female A.*

*Antigua has given me back my identity as a woman, hopelessly lost among recent avatars. It has given me rest, at last, and has made me smile.*

*Besides that, I am not a slave to my body any longer. Only by understanding that erotic space is not the only place that limits are erased, I have grown. Union can take place at other levels.*

*I was trapped in the formula of believing that defense of the feminine meant rejecting what we see as being assigned by others. It is one thing to reject the role, something else to reject identity.*

*Antigua has given mine back.*

*I love you always, a lot.*

Violeta

*P.S. I found Cayetana.*

# 5

If Sartre hadn't said it, I would have: *Hell is others.*

People stifle me. The nearness of people suffocates me. I cannot bear the human race in its physical proximity. Its *physicality*, if I may call it that. Men's and women's noises and smells evoke nothing but repulsion when I am faced with the idea of being part of them. How difficult it has been for me to understand Violeta's driving need to connect with other people. My desire has been, systematically, to check them off.

I am being pervaded by a kind of panic. I see it as an amorphous mass advancing toward me to touch me, invade me, infect me, and, finally, to annihilate me. As it approaches, this mass is dividing in half, into two equal sections: Andrés on one side and singing on the other. Andrés's side paints one panic: that he doesn't love me anymore, that he is leaving me, that he is in love with someone else. The other panic, the singing one, seeps into my veins, rises with my blood, races through my intestines. I am getting this terror of exposing myself, a fear that thousands and thousands of people can turn the dial and hear me sing without my being able to control it. Terror that my voice will be public, that it will belong to others, separate from me. I am losing control of what is most mine: my voice. It is slipping from my hands.

That is an author's panic, Alejandro tells me.

As if one never gets used to being public.

Just as Violeta was born with an angel in her eyes, in me words and music spring from the devil.

When I am in the actual process of writing a song, I go into my most genial phase. I respect myself, I like life, and my awareness of limits presses me to give more and more. Creativity envelops me, sheathing life with hope. When after long, hard work and many corrections I think the song is finished, I am possessed by devastating insecurity. As it leaves my hands, the song I have just written becomes ugly, loses its charm. My self-esteem evaporates on the air, vulgarized, and I ask myself once again, What am I doing here? Is this truly my vocation?

The quality of a work lasts as long as it takes to write it.

If at least I were a novelist, that period would be longer.

Sometimes, I regret not having been a simple housewife!

And when I go to the supermarket and am stared at and admired by other women pushing their carts, I think, struggling to breathe: Señora, I am not at all like the fantasy you have of me.

Yesterday some photographers came to take special shots for a magazine cover. I don't like to be photographed. Photographs detect a sadness in my eyes that I never noticed; I never knew I conveyed it until this business of the photographs began. Violeta says that she always

saw it. The sadness. And in recent photos this phenomenon has intensified. Well, the photographers were waiting for me in the living room
and I wasn't ready. This would never have happened if Mauricio had
been in charge. I'm tired of Mauricio's being ill; he feels bad all the
time. The worst of it for me is that I have to maintain my image without him, without his makeup, without his care in selecting my clothes.
I miss him and I curse a couple of times because he isn't there. I ask
Zulema to serve the photographers coffee while I decide what to put
on. Just as I am about to make my appearance, Zulema comes in, looks
at my outfit, and says: "That's a bit off plumb, señora." I turn on my
heel: the right shoulder pad of the beige blouse—it's Cacharel—is
sagging. I look as if my collarbone's broken. Furious, I pull it off and
try on the burgundy jacket, the light silk one, and now the left shoulder pad is crawling up my neck. When I see that the shoulder pads on
the third jacket—a dark bluish-green Anne Klein—don't match and
my shoulders are uneven, I am seized by a rage I cannot control. I
yank off the green jacket and rip out the pads, in the process tearing
a piece of the jacket fabric. I do the same with the Cacharel blouse
and the burgundy jacket. I throw the shoulder pads with the fury of
someone in a jail cell. I open my carefully arranged closet, completely
indifferent to the waiting photographers, and like a wild woman begin
ripping the shoulder pads out of all my clothes. I kick them into a pile
on the tiles of the bathroom floor. I call Celeste, and tell her, meaning
every word, "Burn them!"

Celeste runs out of the bathroom to tell Andrés I've lost my mind.


I have just watched a tape of my most recent TV appearance. My figure is detestable. How can I demonstrate my internal elegance with all
that fat hiding it? I remember the days of the radio, when I was an
amateur, when I sang before a microphone and no one saw anything:
you could dress like a clown for all anyone knew. The recording studio, and me. That was all. For me, the move from radio to television

was what it must have been for silent film actors to begin to speak overnight. Quite a few took a fall, their talent wasn't in their voices. Like them, I am a victim.

I can't diet without dying of hunger, and since I don't have any willpower, I have worked out the following plan: eat, taste, chew, and enjoy, but don't swallow. I began this system a few days back, when I saw the damned tape. It works well for a diet, but there are a few practical problems. You can't eat in the dining room. Where do I put the chewed food without being caught? What would Zulema say? You can't eat in the bathroom in order to throw each mouthful in the toilet; that would be strange, and esthetically displeasing besides. In my office? Not a chance. I began eating lunch in my car; no one controlled me there. I would set off with my lunch box, just like my children, parking somewhere to eat; the trick was not to be seen. I brought with me a plastic bag to toss out the scraps and get rid of them in some street trash basket.

This system lasted a week; I lost two pounds and was recovering my soul. Until one day when I didn't come across my precious municipal basket and left the plastic bag in my car. Truth is, I accumulated several bags, meaning to dispose of them at the first opportunity. One afternoon Andrés moved my car to get his from the garage, and came back wearing a strange expression.

"What is this, Josefa?" He held out the bags, grimacing, holding them away from him with exaggerated distaste.

Instantly, as if struck by a sudden plague, I was hot with humiliation. As if I'd been caught in a crime. If I had told him ahead of time, it wouldn't have mattered to me that he didn't agree: he would have had no choice but to be my accomplice. But to have him find a plastic bag behind the seat, filled with chewed-up food. How embarrassing!

I was certifiably insane.

Furious with myself, I flounced out to a pharmacy to buy pills to replenish my stock, to see if I could find some safe appetite suppressant. I showed my credit card at the register and they handed it back.

"It's expired," the woman told me. What? I have never let a credit card expire! The company takes care to renew it in time. I start for the office, very angry now, and ask my secretary to get me someone at Diners. The answer: they sent the renewed card two weeks ago; they interviewed me over the phone and I personally accepted the card and signed the new contract. Shit! Something like terror washes over me.

I begin to experience attacks of nausea. That is something new. As are the recurrent nightmares in which the Old Fortune-Teller tramp appears, handing me her crutches. Dear God!

How long before I end up talking to myself in the street?


My deterioration worsens. I remember conversations; I have absolute recall of what they were about, but I don't know with whom I had them. Complete phrases come to mind—and the atmosphere in which they were spoken—but I don't know who said them. I do remember what Andrés told me the last time we made love. I was reluctant.

"I have the feeling you don't want to because you're not in the mood," he said.

"You're right. *A priori*, I'm not in the mood."

"When it comes to sex after forty, Jose, it's a matter of awaking the animal we carry inside. Come on, once you get going, it'll be good. Let's wake the beast!"

I remember that well because he hasn't asked me again. It was during the siesta, and the children weren't home.

Because my nights are not planned for seduction. Andrés falls asleep immediately. I have twenty bedtime chores: dental floss, taking off my makeup, moisturizing cream on both face and body. I hang up all my clothes, open and close the closet a dozen times. I drink the nighttime glass of water, look for my glasses and the book I'm reading, clean the ashtray, go through all the rooms, look at the children, check the lights, and turn out the ones left burning. I remember Violeta: she goes to bed like men do. Undresses, and that's it.

But, back to that siesta. I don't think it's serious that sometimes the animal doesn't awaken. My watchword is: *no* to the death of romance. It isn't the sex that's essential, it's the *romance*. Sometimes I lose the enchantment, it becomes eclipsed, and suddenly Andrés's breathing sounds annoy me, even though they're the same ones I ignored yesterday, or I am put off by the slight gargle I hear in his voice when his head is on the pillow in that horizontal position he likes so much and that I never fall into unless it's to sleep. Then I flip the switch. This is my Andrés, the man I love so much. No, it is not the *idea of Andrés* I'm in love with. I am in love with Andrés. (Or is the whole thing just a mirage?) Romance is my commitment, the difficult struggle against routine; it's making that routine meaningful, it's flirting, it's talking to each other in a special way, and enjoying each other. Andrés always said that I was the kind of woman who demands illusions the way other women demand jewelry. Nevertheless, he has always been grateful for my ability to live our romance.

Now that I am shrouded in decline as if with leprosy, I study my body and detest its flab. I loathe the fat that appears where it shouldn't. And I go back to the concept of romance: the only decline I can conceive of loving is that pertaining to Andrés's body. He isn't the thirty-year-old swain himself; sometimes his back is a little bent, sometimes the wrinkles under his eyes are deeper, sometimes his square face looks puffy, and a purple vein stands out on his legs. And I love all those details. His is the one decline I can abide.

Hopeless, love in me.


I write a long letter to Violeta, unburdening myself. Within a few days I receive a fax at my office. Only one sentence, written in a heavy pen.

Alejandro brings it to me, frowning.

"What did you write to Violeta? That you're not going to sing anymore?"

I read: *Have you forgotten our poet Rafael Alberti so soon? No one on this earth is alone if he is singing.*

Pure outwardness.

I am terrified by the demands of affection, its endless pressure, even that of my children. I am indebted to everyone.

I try to get in touch with my inner being, but to no avail. I find myself preparing for the next occurrence when I have barely finished the present one: pauses in time are determined from the outside, never within me. I am a sum of "events," all sparkling. Time, oh, God, time is what I ask for! I haven't had it for years. I gave it up to leave opacity behind. Once I was discussing wealth and values with Violeta, the pythoness. "You're mistaken, Josefa," she told me. "At this point, or at least tomorrow, wealth won't be measured in power or in money. It will be measured in *time*."

I am so physically exhausted every night when I come home that I fall into bed without strength enough to focus on the words on the page of the unread book that stares at me accusingly from the night table. Since I am too tired to sleep—I never have the placidity of sleepers— I pick up the television remote with the hope that the various languages on the cable will lull me to sleep. Nothing would leave me with such a clean conscience as having worn myself out with the domestic chores of a good housewife. But that isn't how it is, and to top everything off, I have to sleep with the guilt of not being that *good housewife*.

The night has passed. I have passed the night. But I am always tired when I wake up. I open my agenda: a new day. And ask the dreaded question: Where did the joy go? The passion?

I get home late, me in my elegant lamé. Andrés is in the study. I tiptoe in. He is listening to music, a Whitney Houston tape. It makes me laugh. What is Andrés doing at one in the morning listening to something besides Brahms?

"I bought it today," he answers.

"Since when do you buy cassettes? That's the first time since I've known you."

"I don't know, I wanted to."

"And since when do you like Whitney Houston?"

"I heard a concert of hers on the radio as I was driving home last week, and decided I really like her."

Something fishy here. Cassettes—not CDs; you listen to those at home, to cassettes in your car—are typically a secret lover's gift.

Lunchtime, one Sunday. We are all in the kitchen. Borja, in charge of setting the table, opens the pantry and takes out wine, one of those cardboard containers I keep for emergencies but detest—as if the mere vessel could alter the exquisite sensuality of a good wine.

"Aren't there any bottles left?" Andrés asks.

"No, just these."

"Josefa doesn't like them," I heard Andrés say as I look for a funnel so I can pour the wine into a wide-mouthed green bottle. *Josefa doesn't like them,* a short, simple sentence. A declaration of love that warmed me for a while.

And because I retained that warmth, I dared speak to him after lunch.

"Andrés, why don't we go back to the mill house again? I miss it more each day. If you only knew how nostalgic I am for those rainy days, the scent of the salamander stove and boiled milk mixed with damp wood."

"We can't go back because that's not a house we can share with strangers."

"We can share it with some friend . . ."

"Do you have a suggestion?"

"I don't know . . . maybe Pamela. She has children the same age as ours."

"No way." His way of answering was strangely harsh, and Andrés is never harsh with me.

"Now that she's working with you, in your office, I thought she might turn out to be someone you are closer to, someone easy to get along with."

"That's precisely why I couldn't stand it."

"Why are you so angry? It's a simple suggestion."

"Because your naiveté amazes me, thinking Violeta can be replaced! I don't want to go back there. It was hers. It was a gift she gave to us. Without Violeta there is no mill house."

"The cranberries, Andrés. Do you remember the cranberries? It was all due to the magic of that enchanted house," I insist.

"Don't you get it? The magic was Violeta's."


Andrés's birthday. Sure as I am of my deterioration, I decided to make a gesture toward trying to counteract it. I got the children together and proposed that we surprise him. We bought thousands of presents of every kind and wrapped huge packages. Diego, in his childish hand, painted an enormous HAPPY BIRTHDAY sign. Streamers, balloons, a Pompadour cake on a large tray in the middle of the carpet, surrounded with presents, eight little candles (skipping the other forty seems elementary good taste), and crab canapés with a variety of fruit juices. Everything he likes. And it is all in the study, with the door closed, so when he comes home he won't notice anything; we will make him think it is just another birthday. The children were excited, especially Diego.

"What time will he get here, Mama?"

"I don't know, sweetheart; we didn't set a time. But he will be here sometime before seven. Be patient."

(We didn't have that daily call anymore, wherever we might be, when I'd say to him, *You still love me?*, and he'd answer: *I do nothing else.*)

At nine, Diego fell asleep.

At ten, Borja and Celeste got bored and went to bed.

At eleven, he arrived. They'd had a party for him at the office, how could he not stay? They hadn't invited me because they knew I had a date with my producer. Right, I hadn't thought it necessary to tell him I'd cancelled it.

And all the things I'd forgotten, I remembered his words on another birthday when after the festivities we had a delicious talk in bed: "Sometimes I talk with you, Josefa, as if I were talking to myself. I know that's not who you are; what amazes me about you is that you're not me, you are what's different from me, *other*."

Is this the same man who told me that?


The next day I am interviewed for the women's page of a newspaper.

"What is happiness for you?" the reporter asks.

("Don't ever give a sophisticated answer on that subject," Violeta had warned me once. "Suspect anyone who doesn't answer that question simply!")

"A rainy day in the south," I reply. "The light at two in the afternoon, warm soup, and everyone around the table. That is happiness."

Which I am losing, or have already lost. But that I don't tell the journalist.

A morning of honey, a morning of love: that is an answer, too, isn't it, Violeta?


We are going out to eat. While looking for the cigarettes I always keep in the glove compartment in Andrés's car, I find a pair of sunglasses.

They're large ones with black frames, gold trim around the rim, and dark lenses.

"And these glasses?"

"Which ones?"

"These, Andrés. These are a woman's, but they're not mine."

"I have no idea who could have left them there."

"But what woman has been in your car? How could you not know?"

"How can you think I remember? I don't have any idea."

The next day they were gone.


And what if I pay him in the same coin? What if I break my strict monogamy? It was never dictated by standards. No. It was a choice, free and white and pristine, following our long clandestine romance when he was still married. ("I don't want to hurt anyone, Andrés." He looked at me and answered, "That's my problem, and I will take care of it." And despite the denigrating offers from his first wife—that he continue our affair, she accepted it and would keep the secret; anything as long as he not leave her and they save their marriage at any price— Andrés arranged everything without involving me, very cleanly. I don't know how, but he worked it out so that the inevitable ugliness of a moment like that would not invalidate me.) He laughed when once— a long time ago—while watching Meryl Streep on the screen, I told him, "I've changed sides, Andrés. I don't identify with the lovers any longer, I'm on the side of the wives." That's when I began to be monogamous. A choice that has given me power, strengthened me. Unfaithful to Andrés? The mere idea throws me off balance.

The only place I like men is in grand hotels, those same men I ignore in any other situation. I look at them. The length of their legs, the breadth of their chest, the line of their shoulders, the cut of their hair. No, not young men. They aren't attractive to me, and besides, they don't frequent the good hotels. It's mature men I look at. I want to smell them. Those snowy white shirts excite me. I imagine those men in the shower (just like the one in my room in the same hotel), naked, wet. Kissable. A combination I find irresistible. These so serious men at conferences, always in groups of others who are equally serious, denote a masculinity sometimes contained, sometimes aloof. If ever I were unfaithful, I have thought, it would be with one of those men in grand hotels.

Until I realized: those men *are* Andrés. They are the image of the serious criminal lawyer, handsome in middle age, with an air of thinking important thoughts: a dignified gentleman in a dark suit strolling about a conference I'm not attending. The eyes of other women in hotels see him that way.

Even to be unfaithful I look for him.


The fax machine has facilitated continuity in my communication with Violeta. Since I have neither time nor peace, letters are out. I tend to send her silly little messages, snippets, trite but true thoughts, like every cliché. She appreciates them, understands these modern smoke signals, carrier pigeons that say *I haven't forgotten you.*

*Viola, it's forbidden to be sad because you're not living in this country. You're not losing anything. 1994 will be enshrined as the year of great national boredom.*

*Dear heart: now not even the famous Cordillera of the Andes belongs to us. We can't see it for the smog. There's nothing left, if you know what I mean.*

Other times pain outweighs humor.

*This is the only possible hell. That other one doesn't exist, doesn't matter. Doubt and disaffection. That fringe I learned about thanks to*

ny jacket and purse and, in desperation, run toward the
cross the peaceful hall of my house, in a blur I see wall-
ntings, I don't focus well, perceive only dim shapes, yet
they look like because I have seen them every day of
of every year and I do not need to focus to know that
paintings in the hallway of the house that is choking me,
g now, I don't want anyone to stop me, I open the door,
he garden, and finally I am in the street, the walls that are
me are behind me, I am free, the street, I am here.
ave nowhere to go.

re at four o'clock on a Sunday afternoon, such a familiar
the likely aroma of cake baking in the kitchen oven.
o go on a Sunday in autumn without drowning. I walk
wn the sidewalk; I don't know where I'm going, but the
that my legs are so springy that the choking is going away,
ve steps—purposeful these steps that do not know where
;oing—allow me to breathe, clear my throat and my chest
ead, spinning, spinning, drowning.

e, Violeta told me; *when you are desperate, write, use your
on. Work is the only thing that will get you through. Believe
fa, the only thing. There is nothing work cannot get you past,
worst moments.*) I sit down on a bench in the plaza where my
g has brought me and take out the pen and notebook I always
hand. Words burst out just as they are, clothed, dressed for
. I write stupidly, madly. No matter. I don't know that I am
ing my best song. And last.

n don't realize that their creativity is born of small things, of
allen things. Their inspirations, small breaths of light in the
ss of the quotidian. Never grand, total, sublime illumination.
y step, interrupted, punctuated with trivia, like every hour of
lay, that is woman's creativity. Never believing in it, never giv-

*you: reserve. I don't know where I'm going, Violeta; I <u>don't know who</u>
loves me. And what's worse, I <u>don't know whom I love</u>. The next article about me should be entitled "The singer, or shrouded sensibility."*

She answers immediately.

*It's essential to differentiate between pain and anguish. Anguish
immobilizes, pain makes us grow. And listen to who's telling you this:
one who knows!*

Alejandro always reads my faxes, because he gets to the office
before I do. His inevitable question is, "Who's the crazy one? Violeta
or you?"

ing it much importance. Tapestries, or patchwork quilts, the creative ideas of women added one by one with the illusion of building a whole that will make sense; each piece a drop of light eagerly stolen from a small, invisible, silenced life.

I come home transformed. I have finally written a song after a long period of sterility, months and months of humiliation as Alejandro tells me that my sales are falling off because I haven't brought out a new album since the one I dedicated to Violeta. The humiliation of knowing that in two years I've been unable to come up with enough new songs. I have obstinately refused to sing songs written by anyone else because I don't have the energy or the desire to find coherence among them. I know that my decline has already begun, my imagination has been put out to pasture. But today I come back to Andrés feeling light, the drowning dissipated. On the air, a sweet scent of cumin.

"Do you know, Andrés, that artists, or—not to sound pretentious—people close to the act of creating, are given moments of sensitivity and self-awareness that other mortals don't usually have? Well, today I had a ray of lucidity, I've written a song and . . . I have realized the extent of my love for you."

Andrés raises his always generous eyes and looks at me with a mixture of tenderness and compassion.

"That's too bad, Josefa. Mine is weary."

After forty, there are many more reasons for suffering than for enjoying. I age a little every day, and every day the world is more malign.

Mauricio, my faithful and eternal Mauricio, is ill.

It is the AIDS virus.

I come home undone, battered, every member torn from my body, disintegrating, sick of pain. Andrés gathers me in. I sleep in his arms. Physical touch reignites affection.

"Do you know, Jose, what the great Socrates said?"

"What did he say?" My voice is barely audible.

"That love is loving something different from oneself, something one does not possess."

Does he say that for Mauricio or for himself?


Celeste has walked seven long blocks and suffered more than seven stubborn oglings of breasts outlined by the T-shirt bearing the face of Jim Morrison subjugating the universe, the one beyond her breasts. A number of necklaces interrupt Morrison's stare.

When Celeste bursts in, I'm lying on the sofa listening to the damask voice of Howard Keel on an old recording. When I see her, I smile. She is like me: that healthy air, pleasingly plump, as Zulema would say. But her look is not peaceful.

"Did something happen?"

"Yes. I want to tell you that I'm never going to eat again for the rest of my life."


Dinner at home. Seeing people is the price I pay for having them love me. But if I had my choice I wouldn't see anyone. The guests were perfectly charming, but I was incapable of playing my usual role as hostess, the one who fills the holes in conversation, the one who asks each guest what that guest wants to be asked, the one who is attentive to having the glasses filled again and again, the one who laughs and always tells some entertaining anecdote that puts everyone at ease. The one who provokes the discussions that somehow impassion some fiber of the drowsing brains of the nineties. As the evening progressed, I could feel the palpable boredom: not just mine, everyone's. Andrés is so used to my doing the "socializing" that he had no repertory to call upon. Indifferent in my chair, I counted the minutes till everyone would leave.

"I'm not entertaining anymore," I tell my husband when the door closes. I am lying full length on the sofa. "I'm not capable of being charming."

"It doesn't matter, you don't always have to be sparkling."

"I can't do it anymore, Andrés. It's a pain, I don't care if they are bored. My superego lets its guard down."

"You're tired, Jose, that's all."

"This is the first time in my life that I've been too tired to undress. I don't want to undress. I'm going to sleep here."

Andrés, untypically, does not try to convince me. He brings a throw and covers me there on the living room sofa. (Does he want to sleep alone?)

"Andrés, I can't go on."

Intoxicate me.

Sanctify me.

Save me.

My little Diego comes in, happy, showing me a picture of Andrés in today's newspaper. The occasion is a lecture he gave in the law school.

"At last!" says Diego, sticking it in my face. "My papa is in the newspaper, too."

I am swamped with guilt. And, in passing, I understand the anger that has built up in my son.

I get almost no sleep these days.

I remember one Christmas when Zulema—who is unmarried and lives alone—came out impeccably dressed after preparing our dinner.

"And you, Zule?" I ask. "Are you going to have something delicious tonight?"

"Yes, I cooked the turkey ahead of time, everything is ready."

"And are you going to get together with some of your family or friends?"

"No," she answers, emphatically, her mouth screwed tight. "I didn't invite anyone. All people do is dirty up everything and make a mess. I'm going to eat by myself."

Today I feel on my fingertips the memory of that order, that void. I touch it, I caress it, terrified, ensconced upon my fear.

My hours of wakefulness troop among these images: Zulema's Christmases and the Old Fortune-Teller of my childhood.

Free fall.

Every night I sit in the living room and say good-bye to the things around me, each painting, each piece of furniture. Then I go into the rooms of my three children, and tell them good-bye. I say good-bye to everything real.

And invariably, as I do so, nausea pays its visit.

*We don't appreciate what's great until it's too late*, my grandmother Adriana always said.

Pamela. My heart tells me. She is Andrés's new love.

The reason I most detest her is that she feels, and shows she still is, sexually competitive. She is my age. She is a captivating woman. Wasn't that what they used to say about me? Resignation and despair are not my natural states. And it is in regard to Andrés's body, that body, my only body, it is in regard to our erotic couplings, that my lack of power maddens me. I'm not ready to lose that. Nevertheless, maybe I should resign myself to that moment that comes to every couple: the death of passion.

Pamela.

There is nothing I detest more than a woman martyr. I will not be one.

Someone would say that the feminine is a blend of howl and abstraction: melodrama. I won't go there.

That was what Henry Miller recommended Anaïs Nin avoid: stridency. Despite the maleness typified in recommending that to a woman, this time I think Miller is entirely right.

Consolation. Oh, that I had it.

Andrés and I are at a point when it is impossible to penetrate the fissures. We are——we have been——such good friends and so respectful of one another that if he prefers not to speak, I must not force him. I prefer silence. At least it elevates one.

Dignity, in the end, is a problem of self-esteem. It has to do with the way a woman looks at herself, not with what is external. I must keep my dignity if I am not to wallow in a probable pool of filth. And maybe recapture his love.

If I were brave, I would go away.

I received the following letter.

*Jose:*

*I am killing time, Bob's plane is late.*

*The vulgarity of the line of the abdomen. I am looking at a woman in the airport, across from me, and thinking: what if I had been born of her . . . The woman has her little girl with her, a tiny thing; she falls and hits her mouth. The father picks up the shrieking child. The woman looks at the husband, half annoyed, accusing, bored. She never even touches the little girl, who is crying and crying. The woman's T-shirt is green and tight; sagging breasts and nearly nonexistent waist. She sits with her legs apart; she's wearing needle-heel shoes and each foot is pointed toward a different side of the airport. I keep watching her, waiting for some move toward the little girl who has fallen; I linger at her hair: thin, dyed. Not a single point of attractiveness or warmth. And I think, terrified: she could have been my mother. Why not? And then . . . who would I have been?*

*Talk about the absence of dazzle!*

*This goes to forgiving Cayetana anything.*
*They've announced the arrival of the plane. I'll leave you.*
*I love you, always, and expect to see you.*

*Violeta*


I put the letter back in the envelope, as always postmarked Guatemala, and think: to every madwoman her aberration.


I visit Mauricio. On the way I look at myself in the rearview mirror. No, wrinkles don't matter. Mauricio can't stand lifts. "You have to leave them alone," he told me. "They're the marks of sin; you have to show the stigma of lust."

It's strange to find myself here; it has always been the other way around. In all these years I have never come to his house before. It is more modest than I had imagined it, since he is such a sophisticated person.

He is very thin, he who was always fighting his large, heavy body, and who spent his life sharing diets with me. He is in bed. How the illness has progressed!

Or has a lot of time gone by? Is it also that I didn't notice?

I sit down beside him and we talk generalities. He asks me whether I'll be going to the United States, because he senses he won't be going there again. His mad dream has always been that country: Mauricio had his eyes permanently there, in the other hemisphere. In wintertime he used to say, "I can't stand to be cold while developed masses are shitting from the heat."

He takes my hand.


Celeste isn't eating anything. Anorexia, according to Andrés. I have taken her, kicking and screaming, to see Phillipe, who believes it's depression. Borja has come to speak to Andrés and me together. (I know that Pamela is on a trip. Is it my obsession, or is it true that Andrés is getting home earlier?) My son does not want to enter the university immediately; he thinks he needs to refine his career choices before making any decisions. He asks if he can spend a while outside Chile; he wants to work and earn some money. Could we help him a little?

"Where do you want to go?" Andrés asks him.

"I want to travel through Latin America."

Something turns over inside me, but I hide it.

"Is it your plan to stay in one country for a longer time?" I ask timorously.

"Yes. I've been thinking about making Guatemala my base."

Andrés looks at him with an understanding smile.

"Violeta, right?"

"Yes."

And although I am the mother, Andrés looks pleased and gives his immediate blessing to the project.

"It will not be a lost year, Borja," he tells him, ruffling his hair, brusque and affectionate at once. "I'll help you with the expenses. It seems to me you're looking for roots, learning about your origins, and that's well worth while."

Borja is radiant. Borja has grown up. He is not my little boy anymore. At any moment, he will be a man and separate from me. I look at his long hair, his legs in the filthy blue jeans, the sweatshirt with NIRVANA emblazoned across the chest. My efforts to make him dress like a normal human being have gone for naught. I buy him clothes with the best labels, but he somehow manages to look like a bum. (Last week Andrés's niece got married. I asked my children to dress up for the wedding, because it was formal. Andrés's family has never been able to take their eyes off me; I don't know why they are so impressed that he married a singer. I knew perfectly well how closely they would be observing us. "I want you to look handsome," I told them. They objected. "I'm not wearing a suit, not even as a joke," Borja resisted. "And if you think, Mama, that I'm wearing some satin thing like you on TV, you're crazy," Celeste told me. "Besides, that wedding will be a bore, we don't have anyone to talk to, and all those old snobs are a pain." "Better if we don't go at all," Borja backed her. "When Mama wants us on our best behavior, it's unbearable." I complain. "Don't be like that. You won't have to open your mouth if you don't want to. I promise not to make you do anything. But wear something decent. What does that hurt? I just want to show you off.")

Violeta will have Borja, not me.

Fax to Violeta: "Let's give credit to Signoret, who in her old age says, 'Nostalgia isn't what it used to be.'"


I have to go see Phillipe. Self-diagnosis: sick potentialities.

There is an element of female neurosis that I particularly fear: its loyalty to misery. If that yields, what space does it leave behind?

Violeta would answer: Get out of there with the help of the goddesses, don't under any condition allow yourself to fall in love with your sickness.

I asked for a personal appointment, none of this telephone consultation. I get in the car and go. The day itself makes me sad. I have the sensation that everyone is about to burst into tears: women clinging to their steering wheels at the red light. The trees in this increasingly dirty and gray city are angry.

At the next red light I see a woman standing on the sidewalk; she is dressed in a red taffeta vest over a flowered housedress. How can she? Why would anyone dress herself like that? An unexpected tenderness spreads through me, I feel the innocence of that taffeta gesture. The woman I'm watching has gray hair, and is happy. Not like those hiding behind the steering wheels. The taffeta is transformed into humanity.

It is not for nothing that I was named and baptized Josefina Jesús de la Amargura. Why would anyone name a child Josefina Jesus of Bitterness?

"You're wiped out," Phillipe tells me.

"But . . . but why?" A stupid question.

"You tell me."

"It's absurd, I'm living my usual life. I came because of my fatigue, that's all. Did you know I had an attack of fatigue before my last recital? We had to cancel it. That's why I'm here."

"Yes, I read about it in the paper. But you're also here because of dizziness, right?"

"Yes . . . the dizziness."

"And the nausea."

"Yes, the nausea."

"And the headaches."

"Well, it came to me all at once that I might have a brain tumor. Do you know that I forget everything? Things I've said two days ago, appointments I made the week before."

"And you can't concentrate . . ."

"Right, I can't concentrate. I've been stuck in the same book for a month, I can't get through it. A novel by Gail Godwin. I read and read, and when I close the book and turn out the light I realize I haven't any idea what I've read. The next night I start the same chapter over again. I've come to hate the author!"

"Josefina, you are a picture of severe *surmenage*. Stress. Call it what you will. But you are going to have to stop. Now."

"I'm sorry, Phillipe, I can't."

"What do you mean, you can't?"

"I have a tour scheduled for next month."

"Cancel it."

"Are you crazy? The record label has put all its energy and expectations into this tour; it will guarantee my comeback."

"You've done your part. Leave the promotion problems to them."

"And how are they going to promote anything without me? I can't. I have to be responsible for my own mistakes."

"What mistakes?"

"Not recording a new album. Cancelling the last concert. This business is much more complex than people think, Phillipe. It isn't enough just to sing. Give me something to make me feel better, and I'll be off."

"Not this time, Josefa."

"Did I tell you Mauricio is sick?"

"Yes, we talked about it."

"That's what's got me down. Ten years working together . . . It's terrible, Phillipe. He's going to die any minute."

"That's how AIDS is."

"He can't even do the ponytail in his hair anymore. He doesn't have the strength. Yesterday I had to comb it myself."

"I'm sorry. But let's get back to you."

We stare into each other's eyes. No truce. There won't be any.

"I've dried up. I've written only one song in months. And I can't sing. My success is fading. Celeste hates me. I can't stand myself. And on top of that, I feel that Andrés doesn't love me. It's as if love had some kind of energy that frees one so the creative juices can flow. And now I don't have that love. And I want it back: not any love, but *that* love. I want *that* love to give me *that* energy."

I repeated it to myself: that fertile, abundant, fruitful, prodigal, fecund love. That's what I want.

"Andrés is the perfect counterbalance to my fervor. If he hadn't been committed to seeing it through, he would never have invited me to share my life with him. In that sense, he is a serious man. And I entered into that commitment, Phillipe. Can he take it away just like that?"

"No. And what is happening is happening because he hasn't yet withdrawn the invitation. And it's my impression that he's not going to. I think, I *do* think, that Andrés is tired. Of you. But that tiredness doesn't necessarily have anything to do with love. You are a difficult woman, Josefa."

Phillipe's diagnosis was clear. Stop. Cancel everything. Go away.

"Where?"

"Wherever you think you can make a true recovery."

"And if there is another woman, won't that be handing him to her on a silver platter?"

"Just the opposite. If that were so, and that's something we don't know, your absence would take away a good part of her dazzle. And last of all, if it's a hot passion, let it burn itself out."

"You know, Phillipe? There is one thing that still gives me hope about myself, makes me think I'm not all bad: I don't want to stay with him at any price, like his first wife. I don't, like her, want marriage *per se*, not caring *what* it's like or *how* it feels."

"That speaks well for you. You see, you *are* capable of going away."

"And abandoning Celeste at this time?"

"Leave Celeste to me. Your absence will be good for her. Am I treating her, or not? I'll keep an eye on her, and with Andrés see how to proceed."

"I can't leave before Mauricio dies . . ."

"But we don't know how long he can last, Josefa. Go on. Save yourself since you can't save him."

As we said good-bye, he put his arms around me.

"Take a chance. You won't be sorry."

It wasn't until I was outside, alone in the car, that I thought about something he had said: "You live run through by a double-edged sword, Josefina. Do you know Adrienne Rich?"

I answered with a melancholy smile. Was it worth the effort to tell him how sensibilities and lives intersect, how in the end we are all the same, how the same Adrienne Rich he wants to use to define me has done that for Violeta for centuries and centuries? I nod.

In one of her poems she says: *Her wounds come from the same source as her power.*

Sometimes, the everyday sound is the only one that can calm us and make us feel part of the human race. Other times, it is its absence that elevates and solemnizes.

For light to come, silence is necessary.

I must go.

Antigua.

# 7

$\mathcal{A}$ lightning storm in the heavens between Colombia and Guatemala. Probable moment for reflection. I reject it. When my mouth feels dry, I think of the scent of *membrillos*, of purple eggplant, of snowy floating islands. This time I don't have to scan the newspapers of the country I'm flying to, I don't tremble at the thought of my arrival, of my press conference, of my concert. On this trip I am not a star: something that hasn't happened to me for a long, long time.

In Bogotá I suffered the last—I hope—"star" experience, and because of it I will not get to Antigua tonight, as was planned.

As it happened, I took a Ladeco flight. On arrival in Bogotá they announce that owing to a cancelled flight they don't know when we will be leaving for Guatemala. I'm a little upset. I must notify Violeta. It makes me nervous to picture her, with children, waiting at the airport for a plane that will not come, with the resulting drive back to

Antigua at night, which Violeta has told me she doesn't do for safety reasons. In Guatemala it gets dark at six. I can't call from an airport phone, so I go to the airline desk to ask for help. On the verge of tears, I explain that I am stuck in this airport without any knowledge of when my flight will be leaving and that I have to get through to Guatemala. Since I am not allowed to use the telephone, they offer to send a message for me. I write it out and sign it—as is natural—with my name. The clerk goes into the office; I breathe more calmly. But within seconds, out of those same offices comes a man in black trousers and an impeccable white shirt; his light hair is cut very short, he has blue eyes and a voice of command, and he yells: "Where's the singer?"

"Here." I go to him, puzzled.

"Do you think because you're famous you have the right to send this message? What does this 'I'm stuck' mean, when the company is taking care of you?"

"I'm sorry, señor. Who are you?"

"I'm the Ladeco manager for Colombia."

"And why are you so angry?"

"Because you're making a scene in front of all our customers. If what you want is for everyone to know that the famous Josefa Ferrer is on the airplane, you've succeeded, with the fuss you're making."

"Señor, I haven't made any fuss, and I haven't made a scene. Look, get a grip; there's only one customer at your whole counter. All I did was talk with the clerk."

He is purple with rage. I suppose that the flight isn't anywhere near ready to take off, and he clearly doesn't know how to handle the situation; he's in over his head and he's taking it out on me. I feel very vexed. This man is yelling at me and he has no right to do so. What is he really afraid of? That I will send a letter to authorities in Santiago saying that their manager in Bogotá is inefficient and, besides that, he has no idea how to handle emergency situations, that he completely loses his cool and yells at someone who has millions of listeners?

"You are abusing your power! You can bet the embassy will hear about this!" The man cannot contain himself.

"What abuse are you talking about? You're the one who's being abusive."

"Stars!" he snorts, beside himself, and stomps back into the refuge of his office.

The clerk behind the counter stands staring at him, not me. An Argentine, the one customer standing beside me, says, amused, "*Che!* So you are Josefa Ferrer! That's good to know, I'm delighted to meet you. By the way, please tell your compatriots to be more careful in choosing the personnel for their airlines."

I am furious. I have never taken advantage of who I am, that's the last thing anyone can criticize me for. The Argentine invites me to have a cup of coffee.

"I have a card for international calls. I'll lend it to you."

Thanks to him, I'm able to reach Violeta before she leaves home, and explain the situation: she took it happily.

"I have a fantastic idea," she says, cheering me up. "I'll leave the family here and come to Ciudad de Guatemala by myself. I'll get a room in the Hotel El Dorado—it's near the airport and you'll like it. I'll wait there with a good book until you come. The time won't matter. And it'll be cool to have a good talk alone before we get to the house. How does that sound, Jose?"

"It sounds great."

I smile, calm down, and go to meet the Argentine who has rescued me.

As I was saying, I refuse to reflect on the storm in the heavens. I am perilously tired; I need to leave the singer on this plane and get off as *someone else*. Someone I'd like; for instance, the little girl with the shy, dark eyes who, when they put an arithmetic test on her desk in school, looked at it, did not know a single answer, then realized that from the closet beside her desk, the new schoolmate with the pixie eyeglasses, the one with whom she had never spoken, was, from the closet where she was hiding because it gave her total fits to participate in class, passing her a sheet with the answers. She'd scored a seven, and that was why she had gone to her new friend's birthday party. Yes, that same little girl who fearfully asked the other one a couple of years later if it could be true that Adam and Eve had been driven out of Paradise because they tried to have a baby, if *that* could be the famous sin.

That girl, now grown, arrives in this country she does not know with the illusion that something new may still await her in life. She goes to the hotel El Dorado, meets her friend in the room, which of course is filled with flowers and where a bottle of champagne is chilling; they embrace like two starving women, call room service twenty times during the night, do not move from their respective beds, or sleep, and she lets it all out, facing the one person she can do that with, and talks and talks about all the things she has been storing up since the day she was born.

And that took the whole night.

# 8

$\mathcal{V}$ioleta lives on Sexta Calle Oriente, but in the city they still call it by its original name: Calle de los Peregrinos. It is an old colonial house with ocher walls, closed to the outside world, enormous and bright inside. The person who enters is assaulted, unexpectedly, by great space, beginning with the classic garden: flowers of every color, exuberant plants we don't even know the names for in the Southern Cone, brilliant green grass, and a large tree on one side—in this case a cedar. Of the four walls that compose this large rectangle, only one does not feature wide, furnished galleries: the wall of the fountain.

"The one difference between Antigua and Spanish architecture is that here you find fountains embedded in a wall, not in the center of the garden," Violeta explains.

The color of the stucco is red, that colonial red that is not quite terra-cotta. The wall of the fountain is white, with a band of the same red across the bottom, right at the ground. The water is turned off only at night.

I look at the numbers of doors opening onto the galleries.

"What do you do with so many rooms?" I ask, almost with envy. I remember the house on Calle Gerona and Violeta's telling me that there are never too many square meters, never.

She points to the gallery to the left of the large entry door.

"It's easy, you won't get lost. All that wing is ours: Bob's and mine. This one, opposite the fountain wall, is common space. Behind the kitchen are the service quarters, which include a stone wash-trough, one of the traditional ones, you'll see it. Tierna despises the washing machine, she likes to pound the clothes on stone."

We walk toward the right wing, the one for the children and guests. As she is showing me Jacinta's and little Gabriel's bedrooms, I see a guitar leaning against a chair in Jacinta's room. I shiver: I will not play it, ever, I say to myself, half angry. As we walk on, I watch Violeta: she glides through these spaces with a body that is completely at home. From the neck of her dress hang her eternal "Mia Farrow" eyeglasses, as we called them years ago, and she still has that faraway, distracted gaze typical of astigmatism. And although I have been told that it is never cold in Antigua, she has kept the habit of dressing in things that flow: various rich cloths undulate as she walks, whether as scarf, kerchief, belt, or shawl. Square meters of house, meters of cloth on her body: abundance and variety of spaces and textures. Between two bedrooms, a dream of a small room with a light-filled patio, all in stone, illuminates that part of the house.

"And whose room is this?" I ask as I pass from Gabriel's bedroom to another, obviously masculine.

"It's Alan's, Bob's son. He comes to see us two or three times a year. He's about Borja's age."

I see some familiar articles of clothing on the rug, but more than the clothing I recognize this way of dropping things on the floor.

"Borja is living here?"

"Yes, since this room is empty almost all year, Jacinta's friends use it. But let's go on toward the back, I want you to see your room."

"Is it the 'official guest room'?"

"You can call it that. But I was thinking of you and Andrés when I decorated it. Imagine how excited I am that you're finally going to use it!"

I see my suitcases. Who brought them in? I can't help stretching out on that inviting bed, wide, attached to two heavy wood columns.

"Apparently it's Spanish, from the last century. If the antique dealer who gets furniture for Bob is serious, you'll be sleeping on a relic."

The doors are open to the gallery and I breathe in the scent of the plants. Then I discover a rare flower on my dressing table; it is pink and the green leaves are thick, firm, and erect.

"What is this marvel? I've never seen one like it."

"It's an orchid; its name is cattleya. From this area. Orchids grow like wildfire here."

I get up, moved. I hug Violeta.

"You haven't changed at all. Every little detail . . ."

She smiles. She looks so beautiful. She hasn't aged; she doesn't have a single wrinkle more than she had three years ago. Or gray hair.

"Come along, I want to show you my part."

"Wait, let me see the bathroom." I open that door and find myself in a bath all brick and painted tiles, something I have seen only in Mexico or Seville. An antique dark wood beam encloses the area of the tub which, of course, also is trimmed with a row of tiles.

"It's gorgeous, Violeta! It must have cost you two a fortune to do this house."

"Well, the house in Ñuñoa sold well, remember? It was so pretty! With that money we bought this one. The remodeling was almost as expensive as the original cost. Bob financed it, following my plans and designs. It was a two-party adventure, I couldn't have done it alone."

"And at last you fulfilled your dream of having a house in one of the places you've fallen in love with."

"I did it here, since I could never have done it in Llanquihue. I feel that each brick is mine, Josefa. And I've had it only two years. It's as if it was and will be my house forever."

"You dare to still use that word? *Forever?*"

"Yes." I hear a slight tone of apology. "In spite of everything, I dare."

We go to the left wing, hers. I cannot contain my enthusiasm. Her hand is visible in everything from the broad architectural features to the smallest details.

The room was enormous. How many could fit in that bed? An arch with a door made of iron bars and wooden spindles, letting air and light through, separated the bedroom from the study: a separation more psychological than real. Against one wall, I recognized the wicker trunk. I saw hundreds of books, tall bookcases from floor to ceiling, with a small ladder. Flower-upholstered armchairs, two large tables that acted as desks, paintings and tapestries on the walls. The sunroom in Ñuñoa came to mind, because of the light and the warmth of the wood, the fireplace laid for storms, and the desk facing the fire, with clean paper and prettily-bound notebooks on top. That was hers, I had no doubt. I walk closer and read the page she is working on.

> *GUARECER/ to aid, to succor, to assist*
> *to guard, to preserve*
> *to cure, to treat*
> *to take refuge, to escape from danger*

"Come on, Jose, don't be a bore; we're looking at the house . . ."

"And that door behind the books. Where does it go?"

"To my workshop. No one goes in there."

And she led me into that space—one mass of light, light everywhere, total light—surrounded by a small interior garden and ringing with birdsong. Two of the four walls were entirely glass. It was a nearly hidden space, ample and empty. There were several looms of various kinds and sizes; wools, silks, cottons, also cords and rougher materials. And in the middle of the room, an enormous stretcher, approximately two by three meters, holding an unfinished tapestry. I could make out large areas of color, and, clustered along one side, small areas thickly embroidered with flowers of every shade.

"Mixed technique," she says before I ask, one hand on her hip, studying her work as if it were someone else's.

A carousel of colors.

"Violeta, this is Paradise!"

"It's true, isn't it?" she replies excitedly. "Finally I've found the place."

Violeta and her places.

For a long time I looked at the work, without saying anything, as if ancient perceptions were taking shape in my mind.

"Come on. I want to take you to one more place in the house," she said. "You can come back to the workshop later; I promise to let you in."

She led me to the culmination of her joy with this architecture: the *azotea*, the enormous flat roof. In the middle, an ancient tower rose from the flat open space.

"It's the roof of the kitchen, don't think it's a bell tower."

I look out over neighboring tiled roofs, a wash of tiles mixed with the green of the hills and, in the distance, majestic, the volcano. The Volcán de Agua.

As if she were following every movement of my eyes, Violeta tells me, her voice low and intimate: "You know? When sometimes I don't wake up feeling good and think I'm losing something of the 'wide,

wide world,' I climb up here to the *azotea* and look at the volcano. Believe me, Josefa, just looking at it is enough. I feel peaceful and renewed. There's no pain it won't carry away. On a normal day, the volcano makes me happy. It's essential to all of us who live in Antigua."

"And it must remind you of the volcanoes in the south of Chile?"

"It's strange, my places always have volcanoes."

Violeta tempts nature. Isn't it strange that with her history she chooses to live near them? Isn't that some sort of provocation? What would Cayetana have thought of them? She also points out the Volcán de Fuego and Acatenango.

I looked at her, straight-spined high above the city, and she reminded me of a queen. Antigua, she had said, the Sleeping Beauty of America. She loved her Beauty and wanted it to watch over her sleep. To be the woman she was, and to have done what she had done, and to have lived what she had lived, she seems too whole a person. Violeta: alive and with so much death!

"You see that church, there where the yellow flag is flying?" She interrupts my thoughts. "That's San Francisco. Brother Pedro is buried there, the saint of the poor. He isn't an official saint yet, but it appears that he's going to be canonized soon. We'll go ask him to look after Andrés."

I sat down on the edge of the bell tower—that's what I called the roof over the kitchen—to soak up the sun, and regarded my surroundings. Could this beauty be true, or was someone going to wake me to say that it was just a dream? Coming from Ciudad de Guatemala, after being up all night and with my heart protected, the green of the hills began to soothe me. And arriving at the high plateau, I was filled with calm. It is surprising that a half hour outside the capital you can find a corner of the world where history has stopped. Large old homes, cobbled streets, some ruined churches, others still standing, sixteenth-century architecture, the uniformity of the period, the absence of anything modern, introduced me to this jewel I have come to almost on my knees, hoping for its mercy.

Its quiet . . . can it heal me?

"What do you aspire to, now that you have almost everything?" I ask.

"For my burden to be lighter each day."

"May God help you, Violeta."

# 9

Chichicastenango isn't a place, it's an experience.

The definition is Violeta's, and she was right.

Although Antigua began to stir at six in the morning, I refused to change my habits. Violeta brought my coffee to the bedroom about eight; she had already showered, dressed, and eaten breakfast. She's become a native, I thought.

"Coffee isn't great everywhere in Guatemala. It's a privilege of Antigua. We're surrounded by coffee plantations."

We set out, Violeta at the wheel, to explore the famous mountain town that every Thursday and Sunday is transformed into a market. Market-town, the prettiest in America, Violeta states without hesitation. Even Mexico would love it. And that's saying a lot.

Minibuses suddenly appear along the winding road, like a menace.

"One day I inquired about the minis to Chichicastenango," she tells me, "and a driver told me that he brought his out only on Sundays, because that was the one day they didn't check tires. His were totally slick. How about that?"

As we drove I surrendered to the landscape: enormous ravines, green cliffs, proud forests. Where could Andrés be? Last night I had broken my promise to myself and called him. I waited and waited, my throat dry, hiding from Violeta. No one answered. It was twelve o'clock midnight in Chile. What would I have said had he answered? I am left with the panic, the fantasy of his hands on another body, but also the dignity of silence. What would my tone have been? Tears, blame, or a single cry: that he come save me.

Violeta points out a stucco hut, round, with tiny windows, something like one imagines sentinels used in the Middle Ages.

"You see it?"

"Yes, I've seen several."

"Well, those were the lookout posts PAC used during the guerrilla war. PAC is a corps that was created for civil defense. Now that there's no war, no one knows what to do with them. They are wickedly armored, and they've weathered right down to a pile of stone, a real danger. I can guarantee you they've been used in kidnappings and various other of this country's criminal dramas."

This is the old Violeta. I smile. Still impassioned by all her causes, lost or social. Come what may, she will be on the side of the guerrilla fighters. I remember how impatient I always was with her lack of skepticism, and am aware, to my amazement, that now I don't ask anything different of her: it doesn't bother me anymore. It isn't as if everything had gone so well with me, after all. And I feel an immediate sense of relief.

"Are you still moved by hymns? Do you still cry when you hear carols and the national anthem?"

"Yes, even though you think I'm nuts," she replies, laughing, her eyes on the road.

My tone changes: "Aren't you afraid to live in this country?"

Now she turns and looks at me with a meaningful expression. "And weren't you afraid to live in yours the last twenty years?"

I hesitate. On this subject I prefer not to make the mistake of answering spontaneously. But Violeta presses on, not waiting for me. "This country has as many wounds as ours, but they're out in the open. All the nastiness exposed to the light of day. The air will heal them, I think. They aren't hidden beneath protective bandages intended to make them invisible. Pestilence here stinks; Chile's wounds, in contrast, are sanitized. Tell me, which will heal first?"

"Don't preach at me, Violeta. I'm closer to your thinking than you imagine. The 'new times' have begun in Chile, and apparently the transition is over. Everything is fine. Things seem normal. Entrepreneurs are producing, politicians are politicking, students are studying, workers are working. Things are marching along. We have all the gray of efficiency, now everything is competition and we're all cut and dried. Basically, it's a pain."

"The transition . . ." she murmurs, in deep thought. "It should have taught us one thing: that we have to go back to the classifications of good and bad. Anything more subtle leads to surrendering your soul."

"You may be right. The thing is that I'm tired of trying to see things in relative terms. It hasn't helped me at all."

We fall into an hermetic silence we both find comfortable.

For several kilometers I am obsessed with the greenness of the countryside. I had called an hour later last night, fearful that Violeta would catch me in this act of childish, unnecessary control. Nothing. Empty, that bed with the telephone beside it on the night table. Dear God, what am I going to do? I can't lose him, I don't exist except in him. I feel his hands on my hair . . . The nausea returns. How I long to be free of this fear, this nightmare. Andrés, I'm drowning!

I try to come back. Finally, determined to be where I am, I ask:

"What does the name of this town mean? It's so difficult. I mean, the town we're going to. I can barely pronounce it."

"Chichicastenango? *Tenango* means 'the place.' The *chichicas* are those plants growing along the road, those thistles. 'The place of the thistles.' As Quetzaltenango is 'the place of the quetzal.' The quetzal, besides being the national coinage, is a bird. You will see it in the embroidery; it's an icon that's repeated over and over. The spirit of Guatemala. It's like our condor," she laughs. "But the quetzal is prettier, and more appealing."

"I'm struck by the poverty, Violeta," I comment as I look through the car window. "But the children have taught me that poverty or no, any price can be negotiated in this country. Is that true?"

"We all do it; I did it myself. Until one day in the market in Antigua, after some hard bargaining, a man, worn down, says, all right, why don't we settle on the price I offered him. When I handed him the filthy bills, he said, 'I'm only selling this because I'm hungry.'"

We reached the town around eleven-thirty. My eyes were nearly blinded, like Moses's when he saw the burning bush. The fiesta of colors that greeted me is beyond description. I was inundated by the golds, sepias, earth tones, olive greens, blues, the entire gamut of lilacs and purples, of hundreds of crafts stands. One after another, squeezed together as they were, it was impossible to count them or tell where one began and the next ended.

"I always find inspiration here," Violeta said when she saw my face. "Come on, we'll go to the market later. Right now I want to take you to the church of Santo Tomás. This way."

We walked a while through steep streets and suddenly, there was the church, magnificent with its stone steps, that gray of true stone. Opposite it, I saw another church.

"Are we going to both?"

"No, just this one. The one you see over there is theirs, the one the Indians go to. It's called El Calvario. They go there to find Sajorín, or

Chukajau. He's the head priest of the Mayas, the wisest and oldest, and sometimes the most prosperous. They visit him in the church and he gives them advice and heals them. It would be disrespectful to go in there. I never have."

"I don't understand; if both churches are Catholic, why do you speak of them as if they belonged to the Indians?"

"Because they do. The Spanish weren't totally stupid, after all. They were satisfied with the bizarre fusion they achieved between their God and the gods of the Indians. Remember, it was only in 1542 that the Catholic Church acknowledged that Indians had a soul like other human beings. Where Santo Tomás stands, for example, was a Maya temple; the Spanish didn't destroy it. They built their church over it, respecting the ancestral Mayas buried in the floor of their Catholic church. Watch how the Indians pray. They pray toward the ground; they know that the Maya gods are buried there."

You could scarcely see the steps of the church for the clouds of copal incense swirling over everything. I saw that one of Violeta's shoes was untied; she nearly stepped on the lace.

"Lift your foot, Violeta."

"Oh," she laughed. "It's because Bob isn't here . . . He ties them for me."

Violeta never learned to tie her shoes. "No one taught me," she would defend herself, "and it's too late now to learn those mechanical skills." A thousand times, all through our long history, I've had to ask her to lift her foot when I saw her about to trip over the laces. Very carefully, I tied the bow. And as I perform the familiar action in this faraway town, I understand that Violeta and I are the same persons we have always been. Apparently greatly changed, yet forever the same. And in a hundred years I would say the same, I'm sure. This feeling comforts me.

We walked into the great nave of Santo Tomás, dark, with few benches. In the central aisle I saw clusters of candles fixed in wax on the floor, and Indians praying aloud and protecting their candles—hardened sperm or melting flower petals. I looked toward the altar and was amused to see that Christ had not been assigned the central place: he was to one side. I was greatly moved by the fervor and devotion. Andrés was again in my thoughts, without nausea, without fear, only a sharp pain in my breast. When I had called the third time and there was no answer, I sat down and wept, clutching the phone to my bosom. I must hang on, I can't go down. I look at the Christ clad in cloth robes, and beseech Him: Lord, give me strength! My body expands, and for a second something painless seems to emerge.

"What a strange church! This isn't Catholic ritual."

"Catholics have been tolerant here, a rare thing . . ."

"How, tolerant?"

"They even used to allow some rituals with liquor. The Indians would come in with their bottles, which they used to be closer to God . . ."

"Liquor, to be closer to God?" I am aware that I am asking stupid tourist questions, but Violeta doesn't mind. I am transported.

". . . Because God is spirit, and when you drink alcohol the spirit is liberated. They used to come in the church, take a drink, and spit three times. The first to the left, for their god Maximon. The second, to the right, for the Maya family that looks after God. And the third to the middle, for themselves. Can you imagine the floor of the church with all that alcohol spit!"

"But Violeta, that's paganism."

"It isn't paganism, it's mysticism."

She walks to an altar at the left of the nave. There are several figures carved from wood, and those at the end of the grouping, on each side, are pregnant women. Violeta, very serious, lights a candle.

"What are you doing?"

"This is the altar to fertility. Here's where you light candles when you can't have a baby. I light a candle every time I come, as thanks for Gabriel."

What does Violeta believe in? She makes a prayer, indiscriminately, to this saint in the Church of San Francisco and to a Maya god. It's all the same to her. And says she is agnostic.

"By the way, Violeta, we need to organize Gabriel's baptism."

"Yes, we have to invent something."

"Invent something? Baptism is the same wherever you go."

"Oh, Jose, don't be so rigid. I couldn't take a Catholic ceremony."

"Why not?"

"I don't know. God is so difficult!" She sighs.

Once she has completed the ritual of the candles, she leads me outside the church and then to the internal patio of the rectory. We sit on the floor. Violeta lights a cigarette. She offers me one.

"Do you still stick to your five cigarettes a day?" she asks.

"Since I haven't been singing for a while, and haven't any desire to do so, I smoke when I feel like it. I don't want any more privations than those my poor soul is already suffering."

She lights my cigarette and her enthusiasm builds again.

"You're going to like this: something very important happened in this place. At the beginning of the eighteenth century. You know what a priest found in this church?"

"What?"

"The *Popol Vuh*. It was right here that it was found and translated."

"I don't believe it! Here?"

"Well, it's not so strange. After all, we're in the land of the Quiché, and that's where all the stories in the *Popol Vuh* come from."

That did impress me. "So we owe this Maya gift to humanity to a Catholic priest of Santo Tomás. Amazing! Tell me, do you still have the card from Cayetana on your dresser?"

"Yes, and I always wonder where she bought it. Do you realize it could have been in Antigua?"

"I do."

How long had Violeta's head and heart concentrated on this question? She had wanted to follow Cayetana's footsteps and untangle her mystery. That was her choice. And if it has given her peace, all blessings on it.

# 10

Torrential. Clamorous, this rain. As if instead of water, small rock showers, stalactites, were falling. In the background, like the companion husband to the water, the thunder. Titanic, haughty. If I hadn't known this house had survived a couple of centuries and more than one restoration, I would have raced outside.

"Violeta, are you sure there's no danger?"

Violeta laughs and invites me out to the gallery so that in its protection we can enjoy the storm and fresh air. Seated on the banquettes, we gaze at the watery curtain. Neither music nor voices have meaning, the rain brings its own. In Chile, this would have meant catastrophe, with floods and victims, power outages, and rivers over their banks.

"I'm not young anymore, Violeta," I said suddenly. "If anything important has happened to me since the last time I saw you, it's that I'm no longer young. And, as an aside, thank God."

I gave her my latest observations on a subject that has always obsessed her: time. I explained that I had left youth behind the day I stopped consuming minutes, living them swiftly, hurrying them along in order to know what came next. I ignored the event I was experiencing to leap to the next, always eager to live what I supposed life was dealing me. The north of my compass was clearly the future, which consumed the present without treasuring it. Without living it. When I discovered the pleasure of holding each moment, of clinging to it intensely, concentrating on it as if never to let go, inhaling it as if it were opium or the fragrance of orange blossom, that moment I left my youth behind.

"As you say so well, Jose, thank God. We're at a great age. Unfortunately, we enjoy life only when we learn how ephemeral it is. That's a cliché, but wildly true. And very difficult to comprehend in the bloom of youth."

"But you never devoured time without enjoying it, the way I did. You know the only place where you didn't outdo me?"

"Yes, in the mill house."

"And do you know, Violeta, that *I cannot forgive you for that?*"

"For what?" She seems surprised, almost fearful.

"For the mill house. The one thing I hold against you," I said from my heart, "is that you took that away from us."

"That's not fair, Josefa. I didn't take away the place, I just went away myself."

"It's the same thing."

"You could have re-created the summers, you didn't need me for that."

"The problem was that I needed *you.*"

"I was that important there?"

"That first summer, early in '92, I remember as a nightmare. I think after you killed Eduardo, my life went straight to hell while yours got better. Doesn't that seem crazy to you?"

"No, Jose. What happened was that you had to take a nosedive. If you feel that I took away the only place that could calm that voraciousness of yours, I offer you this one: Antigua."

Neither of us spoke. I believe that Antigua is the station of the soul that perfectly fits Violeta's tastes and talents. ("Postmodernism is *nothingness*, Josefa. That's its sole charm. And also why I hate it!")

It is Violeta who picks up the conversation.

"The difference between us was that I was desperately looking for time, and you, with the same desperation, were consuming it. What I've done is to transport the month of February, the temporary stay at the mill house, to a permanent condition."

"And how have you done that?"

"By finding the place. Just as I did in Llanquihue a couple of lifetimes ago. I realized very soon, Jose, that the noise of the world steals time, devours it, minimizes it, and finally makes us live half of a whole: half, not all. Here I live time twice over, each of your years in Santiago is equivalent to two of mine here, if not three. You know why we have so little time? Because we've given it to noise."

Borja and Jacinta arrive. They are happy, they nearly always are like that. I fear that Borja has some hidden agenda. He shies away each time I talk about going home to Chile. They offer us rum. Happily, we accept. While we're waiting, I pose one last question to Violeta. "You were so tied to your roots, Violeta, hasn't it been hard for you to abandon Chile?"

She looks at me, pensive, as if she did not want to answer my question lightly.

"No. It hasn't been hard. Because the boundaries of my origins have expanded."

# 11

The inevitable moment arrived: Cayetana.

"I'd like to visit her grave, Violeta. Will you go with me?"

Maybe in the cemetery itself, beneath the cypresses, she will tell me about it calmly. But I have to get her outside this house; it is too beautiful, too comfortable; it makes her nearly complacent. I must understand the road she has traveled to reach this apparent peace.

It's a Sunday, four in the afternoon. We drive down Calle de los Peregrinos to the long Calle Sucia, and park beside the walled cemetery.

As we walk, I think about Cayetana. Today I understand her better than ever, her conflicts with maternity. She hadn't realized that having a daughter would mean amputating her own life. That is the root of my identification with her. At an age when I should have been more free, my children bind me to them. Poor things, it isn't their fault, I brought them into this world without consulting them. But somewhere deep inside, I resent them, I am resentful for them. When one day they absolve me of the arduous task of being a mother, I won't want to be liberated; I will probably be an old woman whose energy is long gone, and who no longer cares about freedom.

"Why did she have me, then?" Violeta spit out when I told her my thoughts. "When Jacinta was born, I wasn't a lot older than she was. And I didn't have my child to abandon her. Her existence is *my* responsibility."

"She never managed to bring you to Central America, true. But, contradict me if you want, Cayetana would have been capable of killing a man for your sake."

Violeta is surprised. "I'd never thought about that."

"Well, think about it now."

She stares hard at the paving stones and keeps on walking. After a while, she speaks again.

"You're right. She would have. You know what? That's a consolation to the part of me that's a mother and the part that's a daughter. Cayetana would have killed for me, too."

What Violeta hasn't recognized is that her chief greatness, her horror of enduring petrification, she inherited from Cayetana. As well as her honesty and courage.

And I remembered her words that afternoon, the first time they let me see her in the jail. "I think I was born bad. My mother was bad and I was born of her."

Was that very different from what Jacinta told me when she came to take refuge in my house after her mother's crime?

"It's the anger, Josefa! The anger has passed from one generation to another through the blood of its women."

I held her very close and stroked her hair, that light chestnut hair so like her mother's.

"No, Jacinta, don't say that. The best part of you comes from there, too. You will be a vigorous, strong woman, secure and generous, because you have in you the blood of Carlota and Cayetana and Violeta. You will be a stupendous woman because you come from them."

"Or cursed because I come from them."


We reach the cemetery entrance: solemn, a wide gate and high walls for the final rest.

"Has it already been twenty-eight years since she died?" I am frightened by the passing of time.

"And thirty since I saw her," Violeta answers.

We walk through the opening in the thick white walls. We are on a stone path laid out in perfect perspective, with plants bordering the grassy areas and cypresses, acacias, and other trees I can't identify on either side. In the distance, a large cross, also of stone, like the anteroom to the final room: the church. White, colonial—or at least adopting that style. The scent of cypress was everywhere.

"What a shame the dead have no sense of smell," I say to Violeta. "The worst part of death is never to smell again. I remember Roberto. Doesn't that happen to you? Doesn't it destroy you to think we can never smell their scent again?"

"I've carried Cayetana's scent with me forever; I would know it if I passed it in the street: that combination of tobacco, grass, and roses."

We walk among the tombs: small white houses, the mausoleum as the final house. A Latin American cemetery, they're all the same. None of those European graves in the ground, with the stone and grasses growing wild. Nearly all of them have the name of a family in the center. The dates of the earliest mausoleums are from the last century. The farther we go, the more recent the dates of the dead. I follow Violeta; suddenly, very sure, she turns left. At last she stops.

"Here it is."

She points to an isolated rectangle of white cement, small in relation to those around it. The base is green tile. At the highest point it reaches no farther than Violeta's knees. On top is a cupola, and on that a cross as the one adornment. There is a sort of receptacle on each side, but no gargoyle figure: they provide a place for flowers. There are no flowers; the containers are empty except for a trace of rain water inside. The white of this tomb is the only mossy white in the area. No one has painted it, and some crumbling has produced dark stains.

"In the middle, between the Moreira and Fernández families," I hear her say.

"What?"

I notice an important detail: there is no name on the tomb.

"But Violeta. Why isn't there a name?"

"Because she wasn't a Palma, the family that buried her."

"And when did you learn this was the grave?"

"After Eduardo's death. When I came to live in Antigua."

"That recently . . . That's not right! Isn't it the least a daughter can expect, to know where her mother is buried?"

"I knew it was in this cemetery; that's what it says on the certificate my father brought back to Chile. The problem was to locate her."

"How did you, since there's no name?"

"Because my obsession brought me here. Here, let's sit down."

She takes her cigarettes from her purse, offers me one. I accept it. She sits on Cayetana's tomb and makes a place for me.

"You think it's all right?" I ask timidly.

"Cayetana smoked twice as much as the two of us put together." She laughs, and adds, "And she wouldn't have minded if we sit on her grave. Besides, when I went with her to my grandmother Carlota's tomb, she sat on the ground and started talking to her. She said that's what we would have done if Carlota had been with us."

"Well, so how did you find her?"

"Let's review a minute. It's 1964. Cayetana goes off with her Guatemalan *guerrillero*, leaving her daughter with her legitimate father. Right? Together, they go off to the war. Cayetana is torn between her spirit of justice, her hatred of my father, and this daughter who's beginning to get in her way. She wants to be involved in the struggles for liberation—it's the sixties—but she also wants to have her daughter with her. Difficult, the two things at the same time. Rubén, the *guerrillero*, promises her things he doesn't follow through on."

"How do you know all this?"

"Bob and I came here together from Huatulco, Mexico. It was a secret trip. Eduardo never knew. Bob loved Antigua as much as I. He had studied Spanish here and his subject was Central America. It seemed monstrous to him that I had never found my mother's grave. And with his contacts, in those few days we were in Antigua he located a member of the Palma family. That person was out of town just then, but I came back to Chile with his name and address. It gave me the peace of mind to make long-range plans. While I was in jail, Bob wrote this man and told him my story. When I came to Antigua, the first thing I did was go see him."

"Who is he?"

"Emilio Palma, Rubén's brother. He's almost seventy today. If Rubén had lived, he would be sixty-five. And Cayetana sixty-two."

"Cayetana an old woman! I can't imagine it."

"No, that's the eternal spring of those who die young. Their images are frozen for all time. Deterioration and Cayetana are not compatible terms."

"Go on, then . . ."

"Emilio Palma. I knocked at his door one Friday afternoon. Bob was with me. Emilio lives in a very pretty house on Calle de los Duelos, almost on the outskirts of the city, behind the Hotel Santo Domingo. A maid came to the door. I asked her to tell him that I was the Chilean woman, Cayetana's daughter, and that I needed to speak with him. He sent me a note, after ten long minutes; he would receive me the next day, Saturday, at six P.M. He was correct; I didn't have any right to burst into his house the way I did, but I was burning with impatience. You know what I did? I went to one of those wonderful boutiques in Antigua and bought a cotton dress with a look of Charles Dickens, something a character in *Oliver Twist* might have worn. It was strange that at my age I would have picked out an orphan-girl dress to impress this gentleman who was the closest I had come to Cayetana.

"That Saturday, at exactly six o'clock, I walked through the gate of his colonial house. Alone.

"Emilio Palma was waiting for me. The same maid showed me to a large drawing room, very beautiful but a little overdone and dark for my taste. This man appeared. I was surprised by how tall he was. Why had I imagined he would be short? He had thick white hair and was wearing slacks and a well-cut white shirt. He emanated a refinement I hadn't expected.

" 'Violeta Dasinski?' His voice was measured.

" 'Don Emilio?'

" 'Emilio is enough; no *don*, please. Do you want to sit here, or would you prefer the gallery?'

" 'I would like the gallery, if you don't mind.'

" 'This way.'

"I followed him outside. At that moment another gentleman appeared; he, too, was good looking, a little younger, and he had a rather distinguished air. I was introduced.

" 'This is the daughter of my brother Rubén's Chilean comrade; I told you about her. This is Raúl Baeza, an architect who specializes in restoring houses and monuments in Antigua.'

"I commented, spontaneously, that I was an architect, too. I think this was an important element in the smooth progress of our meeting. I told him about my plan to buy a house and restore it. That interested him greatly, and he gave me various bits of information while Emilio watched us, delighted. We were served rum with ice and *limón,* the way they drink it here, and various fruit juices. After twenty minutes,

Raúl—who in fact did help with the restoration of the house and who is one of my few Guatemalan friends—got up, saying that he would leave us to our business. But by now the ice had been broken, and after he left I wasn't afraid any longer of facing Emilio Palma. I went right to the heart of the matter as soon as we were alone.

" 'You knew my mother?'

" 'Yes. Not very well, because she and my brother were usually in the country, in the villages. I was living then in Ciudad de Guatemala; I hadn't as yet inherited this house. But we met, right here in fact, in Antigua.'

" 'In this very house?' I could scarcely speak.

" 'Yes, in this very house, which she liked very much. But they didn't stay here, they joined some of Rubén's friends. He never seemed very interested in us. After all, his activities were clandestine, and attacked the customs of our family. You must realize that although Rubén's was not an isolated case—the same happened in many traditional families in Guatemala—my family never recovered from the stigma of having a *guerrillero* son.'

"I wanted to pay attention, but I was in a frenzy over the thought that Cayetana had been here in this house, maybe sitting on this same bench, facing the same gallery.

" 'When we received the news of his death, my parents went out to the country, into Quiché country, to take charge of the situation. They returned with two sealed coffins. Their humane gesture—they were very sensitive people—was to look after her. They didn't have the heart to abandon her without assurance that someone would come to get her. My father personally called her former husband in Chile; that must be your father, isn't it, my dear?'

" 'Yes.' I was relieved that he had begun to loosen up a little with me. After all, I was a kind of niece, wasn't I?

" 'Well,' Emilio continued, 'he arrived with a chip on his shoulder, and he gave everyone the impression that he was indifferent to the entire subject. That was why we determined to bury her here; your father was going to leave as soon as he had the certificates. They couldn't just leave the coffins waiting in the meantime.'

" 'How vicious,' I commented. I was inwardly raging, swept with waves of hatred for my father. 'Cayetana lost all her family in an earthquake in southern Chile, and her parents died the year she left for Central America. That's probably one of the reasons she left. There was no one in Chile to answer for her; only me, and I was still a child.'

" 'She told us about you.'

" 'Really?'

" 'They had a small discussion about that. She wanted to leave Quiché territory and move here to Antigua. I gathered from the discussion that Rubén had made promises he hadn't kept, and that she had had great expectations in regard to those promises. When I asked her why she wanted to live here, a place that was so dead in those years, she answered that she had a daughter and that her only wish was to bring her to Central America. It seemed to her that the tranquility of our city was ideal for you to grow up in. She wanted to leave the guerrilla war specifically to be reunited with her daughter. Rubén did not seem very understanding on that point.'

" 'What, in your opinion, would have happened if they hadn't died?' I dared ask.

" 'Who can say? Maybe their conflict would have intensified. I can't imagine Rubén's abandoning that struggle. He was a fanatic.'

" 'Like everyone in those years; you have to judge him in that context.' What was I doing defending Rubén Palma, the man who had stolen my mother away? I am totally mad, I told myself.

" 'Maybe she would have gone back to her country, or maybe they would have set up a kind of general headquarters here in Antigua, with Rubén coming and going. That might have been the most workable. She was a formidable woman. Not submissive or timid, like so many Guatemalan women. I remember I liked her strong presence, her ability to talk on any subject. She didn't give me the impression that she was entirely obsessed with the idea of the revolution . . . I would say, rather, she was more like a woman in love. She liked poetry. I am a poet, although I make my living as a physician. I remember we talked about Gabriela Mistral, about Neruda, César Vallejo, Rubén Darío. Your mother was no fool. And, I must tell you'—he looked at me with a certain tenderness—'Rubén loved her. My God, how he loved her! If you have ever lost any sleep over that, don't ever do so again. I am a man who is perceptive in matters of the heart, and although I saw Rubén very little during those years, I feel that he became more human. Something very decisive must have happened to him while he was with that woman. My mother analyzed it several times when we were together; I was the bachelor son who kept her company. At night she would talk about her beloved son—with my subsequent fits of jealousy. After all, I hadn't abandoned her, he had. But she adored him. My brother was very handsome. Did you meet him?'

" 'Yes, he came to our house once, our house in Chile. He was invited by my grandfather, who introduced him to Mama. I remember him perfectly. I was twelve, and I noticed how my mother looked at him. As a result, I looked at him, too. I remember those green eyes, like yours. He had beautiful eyes.'

"Emilio smiled, not without vanity.

" 'A little later I will show you photographs of him. Rubén, ever since devoting himself to politics, had never taken women seriously. He used them for his appetites, nothing more. His cause did not allow more. He never married or had children. Nor did I. Since the rest of our family were females, my mother was inconsolable: the family name would die out. When we learned that he was living with a Chilean woman, that he had actually brought her with him from Chile, we were very interested indeed. His lovers never lasted more than a month or two. My mother wanted to meet her.'

" 'And did she?'

" 'Yes, the same time I met her, here in this house.'

" 'And what did she think of her?'

" 'Since my mother took charge of her coffin, you may imagine she was not unimpressed. She hoped that this woman might lead her son to his senses. She was very happy to know that you existed, this girl who seemed so important to her mother, because that might be one way to lure the prodigal back home. She supported Cayetana in that little argument they had. Rubén was uncomfortable, I do remember that.'

"Emilio's words were like honey, balm, anaesthesia for all my stored-up misery! Finally someone was addressing the very fibers of my pain. Finally *someone* knew something about my mother's feelings.

"Suddenly I remembered the main reason for my visit.

" 'Where are they buried? I've looked for her grave in the cemetery, without any success.'

" 'Ah! The story of the mausoleum. Rubén is buried in the Palma family tomb. When they discussed the matter of where to bury Cayetana, there were different opinions. My father's won out: they were not married, there was no legal bond between them, it was not proper for her body to lie in the family mausoleum. So then he looked for the closest empty plot to ours in order to bury her in a separate niche. The problem was that because mine is an old family, our mausoleum was already surrounded by tombs. They found a small empty space between the Moreira and Fernández families. They bought the spot and built the tomb there for your mother. When it came time for the stonecutter to add the basic facts about her, no one knew how to find them. When had she been born? How could we find out, when we'd barely come up with her surname? Then my mother said: between the Moreira and Fernández families. Don't forget. I didn't forget.'

" 'You mean that my mother's grave is unmarked?'

" 'Yes.'

"There was a brief silence.

" 'Although my mother—may God hold her in His holy kingdom—had a romantic turn and wanted my father to bury them together, he objected. And his opinion was never questioned.'

" 'Please, I'm not asking for explanations. I'm just upset her name was never incised. I wore my eyes out looking on those tombs—there are so many of them! I would never have found her if you hadn't told me.'

" 'You're right about that.'

" 'One last thing.' It was getting late and courtesy demanded I leave. 'What did she die of?'

" 'Typhoid fever.'

" 'How do you know that, since the coffins were sealed?'

"He laughed. 'I can see you don't know this country. Do you think my parents were going to be satisfied with the government's version? Of course not. Through his influence, my father managed to have the coffins secretly opened. No. No gunshot wound. No aggression of any kind. It was in fact the damned fever. They were isolated in a peasant camp where there were no antibiotics, and were not treated in time. My father found those campesinos, going against everything the government had warned him of. Later they were wiped off the map, should you be tempted to look for them. But he, lord and master in his land, did whatever he pleased, and he found the peasants, going on descriptions Rubén's comrades had given him. The information is accurate. They were isolated; they had planned it that way as part of the strategy. No one had counted on that terrible microbe. Oh, one fact that may interest you, in case you are a romantic woman. Your mother was the first to get sick, and Rubén became ill nursing her. It was fast, so don't agonize over that. It wasn't a bad death, given the expectations my brother had. The one bad thing about that fever was that it robbed him of the opportunity to be a hero, to take his place beside all the Latin American heroes of those years.'

"I noted a light tone of sarcasm in his voice. Was he still jealous of his brother, after all these years?

"I got up discreetly, spoke the usual courteous phrases, such as thanking him for his time. I felt as if I had ascended and descended Mount Everest in one afternoon. Exhausted. Emotionally exhausted. I decided on the spot that the tomb would remain unmarked. It seemed absurd to add her name twenty-some years after the fact; it isn't as if Cayetana would have cared. As I was walking out the door, Emilio said, 'So you plan to stay in Antigua?'

" 'Yes.'

" 'Alone?'

" 'No, with a foreigner. And with my daughter, who will be arriving soon.'

"He looked at me with curiosity.

" 'Repeating your mother's story?'

" 'No. Well, close.' "

# 12

$\mathcal{V}$ioleta periodically went to San Antonio Aguas Calientes. I wanted to go with her today, as I want to go everywhere she does. In addition to my interest in getting to know the place, being with her gives me a peace I've never known, as if in forging a bond with Violeta I was forming myself.

The first thing we came across leaving Antigua was an enormous Nestlé plant.

"Nothing escapes today's globalization," she commented. "In the middle of this colonial ambience, the first thing you notice driving into the city from the opposite direction is that unbearable sweetish, butterish odor from Nestlé."

We turned onto a small dirt road, impressively green, entirely surrounded with coffee plantations. When I first saw them, I was surprised to learn that the coffee "trees" were those shrubs beneath the taller trees planted to protect the harvest. Then ten kilometers later, in which the only danger had been the crammed buses racing along at demonic speed, we drove through a miserable little village called San Lorenzo. Terraced land, houses with medlar trees, palms, and orange trees. Everything else was huts, poverty, and dirt.

"This is where I planned to stay when I first came to this country," Violeta says.

I am surprised. "What could draw you to a place like this?"

"Because it was pure *nada*. Nothingness. The last hiding place in the world, the most lost, most alien, most inaccessible of places. Its very misery attracted me, like an expiation. I was so low, Josefa, so lost, that burying myself in this geography seemed a way to survive. Every time I come to San Antonio Aguas Calientes, I have to drive through San Lorenzo. And still today, after all this time, I tremble a little when I remember. How strong the pull of *nada* must have been for me to have wanted to lose myself here!"

I recalled a friend who was sick with guilt for having left his wife, whom he didn't love, who, although he was able to pay for the best apartment, chose after he left home to live in a basement room filled with cockroaches.

"And did you try it?"

"Bob stopped me. He proposed that I build the most civilized life I could while trying never to hurt anyone. That was our motto."

"Are you in love, Violeta?"

"Oh, yes. Absolutely, *yes*."

"I can't believe it! Someone over twenty who still says she's in love."

"Do you know, Jose, the real value of our relationship? When I came here, I didn't want to deny the differences between men and women, those things we both know about, those things we can't squint at. All I wanted was a new way to deal with those differences. And Bob understood my eagerness to replace fear with understanding. I suspect that we have a pretty even balance between passion and esteem."

"You're very lucky . . ."

Violeta ignores my bitterness; I know she is doing it on purpose.

"You see, we met at a point in life, right in the middle, when we were on the way to becoming skeptics, or disbelievers. We restored faith to one another. And what best describes our present situation is that we complete one another."

I sit meditating on the business of completing another person. I like the concept. I think that in fact that had once been true of Andrés and me. Why wasn't it now?

I am distracted by an enormous sign—almost elegant in these surroundings—with facts about the town: 10,000 INHABITANTS; FOUNDED IN 1528; LANGUAGE, KAQCHIQEL . . . I point to it.

"Of course, this road was constructed in the eighties," Violeta says, "when all of Central America was ablaze with *guerrillero* movements. That crisis was the argument for upping North American aid to this country. But I'll bet you that the officials of the aid agency that came to San Antonio Aguas Calientes limited its contribution to these hundreds of meters of paving stones and that enormous sign with its useless facts. Since then, the inhabitants of San Antonio have continued to live in their usual poverty, and since the majority of them are illiterate, they've never even been able to read what the sign says."

"And those small buses I've seen everywhere in Antigua, the yellow ones that say 'School Bus'? Are they part of the aid plan?"

"They must be; I guess they forgot to paint over the English."

The road became more and more twisting, and at any one of the curves I could see the town in the ravine down below, set at the foot of a chain of hills and verdant, tree-covered volcanoes that made me think of the nearly always dry mountains and the high and untouchable clouds of my homeland. Here the clouds hung low, right across the road. And here in one hour they receive the rainfall my country accumulates in a year's time.

We drive past the plaza and the market and turn onto a very poor dirt street. Violeta parks the car in front of a small patio filled with trees and palms. It is surrounded by protective cane reinforced with adobe. A woman comes out to welcome us. This is Anacleta, the mother of Tierna, who cleans for Violeta. She is thick-bodied and old-looking, with few remaining teeth; she is wearing a beautiful garment of different cloths and embroideries. (She is younger than we are, Violeta will tell me later.)

I watch them both; their manner is that of old friends. Anacleta invites us in.

"Just there to the right."

The three of us take a seat in a kind of patio. I try to look into the dwelling but see very little; it is very dark inside.

Violeta asks Anacleta if her other daughter, Irla, can come to us for a few days; more guests are coming and Tierna cannot handle so much work.

"She is silent these days," was Irla's mother's comment. Sure enough, when she came home with us, we didn't hear a word from her all the way home. And I think if I ever write a song again, I will call it that: *Silent*.

Violeta and Anacleta are going through a pile of embroideries. Violeta takes a few notes. For some reason I cannot decipher, the scene moves me.

"Look, Josefa," Violeta calls to me, and holds out a *huipil* to show me, the traditional tunic Indian women wear. "I want you to recognize the different patterns of the embroidery."

"Patterns?"

"Or borders, or stitches. This is a *huipil* from San Pedro."

Anacleta intervenes, and with her thick finger points out each new line of stitchery. Since they fit together so well, I hadn't noticed that in fact they can be separated, row by row.

"This is *dog's foot*," she tells me. "The next one is *the comb;* the third is *roses*," and her finger runs carefully along each one. "This is *chocolate*, this *the seed*, and it ends with *the scissors*. It's done with a silky thread, so this one costs more."

I take it in my hands, and sink into those colors. They flood through my eyes and soon my senses are drenched.

When we are on our way back, laden with thread, yarns, and cloth—in addition to Irla—I ask Violeta about her new craft.

"I have the strange sensation that I've been a tapestry maker since I was born. It's come with such naturalness and ease, with such *rightness* . . . It's as if I had disguised myself as an architect for many years, only to wait for the tapestry side of me to emerge."

The word "emerge" startles me. For some reason I associate it with my nausea. Last night, nearly crazed, I called Pamela's house. She answered, half asleep; she laughed when she heard the silence on the line, and hung up. That laugh . . . she's happy . . . she's with Andrés. I tremble, I get a flash of Andrés, naked in the bed in the mill house, opening his arms to me. The nausea turns into vomiting. I throw up as if emptying myself of all my history, everything . . . Enough! Violeta's tapestries interest me more than all this shit oozing out of me.

"When, Violeta? When did you suspect? It's more than changing professions. You were so serious about your architecture."

"It was in the solitude of my cell. From staring at my hands so long, I realized they could be of use. It had to be in that lonely time, Jose, when for hours I stared at them, bone by bone, every centimeter of flesh. Only then did I know them, know what they could do, what they wanted to do."

Violeta has no idea where her tapestries are going to end up when they are sent to New York, nor does she lose any sleep over it. She knows they have a destination, that they are not mere visual games for her own complacency, and that strips them of abstraction, makes them more valid in her eyes. When checks in dollars arrive, she looks at the hanks of thread and accurately calls her pieces "work."

"But, Violeta, do you have fun with your tapestries?"

"That's a strange question, Jose. Didn't we promise each other years ago that we would never do anything that wasn't entertaining?

Believe me, they give me pleasure. But when pleasure is paid for, it passes automatically to the category of work."

How well I know her. She answers as if she were following my line of thought. "You're so puritanical! Then you think it's legitimized, is that it?"

She laughs as if she'd been caught in something naughty. I am back in the present, the pain has receded, peace returned. Violeta turns serious, with this new air of serenity that seems never to leave her.

"I want time, Jose, I want time. At first I dreamed that I could embroider because of others, for others, and not just my personal pleasure. The experience of being accepted and distributed showed me that in fact that I wasn't doing it just for myself. And the dimensions of what I was doing broadened. It was the work that was making me an artist.

I know what she is trying to tell me: work is the only thing that reduces anxiety, the one thing that gives you the distance you must have to face the outside world. And I can't, I don't want to work. Then I am filled with envy, and rage against myself; I tell myself all is lost. But Violeta doesn't feel that way; her last words are optimistic, even jubilant.

"It's the joy, Josefa, the joy that no one knows better than you! My tapestries are like your songs. We are two privileged women! Do you realize how much passion we put into what we do? And we both know very well that *passion* is what generates energy. We are blessed!"

# 13

"Some women really hate men!" I look back over my shoulder to speak to Violeta.

We are walking single file because the sidewalks are so narrow.

"Are you talking about my friend Barbara?"

"Yes, she made quite an impression."

"Well, she has good arguments. At any rate, she has the theory that four thousand years ago men discovered that women were definitely superior, and that was when they stepped on them, terrified they would be eaten alive. She believes that the eternal history of abuse and discrimination is owing to the deep hatred men feel for these beings they fear, that they could awaken somewhere, rise up, and crush them. That is, the all-too-familiar theory of threat."

I'm uncomfortable trying to have a conversation while I keep looking back.

"Is there some place near where we can get a good cup of coffee?"

"We're almost at the Doña Luisa; let's go by there and we'll buy some sweets on the way. You have to know Doña María Gordillo's shop, it's one of the high spots of Antigua. I want you to eat a *chimbo* egg; they're made from a recipe that goes back to the time of the colony."

We find a seat in the Doña Luisa. The place is filled with foreign women with light hair and eyes and exotic hats. There is no room on the wall for another single notice: from houses for rent to classes in anything conceivable. We have with us our box of María Gordillo's candies: caramel, marzipan; *chimbo* eggs, crystallized guava, and several other delicacies. We order our coffees.

Today I had met Barbara, one of Violeta's two friends in Antigua. She has lived here six years. She is Canadian. Fleshy, voluptuous, she has warm eyes and a ready laugh.

"How did she come to live here?" I ask Violeta.

"She was working in theater, in Toronto. One day her closest friend got a divorce, and to get away from that painful process decided to go to Mexico. She stopped in Isla Mujeres, and from there called Barbara. 'Come on down,' she told her. 'I'm building a house with my own hands.' Barbara, who at that moment was 'fresh out of ideas,' as she put it, sold everything she had and left Toronto behind. They lived six months on the island, in the most primitive conditions. When their visas expired and they had to go back across the border and re-enter, they decided to come to Antigua to learn Spanish and support themselves teaching English. They stayed a couple of months. The day before they left, as Barbara was rather reluctantly packing her suitcases, they learned that a hurricane had lashed Isla Mujeres and leveled their flimsily constructed house."

"And they stayed here?"

"Yes. Barbara opened a clothing store that over time evolved into the sophisticated boutique you saw today. She combines native materials with her original European designs. Things began to go well for her, and today she exports her clothes to Japan and the United States."

"Does she live alone?"

"Yes, with two cats, one of whom is going to have kittens. She just introduced the first male component into her household: a dog."

"Why can Canadian women do this and we can't?"

"Because we have a strange sense of our roots. But the point isn't whether one is Chilean or Canadian. The point is options," Violeta answers, playing with her *piedra cruz* ring.

"What do you mean?"

"Barbara didn't opt for either marriage or motherhood. That's what gives her that air of freedom you notice in her."

"I could never live that way. There's Santiago, my mother, Andrés, the children . . . Everything ties me down, pulls at me, strangles me. Why the hell wasn't I born in Canada?"

"Even if you had been . . ." Violeta laughs at me.

I order a second coffee, mulling over the idea of my roots, with overt envy of people like Barbara, of everyone different from myself.

"Besides Barbara and Monica, your Argentine friend, do you have any strictly Antigueña friends?"

"No."

"Why?" I can't stop asking her questions, impatient to understand life in this city. You learn about life as you live it, Andrés would have told me. But I want to know in advance.

"Because three strata co-exist in Antigua: the native-born Antigueños, the foreigners, and the Indians. Those are three distinct worlds with very little interchange among them."

"And the Antigueños?"

"They've been here forever; there are families that refused to move even after the earthquake of 1773. They live in those large, walled houses, their whole lives turned inward."

"They're in luck! They probably don't have a notion of what neurosis is."

"Don't you believe it, and they're damned boring. The inside of their houses is the core of their activities. The children do all their pre-college work here, and when they do go to the university—if they go at all—they study in Ciudad de Guatemala."

"Like Jacinta."

"You see? The women our age aren't professionals, none of them. Their destiny has been utterly traditional: they marry young, have a husband, a house, and children, and devote themselves to that. They are a closed society, and aren't noted for their intellectual curiosity."

"That's true anywhere in the provinces . . ."

"Jacinta tells me that in their houses—I've scarcely been inside one—there aren't any books. In Antigua itself the book business is almost nonexistent; all we have are a few secondhand book stores run by North Americans. Can you imagine the hunger?"

"I'm not surprised. And I don't think that's only because Antigua is in the provinces. A friend of mine who's a photographer was asked to photograph the most beautiful and expensive houses in Santiago for an architectural magazine. He poked into every corner of those houses, looking for the best angles. When he was through, he was scandalized: there wasn't a single book in all those wonderful houses. Not one."

"Where do they get their ideas, do you suppose?" Violeta asks, very serious.

"And where do they get their pleasure, that's what I want to know. And you, how do you manage?"

"Well, for one thing it helps to have a father who has a bookstore. He sends books to Ciudad de Guatemala, to Bob's post office box. You can't count on the mail here in Antigua. Other than that, I rely on Bob's subscriptions to things like *The New York Review of Books*, and when he goes to the States, or his friends come here, I put in orders. I supply books to a large sector of the foreign colony; mine are always on loan."

"Why are there so many foreigners here?"

"Because of the language schools. Look, out of the thirty thousand inhabitants in Antigua, foreigners make up at least ten thousand. They're not always permanent, it's a floating population. Of all this part of the continent, Antigua has the most organized system of teaching Spanish. There are some eighty schools in this city! Most with very personalized instruction. There's no shortage of women who, even though they aren't teachers, take that job in order to marry a gringo: that's the primary goal of Antigua's girls."

"But there are foreigners like yourself, aren't there, who don't have anything to do with teaching Spanish?"

"Yes, but most are people who came to study—North Americans, Swedes, Norwegians—fell in love with the place, and didn't go back. Antigua is magic, Jose. They can't help coming back, and they end up staying here. I have one friend, Elizabeth, whose father brought her here to live when she was fourteen, at the end of the sixties, when this was the end of the world. He came from the United States to write an article, fell in love with it, and never left. The truth is that anything sophisticated—the restaurants and studios of the city—we owe in large measure to the foreigners who have loved the place."

"It must be a thrill to live in a city that is the patrimony of humanity. I would feel very important."

Violeta smiles.

"But you're one of the group that influences life and culture in the city, aren't you?"

"Well, yes . . . You'll never see the Guatemalans who live in the capital and come here for the weekend, nor run into them at any event. They don't come to our galleries or our cafés. We live in parallel worlds that never meet."

"And the two never clash?"

"Never!" she exclaims emphatically. "The people of this country are the most amiable in the world, as you will have noticed. And Antigua is a city with zero aggressiveness, quintessentially peaceful. It must be one of the least violent places in the world, and that's nothing to sniff at these days."

"Knowing you, that must have been key in your decision to live here."

"It was. Would you believe that not even politics penetrates here? Not the guerrilla war, not coups . . . nothing. The Antigueños know there's a President of the Republic only because those presidents have weekend houses here, and when they come you see soldiers around in the streets—that's the only reason."

"It gives me the impression of great isolation, a place frozen in time."

"It is. Time stopped centuries ago in Antigua. That's part of its beauty. It is a city that watches people come, live, and leave."

"But that's sad."

"No. Not if you have what you love around you. When things are serene inside you, it doesn't matter that others leave."

I feel I hate her a little. How can she be so sure? Does she really believe she has solved everything? Does she forget she murdered a man?

"I don't have much to do with the outside world," she continues ingenuously, untouched by my evil thoughts. "Just what's indispensable to keep me from feeling like a wolf from the Russian steppes. I live like an Antigueña woman: my house is the center of my life, I spend a major portion of my time there. For my mental health, I go to the capital once a week. And at least once a year I travel out of the country."

"It's a different sense of time, isn't it?"

"I don't keep an appointment book. That explains everything, doesn't it?"

"But, Violeta, how can a human being in the twentieth century live without an agenda?" I ask, horrified.

"I'm not sure I am living in this century."

"You have a telephone, a television, even cable; Bob has his computer and his fax . . ."

"Agreed; we take advantage of end-of-the-century electronic toys in order not to have to live in it entirely."

"Do you consider life lived this way is more worthwhile?"

Violeta hears something in my voice.

"I'm not criticizing you, Josefa. I'm not saying that one option is better than another. This is what I needed, you know that. I have spent my life looking for coherence in the way I live, and I feel I've found it. There are thousands of possible options."


We go home. Violeta still had something stuck crossways in that bundle of live matter that is her mind. I know her. It would come out at the hour for rum.

In the meantime, I lie down upon my Spanish relic and picture someone I know: a square chin, strong hands lacking the pianist's fingers I would have chosen, a chest with just enough hair for me to rest my cheek on, hard thighs and strong, well-proven legs, a penis peaceful when resting, crazed when primed. Does anyone know that body as I do? His ex-wife . . . No, she didn't know every inch of him, not that way, did she? Maybe she did. The two of them in bed; it's insufferable to share a body, even in different time periods. Little by little the insecurity begins to creep in, a tiny suspicion about the person I am, about my erotic performance. Does the woman exist who can honestly say she feels spectacular in bed? Well, time leaves its mark. It wasn't the same eight years ago, or ten, when Andrés reacted simply by putting his hand on my back. Had his eros been reactivated touching Pamela's?

I have a second memory, a body memory. Desire: the most irrational and irrepressible of impulses. And how frightening it is to come to the moment that cannot be suborned: the depletion of desire. Maybe at one point we begin to ask little of each other, after having believed in that impulse for so long. I must irrigate the dead zones of love and eroticism; that will be my task if he will give me the chance. But there is one thing that, fatigue or no fatigue, cannot go unnoticed: we always *feel*.

Who will win this battle? Who will end up with the shining trophy, as I was taught as a little girl? She, present, or me, absent? The void is not advancing toward me anymore, as it was in Santiago; at least I have won that much. And that's no little thing, according to Violeta. She's betting on the best of Andrés, that is, on the happy ending. But only if I stop being the impossible woman I've been all these years. At any rate, Andrés has nothing to do with that. If something important is happening to me, it is that, win or lose, I must leave that woman behind for my own sake, not for his.

The sun has gone into hiding. Now the spirit rests.

The hour for rum arrives. Violeta seldom eats pistachios anymore, they're hard to get. She has given them up for cashew nuts, which are sold, very fresh, delicious, though not cheap, on a corner of the plaza. She serves them with drinks in the late afternoon, on the gallery. They are a vice; you try one and you can't stop.

Violeta holds the glass of rum near her face, and they are one color.

"I want to tell you a story."

"Go ahead."

"My old friend, Ernesto Martínez, came through Antigua. You know who he is; he's a man who has bled in his quest for power. When the democracy came in, he was appointed to nearly every post, and now he is a senator. From all appearances, a story of pure success: first, getting ahead inside his party, then, outside it, among the region's voters. His last campaign was difficult, he told me, and the election very close. But despite unfavorable predictions, he won."

"I remember something about it, he was supposed to lose."

"The interesting thing, Jose, is that he confessed to me that on the night of his victory, at four in the morning, and by then in bed, he was gripped by the most ferocious emptiness. He didn't know what to do with himself. He tried desperately to rationalize the meaning of that feeling. He, who was already quite familiar with the reality of power. And its relativity."

"Did he talk to you, too, about his appetite for power?"

"It was more about the changes in politics in this new world of trade-offs and consensus, in this new formula of pure image and a dearth of ideas."

"Well, my impression is that true power is based in private enterprise and in the communication media. I say that intuitively, not knowing much about it."

"You always have understood more than you appear to," Violeta comments with irony. "But what surprises me, Josefa, is that the one question he asked himself the night of his triumph, lying in his bed at four in the morning, was, What do I do to lead a worthy life? That was his obsession."

"I find that surprising in him. He seems so ambitious."

"Well, the way that Ernesto finds to live worthily will not, obviously, be by leaving the world to come live a bucolic life on a plain in Central America. Nor is he going to enter a monastery. He will see how to do it; he will resolve the dilemma in his own way."

"Why the hell doesn't he devote himself to the poor? That would be a worthwhile project for a politician."

"Each of us will learn what his way is. The important thing is to learn in time. You will find yours, and I won't discredit your choice, nor you mine. Isn't that right?"

I nod. I know why she's told me about her friend the senator. I know why she told *me*.

"Well," Violeta sighs, "we already know we can't change the world, that's for sure. That has been the unkindest cut of all for our generation. Our goal disappeared when we were halfway along the road, when we were still of an age and energy to effect transformations. Politics today isn't the old politics. Today it's power for power's sake, with a few individual characteristics depending on the group, but with no substantial differences among them. Which means that the only thing left for persons like Ernesto is to ask himself humbly, Where do I find dignity? And to cling to that, if there is nothing else to cling to."

Violeta and I look at each other. We measure one another, recognize, evaluate, appraise one another. And I choose to clear the air.

"And the Last Forest, Violeta? What happened to that?"

"It is my dream, my welcoming Utopia. I believe, Josefa, that it's in the Last Forest that one finds dignity. And that those forests are not far from here."

# 14

*W*alking a few steps toward the church and convent of Santa Clara is synonymous with certain moments. For one *quetzal*, I have hours of retreat and silence in my refuge: the garden behind the home of the Clarisa nuns. I breathe deeply beneath the shade of six large acacia trees. ("Violeta, did you know there are acacias in the ruins of Santa Clara?" "Yes, I know them." "All you need is your hammock. What did you do with it?" "I brought it in the shipping container; I have it; I think I'll put it up on the *azotea*.") I become friends with the medlar tree and the palms, and sit on the large stones.

My mind travels back toward the end of the 1600s. I try to imagine the first Clarisa nuns to have arrived from Puebla. What were they like? What would they have eaten? At least they wouldn't have been cold, a great gift of this city. How generous these enormous cloisters and fountains can be without cold! Did they come out of love for

God or because their families made them? Or was it because of an unfortunate love affair? I concentrate on the last, in order to identify with them.

Almost no one comes here; maybe some tourists wandering through the ruins, but I don't see them or hear them. Again I breathe in. But this time it is the abyss. Because every breath is agony when the images flash into my mind: those images. The sunglasses in Andrés's car. They were a woman's. From *Ted Lapidus*. What were they doing there? Does Pamela wear *Ted Lapidus?* No, I would remember; they were handsome glasses and I would have noticed. Those sunglasses haunt me.

I can't stay calm. I walk toward the entrance of Santa Clara. Just across from it are the public wash-troughs, the enormous pool of mossy green water, and the impeccable order of each of the stone receptacles for Indians to do their dirty wash. I am fascinated by the perfect distribution of the stone in each unit. A woman is busy at her chore. I watch her. She is talking to her little girl as she scrubs each piece. She laughs, and I see she has only two teeth, enormous, long, as if about to leap from her mouth. She splashes water with her hand— beside her, another Indian is washing her hair—and repeats the same motion to wet and rinse her laundry. From one wash-trough to the next, I recognize that coffee-colored soap I saw in the market; it looked like rocks. It's for lice, Violeta told me. (In my country there are lice even in the private schools, but it is not acknowledged, and soap to kill them isn't sold in the stores.) I am mesmerized by her movements. No scrub brush, just her hand. And my history as a singer betrays me, because without summoning her, without inviting her, Violeta Parra comes to me, and this silent voice begins to sing, as when Violeta and I sang together at the university: *Here come I with my basket/ of sorrows to wash by the stream of lost memories/ let me, please let me, pass by./ I am the simple washerwoman, I spend all day at my task,/ love is a stain you can't get out without pain/ sweet moon, bright moon, keep shining down on me*. I begin to cry. A slow, absurd weeping. No, I can't keep crying, I tell myself angrily: I am strong, self-sufficient, independent, I repeat, and the words cascade into the water, empty. My tears mix with the water for the wash-troughs. I put my hand into the stone basin, and splash my eyes. The Indian woman looks at me, and I look back at her. Again I dip my hands into that green water, and she keeps watching me.


July Fourth, Independence Day in the United States. A day like any other.

I walk to the plaza. It's jam packed, what is going on? Why are there so many people? The lines at Guatel, the telephone company, and the Banco del Agro where I change my dollars, reach out into the street. The sidewalks are filled with colorful trinkets for sale. I move toward the phone company; maybe I can call Andrés from there and talk with him, certain that no one is listening. The line is enormous; at the same window where you place international calls, people are paying their bills and their local calls. Why don't they have separate windows for the two functions? I will wait a while in the plaza.

I choose a bench near the central fountain. I listen to the running water. I rest. I am always exhausted. I watch the little native girls (they're not *natives*, they're *Indians*, Violeta would correct me; calling them *natives* must be politically incorrect). They walk past me with their enormous baskets on their heads, never touching them with their hands, beautifully erect. I observe the perfect line of neck and back. How do they do it? They're only children, so tiny. "They know how because they've been doing it for five thousand years," Violeta told me yesterday. "You and I would spill the whole mess."

I watch a tourist with a huge belly and skinny legs; he's wearing shorts, a skin-tight T-shirt, and white athletic socks, and his minuscule feet are shod in very proper black business oxfords. He is trying to take a picture of his wife. "More toward the middle," he tells her, but the woman doesn't move far enough, she's a little self-conscious. More toward the middle, he repeats, obsessed with establishing a perfect symmetry between her and the fountain. My God, how can someone marry a man like that, bind her life to a man who brings those feet and legs with him? "Oh, bellies are much worse," Violeta would argue. "You know you have a fetish about legs." No, I answer mentally, a man's belly is horrible, I agree, but in the long run, I can take that. What I can't stomach is this: have you ever seen anything less masculine than those legs? Skinny, hairy, and those pristine white socks and little black shoes. I imagine him naked, wearing those socks, the very worst situation a man can be found in. God, how unsexy! What will Bob look like?

As I start to picture Andrés's legs, remember every line of them, and suffer, I am distracted by a bird: it lights in the tree nearest me. It is blue. Its throat and head jet black. Everything else completely blue. What a beautiful bird. Where did it come from? It isn't that brilliant blue you see in some books. No. A dark, oily blue. I've never seen a bird like this.

I go back to Guatel. The line is even longer. I am trying to make a decision when an Indian woman sitting on the sidewalk before her merchandise, very close to where I'm standing, calls to me: "Eh, you . . ."

I am startled. Anything unexpected that involves another human being, especially if it's on the street, frightens me.

"Me?"

"Yes, you . . ."

She says something I can't understand. I never understand much of what they say, their Spanish is strange. She is saying something about a man. I turn; a brown-haired tourist is standing beside me. Is she referring to him? Or to Andrés? But what does this woman have to do with Andrés? I must be crazy. Although maybe she's some kind of witch and she's handing me a prophecy.

"What? I don't understand, will you repeat it?"

"If you give me a *quetzal*." This I understand immediately. I hesitate. Should I fall in with her game, or move on? Intrigued, I take a *quetzal* from my purse and hand it to her. This time her words are clear: "The brown-haired man does not belong to you . . . but he depends on you."

"What brown-haired man?"

She doesn't answer. She just sits, totally mute.

"I don't understand," I tell her.

"Buy a *huipil* from me," is her answer.

I leave there disturbed. Forget Guatel. I'm sweating. It's hot, as always, but that doesn't justify my agitation. I walk toward the Calle de los Peregrinos. The brown-haired man . . . Andrés isn't mine, Andrés isn't mine. I am wildly thirsty. I stop at a small café and order a melon squeeze. The café TV is tuned to a soccer match. Brazil against the United States. Yes, I had heard Violeta this morning saying how happy she was that Bob would see the game at home, since she couldn't help being for Brazil. She is always for the Latin Americans. "Imagine," she'd said, "if the U.S. beats Brazil on the Fourth of July. What that would be like!"

Too bad that the time of my trip coincided with the World Cup. Andrés will scarcely notice my absence. I look at the men in the café. Brazil scores the only goal in the match at twenty minutes into the second period. The Guatemalans are hopping up and down with joy, everyone is applauding. Who said that anti-imperialism is old hat?

The Fourth of July, I think as I turn onto Calle de los Peregrinos.

*"Why is it that so many more words have been said about Abraham Lincoln than about any other American?"* Dressed all in pink like a sugar plum, big sash, white shoes, the microphone. The whole

school, students and teachers, in the auditorium, listening to the main speech. And Violeta, in the row of the chorus, reciting with me to herself. The Fourth of July, also a holiday in the school, the student assembly under the direction of the nun who teaches the Glee Club. While the chorus sang the last lines . . . *"while the sun keeps music . . . in my old Kentucky home . . . far away . . ."* I walked onto the stage. *"Why is it . . ."* During rehearsals I was numb with anxiety when the moment came I was supposed to begin. I was thirteen, and still unaware of the concept of stage fright. Then, in rehearsals, Violeta started with me in a low voice; she had studied my speech, learned it with me, and knew it by heart. She did it to convince me that I could do it, to force me to overcome my reluctance to be heard by the whole school. "If you get nervous and forget where you are, I'll whisper it to you. I'll be reciting with you." And when the day came, I walked up to the microphone and couldn't speak; nothing came out. I looked at that huge audience in front of me and my stomach felt hollow. Until, unable to tell from where in that moment of confusion, I heard Violeta's voice, slow, but strong enough to reach me: *"Why is it that so many more words have been said . . ."* Then I could do it. I raised my voice, strong and clear, and recited. I performed my speech to perfection, and when the audience burst into applause, I liked it. I felt a strange vertigo . . . Oh, how I liked it! I had no way to suspect then the number of stages I would climb onto later in life, or how much I would need that vertigo in order to feel alive. And how I would struggle each time—infallibly, each time—to overcome that panic.

And so the first sentence of my speech on Abraham Lincoln came to be a kind of sorcery between Violeta and me: my first radio audition, the first time I sang on stage at the university, the first time I was on television. Violeta, always accompanying me—except that crucial day I won the Festival of Song. And at the moment I began, she would manage to be close by, where my eyes could meet hers, and I recited, almost to myself: *"Why is it that so many more words have been said about Abraham Lincoln than about any other American?"*

The Fourth of July.

A new storm is brewing in Antigua. I walk faster.

# 15

*V*ioleta brings me a cup of coffee in bed. Now with the caffeine in my body I am capable of life. I get up, put on my bathrobe, and go to the kitchen, where all kinds of temptations are laid out for everyone's breakfast. Fruit, steaming coffee, freshly baked bread, toast, cereal, yogurt, marmalade, and eggs. Absent-mindedly, I try a taste of marmalade. "It's *sauco*, elderberry," Violeta tells me. "It grows well here." I taste the pleasing combination of acidity and sweetness, remembering the cranberries at the mill house; the jar is the same, so is the ambience. I choose a mango yogurt and pick up a pitahaya from the tray. I have chosen this fruit for its looks. It could be an illustration for a story; its tough skin looks like a reddish artichoke. It is a fiery red at the heart, turning to brilliant fuchsia lines speckled with coal-black seeds. One of Rufino Tamayo's watermelon paintings would pale beside this beauty. ("Have you ever used them in one of your tapestries?" "No," Violeta answers. "Not yet." "Oh, please do; this fruit is unique, Violeta, you have to *use* it!")

The large table in the kitchen accommodates everyone who comes to eat. I am always the last. The kitchen itself is square; the middle of the ceiling opens into a large brick tower with small skylights to let in light. The walls are covered with painted tiles. ("Large and square; you didn't have to have a reincarnation, Violeta, to get your square kitchen!" "I don't? You don't take my death and resurrection seriously?")

During breakfast the day's activities are discussed. Violeta talked with Bob last night, who will be arriving in three days with his son Alan. "Do you know why his name is Alan?" Jacinta asks me. "Because his mother is a fan of Alan Bates." Borja solemnly announces the matches scheduled for today. Rumania against Germany. The discussion begins about whom we want to win. Jacinta says she can't stand the Germans. I say I hate Rumanians. "Why?" everyone asks, surprised. "It's Violeta's fault," I answer.

"Tell them," Violeta urges.

"Yeah, tell us, Mama," Borja begs.

"It happened during that revolutionary period in our country, many, many years ago. Violeta wanted nothing so much as to lure me into her activities, which, I scarcely need say, didn't interest me. To indoctrinate me, she got me—as if it were a big deal—an invitation to Rumania. I was studying music at the university, and the invitation was to learn how Rumanian schools of music were being run at the time. I felt I had to accept, Violeta had worked so hard with her friends and with the embassy. I went. My stay there is a whole other story; I'll tell you that another time. But my hatred of Rumania began after I was back in Chile. A few days after my return, I receive a notice from customs to pick up a package. What could it be? I set off enthusiastically; I'd never received anything from another country. 'It's a record,' the official tells me. 'You have to pay the duty to claim it.' It wasn't all that cheap. I pay for it: it was a government propaganda record, specifically, Ceausescu's speeches with accompanying translations. Ye gods, was my reflection, that cost me; but even so, I was thrilled that someone had remembered me. The next week, another notice from customs. A second record. Again I pay the duty, this time I'm a little annoyed. The following week the story is repeated; I go to customs and I pay, openly angry. The label says *Number 3*. Alarmed, I check and find that the earlier records were numbered *1* and *2*. My God, how many are there? When the fourth notice comes from customs, I don't go to pick it up. They call me after a few days and explain that it is my obligation; if I leave it there I will have to pay a fine. Bottom line: there are ten records. The whole collection of the Rumanian process, with hundreds of speeches by Ceausescu translated into Spanish. That period in my life I call 'the era of the Rumanian records.' "

Violeta and the children were laughing when the kitchen door opened. I didn't even look, thinking it was Tierna. Violeta's expression changes; she gets up from her chair. I turn and see a man embracing my friend. No, it isn't Bob; in photographs Bob is blond. This is a dark-haired man, apparently Latin, tall, fortyish, with a few gray threads in hair combed straight back into a ponytail.

"Javier!" Violeta sounds very pleased.

"I apologize for the interruption, I see you're still having breakfast."

"When did you get here?"

"Last night. I couldn't resist coming straight over."

"Where are you staying? Will you sleep here?"

"No, I'm at the Santo Domingo."

"But . . . why did you go to a hotel?"

"Well, the magazine is paying. And I have to work. If I stayed here, I wouldn't get anything done. And how is the princess?" he asks, hugging Jacinta.

I tried to identify his accent. Mexican? Guatemalan? I get them mixed up.

"Javier, I want you to meet Josefa Ferrer. Besides being a singer, she's my lifelong friend. She's come to get a good rest. Josefa, this is Javier Godínez, from Mexico; he's kind of a brother of Bob's, they were classmates at Harvard."

"Josefa Ferrer? But what a privilege!"

As he comes to shake hands, I think about my hair, my less than elegant bathrobe, my still-asleep face. This doesn't seem the best moment to be introduced to anyone. I say an off-hand "hi," and finish my yogurt.

"Sheesh, but my mother's famous!" Borja comments. "They even know her here."

"I came in on the middle of something," Javier says. "What was it?"

"The Rumanian records," Jacinta answers.

"What is that? Some new rock group?"

Violeta tells the story, repeating every detail, and there I sit, feeling like a fool. Javier is amused by the descriptions and looks at me differently; he seems to see me as me, not the singer.

"Later I'll tell you a couple of stories about the Soviet Union during those same times; believe me, you will find them funny," he says, speaking to me.

"Then you've been in that part of the world, too?"

"In our generation, is there any intellectual worth his salt who hasn't had some experience with socialism?"

So, right away I know that we are of the same generation, that in fact he is an intellectual, and, if he's close to Bob, one of some importance. And it's likely we'll get along. But just the same, I get up to go shower.

"What time will you all be ready to do something?"

"Josefa is free, and I will be at lunch time." Violeta is probably thinking that maybe this man will take me off her hands for a while.

"You want to come with me, Josefa? Have you visited the convent of the Capuchins?"

"No, not yet."

"And have you had coffee at the Opera?"

"Not that, either."

"Or visited El Sitio gallery?"

I laughed with embarrassment.

"No, I haven't."

He looks at Violeta, amused.

"What have you been doing with your friend. Had her locked up?"

"You two go," Violeta suggests, content, "and we'll meet for lunch at the Café del Conde. I have a taste for some of that cornmeal bread and a basil quiche."

When I got out of the shower I surprised myself by looking for some "outfit." Until that moment I hadn't been out of my jeans, thinking that part of the restorative process of this trip was not to get dressed, or even think about it. I found an ankle-length lilac cotton dress—something I'd bought right there in Antigua—and added a sleeveless silk vest, as Celeste might have done. It looked good, and gave me a youngish look. As I was dressing and the mirror was insisting on reflecting this body I love so little, I thought with envy of persons who feel good about themselves, who don't waste their energy in disguising this or that feature and are right at home in the one skin they have.

Violeta is a woman who is comfortable with her body; she is detached from watching it make its way through life. Not me: I have always felt uncomfortable in my skin. Violeta was pretty from the time she was a little girl. She grew up counting on that, so for her it was never a worry. Her indifference in adult life merely emphasizes what never happened to me. I had to *invent myself*. I remember, with nostalgia, the mill house as the one place I let myself go. The home-baked bread, the cherry preserves and Ensenada cheese making me feel like a normal woman, your run-of-the-mill mortal. Once back in Santiago, I would lock myself in my room for four days, surrounded with pharmaceuticals to help me put up with myself and with the ferocious diet I was beginning. The first day I ate nothing but boiled potatoes; the second, only chicken; the third day was beef, nothing but beef; and the fourth, bananas. I drank liters and liters of water and lost fluids as never before. Despite the sophisticated diets doctors subjected me to, I favored this one, primitive and incomprehensible from a scientific point of view. By the fourth day—vicious, each of those days—I had lost three kilos with mathematical precision. Then my stomach would shrink and I would begin the year and normal life, eating practically nothing.

I had to tolerate being stared at—always, everywhere, people's eyes on me—and my awareness of my body kept pace with the avidity of those gazes. And when I submit to them voluntarily, when I must ask people to look at me on stage or TV, I have to go through the torture of thousands of creams, all kinds of little jars for different purposes, unwholesome makeup, oils, body wraps. That time Violeta went with me to a Festival of Song—one at which I was an invited artist—she stood frozen in my dressing room as she watched the whole process. "But Josefa," she exclaimed with desperation, "they *construct* you each time, they take you apart and put you back together again!"

It seems to me that the whole world is filled with overweight women who wanted a different fate for themselves—no one is voluntarily fat—and their lives are ruined, all those doors closed to them, because of a seemingly innocuous problem: too many inches. Thinness as the supreme value. How did we get to the point of a cultural madness that plunges eighty percent of women into worry and strife and repression? We should have murdered Twiggy years ago.

In Antigua no one knows me. What a blessing. It's like the mill house.


When we had driven nearly across the entire city (the convent of the Capuchins is on the opposite side of town from El Sitio gallery), we approached Sexta Norte by way of the plaza. At last, the Café Opera.

The hour of the day, the sunshine, the unusual exercise, and the emotion of so much visual stimulus, has made me crazy for strong black coffee. Up till that moment, we had talked only about abstract, objective subjects, as befits two people who have known each other only a couple of hours. But there was no doubt that while I was showering, Violeta had given Javier a summary of my life.

"You've sung in Mexico, haven't you?" were the first words he spoke to me over the steaming coffee.

"Yes, in Mexico and in the U.S., and everywhere on this continent." I curtly dismissed that subject.

"We won't talk about that if you don't want to." His diction is perfect. "Are you going through some kind of crisis?"

"Yes. Everyone knows me as a singer; everyone wants something of me because I sing, they all want to hear me. And I don't want to sing anymore."

"Everyone?"

"Everyone." A brief silence. "Except my daughter. When she was a baby, I used to sing her cradle songs. She would begin to pucker up with the first notes. Do you know what 'pucker up' means? I don't know whether you say that in your country."

"Yes, I know."

"Well, every time I sang she would start to burst into tears. Violeta consoled me by saying the child was protecting herself from the emotion my voice evoked. When she was older, she would put her little hand over my mouth and make me stop. She has been the one creature on earth who can't bear my voice."

Why am I talking like this? It's the first time I've ever told that about Celeste.

"And today how is that child doing?"

"She's suffering from anorexia. Or maybe it's only depression, and I'm exaggerating. But she can't stand being my daughter."

"And you, can you stand being her mother?"

"Barely. It's one of the reasons I'm here."

"You want to tell me the rest?"

Well, why not, what does it matter? What image do I have to maintain?

"Yes. My son prefers Violeta to me as a mother. I can't write a song. In my last recital I had such an attack of stage fright that I fainted so I wouldn't have to experience it . . ."

"That's pretty serious."

"Since everyone expects women to lose control, I was allowed to swoon."

"And is anything else disturbing you?"

"I don't have the strength to sing again. My husband apparently doesn't love me anymore, he's fallen in love with another woman. Do you think that's enough?"

"And success is to blame?"

"Success? I don't really know what that is. I remember it as a monster that gets inside you and begins to give orders; it commands and the rest of the body obeys. It goes along changing your whole being to meet its own needs. When it wants love, it grabs it. When it doesn't, it tosses it away. And in the end it is transforming *me* into the monster *it* is."

"But this monster didn't come along without being invited, isn't that right?"

I smile at him with a certain humility.

"No. I invited it. I wanted to be stupendous in what I was doing. I wanted to avenge my mother's insecurities. And then wreak my own vengeance on my schoolmates, who had always shut me out. I needed to be dazzling for myself and not for someone else, because I had the experience of having that "someone" disappear, and of the hunger and vulnerability that came afterward. No, that couldn't happen again. Maybe I also needed the monster in order to marry again, and to catch the best possible husband. And that, in vulgar terms, is what they call ambition, isn't it?"

"Probably; that is what a man usually wants. In a woman, they put a different name to it. But the problem is that there is no end to ambition."

"How is that?"

"Ambition is like a floodgate to the soul that never closes: gusts of wind blow in, swirl around madly, sometimes choking, sometimes freezing. Always, first, throbbing with anxiety. An ambitious soul is nearly always exposed to the elements; storms hover about it."

He looks at me with warmth, and I comment to myself that Mexicans use the language better than we do.

"Ambition leaves no room for serenity," he concludes, almost to himself.


(Celeste. That time I came back from Istanbul, one of the most beautiful places on earth, because I couldn't be away from her. I traded the Bosphorus for Lake Llanquihue, and came home to hug them, my three children. Serenity? Yes, I know it. I know it.

That well-being, in the mill house. That well-being specific to the south of Chile, those rainy afternoons when the children ran around with their friends beneath the chestnut trees and I, from afar, heard their happy cries. Andrés reading in a bedroom curdled with light, lying on the yellow coverlet with green flowers, the one we'd had for eight years. Nothing changes in the mill house. Dusk is coming, I close the door to the one little living room in the house, the fire lighted, the temperature just right, warm but not hot enough to give you a headache. I sit down at the dining room table—the only table in this borrowed home—I take out my notebooks and favorite pencil case, and the sound of the rain prepares me for composing. The notes and words whirl in my head, but there is no clashing, no racket. I look through the window; five meters away I see the palm tree that the rain has left gleaming, glimpse the roof tiles of the House of the Chestnut Tree and the smoke from its chimney. We are all together, we are all fine. Both houses a shelter for my children. It is an essential part of my well-being: having them near, knowing they are near. The dementia of motherhood. This same rain in Istanbul, sitting at a table in my suite, looking out at the merlons and towers of the mosques, trying to work: searching for inspiration. But I was too uneasy: my children. How many hours between them and Istanbul? No, I can't work when I'm away from them. Except that the impotence that comes from having them on top of me, interrupting me, blocks me as much as distance from them. I turned down the invitation, I invented an illness, and I came back. Can men suspect what this means? I come back, and that house in Llanquihue gives me what the most magical city in the world cannot: serenity, *that* well-being. The calm of those rainy summer afternoons in the south.

A precise notion of well-being.)

# 16

The house awakes in a stir because of Bob's arrival. Violeta decides to have a formal dinner. She loves the house filled with people, she doesn't complicate things or complain. She still hasn't learned to set the table; where does this fork go? this knife? she asks me. Which glass is for the white, and which for the red? The fragrance of corn tortillas and beans wafts from the kitchen. Javier has helped with *chiles en nogada,* it hasn't been much work for Tierna to cook them. The formality of the set table makes the dining room larger; it looks enormous.

"Javier will sit here, and Borja and Alan here, we'll let Gabriel eat at the table . . . Bob, Javier, and you. Me, at the head of the table. There's room for everyone."

What she always wanted; a large table occupied by a family. With her at the head. Abundance never seems excessive when it comes from Violeta: abundant physical space, cloth on her body, measurements in tapestries, food in the kitchen, people at the table. Violeta has never been greedy for abundance *per se;* hers is a phenomenon totally opposite from that of hoarders; she loves to give it away.

At seven in the evening I hear the big front gate; a car is driving in. Violeta has driven to the capital to pick up Bob. We all go out to greet him. I'm surprised to find him so much as I imagined him. He has that candor in his eyes typical of a certain kind of man born in the States, the ones women really like, the ones who don't buy the story of arrogance or of the American dream. He is tanned by the sun and his hair is blonder than the photographs show. He is shorter than I had guessed, but more muscular. He seems a strong man, informal, and quick in his movements. I don't see any jarring note between them, and I recognize one of Violeta's traits in him: that open, honest, gaze. In one second, the whole story of those two makes sense to me. I can see that his smile comes easily. No, he is not the Hollywood lover boy. He is a normal, approachable man with whom one can feel at home.

He embraces me warmly. He looks at me complicitiously, as if we were victims of the same bewitchment.

"At last we meet!" he says in his perfect Spanish. "I know more about you than you know yourself."

There is anxiety in Violeta's eyes. It is important to her for Bob to love me, and for me to love Bob. Wasn't that how it was with me when I introduced her to Roberto, and then to Andrés? And I have a strong desire to hug them both, to express somehow what I am feeling: that rare gratitude that there are people like them on this earth.

After a magnificent, strictly Mexican dinner we "grown-ups" went to the study and the "youngsters" went out. Gabriel was fast asleep, excited and exhausted by the arrival of his father, his half-brother, and all the gifts. I remembered that I had brought a gift for Bob, and got up to go find it: a recording by Violeta Parra. I thought it would give Bob insight into the origins of his own Violeta and, in passing, pay homage to her. In fact they didn't have one of Parra's records, and our Violeta wanted to hear it then and there. Javier and Bob yielded docilely to her whim; Javier even knew the lyrics of the songs. The rum—infinite, the quantity of rum consumed in this house—was served in generous portions, neat, with a little *limón* and ice. All of us listened holding, or caressing, our glasses.

Violeta grew visibly melancholy. Had I done the right thing in bringing this slice of our land to the serenity of Antigua? After the last chords, she broke the silence with an explosion of sobbing, like a child trying to hold back the tears.

"Oh, my God, such nostalgia." She looks at me sadly. "You brought me a piece of a Chile that's gone."

"Why gone?" Bob asks.

"Because we seem to be a country that packs everything away, incapable of dignifying its own past. And that's painful to me."

"Are you stuck in the past, baby?" Javier laughs.

"I'm not interested in the past as such. I'm interested in it in order to know who we are today."

"Because without memory we're nothing, isn't that right?" says Bob.

"I'm trapped in a strange space, a no-man's-land. I don't want to go back, like the extremists in so many places, but neither am I comfortable with today's pragmatism or the total absence of ideology."

"Violeta, Violeta!" Javier exclaims. "Who among us is? We're children of the sixties, after all!"

"I don't want to make everything relative, because it will frighten me if tomorrow I can't tell who is suffering and who isn't."

"And what's to prevent you, my dear? Why is that going to be a source of sadness?"

"Because I don't have anywhere to weep over our old music,

the beliefs that elevated us, telling us the world was broader than any of us."

Bob keeps a respectful silence. His traveler's eyes have seen everything. They embrace Violeta.

"I have the impression that Chileans, in their success, are like the blind," says Javier. "Their eyes are clouded and they can't see when the sun comes out."

"But," Violeta continues, "who will tell Jacinta's children what the world we aspired to was like?"

"They can never know that." Javier's gesture is skeptical. He sips his rum.

"I think it's a good thing for Berlin to be one city. But did the Wall have to take such a good part of us with it? Is the world better today because it came down?"

"Yes and no," Javier answers. "Yes, because freedom in itself is always good. No, because along with the Wall we lost the hope of building a better world. You, Bob, do you believe that this postwar epoch is worse than what came before?"

"Deep down, I think I do," Bob says. "But it's a relative and complex subject. The forces of nationalism are the worst of this era, worse even than those of imperialism. Besides that, cynicism today knows no boundaries. After all, Communism acted as a limiting factor for everything else, because it was feared."

"And people are more insensitive and unjust now because they don't have that fear," Violeta interrupts, encouraged by her husband's words. "You're absolutely right, Bob, you have a point. That's how they are now: naked; they have shown their true faces, the ones Communism helped them hide. Since their conduct then was moderated by fear, they made concessions to prevent the threat from materializing."

"And now that they know there is no threat, they can act with total impunity." Javier completes the idea, looking toward me, trying to draw me in. I don't have anything to contribute to this subject, I know only that he is sitting very close to me and something seems to dissolve inside me.

"Last night on television I saw the most heartrending scene I've seen in years," Bob interjects. "In Rwanda, in one of those refugee camps. I saw a group of men killing one another, yes, clubbing each other *to death* for a piece of bread. I have to ask whether the world would have allowed those two million hungry people twenty years ago."

"The Soviet Union would have tried to intervene to capitalize on the situation," Javier responds, "and other nations, in turn, would have acted first to prevent the Communists from gaining any advantages from the drama in Africa."

"When you come right down to it," says Violeta, "the USSR and Communism were principal factors in triggering the guilt of the wealthy nations. Now there is no guilt because there's no power that elicits it. Now we see them as they truly are."

"And also what we were," Bob adds. "Our ideas were probably those most contrary to human nature."

"Nevertheless, they were born of pure humanity," Javier replies. "We former Marxists were the true believers, more than the right itself. To such a degree that when they told us the poor were poor because it was God's will, we called ourselves atheists. We protected God."

He smiles at all of us. Violeta continues. "For me, being on the left in this ridiculously confused panorama today has come to be a phenomenon of pure chemistry. And at this point, my leftist tendencies are located in my pores, not my head."

"It is really difficult to live the end of an epoch," says Bob, as if answering, or consoling, Violeta. "I wonder why it happened only to us?"

"Intellectuals are pondering that point, without much success," Javier says. "Every end-of-epoch produces what thinkers call 'the malaise of civilization.' Not knowing exactly the consequences of the present, not having a clear awareness of what awaits. And nothing of what is happening, to the world, to us, is immune to this crisis, this malaise."

"You can't visualize the future. At least I take comfort from thinking that not understanding it is different from condemning it," Bob says, and he refills our glasses. Violeta thanks him, looks at him and, as if speaking to herself, closes the subject with her last thought.

"Antigua is my salvation. Here I can cling to the beauty of everyday life, at a determined tempo, and manage to save myself a little from that sense of the immediate."

"But you suffer just the same." At last I put a word in.

"Yes, I suffer just the same. I suffer for my world, which inexorably disappeared, and I don't know whether humanity will be any happier without it. I'm not sure. It has left me naked as water. Oh, shit, what a tormented continent! Halfway to catching the brass ring, halfway to being a developed nation, even if there are black holes in that development, facing the problems of modern countries while carrying the burden of sorrows of undeveloped countries. It's clear that among us there is a south for every north—a poor relative for every rich uncle."

She gets up, opens the door to the bathroom, and disappears. Javier stands up also, stretches his long legs, and holds out his hand for me to follow him.

"Where?" I ask slowly.

"Let's leave them alone. We'll go have a drink at the Santo Domingo."

Since Bob doesn't protest, I leave with Javier.

We find a seat in the salon in front of the gigantic fireplace with its majestic, massive, hammered copper hood. I order a margarita. I am exhausted. Javier's fingers—very delicate those fingers—touch my chin and slowly guide my head to his shoulder, where I find the precise place to rest. I don't ask myself what I'm doing here, who this man is, why I am leaning against a body that isn't Andrés's if no male body existed in my consciousness that wasn't his, if each and every one had vanished from the face of the earth. Wasn't it true? Weren't female bodies still circling in his orbit and I just couldn't see them? Pamela has long, slender fingers covered with rings. Pamela's breasts are better than mine, Pamela . . . this is madness. I sink into the comfortable shoulder of this dark-skinned Mexican, a mixture of Aztec and Andalusian, he has told me, proud blood that throbs and warms. As long as we have a pair of arms to hold us, we are safe. The point is to have those arms, it doesn't matter whose, and we will be warmed. I submerse myself in those arms.

And there amid old convent walls, wood saints from the 1600s, Gregorian chants, candles, and calla lilies—they call them *alcatraces* here—Javier focuses beyond me. He breaks that rare personal spell to return to Violeta.

"Amazing, the strength of nostalgia."

"No," I answer, feeling that Violeta is creeping into this narrow— oh, so narrow! crevice of my personal life. I rise up from the fantasy of that cozy sofa and say, in no uncertain terms, "It isn't nostalgia. It's longing. And believe me, that isn't the same."

# 17

Doña Beatriz de la Cueva de Alvarado.

Sitting on my bench in the museum in the centuries-old Universidad de San Carlos, waiting for the concert to begin, thinking about Beatriz de la Cueva, that strong, level-headed, ambitious woman who—in the mid-sixteenth century!—succeeded in being named governor of the Kingdom of Guatemala. What must the reaction of the rest of the Council have been to a woman as commander in this lost corner of the Viceroyalty of New Spain?

This morning Javier took me to the mirador. The skies cleared. And once the rain had blown away, the air became crystalline, transparent. Breathing was not merely breathing; it was inhaling, exhaling, animating, ventilating, conquering, alleviating, almost moaning. Two vibrant bodies, together we appreciated the city in all its expanse. Nearly hallucinating, I felt its accessible size, its still-cobbled streets, its colonial, nearly all single-storied buildings, its ring of verdant volcanoes, calling to me. Like a whispering. Calling me, in their peace, to a strange surrender, a repose, as if in their millenary silence they were promising unknown fluidity, coming serenity, adventures of the spirit, that could not help but pacify. Andrés, Andrés! Are you giving me up?

The statue of Santiago the Apostle seems to watch over the city.

"Why not one of Pedro de Alvarado's wife?" I ask.

And he tells me that this city was once named Santiago; that it was founded because the first Santiago, the one over which Don Pedro de Alvarado had reigned, was washed away by effluvia from the del Agua volcano. El Fuego and Acatenango were never that treacherous, he explains. And the figure of Doña Beatriz appears, and the legendary love between her and Don Pedro. When he died, she dressed in black from head to toe, ordered her palace painted black, and hung black drapes at all the windows, closing herself in to weep over him. That was love; not these pseudo-intellectual, pseudo-psychological, light-weight affairs of today! Shortly afterward, the volcano carried her off: palace, city, and all. In 1543 the new Santiago was founded, which today they call "la Antigua," the "Old," capital of Guatemala, which it was until the infamous earthquake of 1773.

This iron woman, this semiheretic, with as much ambition as passion, came to these savage hinterlands from the sophisticated Spanish court . . . how much could she have loved this land? And did the land return her love? I wonder, was it worth it to her? The volcano didn't love her. No, that is established.

"History rumors that she made pacts with the Indian gods."

"Would they have served her?"

Javier looks at me, stirred by that idea, and says, "There is a Maya curse you may find useful."

"What is it?"

"It's the spell of the black candles. You light them to annihilate your enemy. But you must be very sure when you do it, and fervently wish the destruction of that enemy, because from that moment you yourself will be vulnerable to spells, and your enemy can cast one on you. Beatriz risked that. Are you ready?"

I think about Pamela, and am sorely tempted. My body trembles; I don't have Beatriz's fortitude.

"No!"


The walls and the black drapes stay with me until I get to the concert. Violeta has insisted I come; she says it's a present for me.

I feel a certain consonance among the stark white of the old Universidad de San Carlos—the first in Central America—Telemann, and the oboe; behind the violinist is the Virgin of Guadalupe, the dark sovereign robed in gilt and green, her skin dusky against white arches like pierced, solidified meringue rising to the ceiling of the dome of the university and its crème Chantilly cornices. The cello solo begins. Such a difficult instrument, the one I like least of the baroque—and I don't know where I am, again I don't know what I am doing here. I look to my right and see the bright face of Bob. I have known him barely three days, but he seems an old and beloved member of the family, *my* family. Then to the left, I meet the reassuring eyes of Javier, strands of gray in his ponytail, slender, dark hands, and that athletic body, that friend-body, body on the verge of becoming more than a friend. It's very clear that I'm not much in touch with myself. All this is so new, and yet it seems to have lived in me forever.

After the intermission, they announce some Guatemalan songs from the mid-1700s. A singer comes onto the stage, beautiful, with dark skin and hair, about my age, handsome in her creamy-tea-colored satin dress. Her voice lifts in an elaborate, ornamented baroque piece composed on this continent as Bach and Telemann were composing in parallel time. It sounds a little like a canticle, and my stomach begins to tingle. I look at Violeta and she returns my look. Hopefully? She knows what is about to happen to me; what's more, I suspect she planned it to happen. After that hymnlike song in which the dark-skinned woman calls to Jesus, they announce a *chapín*, a Guatemalan folk song, less sacred, gayer: the singer's eyes sparkle, her marvelous voice intones: *"Gitanilla viene, gitanilla va, gitanica que viene y que va . . ."* Something sweeps through me; I want to sing with her. *"Gitanico hermoso, ángel celestial, en dulce armonía les hacen hablar, morenica del sol más hermoso . . ."* A familiar strength glows in me, as if my blood were bubbling from my nerves to my gut: "Let them dance gracefully to the song and the beat." I concentrate so hard that I am breathing along with the singer, I breathe from my diaphragm at the same time she does, I follow her as if her vocal cords and her veins were my own.

The brief concert ended with an old song, *Los negros de Guaranganá.* With my feet and my temples throbbing to the beat, alive now, alive with ancient life, American life, *mine,* I am seized with an unexpected and consuming eagerness to possess all this for myself.

Spontaneously, I hug Violeta as we leave.

"I have the feeling you have a lot to do," she told me. "And I have started you on your way. A friend of mine named Lavina researches old songs. I want you to meet her."

She goes to look for her, introduces me, and we set a date to meet.

Walking over the paving stones at the exit from the university, I drift away from the others, burning what passes beneath my feet, left behind, fading . . .


I believe it was the fault of the concert. Of the music, the beat that gripped my body, of the dark-skinned singer who exorcised me, of Lavina who tempted me. I did not go back with Violeta and Bob. I went directly to the Hotel Casa de Santo Domingo. It was also the fault of that place, of that ruined convent that had been reconstructed as a hotel. As I told Javier, I am sure I am in one of the most beautiful places in the world.

In front of the same hammered copper fireplace, I ordered the same margarita I had three nights ago. Javier asked me to tell him two things: my treasure—what was it?—and my fantasy.

Javier's questions merely tell me that my intuition is correct. That with him my vulnerability doesn't matter: he is a noble man, I have nothing to fear. I have fallen into good hands. His hands will not be rough, they will not torture, only shelter. If I have to shoot a dart or two at Andrés, at least the man I use as weapon will be worthy.

"So . . . Have you ever thought of the medieval moat as a symbol of liberty?" I ask.

"No, but I'm open to the idea, if you convince me."

"You do know, Javier, that we women have been taught to fear solitude?"

"That I do know."

"Men have wanted to lock us up in moated castles; solitude, the tower; solitude, the water: the great nightmare, us inside. Alone. But they lied to us, in this as in so many things. Because, although the moat is daunting, it protects us in that solitude. If freedom for men begins far from the castle, in air and movement, mine, though it seems strange, originates in that very moat. The moat guards the treasure, it stands between it and the world."

"So your treasure is your solitude?"

"Yes," I reply, very serious.

He looks at me, a spark of amusement in his eyes.

"Truth is austere, my lord, as Stendhal said."

"Yes, it is."

"And your fantasy?"

I take a swallow of my drink; this man doesn't let me breathe. But he listens. How wonderful and strange a man who listens can be!

"Did you see the movie *Lily Marlene*?"

"Fassbinder's? Yes, I saw it."

"Hanna Schygulla, Lily Marlene seen through Fassbinder's eyes. That is what I would like to be. All the ambiguity in that song. Ears listening in the trenches. The great velvet and chandelier-lighted halls, the power floating in the air Lily breathes. The Führer makes her breathe: to give herself is faster and easier and . . . it can be beautiful. The king and his slaves, the Führer and his soldiers, all listening to that voice, imbibing every note. And the others, the soldiers in the trenches on the other side; they are listening, too; they, too, adopt her and venerate her in the fragility of that night of war. Lily Marlene for everyone, cloaking everyone. Lily Marlene on this side and on that: the one bond among all the powers in that war, the one thing that makes brothers of the soldiers of both armies at that hour of the night when her voice swells and the song envelops them, traps them, holds all of them equally, becoming the depository of all a soldier's nostalgia and sorrow, which in the end are the same of those of his brother, the enemy soldier. All through the power of song."

"Difficult woman," murmurs Javier.

"Now it's your turn. Your fantasy, your treasure."

"May I be contingent, immediate, and, uh, not too serious? Do I have your permission?"

"Please. Go ahead."

"The one possible fantasy—no other comes to mind—is to make love to you tonight."

"What! You call that 'not too serious'?" I feign aplomb to gain time.

"Look, Josefa, you told me about your moat: now I will tell you about my well. Every time I hear that word, I think of human relationships. A bottomless well. The only bottomless well among all those that exist with no known or specified level, nothing but its viscous waters."

"Javier, now I'm the skeptic."

"I live tormented by that . . . viscosity. Then when I find warmth, I recognize it immediately. And it seems a crime to miss it, to let it go by."

"Warmth . . . There isn't a lot of that, in truth. It's a rare luxury."

In one minute, like an avalanche, all the elements that have composed my life these last years come tumbling down on me. I pose them against this warmth. Are they compatible? I think of my muddled affections, of my no longer innocent relationships, of envies, rages, struggles for power and prestige—for fame. Behind that come pragmatism, my unrestrained individualism, my ambiguity, my fear of dissenting, my self-criticism . . . and all of it rests upon a terrifying dimension of mortality. (I see the ceiling, Violeta; for the first time. I'd never had time to look. There is so little real time left. Why did I undervalue what I thought useless? After all, what does *anything* matter if we are going to die?)

"Don't agonize, Josefa Ferrer, let's for once act on that basic animal impulse of the 'you and me.' "

Just that?

A lie. It is never just that.

"Let's," I say to him.

The walls of the rooms in the Santo Domingo are an indescribable color: white, cream, eggshell, butter.

"Turn out the light," I said, in a tone that brooked no argument. "It's been many years since I made love with another man, and I'm not at an age to do it with the lights on."

Javier laughed and turned out the light.

I closed my eyes.

That last morning in Chile. Andrés had gone out looking so handsome; I would have liked to touch his leg, like this, just reach out and feel his strong muscles through the gabardine of his suit. Yet it is another hand that touches my neck, then lower, my breasts. And why only Andrés's thighs? Why not Javier's, which are also firm and beautiful? How many years do I have left to yearn so savagely for a desired and impossible body, how many for my hand still to be welcome on a man's leg? Oh, God . . . Time! And that dimension is erased, extended by another hand . . . put your hand here, Macorina, the one toying with my nipple, the right one, my favorite. How can I breathe, swallow, be alive, when in the morning I study myself in the mirror and am unable that same night to take off my clothes in front of a man? It is these muscles, these legs, that are slipping into the bed in the Santo Domingo. What was I doing all these days, all these long days, that I could not recognize that involuntary movement of my desire for what it was? I did not hold out my hands because I thought I would not know how to articulate them; now I know, and these legs are at my bidding, seeking me, opening me. I want to see him, see his mestizo nakedness as I have not wanted to see another, I am alive down there, naked, this large, dark man, oh, I want to feel him inside me, with the light out, want him so deep, deep in me, black eyes, great, erect penis, I can sense it, put it there, there where the throbbing is, unlocking myself I take this body, not only Andrés's, why only for Andrés if I am many? I am milk, I am honey, let men take me, enormous sword impaling me to assure me I am alive, that I have time, a sunflower, a trumpet of love, heat, color like chemicals, I can even let go, spill out, that outpouring will make my vagina and soul come together, fucked until I lose control. I'm burning. I am on fire.

# 18

This was as they were celebrating the twenty-fifth anniversary of man's first moon walk.

But that is not strictly what interests me. It is something the news is saying about the last fragment of a comet that is going to crash on Jupiter. Yesterday, or day before yesterday, four brilliant fragments smashed onto that planet. Three had already done so. The glow was so intense that it saturated the observatory instruments. It generated splendors.

I run to see Violeta.

I hear the soothing sound of flowing, nesting domesticity. I walk into the kitchen. Tierna informs me that Violeta has gone to San Juan del Obispo to look for cloth.

"Don't be sad, she'll be back for dinner."

I ponder the way Guatemalans say "don't worry": *don't be sad.* I feel sadness always near by, but I am not always worried. Sadness is better.

Twenty minutes later Tierna appears in my bedroom with an elegant plastic box. Inside is a flower.

"It's for you." She seems excited.

"What flower is this, Tierna? It's absolutely beautiful!"

"It's an orchid, the 'white nun,' our national flower."

I wait for Tierna to leave before I open the envelope. I like the black writing on the rough paper.

> *Is this how I am to go?*
> *Like the flowers that have died?*
> *Will nothing of my name remain?*
> *Nothing of my fame here on the earth?*
> *At least flowers, at least song!*

*SONGS OF HUEXOTZINGO*

The signature isn't on the sheet of paper, I see Javier's name on the back of the envelope. An orchid for a night of love. At least flowers, at least song.

The electricity is off. I go to the telephone, afraid it isn't working. (In Antigua something is always failing, either the lights or the water or the telephone—Violeta warned me—but never all at once.)

I picked up the phone. I had sworn not to do it, that's why Borja makes the calls; he tells me how many grams Celeste has gained, what clever new thing Diego has done and what grades he has made in school, how many millimeters of rain have fallen in that faraway winter.

But today I must talk. I have only one thing I must say. Only one.

"Andrés, we are losing each other."

That was all I said.

"Yes." Silence on the line, his breathing ragged. "Is that the cost of your getting better?" my husband asks, thousands of kilometers from me.

I don't answer.

"Are you better?" he insists.

"Yes."

"Do you think you can come back?"

"I'm afraid."

"Celeste and Diego need you."

Again silence, blended with distant voices.

"I don't want to talk anymore." And that is true, not manipulation. I don't want to. Either I talk about Pamela, about Javier, about Antigua, about love, about truth, or I don't talk at all. "I think I have found the new mill house, and you and I are losing each other." That was all I said.

That was already a lot. I hung up.

Must I dress in black, paint myself black, blacken my palace and my drapes?


My romance goes from rhythm to songs. These from Seville. I found him drinking coffee in El Patio, after the orchid.

"Hey, you, Andaluz girl, do you know any *sevillanas?*"

"Of course," I answer, on the verge of arrogance.

*"In the magic of your eyes, I am lost forever, I live only in the shadows where I first met you."*

That void left by the friend who goes away . . . I am filled with *sevillanas,* I know so many.

*"Do not leave me yet,"* I sing to him, Andalusian to the core. *"Do not leave me, I beg you."*

That night, the first night in the Santo Domingo, the day Bob arrived . . . Violeta's longing had not put a damper on things the way I had anticipated. No. The subterranean currents rose through our bodies until, indecent, they manifested. But at the end of that night—that night—we were not the protagonists. No. My control was.

Do you realize what we did, my beloved Mexican? Do you know the dimension of what we shattered? Fidelity is not to be taken lightly. You told me that first night: "I don't want to force you and destroy something so deeply rooted." And because you realized that emotion was profound, I was later able to. Your understanding empowered this mistreated, loyal body. When, on that night of longing, you did not make love to me, you said, "It is a rare thing to find loyalty; it's all too scarce, you know? That's why I'm not going to press you; that is my gift."

You gave me the gift of my own faithfulness. And when you took it from me, you also said, "I know I can push you, Josefa, it's merely a matter of pressing forward over terrain that's already been prepared. And I believe that this is the moment. But I don't want to take anything from you, I don't want to steal anything, just love you." Then, magically, control lost its meaning.

Oh, Javier, when I think of you . . . That respect, dissolved in the obvious passion of two bodies . . . Was it broken? Or put back together? Like a child in no one's arms am I.

The memory of that love will not be a dagger, as it is in the *sevillanas*. That pierces my five senses, that will kill me. The Andalusian in me will resolve it, Javier. I promise.


And then, the whirlwind.

Celeste, compiling the songs, the cemetery, Javier, the baptism. The farewell.

But I need to go one step at a time.

Two days after I talked with Andrés, Violeta announces a surprise: my daughter Celeste. Violeta has invited her to the fiesta for our little archangel. A week in Antigua as a gift for my daughter. I have no doubt that this was plotted with Andrés behind my back. I touch her, feel her meager flesh. She is better, her spirit as well as her weight. Always a little reserved with me, she is expansive with Violeta. Jacinta, Borja, and Alan have integrated her into their group, and Antigua has begun to exercise its magic when I see the slow return of the smile I had thought was lost. Until she says to me, very convinced: "Mama, we should come back every year."


Jacinta, Celeste, and I, all in my bed watching the video of *The Sound of Music*. As Maria dances with the captain for the first time, in her blue dress, Borja comes into the bedroom and says, "Mama, I want to talk to you." I rise out of my drowsiness, leaving dreams of song in Salzburg for the girls.

Borja will stay and study in this country. He wants to enter the university in Ciudad de Guatemala: architecture. "What better place, Mama, living in Antigua?" Everything repeats itself, turns back on itself in this story of mine. We reach an agreement about some practical matters.

("Doesn't it worry you, Violeta, his relationship with Jacinta? Don't you think they're too close?" "No, it doesn't frighten me; to the contrary, they are very good for each other." And I hear her mischievous laugh. "Sometimes I think they'll end up getting married, Jose, be ready! How do you think we'd be as mothers-in-law to each other's children?")


Bob cooks dinner for us. He makes a Japanese-Antigueño salad: vermicelli, mushrooms, chives, sesame, and a dressing of soy sauce. Then he goes to his desk to send off an article. Violeta and I are left alone.

"Violeta, there's something I've been thinking about and would like to do with you before I go back to Chile."

"What is that?"

"It's about Cayetana's tomb."

"What about it?"

"We should inscribe her name. Cayetana Miranda, in bold letters, you know? You have chosen this to be your land; it will be your children's, too, and probably your grandchildren's. We shouldn't leave the grave without a name, as if Cayetana had been a pariah."

She holds my eyes for a long time, bites her lip as she always does when considering something.

"You may be right. Let me think about it."

I haven't made any more of those desperate night calls to Santiago de Chile. My fingers have calmed down.

I'm still collecting the *sevillanas*, the ones Javier and I have sung through the streets of Antigua. Our ancestors would have asked us to, it couldn't have been any other way.

He drops by Violeta's at siesta time.

*"How cruel you are to me, my dark-eyed girl. Do not be cruel to me. I do not have the soul of a saint, I cannot repent for having loved you—even the stones in the courtyard hear your voice."*

I spend siesta at the Santo Domingo.

Both of us hear castanets.

Violeta is sitting in one of the large chairs on the gallery with a book in her hand, soaking in the sun.

"Only a blend of history and geography can produce a genius like this," she says, showing me the cover. Juan Rulfo, his *Pedro Páramo*. "Mexico can."

"Our great shared love," I remind her. "The day I decide to retire, I might choose that country."

"I hope it won't be in San Miguel de Allende, repeating the story of your singer friend," she says, laughing. "Why don't you choose here?"

"It's a way off . . . Come on, get up. Let's go to lunch."

We take our table in the Albergue de Don Rodrigo. The chords of the marimba welcome us. My legs follow the African-American beat on their own.

"You know, Violeta? My meetings with your friend Lavina have been tremendously helpful."

"Have you seen all the music she's collected?"

"Yes, we've gone over it together. I'm bursting with ideas. I don't even have to pay rights to reproduce it."

Her look is a blend of sweetness and wickedness.

"And you will reproduce it, won't you?"

"Yes. That's why I want to go home. After such a long, sterile period, I'm dying to get to work."

"Do you feel you're ready to face Andrés?"

"I feel as if I'm ready to work, and with a different set of criteria from what I used before. That's what's giving me courage. I suppose the business of Andrés will take care of itself."

"Bravo, Jose."

"The truth is that I'm fine, Violeta; I'm feeling good, but it frightens me to be building up my hopes, considering how neurotic I am."

"Well, all neurotics have to get over it some day."

"When?"

"When they invest a hundred and get back a hundred and ten. A neurotic invests a hundred and gets sixty in return. And invents the remaining forty."

"I'm frightened just the same. This question of love . . . I'm afraid . . ."

"We love as opportunity allows," she tells me vehemently. "And for that reason we're afraid. Isn't that our destiny? Remember, Jose, in the end we will all be judged for love and because of love. Nothing else."

With no further words, I pick up my fork, savor my salad of avocado with *limón*, tomato, and onion. What Violeta says is true. In the end, all truths are simpler than they appear.

"God willing, as my grandmother Adriana used to say, it won't be long before I can give more exclusive time to Andrés—if that's what he wants. Borja has already made his choices, and Celeste will enter the university next year. It'll be just me and our little Diego. The house will be more peaceful, and so will I."

"You hope!" she interrupts me. "The children of this generation don't move away from home. That's the latest trend."

She sips her watermelon juice in its enormous round glass, and picks up the thread of our conversation.

"About the old songs; we could select the ones for your next record together. I would love to do it with you!"

"I'd like that, too. Let's look through them tomorrow morning when you get through working in your studio. By the way, why don't you let anyone come in? Not even me . . ."

"I'm making a beautiful hanging, and it's a secret."

I laugh.

"What title are you going to give the CD?" she asks.

I look at her, serious.

"You remember what I called the last one three years ago, don't you?"

She leans forward in her chair and hugs me.

"How important you made me feel, Jose! It's the greatest thing anyone ever did for me in my whole life."

"I thought the greatest thing had been to hide your box of papers under my bed when you were moving." I pull back; demonstrations of gratitude embarrass me.

"I'm serious, Jose."

"It was the logical thing to do, Viola. After all, no one has done as much to encourage my music as you."

"How happy it makes me that you know that. I've always known, but that's different from hearing you say it."

(When I was the *voyeur*, reading her diary, one passage engraved itself in my memory. *Josefa's singing is a gripping experience. She always recharges me. I listen, and little by little my body grows static, I cannot take my eyes from her, energy is like balm on my skin. That voice falls from the sky like lightning and illuminates the very center of my being.*)

"Well, back to the title," she says.

"Who better than you, Violeta, knows that there are twenty ways to say Antigua?"


I see Violeta in the garden with the hose. She's watering the grass, so it can drink, too.

Tomorrow is the baptism, day after tomorrow I leave. I walk toward her.

Abruptly, I ask the question that is burning in me.

"Will you come back to Chile some day?"

Violeta turns; a ray of sun falls on her amber skin, on a cascade of brightest chestnut.

"No. And it isn't the fear of being pointed to as a murderess; that would concern me for Jacinta's sake, not mine. The real reason is that Chile has become an indifferent country. And that has nothing to do with me."

I looked at her and again I saw the fuchsia frost on her harlequin face, gold and red confetti on her neck, the ribbons in her hair, the fascination of a colorful mask on that infernal night. Will I someday forget those colors? Desolate, Violeta's expression, desolate her words. Desolate as well our country, there on the Andean fringe of the Pacific?

With her free hand, the one not holding the hose, she takes mine.

"Do you remember, Jose, my obsession with that poem by Rich, with finding the missing part of that first line?"

I look again. The frost and the confetti have disappeared; just Violeta before me.

"You don't have to tell me. That line is being written, I know that."

"Why did I need two lives, as the prophecy said, and not just one, to be able to face what was missing from that line?"

"Because I think that the only things that happen to us are those we are strong enough to bear. And you have been, are, very strong. That's why."

# 19

Preparations for Gabriel's baptism cover over the sorrow of my leaving. Celeste will not be going back with me. "A few more days, Mama, please." I think it will be good to have the house in Santiago to ourselves, just me, Andrés, and his son, his son and my son, the three of us. I agree.

Javier, as godfather, can't leave before the festivities.

The matter of the ritual occasioned a discussion.

"The ceremony of the Catholic baptism is beautiful, let's use it," says Violeta.

"Either you're Catholic or you're not," is my argument.

"Don't be difficult, Jose. In the long run what matters in religion is the attitude, not the form."

We have decided to have a large luncheon. We have taken great pains with the menu. The pièce de resistance is to be melon with crab, and we will have that indispensable Mexican dish, *huitlacoche* crèpes; among several desserts, crystallized guava. Tierna was sent to the market for *ocotes*—kindling; a fire must be laid in case of a storm. Water, too, in an antique jug with local motifs. Water and fire for Gabriel. Also candles in colors of the Maya culture.

The candles were lighted at the moment that Javier and I, one on either side of Gabriel, sprinkle him with this water that is not holy. Through the child, Javier's and my hands, desiring one another, communicating what only we are aware of.

The black candle: to drive off the enemy. The purple: to dispel bad thoughts. Green: for success in one's endeavors, whatever they be. The red: for love. The white for children. ("For *his* childhood or for the children he will have some day?" I ask Javier quietly. "I don't know," he answers. "I don't think it matters.") I never learned what the yellow candle signified, probably good fortune; I invent one, anyway: passion.

Jacinta gives the child the mermaid of abundance; Bob provides the serpent of fertility. Violeta, a replica of the Huichol bird to protect him.

When the simple ceremony is over, Jacinta appears in one of the gallery doors with a guitar in her hand. I feel something akin to panic. Bob takes the guitar and comes toward me.

"I have heard you only once, years ago, in Radio City Music Hall. And I didn't have Gabriel with me. Will you give him the gift of a song?"

I see the expression on the faces of those I love, Borja, Celeste, Jacinta, Javier, and I look toward Violeta. She smiles, and says, very low: *"Why is it that so many more words have been said about Abraham Lincoln than about any other American?"*

I return her smile, touching this instrument that has betrayed me, or that I have betrayed, I've never been clear which. From Tierna and Irla to Barbara and Monica, all are waiting, expectant, in a sepulchral silence. I breathe from the diaphragm, as I always have, look at the small, blessed Gabriel, yes, blessed, and immediately know what I must sing to him. My voice rises—it is true that my voice is beautiful. I sing *"Gracias a la vida."*

Never have I had a more attentive audience. Or more appreciative.

Never have Javier's eyes observed me so unblinkingly.

After the guests left, we sat down on the gallery with rum and coffee; I asked Bob to come sit beside me. Caressing the guitar, I told him about the thousands of times that Violeta and I had sung together.

"Ask anything you want, our repertoire is vast and varied."

Bob couldn't believe it; suddenly the stars in the sky were being offered to him.

"Violeta, let's begin with *'La pericona se ha muerto.'* Do you remember the second part?"

"Of course, you start . . ."

Nothing interrupted us but an occasional forgotten verse, or laughter; the children joined in, and Javier with the words he knew.

"Mama," said Borja, after many songs and great revelry, "this is how you used to be those first years in the mill house, when we all used to sing together. What's happened to you?"

"It's the humidity," I answer. "Here in Antigua my pores open up, isn't that it, Violeta?"

I feel a delicious, long-forgotten fatigue. How long it has been since I've sung!

"I want to end this fiesta with a gift for Bob." I turn to him. "Nicanor Parra, one of our great poets, wrote a poem about his sister, Violeta. Later it was set to music. It's very long, so I'm going to choose a few stanzas. Here it is, my friend, for you."

> *Sweet neighbor of the green jungle*
> *Eternal guest of flowering April*
> *Great enemy of the harmful bramble.*
> *Violeta Parra.*

*You have wandered all this land*
*Unearthing jugs of marl*
*And freeing birds from traps*
*Set high among the branches.*

*But the politicians do not love you*
*And they shut their doors to you*
*And they declare war unto the death*
*Sorrowful Viola.*

*Because you cannot be bought or sold*
*Because you do not play the clown*
*Because you speak the earth's own tongue*
*My Chilean violet.*

And my voice sang on, issuing on its own, nearly independent of my will, stealing the poet's words, singing to the admirable Viola, to the volcanic Viola, to my sister, offering my intensity, and ending: "Where shall I find another Violeta, though I search through field and city . . ."

With Bob's hug and the only tear I have seen in Violeta's eyes since I came to this city, I reached the end of the song . . . the end to everything. The parting with Javier awaited: the most dreaded. The flesh does not come gratis, intimacy is not without cost, and he knows it and I know it.

Our bodies meld at the front gate, far from prying eyes. We kiss. We are locked together, each piece of one body fitting the pieces of the other. As in a dance. I took both his hands and placed them on my breasts, so he would caress them, take his leave of them, pay homage to them, Javier . . . may they please him, may he make them breasts able to convoke, to cleanse all rancor.

"I am leaving with your song here," he told me touching his heart. "Thank you for this afternoon, and for all the rest." Fearing the tone this good-bye might acquire, he lightens it. "Any time you need me, beautiful, *I'll be around*."

"I know," I murmured in his ear. "We will have each other forever, in whatever way, we'll have each other."

And when I closed the gate, on my way to a good cry, I realized that I had used a forbidden word: *always*. Did you hear it, Javier? What have you made me do? Javier? Have you left? Did you go? Javier?

Thinking of the dramas that await in the morning, when I tell the others good-bye, I walk past starkly white walls, look at each object as I go by, feel that inanimate objects are taking on life to become the signposts of all identity, something this place will never lack. I go out to the garden and walk across the grass toward Violeta, who is waiting. The last words of a novel by Mishima dog my steps and catch up to me. *"The music plays on. It never ends."*

Never end, Javier, never end.

Never end, Violeta.

Never end.

# 20

July 28, 1994, dawned cold and brilliant, the sharp outline of the cordillera turned to silver. The airplane descended over the city of Santiago.

In my lap was the package Violeta had handed me as I left. I had unwrapped it the minute we took off from Ciudad de Guatemala. I hugged it, weeping for women—certain women—incapable, by themselves, of finding their interior being. Because, lamentably, I am one of them, of those who cannot achieve that except in the reflection of a sister. Because I have not learned to look directly at myself, because I have needed another feminine presence—even though my opposite—to make my own story.

I ran my fingers over the edges, and they protected me in that night of pure air.

It was a weaving, a rectangular tapestry of ample proportions.

How many minutes of Violeta's eyes, of Violeta's hands, were in it? How many of my "sweet neighbor of the green jungle's," my blue, green, and garnet tapestry maker's?

Large green areas blend together, a thousand tones of this dancing, floral color, with small patches—always green—encroaching upon each other. How many greens had Violeta found in the silks, the wools, the cottons? A few fine, gilded threads splashed the lower edge with golden light.

On the right, almost at the bottom of the tapestry, blaze tight groups of assorted flowers in the colors of Antigua's artisanry: blue, yellow, green. The petals of each flower press against its neighbor, probing into it, filling every space. In the center of these blossoms, its large arched wings outspread, is the Huichol bird. It was as if I heard Violeta's warm, enthusiastic voice: it is the one that closes the gates of heaven, Josefa, to keep evil from visiting the earth.

("I am a mestiza," were her final words last night, her conclusion. "As were my mother and my grandmother. Through them, who join with me and shelter me, I reclaim the speech of the first women inhabitants of these American lands.")

On a small sheet of rose paper, paper we bought together in the Casa del Conde bookshop, pinned at one side, she had written: "The trail of green was laid for me from Llanquihue in the south to Oaxaca in the north. Antigua formed the forest." It was then that I saw the letters embroidered in black that leapt from the bottom of the cloth, those letters I have known from time immemorial. I read: THE LAST FOREST.

# Ora pro nobis

We, *the others*, were given a past and memories. They deprived us of the present. Today, for the first time, they accept us as witnesses of this side.

A slice of sky showed through the windows of Violeta's studio; at that hour the sky of Antigua was made of birds. And it was at that hour, after the festivities of the baptism, that four women stole into the sanctuary of the creation. Mysteriously empty, the stretcher—for the first time without cloth in it—is set against the wall; vast, empty space, high walls and cool floor. In the distance, the sound of some bell tolling the hour.

Tenebrous light saw the four women sink to the floor on their knees. And although that light was fleeting, it watched as they took one another's hands and formed a circle.

The voice of one of them rose . . . in prayer?

And the spirits—they, the tutelaries—seemed to filter through the windows, seeping into the ritual space of the evening, whispering a canticle of celebration, of healing, through their forgotten names.

Until we, *the others,* heard the litanies.

"I am Violeta, mother of Jacinta, daughter of Cayetana, grand-daughter of Carlota."

"I am Josefa, mother of Celeste, daughter of Marta, granddaughter of Adriana."

"I am Jacinta, daughter of Violeta, granddaughter of Cayetana, great-granddaughter of Carlota."

"I am Celeste, daughter of Josefa, granddaughter of Marta, great-granddaughter of Adriana."

And the polyphony began, the call of the voices blending together, intertwining, weaving the alliance among them. Until the last faded, the first, the one that repeated, making the ring eternal:

"I am Violeta, daughter of Cayetana, granddaughter of Carlota . . . I am Violeta."

I pick up my jacket and purse and, in desperation, run toward the street door. I cross the peaceful hall of my house, in a blur I see wallpaper and paintings, I don't focus well, perceive only dim shapes, yet I know what they look like because I have seen them every day of every month of every year and I do not need to focus to know that they are the paintings in the hallway of the house that is choking me, and, hurrying now, I don't want anyone to stop me, I open the door, go through the garden, and finally I am in the street, the walls that are smothering me are behind me, I am free, the street, I am here.

And I have nowhere to go.

Nowhere at four o'clock on a Sunday afternoon, such a familiar hour, with the likely aroma of cake baking in the kitchen oven. Nowhere to go on a Sunday in autumn without drowning. I walk quickly down the sidewalk; I don't know where I'm going, but the illusion is that my legs are so springy that the choking is going away, that decisive steps—purposeful these steps that do not know where they are going—allow me to breathe, clear my throat and my chest and this head, spinning, spinning, drowning.

(*Write*, Violeta told me; *when you are desperate, write, use your desperation. Work is the only thing that will get you through. Believe me, Josefa, the only thing. There is nothing work cannot get you past, even the worst moments.*) I sit down on a bench in the plaza where my drowning has brought me and take out the pen and notebook I always have at hand. Words burst out just as they are, clothed, dressed for thought. I write stupidly, madly. No matter. I don't know that I am composing my best song. And last.


Women don't realize that their creativity is born of small things, of downfallen things. Their inspirations, small breaths of light in the darkness of the quotidian. Never grand, total, sublime illumination. Step by step, interrupted, punctuated with trivia, like every hour of their day, that is woman's creativity. Never believing in it, never giv-

# 6

$\mathcal{D}$rowning.

The drowning I am feeling, involuntary, inevitable, invasive. As if my lungs were shrinking and my arteries obstructed, the drowning feeling comes and air is expelled but this tired mouth cannot inhale. The walls of my room close in on me, the walls of my house; as if they had tentacles, they stretch out toward my neck and strangle me. The sound of the washing machine and the cry of a child seep into this air blocked from reaching me. The familiar lines of each piece of furniture, each rug, each painting—Oh, God, how familiar!—become the ground of an earthquake, the waters of a seaquake, everything that asphyxiates, inhibits, prevents breathing. Andrés's voice chokes me, the way Andrés walks chokes me (in good times his role was that of retaining wall), and this choking, this drowning I am feeling goes on and on, won't stop, it simply reveals my body, in this situation, become *doubly* body.

*you: reserve. I don't know where I'm going, Violeta; I don't know who loves me. And what's worse, I don't know whom I love. The next article about me should be entitled "The singer, or shrouded sensibility."*

She answers immediately.

*It's essential to differentiate between pain and anguish. Anguish immobilizes, pain makes us grow. And listen to who's telling you this: one who knows!*

Alejandro always reads my faxes, because he gets to the office before I do. His inevitable question is, "Who's the crazy one? Violeta or you?"